Praise for *Old Dogs, New Tricks*

"Doug Richardson has crushed it again. His second suspense thriller, Old Dogs, New Tricks, is as brilliant and startlingly original as his award-winning debut novel, Down Wind and Out of Sight. Riveting action, quirky characters and a fascinating finale—an extraordinary reading adventure. BRAVO, SIR!"

—Richard Lyntton,
Author of the *Deception Series*

"Richardson's novel is refreshingly down-to-Earth, drama-tizing in crisp, controlled language the nuts and bolts of fencing, money-laundering, and other crimes...whose criminal heroes are generally likable, the sort to start a non-profit artists collective as part of their scheming."

—Publisher's Weekly *Booklife*

"Douglas Richardson is back with his trademark combination of grit and humor in this compelling and unconventional crime thriller that begins with a plane crash and keeps you on the edge of your seat from beginning to end. Doug has done it again, spinning a riveting story that he tells with eloquence and detail and keeping you engaged, amused, and sometimes horrified. You won't be disappointed!"

—Amanda Lamb, WRAL TV Reporter and Podcast Host,
Author of the *Maddie Arnette* crime thrillers

OLD DOGS, NEW TRICKS

A Victor Harding Adventure

OLD DOGS, NEW TRICKS

A Victor Harding Adventure

DOUGLAS RICHARDSON

Torchflame Books
Vista, CA

Old Dogs, New Tricks: A Victor Harding Adventure
Douglas Richardson
www.douglasrichardsonnovelist.com
dr@counsel.global

Published 2023, by Torchflame Books
www.torchflamebooks.com

Paperback ISBN: 978-1-61153-525-9
E-book ISBN: 978-1-61153-526-6
Large Print ISBN: 978-1-61153-737-6
Library of Congress Control Number: 2023907936

For Pam, yet again.
Who else could it possibly be?
No one.

Whoever said you can't teach
an old dog new tricks
obviously never met this old dog.
—Anon.

1

Lake Central Flight 153

SOMETHING IS STRANGE HERE. From the frost-covered outdoor observation deck of Oshkosh's Wittman Regional Airport, I watch for my brother Colin's Chicago-to-Oshkosh Lake Central flight. I spot a speck in the distance off to my left, coming in from the east. It's the usual antiquated Lake Central puddle-jumper, a dead plane brought back to life with the installation of modern engines. Now, as Flight 153 descends and lines up on the final approach, I see that something is definitely amiss.

The airliner wears Lake Central's bright chrome yellow, but the shape seems wrong and it's flying at a peculiar angle. The aircraft does not flare and lift its nose as it comes in for its landing approach, but rather it flies directly past the tower, wheels down, no more than one hundred feet off the runway, the right wing canted high in the air.

I get a clear look, and I am horror-struck. What I see is... *grotesque.*

Flight 153 has a huge bulge sticking out from its right side, a few feet behind the co-pilot's window. Clearly, the plane has collided with *something*, and a huge piece of that something is now embedded in the right side of the yellow plane's fuselage like an ugly twisted tumor. Protruding from the tumor is...I blink to clear my vision...*the tail of another airplane.* A small plane's entire tail assembly, rudder and elevators, bright maroon, is sticking almost straight out from the yellow passenger plane's flank.

Collie's plane has T-boned a Cessna. The windshield on the co-pilot's side is missing. The right propeller is still turning, but black smoke and a lick of orange flame stream from the turboprop's exhaust, a sure sign that an engine has swallowed something.

My involuntary cry is drowned out by a piercing klaxon coming from the terminal, a deafening *whoop-whoop-whoop* as Flight 153 flashes by the tower, banks sharply to the left, and heads back away from the airport. *My brother is a dead man*, I think. *My God, I'm going to outlive my little brother. I'm going to watch him die.*

—⁓—

Collie had called me a week before, his voice a hoarse whisper. He sounded as if he was afraid he was being overheard. "Got a quiet tip from one of the board members, Victor. The guy says there's a move afoot to ease me out. Monfried has been throwing marbles under my horse, apparently none too subtly."

"Who's Monfried?"

"Yeah, I guess I've never really gone over my current situation with you in detail, Victor. Stephen Monfried is the General Manager of The Landings Club. He's responsible for its six golf courses and four clubhouses down here. As Director of Golf, I report to him. In addition to giving lessons, I run overall golf operations, manage the pro shops, and coordinate with the grounds people. But Monfried is the chief honcho. What he recommends, The Landings Club

Board accepts. Classic white-haired southern boy. Butter wouldn't melt in his mouth."

"And what's he recommending?"

"I'm not sure what his agenda or his time frame is. He calls me into his office this morning, out of the blue, 'just to check in, ya know'. Real off-hand like, he says all the members really like me and the club 'deeply values the ten years I've been put in', but that the club also has to start 'looking to the future'. Swear I could hear an ominous organ chord in the background."

"Wow," I said. "Sure sounds like he's teeing something up—no pun intended. Do you think he'd actually fire you—or get the board to fire you?"

"Oh, no. Nothing as crass as that, nothing that would rile up my supporters, and I have a few. The club runs a real PR risk if they humiliate me publicly after all my years here. But my source says they are talking about bringing in 'an additional senior teaching pro', someone to 'expand their capabilities at the top level'. This is not a 'we're thinking about it' thing, Vic. Apparently, it's a done-deal thing. All this has been done behind my back."

"You know who they're bringing in?"

"Yep, nice young guy named John Whittle. I know him, played him a couple of times last year in regional tournaments. He knocked my socks off. He's past his best years, but he still qualifies for the big ones and can crack the top fifty now and again. No doubt, Vic, Whittle will be a strong membership draw, and they sure need that right now."

"But you get to keep your job, right? You're a lot more than just a teaching pro. So why not let Whittle take over some of that? You get to ease back some, let Whittle play ego games with the young bucks. What's wrong with that?"

"You don't understand how it works down here. Things will be all nicey-nice...at least 'til the end of the fiscal year.

Whittle plays nice, Monfried plays nice, like 'hey, this is a win-win, right?' Then, when the club starts a new budget year, suddenly it's all, 'Holy cow, the whole golf industry is in trouble and we're losing memberships as the old coots here die off and golf memberships are down all across the country and here at the club we're actually thinking of closing two of our courses and gee, Colin, we're gonna have to make some major cuts and so sorry and here's three months' severance. We'll hang your picture in our Hall of Champions.'"

"Colin," I had said, as calmly as I could. "Get your ass on an airplane and get up here. Now. It is time for some serious strategizing."

"Can't, Vic. Got a week full of lessons scheduled."

"Cancel them, Collie. Say there's been a death in the family. Say you'll be gone at least a week."

—◦◦◦—

Now, Lake Central Flight 153 limps back east away from the airport, trailing smoke, its right wing tilted up at an odd forty-five-degree angle, its left wing low and drooping. I race for the ice-covered outside stairway that leads to the tarmac in front of the main hangar. I feel my feet trying to slide out from under me as I hurdle down two flights of stairs. At the bottom, I find a metal door that says *No Admittance*. I tear at the handle, and to my surprise, it opens, triggering an alarm.

I find myself out on the flight line, now lightly dusted with snow, just outside the gaping overhead door of Wittman's huge maintenance hangar. Someone is shouting at me. The klaxon continues to bellow, drowning out all other sounds.

Now well past the far end of the runway, Flight 153 banks around, again heading toward the terminal, still flying with its right wing cocked up at that crazy angle. The right engine is now fully enveloped in flames. The plane descends toward the end of the concrete runway in a series of jerks, and now its nose tips up. *The pilot is actually going to try to land an airplane with another airplane sticking out of it.*

Everything seems to happen in slow motion.

As the turboprop descends to land, its right wing drops sharply. The moment the plane is level, it appears to drop out of the sky. From an altitude of perhaps ten feet, Flight 153 slams down into the runway and bounces back into the air. The tail assembly of the impaled Cessna breaks free, spins backward, then caroms off Flight 153's tall vertical fin. It pinwheels high into the air, twisting and spinning and glinting maroon in the sun.

Flight 153 comes down hard on its nose wheel, bounces back up into the air, and finally touches down on the blacktop shoulder that borders the long concrete runway. I can hear the thrust reversers on the turbines engaging; I see the propellers appear to change color as the pilot shifts the pitch of the blades. The backwash from the thrust reversers snuffs out the flames coming from the right engine—*Yes!* I yell—leaving a detached sheet of orange floating briefly behind the plane. The orange blob of fire looks like a punctured balloon, zigzagging about. Then it vanishes.

The plane slews hard right, straightens itself on the runway for a moment, then seems to overcorrect and swerves off to the left. The pilot jumps on the brakes—I can hear the tortured screech—and now all five tires stream dark gray smoke. There is a loud *bang!* as one of the main landing carriage tires explodes. As the plane skids by me, I think I see a flash of turquoise in the first window just behind the mangled cockpit. *That's Colin.* That is Colin's shirt. *Collie always wears turquoise polo shirts. When he flies. When he dies.*

From the main hangar, a blur of red and silver flashes into view on my right: fire engine, siren screaming, men in gray pants still sliding into their bright yellow reflective fire-coats as they sprint to clamber aboard.

A hundred yards past me, the plane's left landing gear slides off the blacktop and onto the grass. As the left wheel digs into the soft earth, Flight 153 jerks violently around, pivoting around the tip of its wing. It continues its pirouette until it is pointing back down the runway. Then it finally stops.

The left landing gear is buried in mud, bent under the plane, making it look like a crippled old man struggling to regain footing after a fall. The fire truck now circles the plane, looking for something to extinguish. Finally, for appearances' sake, the fire crew sprays a weak stream of foam, nothing more than a piss, really, on the exhaust outlet on the right engine. Then they stand around looking at each other, awaiting further orders that will never come.

I stand rooted to the tarmac of the flight line, perhaps forty yards from the plane, which is groaning and creaking and ticking. My hands are clenched; my nails cut into my palms. My eyes flood with tears and intense weakness washes over me. I think my knees might buckle. Someone rushes by me toward the plane. Someone else is yelling, "Hey, you! Old man!" but I can't hear the rest, don't know where it's coming from. The Klaxon continues its alarm.

Flight 153's fold-out cabin door suddenly pops open, and the stairway begins to unfold like a giant articulated knee. It has not yet touched the ground when Colin Harding tumbles out of the doorway—*of course he's the first out; Collie always sits in the first row*—and, totally out of control, somersaults down the steps onto the tarmac, arms and legs flailing. He lands hard on his right shoulder, struggles to his hands and knees, and begins to vomit violently.

———

Later, as we sit on the blue vinyl seats in the Oshkosh Airport departure lounge, I can't get Colin to stop sobbing.

He's sixty-six years old and he's crying like a baby. He has a yellow blanket with a Lake Central logo draped over his shoulders, and he slumps as if drained of all energy. Colin shudders violently again, launching half his coffee onto the front of his turquoise polo shirt, which is already covered in blood. *Not his blood*, he tells me.

Some Lake Central functionary is waiting to talk with Colin, but I keep waving her away. The other thirteen passengers have now disembarked, and some appear as stunned as Colin. Others clearly are just learning that they have survived a mid-air collision and are shaking their heads in disbelief. One woman has dropped to her knees in front of the refreshment counter and, head bowed, is praying the rosary. A group of five dark-suited businessmen moves rapidly down the concourse, rushing to get as far away from the scene as possible. The remaining passengers are sitting in the gate area, still in murmured conversations with Lake Central representatives or federal investigators or family members who have been allowed through security and are standing about wringing their hands.

The door to the flight line pops open, and two ashen-faced men in blue slacks and white short-sleeved shirts with bright blue Mickey Mouse-grade epaulets step into the gate area. The pilot and—*is this a miracle or what?!*—the completely uninjured co-pilot try to hurry by. The small crowd stands and applauds, but the pilot shakes his head vehemently and hurries away.

Colin doesn't stand, can't stand. He, too, shakes his head hard. "Victor," he sobs, "the Cessna pilot's face was right in front of me, smashed into his instrument panel. *His arm was in my lap.*" He looks at me, his face ashen, a rigid mask of horror. "I had to fly fifteen minutes with this dead guy's bloody arm in my lap."

I drive Collie to Oshkosh Memorial Hospital to have him checked out. He sits in my BMW's passenger seat, panting like a dog, his head lolling from side to side. He won't respond when I try to talk to him. We wait an hour in the ER to be seen, and Colin continues to hyperventilate. Finally, an extremely kindly Physician's Assistant takes him back for an exam, telling me to stay in the waiting room. A half-hour later, they're back. The PA says that his shoulder injury is probably just a strain and not a dislocation or muscle tear, but she straps it up anyway and parks it in a sling. "I'd rest it for two weeks," she says.

Other than that, she says, Colin seems physically uninjured, although his hands continue to shake in periodic short jerky spasms. She administers a mild sedative, and as it takes hold, the spasms soften, and Collie stops shaking his head from side to side. He is still conscious when the orderlies hoist him from the ER wheelchair and slide him into my car, but by the time we hit Route 23 moments later, he is out cold.

As I drive around the front circle at The Boulders, Odell Todd trots up with his goofy grin, ready to greet Collie and grab his luggage. Odie and Colin like each other a lot, and Collie never treats my yardman as anything but a peer and friend.

Before I can say anything, Odie throws open Colin's door, looks at Colin's ashen face, and then freezes, his arms raised as if he's been caught in a stick-up. "What the hell!" he exclaims. "Victor, is he dead?"

"Crash-landing. Everybody lived, but he got seriously shaken up. C'mon, Odie, help me get him up to bed. He's going to be out awhile, and believe me, that's a good thing. He'll be okay, but he's just been through a really crazy scare today."

The next day's *Oshkosh Daily Northwestern* makes a hero out of Tee Bauer, Flight 153's pilot, describing how he alerted the tower with his fly-by, kept the plane's right wing tipped up to counterbalance the Cessna's extra weight on the landing approach, and then cut power to drop the wing level just as the plane touched down. Based on where the Cessna's twisted wing was found in a farmer's field near the town of Black Earth, Tee Bauer had flown Flight 153 thirty-one miles with another airplane embedded in his own.

Co-pilot Stephen Mosley is one very lucky man, the *Northwestern* says. He had been at the controls, with Bauer reading the landing checklist, when the Cessna smashed into Flight 153's galley area, not more than three feet behind where Mosley sat. The bulkhead between the galley and the cockpit buckled but took the brunt of the impact without collapsing. Mosley's seat was pushed forward, and his head hit the windshield, but somehow, he escaped totally unhurt.

The *Northwestern* article contains plenty of quotes from grateful passengers, plenty of hosannas, and plenty of thank-yous and thank-Gods. Colin's is not among them. He was still out cold when the reporter called. Taking the advice of the National Transportation Safety Board and his lawyer, Tee Bauer has declined to be interviewed.

Two days later, things turn sour as the story unspools. The collision was Flight 153's fault, the *Daily Northwestern's* follow-up story claims. The tower, it turned out, had warned Bauer and co-pilot Mosley three times of local general aviation traffic, but they had maintained their landing approach flight path "without attending to local flight conditions and advisories." Flight 153 descended directly on top of the Cessna, whose pilot, nineteen-year-old Wayne Sampson of Neenah, never knew what hit him. Neither did his twenty-one old sister, Ramona, and his best friend, Larry

Scott. All dead, all crushed, all needing their remains to be cut out of the wreckage of their crumpled Cessna.

After an initial hue and cry about adolescent amateur pilots joyriding around the sky, reporters learn that Wayne Sampson had 350 hours of flight time in the Cessna, a twenty-year-old model 172 that he had bought and paid for himself. Instructors described him as a careful, vigilant pilot, one of their best students ever. An anonymous tip lets it be known that Tee Bauer had two previous warnings from Lake Central, as well as one disciplinary action for landing on the wrong runway in Milwaukee, which resulted in his being suspended for a month. Before Lake Central's lawyers shut him up, Stephen Mosley is quoted as saying they heard the small plane warnings, but their vision had been obscured by the afternoon sun reflecting off heavy bug splatters on Flight 153's windshield. Given that the collision took place in January, this seems to be regarded by one and all as a singularly inept excuse.

———

When Colin finally comes to, I try to give him his space, and let him come out of it at his own pace. Hospital social worker Anna Rosen has called to follow up on Colin. She tells me that a variety of emotional reactions are possible, from gratitude to denial, to wanting to give all his possessions away, to full-blown PTSD—post-traumatic stress disorder. "Different people respond to violent accidents in very different ways, Mr. Harding. Don't push him, don't press him to talk about it, but if he wants to talk, listen hard, and whatever you do, don't brush it aside or tell him the worst is behind him now. That may not prove to be true."

I call the golf pro shop at The Landings in Savannah and tell them that Colin has been involved in an airplane accident in Wisconsin, saying it is uncertain when he will return. I say they should cancel his scheduled lessons for at least the next week and I tell them that he will check in regularly to keep them posted. I ask the assistant pro to emphasize to anyone who asks that Colin is fine, with no injuries, just taking a few days to shake it off. The assistant pro seems rather annoyed by the inconvenience; he does not send best wishes, saying only, "Okay, I'll take care of it. Thanks for calling."

I call Christine, not knowing quite what response to expect. Bosom buddies as kids, Colin and Christine have never been particularly close as adults (and given our six-year age difference, neither has ever been particularly close to me). The fact that Colin and Christine are twins does not seem to have much resonance these days. When he's had a few drinks, Collie often refers to Christine as the Ice Goddess, which is not fair. My sister has always been an extraordinarily anxious person, a vulnerability she covers with a guarded aloofness. In her law practice, her surface armor serves her well. With her brother, it has led to an emotional chasm. Colin thinks Christine "has become very New York," extremely materialistic, rather superficial, and not very reliable as a source of emotional support. This was particularly true during his wife's terminal illness, when Colin felt Christine had left him high and dry to care for Susan alone. Their contact in recent years has been infrequent.

As I dial, I expect Christine to be standoffish. But hell, Collie's her brother, and he just almost died, so maybe a little empathy will bubble up from the depths of Christine's generally locked-down personality. But I'll be surprised if it does at this stage of their lives.

Christine surprises me and rebuts my cynicism, respond-ing with genuine-sounding alarm and sympathy. She offers to fly out to Green Lake to "steady" her twin brother, but I know emotional outreach will be a stretch for her. Truth to tell, although Christine is an accomplished trusts and estates lawyer, constantly rendering advice to people anticipating or experiencing bereavement, her bedside manner is not so hot. She is a numbers person, a "quant" who thinks in terms of measures and metrics and rates of return. God never intended Christine to be a social worker or "people person." Basically, a highly-defended introvert, she scoffs at people who speak of "meaningful relationships," empowerment, spirituality, and continuous improvement. She has always insisted that people should "take me as I am," the result being that most people have not taken to her at all. Over the years, Christine has remained isolated and autonomous.

Because of how she is hard-wired, and because I know Christine does not like Green Lake—or me—very much, I let her off the hook, saying I'll let her know if I think her tender ministrations are needed. What Colin does not need right now is a hands-off person pretending to be a hands-on person. For her part, Christine clearly is relieved not to be put on "play-nice duty" for Colin. She says she'll check in daily.

A polite man—for some reason I picture him as a polite *young* man—calls from a Philadelphia law firm representing the U.S. Aviation Insurance Group—the notorious USAIG. I've had experience with similar insurers in construction cases, and my view of insurance companies is a dim one. I regard them as apologists for villains, exploiters of victims. All have the same strategy: deny, disclaim, and litigate until the enemy capitulates. Eventually, they settle the case for a pittance on the courthouse steps.

The young man says his client insures Lake Central Airlines, and he wonders if Colin Harding would consider a quick, quiet settlement for any claims that might arise with respect to the mid-air "incident." No litigation, no need to engage and pay for counsel, just a fast and respectful resolution.

I decide not to put Colin on the phone, deciding I'll handle this myself. "I'm Colin Harding," I lie. "What sort of settlement amount does your client have in mind?"

"Well in light of the fact that no one on the plane suffered a serious injury, but mindful of the distress the incident might have caused, we are authorized to offer you a lump-sum settlement in the amount of $22,500."

"Twenty-two five," I say.

"Yes, that's right," says the young man, "upon execution of a complete release, of course."

"Of course, a release, yes. Well, the consequences of my... *incident* remain a little speculative at this point. I'm not sure what additional symptoms or damages may emerge."

"Well, I suppose that's possible, but this way you have immediate cash in hand, and the whole matter is behind you."

"Hmmm. Would your client be open to a counteroffer?"

"Well, I don't know. We try to be reasonable. Did you have a number in mind?"

"How about four hundred and seventy-five thousand dollars?"

I have to appreciate the young man's aplomb. "Well, that amount is beyond my authority to negotiate. Would you be good enough to take my number and give me a call back if you should reconsider?"

"Yeah, I'll sure do that."

2

Vandals and Locals and Thieves

BACK IN 2008, having navigated the Global Financial Crisis without life-threatening injuries, I believed I was at the pinnacle of my career. Around the world, badly designed buildings still frequently threatened to collapse, a signal for my phone to ring in Chicago. I did not lack panicky clients ringing me up from around the globe. *Call Victor Harding, he's the building crisis architect! Get Victor Harding, the wobbly skyscraper disaster guy!* I had a neat little niche, I had cred, my consulting practice was on firm footing, and I had a few jingles in the bank. I sure wasn't wealthy, but I was...*solvent.* My trusty financial guru, Anil Bakshi, had reassured me that I was "well-positioned for the future and for retirement, when the time comes."

When I reached my late sixties, I decided to celebrate my status and stability by shopping for a summer house, testing the market in midwinter to see if that would bring the price down. For years, I had rented a small cottage up on gorgeous Green Lake, a large and enormously deep inland lake in mid-Wisconsin, savoring the solitude, the quiet, and the company of simple, unpretentious townsfolk. Now, I thought, it was time to up the ante: buy a place where I could drive up and kick back whenever I wanted, where I could leave clothes in the closet, where I could park an old Jeep in the garage and drive it around on warm days, where I could biddy-bum into town to the ice cream parlor, make impulse purchases at the hardware store, and make friends with the local sheriff.

I put Gretchen Suiter, an overly effusive but well-respected Green Lake realtor, on the scent for suitable digs. It took her all of three days to find "the perfect place, Victor, it's *you, it's you.* Big old summer house on the north shore of the lake, six bedrooms, four baths, huge screened porch overlooking the lake, large four-acre lot that leads down to the lake, dock, boathouse, sort of a barn, really, with a sweet little apartment off the kitchen for the help, lots of big oaks. House was built in 1907, beautifully kept up. You'd be the fifth owner."

"And you think that's me?"

"Actually, I do. It makes a real statement, Victor, but it isn't pretentious or showy. Just...*substantial.* The property is named 'The Boulders.' That really says it, right? And...it's architecturally significant."

"Gretchen, there is no such thing as an architecturally significant building in Green Lake, except maybe the American Baptist Assembly."

"Well, okay, *historically significant,* then."

"And just why is that?"

"One of its owners, from 1927 to 1937, was Bugsy Moran."

"Should I know who that is?"

"Actually, you do know who that is. You've heard about the St. Valentine's Day massacre in 1929, right? The one where all those guys got gunned down with tommy guns in a warehouse?"

"I've seen Elliot Ness and *The Untouchables* on TV. I think they had an episode about the massacre. So, this Moran guy is the guy who shot them?"

"No, no, no. The triggermen were Al Capone's guys in the South Side Gang—the Italians—trying to rub out the head of the Irish North Side Gang. One George Moran. *Bugsy Moran.* Anyway, they messed up the hit. Killed a lot of his thugs, but Bugsy was late to the party, and they missed him. Rumor has it he grabbed a bunch of his guys and drove straight up here to hide out in Green Lake for a while."

"Well, that's interesting," I say.

"Yeah, well there's a bunch of wonderful myths about Bugsy's tenure as Green Lake's gangster-in-residence. Tales about stills in the garage and moonshine and surprised people being garroted or suffocated with pillows. There were even rumors of a secret escape tunnel to get down to the lake if the house was ever attacked. Pretty cool, eh?"

"Do these stories add to the value of the house?"

"Victor, don't be so difficult. Please just drive up here and see this house. It's wonderful. I promise you'll love it."

So I drove up to Green Lake, and, yup, it was love at first sight. Irrational, stirring, I-will-never-let-this-go love. This house, this giant, rambling Victorian wedding-cake perched over an elegant lawn sweeping down Green Lake, grabbed me, embraced me, soothed me, and sat me down for a serious talk. I swear I heard a siren's song, Circe whispering softly in my ear, *Home, Victor. This is home, your safe harbor, your safe haven. I'll be yours forever if you'll be mine forever.*

Sounds silly perhaps, but it's absolutely true. I was hooked.

I agreed to buy it before I even asked what the property taxes were, before I researched how much it would cost me to get the lawn mowed, or to take the dock out every winter. At six-sixty-five, the price was plenty steep and would knock a huge hole in my nest egg, but the monthly mortgage payment would be manageable, lakeside property prices were soaring on Green Lake, and my money man, the ever-prudent and invariably reliable Anil, agreed it was a sound investment.

I then took out a giant home equity line of credit and socked another two-fifty into winterizing my treasure and turning the wide screen porch into a magnificent sunroom with floor-to-ceiling glass walls that could fully retract into the side walls and open up the room's entire southern face.

I furnished this splendid living space in a sparse, Japanese style, very Zen, with polished golden oak floors, tatami mats, large Edo-period panel prints on the walls behind a row of low easy chairs that faced the lake. I bought some top-quality antique sculptures of all kinds: bronze, ivory, rosewood, small, but tasteful, each perched on an elegant blown glass pedestal positioned carefully in the room so as to accent but never intrude. I placed a large boulder in the corner whose flat bottom made it look like it was rising out of the floor.

I cannot overemphasize how serene this Japanese vibe made me feel when the decorating was done. I felt like I had worked my life for this. A gratifying acronym, a catch phrase for my current life, sprang unbidden to mind: TATGOD. *These are the good old days.*

In addition to my new home's aesthetic delights, as far as social pretensions were concerned, the house now was a showcase, a unique understated gem. Oohs and aahs at dinner parties, and all that. The truth of the matter was that I wasn't rich, but that house made me *look* rich.

—⁓—

A couple of years ago, over lunch in Chicago celebrating my seventieth birthday, Louie Stutzman, a longtime construction industry colleague, and absolute truth-teller, gave it to me straight. "Time to pack it up, Vic. Your phone is gathering dust, and it isn't going to ring anymore. You've staggered past the big seven-oh, which means that you are officially over the hill. Don't try to hang on, man. The young Turks will eat your lunch, and you'll just get humiliated. Go gracefully, but go."

I knew Louie was right. No point in denial. So, I shuttered my Chicago architectural engineering consulting practice, sold my Evanston house, severed my ties with Chicago's construction industry movers and shakers, bid my circle of high-and-mighty Chicago friends adieu, and retired to a life of full-time peace and leisure at my beautiful Green Lake house.

I was in for keen disappointment.

As I settled into Green Lake life, I found that the social order could be broken into two basic tribes: the *Locals* and the *Vandals*. The former are mostly white indigenous natives whose guiding principle is the old German saying, *was kennt er nicht, isst er nicht,* that is, "If I don't know what it is, I won't eat it."

Green Lake Locals tend to be solidly middle-class, honest, conservative, respectful of tradition, generally unimaginative (except for a small sub-set of locally-grown artists), and unfailingly polite. They don't like spicy food. They tend to like being around other white people. They generally vote Republican.

The Vandals, of which, regrettably, I am one, are *ausländers*. We are a mixed bag of interlopers, transplants from foreign places, bringing with us Land Rovers, big bucks, a casual arrogance, and a patronizing disdain for local norms and traditions. The in-migration of Vandals has flooded Green Lake in a rising tide of affluence. We Vandals act like we own the place, which, increasingly, we do. For decades Green Lake hosted a summer population of fat cats from Chicago who were generally well-tolerated by local property owners. But now party-crashers from distant lands have checked in permanently, tearing down century-old summer houses to build sprawling mansions, demanding the liquor store stock fine wines, and sending lakefront property values forever out of reach to Locals.

We Vandals are fundamentally changing the character of Green Lake, although superficially this quiet town continues to enjoy its leisurely pace and low-key midwestern vibe. In their search for serenity and simplicity, Vandals have trampled Green Lake County culture like thistles underfoot, oblivious to the simple pleasures they say they moved to Wisconsin to enjoy. Vandals' interactions with locals often are patronizing, dismissive, and flagrantly elitist. When confronted by a Local—*and such confrontations are always quiet, always polite*—Vandals, with their insensitivity, presumptuousness, and boorishness, turn snide: "How would you hicks survive without the influx of our dollars?"

On a personal level, I have never much liked Vandals, yet I myself dumped a wad into the renovation of The Boulders, putting a pretty penny into the pockets of various contractors, all Locals. In effect, I bought Leo Wunder his new crew-cab pickup truck and paid off Tom Blasuziak's mortgage. And so, if I walk like a Vandal and talk like a Vandal, should I be surprised if I am regarded as a Vandal by the Locals?

We Vandals, in turn, fall into two sub-clans: the *Lookamees* and the *Exes*. Whether *nouveau riche* or gifted with old money, Lookamees want to be seen, want their marvelous possessions to be seen and envied. Their houses are the biggest, the newest, the most lavish. Lookamees crave what sociologists call "position power"—the perks of status, the torque of economic leverage. Their pathetic attempts at feigning aw-shucks modesty—V-neck sweaters worn with tee shirts underneath, loafers with no socks, vintage Toyota Land Cruisers in the third stall of the garage—are patently transparent. I generally find the Lookamees too vocal, too pushy, too sure of themselves, too oblivious to the feelings of those who do not enjoy their privilege. I have always regarded them with thinly-disguised contempt.

As for me, I now am an *Ex.* That's somebody who was something before but isn't any more. There are a lot of us seeping into Green Lake and raising its economic water table—former judges, CEOs who have accepted the buy-out package, lawyers whose firms kicked them out because of a mandatory age 70 retirement requirement, surgeons whose hands have begun to shake when holding the scalpel. Or, like me, retired architectural engineers whose phone has stopped ringing.

These days, if I socialize with anybody in Green Lake, I tend to hang with the Exes because misery loves company, and we Exes take our fall from high station hard and personally. We have been forced off the front line and put out of action simply because of age. We know that we are on the glide path to senility and death, but we still are sentient enough to know we are—and are regarded as being—over the hill. In moving to Green Lake to "age in place," as the trendy euphemism has it, we Exes have, in effect, put ourselves outside the igloo to freeze rather than waiting to be thrown out by those who see us as nuisances. For us, Green Lake offers a last shred of dignity before we end up in the land of drool cups and fractured hips.

———

The shifting of Green Lake's economic topography has had a spillover effect in terms of crime, the rate of which has risen alarmingly in recent decades. Public safety is still pretty much okay, with little violent crime and armed robbery. But the Vandals' dollar-driven and possession-centric worldview has made them prime targets for the kind of property crime in which they are relieved of various prized high-value possessions when absent or asleep—cash, art, sculpture, jewelry, fur coats, antiques, cars and boats, lawn tractors, and the like. I later learned first-hand that much of this stolen property is fenced—that is, resold—out of state.

The thieves have become bold, voracious, and unafraid that they will be apprehended. They believe that their heists represent only a temporary inconvenience for the well-to-do and know that the victims will be reimbursed by their insurance companies, so repeat hits are becoming increasingly common: *the crooks just keep coming back for more.* The thieves, accordingly, have become more avaricious, more audacious, and better organized.

In recent years, the crime rate for high-dollar thefts has skyrocketed in Green Lake County, just as it has for many of Wisconsin's numerous wealthy inland lake communities. This trend embarrasses the God-fearing and law-abiding Locals, not to mention local law enforcement authorities. Local papers frequently lament that "it's just not safe to leave your door, your car, or even your bicycle unlocked anymore."

3

Gilbert Rennie

DURING MY PART-TIME YEARS of visiting Green Lake before taking up full-time residence, I cultivated a pleasant friendship with Green Lake County Sheriff Gilbert Rennie. One Sunday, Gilbert and I found ourselves paired in a member-guest golf tournament at Tuscumbia Country Club, and we immediately hit it off. In many ways, we were unlikely friends, but we came to enjoy our similarities—particularly our reputation as hard-nosed truth-tellers—as well as appreciate our differences.

In terms of my disdainful Green Lake nomenclature, Gilbert Rennie is a hybrid—part Vandal and part Local. Having moved from suburban Philadelphia to take care of his ailing mother just down the road in the college town of Ripon, Gilbert was, by definition, a Vandal. But now, by virtue of his job as Green Lake's sheriff, he's become a quintessential Local.

Yet Gilbert—*please don't call me Gil*—also is an Ex, although when I first met him, he was a little young to be an Ex. He had retired as the Agent-in-Charge of the FBI field office in Kennett Square, Pennsylvania after putting in his twenty. He then ran a successful private investigation practice in suburban Philadelphia for another decade. His office phone grew silent about the time his mother, who lived in Ripon (the founding site of the Republican party, by the way), had a stroke and needed constant care. So, Gilbert and Jaynie decided—*Hey, what the hell?*—to move to Wisconsin and buy a small run-down farm halfway between Ripon and Green Lake. They also bought a couple of horses, and bought, Gilbert thought, a life of ease, quiet contemplation, and all the delights of being the caregiver for the invalid materfamilias.

About the time Gilbert bought his farm, Green Lake County Sheriff Harold Lemke bought another kind of farm, barrel-rolling his Crown Vic in a high-speed crash while chasing after some punk who had stolen a bunch of pickup truck tailgates. County Commissioner Claybourne Untercoughler heard about this retired FBI agent who wasn't doing much of anything and called Gilbert to see if he might be willing to stand in as interim sheriff until the next election.

"I don't do interim," Gilbert said. "Being an interim anything just compromises your authority and suggests you're just piddling around at the job. I do it full-time, or I don't do it at all."

"Well, you could take on the job now on an interim basis and then run for Sheriff when the time comes," said Clay. "That would give you about seven months to get up to speed and get yourself known around the county."

Gilbert called around to some new acquaintances to see what the job might entail, check out the local crime rate, learn whether the Sheriff's office was respected and the deputies were honest, and interview the auto shop that would be maintaining the office's cruisers. It all checked out, so Gilbert called Untercoughler back.

"Claybourne? Sounds interesting. Let's give it a try."

The moment he said that, of course, Gilbert Rennie became a Local as well as a Vandal and an Ex.

Over the years, I have become increasingly fond of Gilbert Rennie. Similarly, I believe he quite likes me, or at least finds me an interesting diversion. In some ways, Gilbert and I are cut from similar cloth. We're both extremely cynical, for example—although Gilbert calls it "reality-hardened"— and we are both good big-picture thinkers and natural strategists. But we also are different in significant ways. We speak differently. I am verbose and enjoy five-dollar words, I often sound opinionated—because I am—and I am prone to using the gritty language of the construction industry. Gilbert generally speaks gently, prefers short words and short sentences, and often pauses before he speaks. He drops his 'G's" a lot.

Unusual for a law-enforcement type, Gilbert abhors rough language. At one of our early lunches, I started railing about a local plumber who clearly was trying to take me for a ride. I got as far as "that cocksu..." when Gilbert reached out and took hold of my shoulder, gripping me rather firmly. The gesture was not hostile, but it was clear that Gilbert meant some kind of business.

"Victor," he said quietly, "I need to ask you a favor. Although I do not tend to wave my faith like a flag, I must tell you that I am a devout Catholic. This should create no issue, except that you tend to use profanity casually and frequently. And every time you curse or describe someone or something with an off-color term, I have to stop and say a brief prayer for your absolution. And frankly, that interferes with my train of thought. So, I must ask you—around me, anyway—to be more circumspect about using such coarse language. I know conversational use of all forms of the F-word is becoming increasingly common, even in polite company, and I grant that it adds a colorful flair to your speech. But to me, it seems grating and gratuitous and unnecessary. Could I ask for your help in toning your language down somewhat?"

I don't know when I have ever blushed so deeply. I resolved to do better, and Gilbert smiled and lifted his hand from my shoulder.

As one might assume, Gilbert and I generally show different faces to the world. Outwardly aw-shucks, lean, and wiry, Gilbert is invariably affable and pleasant to everyone. Everyone describes him as a nice guy, if a little hard to get to know. Nobody describes me that way; the number of people who have called me—*excuse me, Gilbert*—an asshole over the years is legion.

Gilbert likes to talk with me, both about his job and about life in general, because I challenge him, play the devil's advocate, test his thinking, and reality-test his assumptions. He likes my probing questions, and enjoys it when I cross-examine him and he has the right answers. I sense he has no one else to talk to who is willing to push him and keep him sharp.

When conversation turns to ongoing criminal investigations, we both know there are ethical boundary issues. Integrity and confidentiality are important to him, so he is careful about what he discloses, about where certain investigations stand, and where they are going. He does not feed me insider information, and I've learned to be careful not to ask for it. Many a time, Gilbert has shaken his head apologetically over our regular lunches and said, "Sorry, can't tell you that. Just can't take you there, Victor."

But there also are times when Gilbert opens the kimono a bit and uses me as a sounding board to bounce some ideas off or test-fire some theories. He always warns me when he's about to do this. "Lemme run a situation by you, Victor"— Gilbert Rennie would never use the word 'scenario'—"see what you think. Just informally, 'course. I need this to be off the record, and I'll stop short of improper disclosure. But I'd value your opinion. You comfortable with that?"

I always say yes. Still, even if we're careful about boundaries, in the course of our regular lunches, I learn a lot about what's what in Green Lake, about routine gossip, about crimes and criminals. I'm a bright enough guy, so if, without elaboration, Gilbert lays out some tea leaves, I usually can read 'em. If he provides some lines, I generally can read between them. I can do nudge-nudge-wink-wink as well as the next guy. I know how to add two and two, and I think I generally know what the score is around the town of Green Lake. Gilbert doesn't name names, but I can often infer whom he's talking about.

Bottom line, Gilbert and I play it straight, but we do have some fun dancing around the edges.

4

About Retirement

WHAT A DREADFUL DISAPPOINTMENT the whole retirement thing is turning out to be.

It wasn't supposed to be this way. Like a lot of senior citizens prone to denial, in recent years I had deluded myself with an appealing golden years myth. Part of the mythology that I fed myself was that I really was ready to retire and kick back. I thought I had all the pieces in place—*social, emotional, financial*—to live out the last chapter of my life in serenity and security. To coast. To glide.

All those years of being called on to orchestrate emergency damage control on poorly designed skyscrapers had left me constantly on red alert and made me testy, anxious, and combative. I had been a professional trouble-shooter and crisis manager my whole career, and I looked forward to no longer having major troubles to shoot. As I crossed into my seventies, I thought I had earned the right to ease back and throttle down, to indulge myself and enjoy some just desserts.

On the social responsibility front, I particularly relished the thought of complete disengagement from family demands and expectations. No need to make nice for family's sake, to play God, or play surrogate father to the twins. At least before the plane crash, both little brother Colin and his highly self-sufficient twin were busy toiling away, if not happily, at least financially secure. They could—and should—be able to take care of themselves.

I have always been a borderline recluse, so my Green Lake social milieu was, by my choice, small, and loosely strung. My friendships were friendly, but not intimate or intense. I tended to pal around with about ten guys, all Exes, all in our seventies. Four were reasonably happily married, and their wives were easy company. Six were single: two widowers, four divorced and living alone. To a man, we were intelligent, irreverent, witty, and retired. We golfed some, drank some, pokered a little, rode around on each other's motorboats, and complained about our health a lot in the way aging men do.

Emotionally, I was feeling pretty chipper for a while there. My divorce, long and savage, was finally complete. Yeah, the harridan really took me downtown, but the huge expense of being quit of Magda Salveson was well worth it. Good riddance, indeed, the very best riddance imaginable following all those years of hostility and passive aggression (mutual, it must be confessed).

Financially, at this point, I gave myself a B-minus. I had put some bucks away over the years, and when Anil Bakshi assured me that I had largely dodged the 2008 bullet, I believed him. He said that I could expect my holdings to double about every seven years. He said I would have a decent estate to bequeath to someone when I died, if there was anyone I wanted to bequeath it to.

—⟊∿⟊—

So here I was, ready for those Golden Years, for low-key golf games, crossword puzzles, a few misery-loves-company social gatherings, and travel excursions tailored to geriatrics.

My retirement was supposed to be a new day, and I wasn't expecting stormy weather.

Silly me.

The wheels began to wobble before they totally fell off. As I settled into the role of retired person, what I learned is that the anticipation of *getting there*—of kicking over the traces and calling all my own shots—was not the same as the unrelenting tedium of *being there*. If I lived to be ninety, I was facing nearly twenty years of steady deterioration in mind and body, increasing loneliness, and soul-sapping bitterness. *Retirement was going to be booooring.*

Worse still, with plenty of time to stew, I now realized how deeply I resented the bitter reality of my retirement: *I had not jumped, I was pushed.* Louie Stutzman was right: after years of being considered the fastest, the sharpest, the most creative blade in my profession, I was being consigned to the dust heap—*simply because I was getting older.*

God, *that* sucked.

After a professional career of being in control—*totally in control*—my life was now totally out of my control. I felt demeaned, dismissed, and insulted—not because of infirmity or incompetence, but by the mere fact of age. And there wasn't a thing I could do about it. The seeds of bitterness had been sown.

God, *that* stung.

I decided that somehow, I had to take back control, to appease my lifelong hunger as a challenge junkie. I knew it would not be enough to take up some insipid hobby, to collect stamps or attend single-malt tastings, or to take old-folks cruises on Rhine riverboats. I needed something with purpose, with...*gravitas,* with guts and balls and risks and excitement.

Turns out I should have been careful what I wished for, because I sure as hell got it.

5

Bombs Away

THIS IS WHERE FATE INTERVENES, where the wheels come off, and panic sets in.

The phone rings, and a soft Indian voice introduces himself as Stephen Bakshi. I know the name, of course: he's Anil's brother. I know that he runs a small CPA firm in Albany, New York.

"Victor, I must be providing sad and surprising news. Anil has been forced to cease his financial advisory services, and I am taking responsibility for reviewing his files and closing down his accounts with his existing clients."

I feel as if I have stuck my finger in an electric socket.

"I...I don't understand. What happened? What's going on here?"

"Anil has been taken quite ill, Mr. Harding, and he will not be recovering, actually."

"But...but this is so sudden, Stephen! Did he have a heart attack or something?" My own heart suddenly is pumping hard, banging and thumping and scaring the hell out of me.

"Actually, Anil has been quite ill for some time, only none of us were realizing it. Now the course of his disease has accelerated, and the unfortunate consequences of his condition have come to light. And they are very serious, actually. Not just for him, but for his clients also."

My head spins. "Well, what's going to happen? Are you going to be taking over Anil's clients?"

"In your case, it's not that simple, Mr. Harding."

Now I know what nameless dread really feels like. My flesh crawls. Something really bad is happening here. I feel like I may vomit.

"Mr. Harding, it appears that over the last several years, Anil was developing an unusual form of degenerative brain disease, a form of dementia called *temporal lobe epilepsy.* It's also sometimes called 'ecstatic epilepsy.' Dostoyevsky had it, Lewis Carroll had it. It can advance quickly. It did in Anil's case. The condition is a consequence of the growth of a tumor on the left side of his brain."

"Too much information, Stephen! Tell me what all this means."

"In Anil's case, it means that the left side of his brain, the rational side that deals with reason and logic and detail—*and numbers*—gradually suffered diminished blood flow and began to atrophy, to *wither.* As a numbers person, Anil was definitely a left-brain fellow, you know, so this had a serious effect on both his ability and his personality. As his left brain function deteriorated, the right side of his brain became relatively more dominant. You probably couldn't tell it by talking with him, but his personality was changing in a fundamental way, and over a period of time, his judgment was becoming seriously impaired. When one of his peculiar kind of epileptic seizures occurred, which would usually be at night, his right brain would take over and Anil would first become...*blissful.* Euphoric. Inexpressibly happy. After each seizure passed, Anil would 'come out of it' and appear pretty normal, except a lot of people have told me that he was acting more effusive and optimistic in the last year or so. And he himself was telling me he was feeling more...*creative* these days."

"I hadn't noticed that," I said.

"How often did you see Anil?"

"Since I moved up from Chicago, I didn't see him at all. We had telephone meetings to discuss my finances and our investment strategy. He also sent me summary financial reports, although now that I think of it, I haven't seen one in a while."

"Don't you closely monitor your financial condition yourself?"

"Not religiously, no. Maybe I should have been more diligent, but Stephen, you have to understand how completely I trusted Anil's judgment. Over the years, he made me a lot of money, saved me a lot of money. The adjustments he made to my portfolio during the recession were masterful. I took a hit, sure, but I was back to level ground by late in 2009."

"Didn't you have to approve his strategies and transactions?"

"In our early years working together, indeed I did. But eventually, I gave Anil *carte blanche* to handle my affairs and execute transactions as he saw fit."

There is a long pause on the telephone. "That was a mistake, Mr. Harding. In the last year, Anil became rather... *grandiose*, rather convinced that he had a unique ability to recognize exceptional investment opportunities. In many cases, he was quite catastrophically wrong. He took liberties with your accounts, Mr. Harding, and you have suffered great harm."

—⁓—

Stephen summarizes the bad news in an email, promising a full report and a proposal for what to do with my diminished investments going forward. To make a horrible story short,

Anil had stripped my stock portfolio and liquidated a huge portion of my diversified mutual funds' holdings in order to invest well over three million of my dollars in two entrepreneurial enterprises that went spectacularly bust. A much-ballyhooed company that promised a revolutionary quick-and-easy finger-stick approach to blood testing proved a complete fraud. When the government indicted and convicted the founding "genius," all investors lost everything. For me, that was over two million bucks.

Anil also dumped a bunch of my dollars into a Vietnam-based startup that was going to make electric farm vehicles. After some initial favorable press, the entrepreneurs attempted a premature public offering that opened at fifty-four dollars a share. When the company finally folded less than ten months later, shares were selling at thirty-seven cents. That misadventure cost me another million dollars.

Bottom line: I have not been totally wiped out, but my net worth has decreased by approximately eighty percent. For all practical intents and purposes, I am pretty much broke.

Once my tears dry, I call Stephen Bakshi back to discuss my options. "You can, of course, sue Anil, Mr. Harding, but there would be little point. He invested his own funds in the two failed ventures, and he is well and truly without funds himself. As lawyers would put it, he's 'judgment proof.' He's home living with our mother, and his medical condition is deteriorating rapidly. The tumor is not operable."

I know I should be more gracious about this hard news, but charity comes hard when I feel my future swirling down the toilet. During our good years together, I enjoyed my relationship with Anil, although I never considered us close friends. Now I feel like this epileptic nerd has betrayed me and is abandoning me behind the mists of dementia. No time for sympathy when my own pants are on fire.

"Stephen, I know that you are a CPA. Are you also a Certified Financial Planner like Anil?"

"Yes."

"Does your role in 'wrapping up my file' extend beyond dropping a bomb on my head? Are you in a position to advise me, given the current state of my finances and property?"

"Most certainly, Mr. Harding. If you want to retain me, I would be pleased to assist you. And I have already reviewed Anil's file on your overall financial situation. And I assure you that I do not have epilepsy."

I do not laugh. "Tell me one important thing, Stephen. The most important thing to me. Are we going to be able to protect my house? I spent a huge hunk of my nest egg making sure the mortgage I was carrying was manageable. Tell me, with the financial hit I've taken, is my house at risk?"

There is a long pause before Stephen Bakshi answers. "Well, I must confess that I cannot answer that to a certainty. Victor, because you are now retired, you have no way of generating significant new income, *nah?* So, we have to look at the expense side. If you can reduce your other daily living expenditures enough, possibly you may be able to hold on to the house. But your monthly social security payment only covers about half your mortgage payment. And my heavens, the Green Lake taxes on lakefront property are really quite staggering, you know! There's nothing you can do to reduce that expense. Also, you must be keeping up with your alimony payments to Magda. Last thing you want is her suing you, *nah?* In hindsight, you probably were too generous with the divorce settlement, too much the gentleman. You probably should not have given her the proceeds of the sale of the Evanston house in a lump sum, Victor, but rather used its value to offset your large alimony obligations over time. And those obligations are very steep, yes.

"But what's done is done, *nah*? We must work with present realities, man the pumps to keep the ship afloat. So...I must say that even in this sad situation, your house is your most liquid and most valuable asset. Sell it and put a quick million into your portfolio, and you should be able to ride out the storm as we rebuild your finances. Have the means to live out a relatively comfortable retirement, actually. Just perhaps not in your present house."

The floor drops from beneath me, lofting my stomach into my throat. I try to shake off the horrible mental picture of a small one-bedroom apartment with dusty curtains, threadbare shag carpeting, and stacks of empty foil TV dinner trays heaped in a pile beside the garbage can in the corner of a small Pullman kitchen. A withered figure—*me*—sits stooped in a rocking chair in front of a tiny black-and-white TV. No wonderful Green Lake house, no sweeping vista overlooking the lake, no Zen aesthetic sensibility, no housekeeping service, no Cal, my wondrous cook. No nothing.

I am devastated.

6

A harsh way to die

ON THIS PARTICULAR THURSDAY in early February, Gilbert does not know that I am in dire financial straits, so here we are, scheduled again for our regular monthly lunch, an arrangement in which we always go Dutch. Today I arrive late and find that Gilbert, normally calm and composed, has lost his composure. A half-finished martini sits in front of him in the booth, and his fingers are pressed hard against his temples. Gilbert usually is rosy-cheeked, with an amiable aw-shucks smile. Today he is gray, and he's not smiling.

I glance at the martini and raise my eyebrows; Gilbert Rennie does not normally drink on duty.

"Don't start with me," he says wearily. "Some very ugly shit went down last night. 'Scuse my French."

I slide in across from him, nod "the usual" at the lovely Brianna, and wait silently.

"We had a homicide last night, Victor. A *murder*. A cruel and ugly murder. A young man found a harsh way to die."

He takes a whack off his martini. "Piano wire," Gilbert says, "stretched tight across the road. Set at just the right height to garrote this poor guy as he rode through on his motorcycle. The wire couldn't have been up long, 'cause traffic would have come along, right? Anyway, the wire hits this kid's helmet face shield first, slides down to the throat, and nearly tears his head off."

"Who's the vic?" I ask. In the course of our conversations over the years, I have picked up various bits of cop jargon.

"A systems engineer at Mercury Outboard Motors named Stuart Friend. Moved up from West Virginia a couple of months ago, bought a double-wide on Picayune Road, just up from where he got his big surprise. Neighbor lady says he was polite, clean liver, good grooming, dressed neat, like that. Puttin' it simply, he was a rube."

"Did he have any known enemies?"

Gilbert shoots me a dirty look. This is a standard stupid TV Police Procedural 101 question, and for me to tease Sheriff Rennie with it is in very poor taste. I gesture an apology.

"Okay, different question. Was it a hit?"

"In a way."

" You mean you know who killed him?"

"In a way. I don't know the actual person who strung the wire, but I think I know generally who killed him."

I arch my eyebrows and make a gimme-gimme gesture with my hands.

"You know about Semper?" asks Gilbert.

I shake my head.

"You been coming up here all these years and you don't know about Semper? I'm surprised. Semper is the name of a motorcycle gang based up in Berlin and also the name of the bar they own up there."

"Bad guys?"

"Not too bad. Classic *Locals*, as you would call them. In their day jobs, most of 'em are solid enough citizens. Plumbers, construction, farm machinery repair, landscaping. Like that. They ride their scooters mainly on weekends, drink a lot of beer, then go back to work on Monday. Petty crime, some vandalism, but nothing like this. Their chief honcho is this strange duck named Gunnar Spaaks. Finnish guy. He runs an auto body shop in Princeton."

"I know Gunnar Spaaks," I say. "His shop fixed up my Bimmer when I got hit from behind at the stoplight downtown last year. Very nice work, I must say."

"Gunnar's shop does very nice work, yes," says Rennie.

"So, what makes you think some Semper guy is good for this?"

"I got a motive."

I do the gimme-gimme again.

"First, you got to know that Semper stands for 'Semper Harley.' All the club members ride hogs and have nothing but scorn for what they call 'Jap crap.' Harley Davidson is their religion."

"And?"

"Last night we talked with Stuart Friend's neighbor lady, Mrs. Dora Gidden. She and young Stuart had become chatty-chatty friends, good neighbors. Stuart, just proud as punch, told her all about his pride and joy, his 1980 Honda CBX motorcycle. Don't know if you're into bikes, Victor, but a CBX is a real collector's item, the finest kind of Jap crap. Mrs. Gidden said Stuart's scooter was in showroom-new condition, He told her it had less than 5,000 miles on it. He paid $16,000 for it. He told her it was a steal."

"And?"

"Two things. First, Stuart told her he had gone up to the Semper bar and asked the lads if he could go on some of their weekend rides with them. They told him to take a hike, to use the polite expression. Mrs. Gidden says Stuart thought they were just pulling his leg about riding only with Harleys, that he could make them come around. So he went up there a couple of more times, she says, kind of badgering 'em. Stuart told her it turned ugly."

I laugh dismissively. "They would kill him just because he wanted to ride with them? That's pretty extreme."

"Well, there's more," says Gilbert. "We get up there last night and here's poor Stuart, lyin' in the middle of the road. He's mostly decapitated, only a few strings of his spinal cord still holding his head on. His throat is flappin' open, looks like the top of one of those pedal-operated garbage cans. Like I said, harsh way to die. He's wearing clean-Gene rider gear, no studs or chains or club colors. Simple brown jacket, blue jeans, street shoes. Straight arrow, for sure.

"Then we see the wire stretched across Picayune Road, still drippin' blood. Carefully wound real tight 'cross two trees, neatly wrapped, real workmanlike. Set just high enough to clear his handlebars, but still catch his face. Then we find this deep gouge in the gravel where his bike ran off the road, and we find the underbrush on the side of the road has been all knocked down."

Gilbert pauses and takes a heavy slurp from his martini. "What we don't find is Stuart Friend's Honda CBX."

7

The Joys of PTSD

CLEARLY, COLIN IS IN ROUGH SHAPE, and it soon gets rougher. In "working through" his trauma, he skips all of the intermediate stages of the grief cycle—the gratitude and denial parts—and cuts straight to full-blown by-the-numbers PTSD. Within a week, Colin develops all the classic PTSD symptoms and adds some of his own. He can't sleep, he is awakened constantly by hideous dreams, and he suffers repetitive nightmares where he is cut into pieces and thrown out a window or down a deep well. He often wakes up shrieking, his cries echoing throughout the house. Colin finally gives up trying to sleep at night, instead sitting down at the end of the dock for hours on end, taking long walks into town, or watching the 2:00 AM Monster Feature on WBAY from Green Bay. He takes up smoking.

Dark circles develop under Collie's eyes. Loud noises make him cringe or bolt to his feet. His appetite disappears, no matter what food the good and caring Cal puts before him.

Colin often finds himself grasping for the right word, stuttering, uttering malapropisms, and avoiding eye contact. Avoiding human contact, period. He withdraws. Vicious headaches drop suddenly upon him and then just as quickly disappear. He tells me he feels edgy and angry all the time. He becomes volatile, sometimes erupting into anger or unwarranted attacks. He says he feels like he wants to scream, but doesn't know what to scream or whom to scream it at.

After Colin has been at Green Lake for two weeks, I finally cajole him into a round of golf at Tuscumbia Country Club, a sweet course, a moderately-challenging course. We sign up for an early tee time, Colin muttering, "that way, if it's a disaster, we don't blow the whole day."

It is a disaster. Collie rents the best clubs they've got, and says they have a nice balance, nice heft. For a moment, he seems upbeat. At first, things seem relaxed. It's a super-fine morning. The breeze is soft, the temperature agreeable, and the course is in surprisingly good shape. Colin's first drive is three hundred and ten yards, straight down the middle. I see his shoulders relax; his arms loosen. I drive two-twenty, off to the side near the trees.

My second shot is among the best I have ever hit in my life, a high arc that bounces once and then runs obediently up to within fifteen feet of the pin. Collie's second swing looks tight, jerky, overcontrolled. The ball sails wildly over the back of the green and buries itself in coarse marsh grass. His pitch from the rough proves his mettle as a professional golfer: a soft touch, a gentle run. The ball glides down the green, actually nudges my ball, and runs eight feet past the pin.

To my embarrassment, I then three-putt from fifteen feet away. As Colin addresses his putt, I see his hands begin to tremble. A classic case of "the yips." He steps away, turns his back to the pin, and claps his hands loudly. Shakes his arms. Rotates his neck. He steps back to his putt, appears to steady himself, and eases into the stroke. The ball does not just miss the cup, it *weaves*. It performs an 'S' curve, gathering momentum as it catches the green's downward slope. It ends up twenty feet from the pin.

Colin four-putts the hole. Each time he tries to settle, a wave of tremors courses down his forearms, through his wrists, and into his fingers. His hands describe little ripples, like pebbles dropped into a pond.

"My God," he says. "What *is* happening?"

And so it goes for professional golfer Colin Harding, right up until the moment we agree to pack it in after the sixth hole. For Colin, first hole: seven. Par three second hole: par. Par five third hole: double bogey. Par four fourth hole: bogey. Par five fifth hole: six. Par four sixth hole: lost ball out of bounds, followed by his rented three iron sailing gracefully through the air and splashing gaily into a water feature. Colin just gets worse and worse and worse.

For the first couple of holes, he has been able to smile. Then he tries to bear down. "I'm trying every trick I know, Vic. I can't stop trembling. I have no feeling whatever. Man, if I can't get over this, I'm a dead duck."

—⁓—

We discuss options. Fly back down to Savannah? "Victor, you may think I'm just being a drama queen here, but I'm going to tell you something that is absolute: I will never, ever get on an airplane again. I am just going to have to work my life around that."

We talk of trains: I could drive Colin to Chicago, and Colin could grab an Amtrak from there, connecting through Alexandria. Twenty hours, best route. The bus? Twenty-nine hours. That might work, Colin says, but of course, this would depend on what he would be going back to. The answer to that turns out to be zilch. Nada. Nobody. Nothing. Empty house, empty life.

Against my advice, loyal corporate soldier Colin Harding finally calls Stephen Monfried. I listen in on the speakerphone. Colin is candid with Monfried, detailing his anxiety and volatility issues, as well as the complete disappearance of his golf game. "Steve, I can still run the pro shops and organize events, but at the moment, I am not a confident and competent teacher, and I gotta admit that up front." Maybe I hear Monfried blow a sigh of relief over the phone, maybe I just imagine it. *He's got his excuse.*

Monfried's response starts with promise, then things begin rolling downhill. "It took guts for you to tell me that, Collie. You are an enormous asset to us, and you have been for many years. You have been the face of The Landings Club, both to members and to the outside world. You have been our most popular teaching pro, particularly with our older golfers. They love playing with you, and they love it when you give the young bucks a run for their money. Stan Hitch is always talking about that sixty-six you shot last year in the pro-am. So anyway, I want to do everything I can—within reason, of course--to get you through this tough patch."

Now Monfried's voice turns distant, parental. "You're a gentle guy, Collie, but you've always been an intense competitor. That's what made you successful on the pro tour, and I know you'll fight this thing as hard as you can. But you must admit that you have become something of a loner since Susan died, and I don't know how strong your emotional support network is down here these days. If you're not teaching, I'm not sure it will be helpful—for you or for The Landings Club—having people see you rattle around all alone, processing credit cards in the pro shops. I don't know much about PTSD, but my guess is it won't magically let up just because a lot of people are clapping you on the back and buying you beers at the Marshwood Clubhouse."

There is a long, pregnant pause.

"So...I've talked to the Board, and let's do this. Let's do a leave of absence for a couple of months. A *paid* leave of absence, Collie. You take some time to get the train back on the tracks. Play some loose rounds with no pressure.

"Now don't take this wrong, but I suggest you stay up in Green Lake while you work through this thing. If you're around here, clients are going to want to know why you're not available to play, so when you do get back to teaching again, you're going to have to '*un-splain*' what's been going on. Folks may be put off if their 'professional' admits he's been incapacitated for a while. I think on the surface people may sympathize with you, but I also think you'll find a lot of pressure on you—both as a golf pro and socially. During your absence, I'll see if I can't arrange an interim or temporary hire to fill in the gap. I understand John Whittle might be available. At the end of a month, c'mon down and we'll all sit down and see where things stand."

When Monfried hangs up the phone, Colin's face is a mask of pain. He puts his palms up to his cheeks and opens his mouth in a long, silent grimace—an effect eerily similar to Edvard Munch's famous surrealist painting, *The Scream.* I know what that scream signals, what it portends: *Colin Harding, everything you are, everything you need, your entire life and livelihood—all are going to be taken away from you.*

"Fourteen hours, Colin? *Fourteen hours?* Where the hell have you been with my car for fourteen hours?"

Collie avoids eye contact. "Drove to Minneapolis, then to Des Moines, and then back here. Seven hundred and forty miles. Rest stops for lunch and dinner. Stopped to play with someone's dog."

"I think I deserve better than some wisecrack answer, bro. A person with raging PTSD drops off the map for a day and you don't think people just might get a little bit concerned? Don't you think I'm entitled to be upset? Why didn't you answer your cell phone?"

"Left it here. Intentionally. I didn't really intend to drive all that far. I just wanted to get away for a bit, and when I got away, I just kept wanting to get further away. Look, Victor, I know it was an inconsiderate thing for me to do, but at least I can report some good news."

I plunk myself down heavily in the Eames chair and put my hands over my eyes. "And just what, pray tell, good news comes out of a casual fourteen-hour gallivant?"

"*Peace*, Victor. That's what came out of it. And I am not kidding. And it's not just your spiffy Bimmer, either. I started up Highway 51 toward Rhinelander. Something about the movement, the motion, the...*something*, I don't know, and I felt myself begin to let down. To...*settle*. I wasn't zoning, and I wasn't speeding, and I wasn't on cruise control. I was just... *driving* the car. And the tension began to wash away. I didn't know why, and I didn't care. I began to feel that as long as I was driving...*I would be okay*. I got up to Highway Eight and turned west. Okay, I know this sounds wackadoo, but the more I drove, the more relaxed I got, the more...*serene*...I got. I felt like I could drive—focused and alert, not in la-la land-like, indefinitely. After fourteen hours, I still feel that way. I could climb in right now and do fourteen more hours."

A pitched battle breaks out between my head and my heart. On one hand, this tale is just about the most hair-brained thing I have ever heard. *Driving therapy? I mean, really?* On the other hand, can I, should I, dismiss Colin's report on the state of his own feelings? If someone says, *"Hey! The medicine worked!"* how can anyone say otherwise? And if I say, "oh, this is all just hogwash in your head" ...*well, of course it is!* That's where PTSD lives! Only a placebo effect? Who cares?

Since the plane crash, I have been researching everything I can about PTSD in internet psychology texts and scientific journals and self-help books. In my opinion, they all echo Mark Twain's famed lament that "Everybody talks about the weather, but no one does anything about it." Now I recall a hard-nosed article on PTSD in a veterans' magazine interviewing battle-scarred veterans of the Iraq and Afghanistan wars. One quote stuck with me: "You don't know when PTSD is going to hit, you don't know how it's going to hit. You don't know how long it's going to hit. But, short of clearly self-destructive behavior, if you find something that works on your PTSD, *work it as long as it works.*"

8

Phone Home

A HELL OF A BIRTHDAY THIS IS. Ironically, it falls on Valentine's Day, and I'm not feelin' the love. From anyone. From anything. My seventy-second anniversary is a cruel reminder that death lurks in the shadows for people my age, ever ready to pick us off. Ready to pick *me* off. My seventy-second birthday soaks through my psyche, a sullen whisper of distress and impending doom. Today, there is no joy in Mudville.

Collie has had a bad night, a nightmarish scream-a-thon with multiple wailing, thrashing outbursts. Shortly past dawn, hollow-eyed and exhausted, I pour myself a cup of coffee in the breakfast room, feeling like I've been hit by a truck.

Then I *am* hit by a truck. I pick up the *Oshkosh Daily Northwestern* off the back porch and spread it out on the breakfast table. And there it is, front page, center, an elegant headshot of Xenophon Stakhatos, his warm smile, as usual, embracing the entire universe.

Only now he's dead.

As someone who is not articulate about emotions, I cannot adequately describe what Xenophon—*Phone* to his friends—has meant to me, except to say he is one of the few people on this earth who has ever meant *anything* to me. Armed with all the colorful eccentricities of a well-known sculptor and poet, Phone had always been a full-blown lover of life and lover of people. Quintessentially Greek, he was always genuinely kind, genuinely sincere, genuinely empathic...*genuine, period.* To one like me, who loathes any form of pretentiousness and self-importance, Phone was a highly-actualized human being. I loved him—loved being around him, loved hearing him read his poetry and spout his philosophy, loved watching him craft oversized outdoor sculptures, loved watching him dance when he got drunk, and, most of all, loved how tolerant he was of me and my prickly disposition.

Actually, I first met Phone in my professional capacity as the savior of vulnerable buildings. Phone had designed a magnificent sweeping house up on a high bluff about three miles from Green Lake, challenging local builders to take themselves in directions they could never have imagined. From the street, the house was reminiscent of Frank Lloyd Wright's great turn-of-the-century prairie houses, all sweeping horizontal planes anchored to the earth as if the house was an extension of natural crags and outcroppings. On the lake side, the house was a soaring cantilevered statement of freedom and flight that Phone called "the flying wing."

When the movie "ET—The Extraterrestrial" came out in 1982, Phone's daughter Vilma repurposed a large, abandoned tombstone and had it placed at the entrance to the driveway. Its smoothly polished granite face now was engraved, "Phone Home."

Sadly, the local builders had proved unable to comprehend Phone's complex load calculations and feared the flying wing might sag and collapse if they built it as he designed it. So, without telling Phone until after the deed was done, they added an enormous amount of extra rebar to the house's cast-concrete infrastructure, to the point where the foundation could not support it. When I got the call to come have a look, the entire house already showed sickening signs of sliding down the long embankment toward Green Lake.

My prescription was simple and effective. We injected 40,000 pounds of liquified cement—a product called "grout" in the building trade—under the entire foundation, basically building a mountain under Mohammed. Once the grout injection dried and cured, the house became as solid as my friendship with Phone.

Now Phone was dead, and my most powerful friendship was torn from me.

—◠◡◠—

A decade older than me when we met, Phone claimed to have no fear of death itself, but he said he was intensely put off by the process of dying. Then, at seventy-eight, Phone suffered a stroke that partially paralyzed his left side. Mercifully, for the moment, it spared his speech and his right hand, his writing hand. He was forced to spend his weekdays in a convalescent facility in Ripon. On weekends, Vilma, bless her soul, would drive him out to Phone Home, where she was good enough to feed him and change his diaper.

In the dark of the previous winter, I had received a handwritten note from Phone that said:

> Victor, to pass the time until I die, I have written myself a poem. As I look at it, I suppose it might resonate with you, as well.

TRENCH WARFARE

Accursed enemy sneaks toward me, thinking I won't notice,

Thinking I will look away, but I don't.

It surrounds me now, all about me

It crouches in its shadowed trench, then

Crawls toward me, inch by inch, inexorable,

In no hurry, certain of the outcome.

I marshal what defense I can, but, really,

What I am to do? Where am I to go?

My time has come and will soon be gone.

This implacable enemy may allow me a moment's peace,

But will never make peace, never retreat,

Will just soldier on, bent on leaving no survivors.

I see the spikes on his helmet. Now and again

I espy a dark face that glances furtively

Over the top of that evil ditch,

Then ducks back down, returns to inching toward me.

I cannot escape under cover of darkness.

I can only wait for darkness to cover me.

> -Victor, you seem a sensible fellow. Bad things come to those who wait, so don't wait. Time suspends for no man, and as my present condition demonstrates, we cannot

presume indefinite control. You must act, Victor, you must act! You must take control.

Warm regards at the turning,

Xenophon Stakhatos.

The Oshkosh morning paper provides all the details, tells the tale of Phone's final assertion of control. Everyone assumed he couldn't drive, but it turned out he could, at least well enough to get into town, where he parked his ancient Packard Clipper behind the Wilmot Bait and Tackle store. Somehow, Phone dragged himself into a green rental rowboat, untied it, and sat himself down. He waved gaily to Bud Wilmot behind the cash register in the bait store. Phone could not row, so he just let the boat drift, let the lake currents slowly push him several hundred yards offshore.

There were several other boats nearby—two fishermen from Waupaca, a rich guy in a Carver flybridge cabin cruiser far too large for Green Lake, and a group of teenagers preparing to water ski. They all saw Xenophon Stakhatos brace himself on an oar and struggle to his feet, waver, stand straight for a moment, and scream, "Veni! Vidi! Vici!" They all saw him put a pistol in his mouth and pull the trigger.

This all made quite a sensation in Green Lake, a town not much given to theatrics. I thought the idea of a doomed man taking himself out on his own terms was powerful stuff, but I also found that I could not get my mind around the idea that the man who had jotted a warm personal note on an intensely personal piece of poetry had ended up floating face down on a placid lake in Wisconsin.

Crushing, absolutely crushing.

9

In Which I Start My Life of Crime

"IS IT HOT?" I say, standing on my veranda, my face surrounded by clouds of vaporized breath. It is the day after my birthday. Big deal.

Odell Todd, my trusty lunkheaded yardman, flashes his wonderful lop-sided smile. "Let's just say it's lukewarm," he drawls.

"Is it from around here? I don't want some irate local greenskeeper knocking down my door and sticking a pistol in my face."

"I think it came from New Hampshire."

"How do you know that?"

"There was a repair tag dangling from the steering wheel from some lawnmower shop in Hanover."

"How'd it get all the way out here?"

"Can't rightly say."

"Can't...or won't?"

"Come on, Victor, don't bust my chops. You know how these things go. Anyway, it's a safe purchase. Lawn tractors don't come with titles, o' course. So, you interested or not?"

Okay, here I am on the ides of February, being asked if I want to buy a hot lawn mower. *Is this a great moral tipping point in my life?* Believe it or not, in this moment, I am conscious that perhaps it is. Not just because I'm considering committing a petty crime, but because of the decision-making process involved. I have always tried to appear to be a scrupulously straight-arrow type, absolutely above reproach, not because I am genuinely moral, but because this principled posture minimizes hassles and death threats and random beatings. But these days things are different.

These days I'm feeling angry, I'm bitter, and I'm looking for revenge. *Against somebody, Against everybody.* Following Phone's suicide, I'm feeling melodramatic. I reflect on the significance of this simple act of defiance. Perhaps the purchase of a stolen lawn tractor is a strange way to flip my middle finger to the forces of fate, or maybe it's the face of karma, Green Lake style.

Anyway, here I am, about to tiptoe into the dark world of receiving stolen property. Odell, clearly on the take, is offering me a minor cosmic joke at the straight world's expense, and here I am, deciding whether to cross the line. I think of Julius Caesar's decision to cross the Rubicon: *Alia iacta est,* Julius said. *The die is cast.*

So I know exactly what I'm getting into when I say to Odie, "How old is it?"

"Prob'ly ten, fifteen years or so. Hain't checked the serial number for year of manufacture."

"Looks like someone did a nice job of cleaning it up."

"Didn't they just?" grins Odie. "The Semper guys took it over to Gunnar Spaaks' body shop, and he cleaned it up for us."

I feign ignorance. "Semper guys?"

"That's my motorcycle club up in Berlin. *Semper Harley.* We all ride Harleys."

Proud as a new father, Odell Todd stands next to a John Deere 8500 golf course mower perched on a small flatbed trailer behind his clapped-out pickup. The mower been repainted, and it looks nice. But it looks backward to me. I am used to lawn tractors having big tires in the back, and the little ones up front. The 8500 is just the opposite, and to me, the driver's seat looks like it's pointing the wrong way.

"It looks like I'd have to spin my head around in order to drive it. Like in *The Exorcist.*"

"You don't have to drive it, Victor! I'm the one who's gonna be using it."

"What's wrong with what you're using? Isn't Cub Cadet a good brand?"

"It was a piece of crap when it was new, and it's a complete piece of junk now. The mower deck is rusted through, and when you lower it, it don't come down straight, so the cut is all uneven. Makes your yard look like hell. Also, the motor mounts are shot, so it's throwing the drive belts every time I cut. Throw that thing out, Victor, and buy me a real machine. *Please.* This is a big yard, and as soon as it warms up around here, I'm gonna need a big machine to do my job right."

"What's it going to cost me to 'do the job right?'"

"Well, this one probably cost twenty grand when it was new, and just look how it's been gone over. It's a classic, man."

"*A classic golf course mower.* Now there's a concept. How long will this thing last me, Odie?"

"Forever, if it's maintained good, and you know how good I am at that, even at keeping that Cub Cadet running. I'll do that with this here Deere. This thing will make your yard look like a five-star golf course. Come on, Victor. This is just peanuts to you."

"Odie, it so happens that I'm very low on peanuts right now. I'm running on a real tight budget these days."

Odie nails me right between the eyes. "Victor, as long as you have this house, you have to maintain this house, right? Maybe you can cut back on other stuff, like buying all that fine scotch you're always drinkin', but you can't cut back on quality lawn care. It's gotta get top priority, am I right?"

Odell Todd has never spoken this directly, this *impudently*, to me. He really, *really* wants me to buy this thing.

"I must admit that you have a point, Odie. Just how many of my peanuts do you want?"

"We can let you have it for...fifty-two hundred. Fair market for it is probably eighty-five hundred."

"Who's 'we?'"

"Well, Gunnar Spaaks actually owns it, bought from Kerry Crouch, a Semper guy. I told Gunnar I'd show it to you."

"Gunnar from the body shop in Berlin?"

"Yeah, Spaaks Auto Body Works. That's my day job."

"Well, you guys sure did a good job on my Bimmer. Actually, excellent job."

"You mean Beemer."

"No, Odie, I mean Bimmer. In the world of BMW motor vehicles, 'Bimmer' is the nickname for the car. 'Beemer' refers to BMW motorcycles. Gunnar fixed my Bimmer, not my Beemer, because I don't own a Beemer."

"Stop jerking me around, Victor. Bimmer, Beemer, who cares? Anyway, Gunnar says he knows you. He thought it was cool that I ended up being your yardman."

"Well, Odie, you do great work, and I'm hoping we can continue that. But I got to be straight with you. As a retired person on a fixed income, I have to tell you that I'm very, very short of cash at the moment."

"What, you're firing me?"

"Absolutely not. You're right, the grass will continue to grow whether I'm cash-strapped or not, so your services are not the first expense I'm going to cut back on. But I must tell you—and Mr. Gunnar Spaaks, too—that I don't have five grand in loose cash lying around right now. Ask Spaaks if he'll take three grand. You know, as a returning customer."

"Aw hell, Victor. That's way low. Could you do forty-three?"

"Getting warmer, Odie, but you're not home yet."

"Can't go lower than thirty-eight, Victor."

My pride will not permit me to say that I cannot afford to pay thirty-eight hundred bucks for top-quality John Deere yard equipment. And Stephen Bakshi be damned, I know I have a little cash in my Vanguard brokerage account. Yeah, okay, I can swing this purchase even without hitting the HELOC.

"Okay, I'll go thirty-eight. Just to keep you happy. But Odie? Let's be clear. If after I buy this thing from you guys, somebody turns around and steals my stolen lawn tractor? I'll be coming after *you*. I've heard about that game, Odie, and I won't play. Please don't ever do anything to make me dime you out, okay?"

"I hear you, Victor. I'll keep it locked in the storage garage."

"That's good, Odie. You do that. Keep me happy, Odie. Keep me happy."

10

A Good Day for Gilbert

I WALK INTO MORTON'S for our lunch date, and Gilbert Rennie, grinning from ear to ear, raises a half-empty martini glass to me. Another, this one empty, sits in front of him. I slide into the booth across from him, and gesture at his martini.

"This lunchtime cocktail thing getting to be a habit?"

"Good reason to celebrate. Hell, *great* reason to celebrate!" Heads turn from other booths and tables.

"Do tell," I say.

"We got the Chris Craft. And we caught a lot of other fish, too. Big day. *Big day.*"

Gilbert is alluding to the biggest residential heist in Green Lake history, in which a crack team of burglars had cleaned out the palatial lake house of Rafael Borden while he and his family were in Bhutan. In plain sight at midday, a neighbor saw them roll up to Rafe's lakefront neo-baroque chateau in a white box truck with a magnetic "BYA Residential Services" sign positioned neatly on the side. Dressed in fresh dark blue jumpsuits, the burglars had disarmed the security system and spent over two hours systematically lugging anything and everything of value out of the house—art, sculpture, jewelry, selected furniture, a full set of Herend bone china, Rafe's antique silver flatware, his watch collection, and even most of his clothes. They had left Rafe a neatly lettered note on the floor of the front hall:

> Hope you all had a nice time in Bhutan. In case you forgot it, your security code is 020777. All the best, BYA Residential Services. PS: Most security experts think it is a bad idea to use your birthday for your security code.

As the house was being pillaged, a second team, also dressed in blue overalls and described by witnesses as casual and relaxed, went down to Rafe's boathouse, took the winter cover off his freshly restored 1941 Chris Craft barrelback speedboat, hotwired the ignition, lowered the glistening mahogany beauty into the frigid waters of Green Lake, and, in the dead of winter, motored it two miles over to the municipal ramp. There, they were seen loading it onto a large, galvanized trailer later discovered to be stolen from Stoltzfus Marine and RV in Ripon. They then climbed into their white Ford van tow vehicle and motored calmly away. No one accosted them or asked them what the hell they were doing or where they were taking an antique Chris Craft at this time of year.

It was ten days before the brazen burglary was discovered. The *Green Lake Register* had a field day with the story for days, and Gilbert Rennie had found himself unjustifiably ridiculed, as if he had stood by with his finger in his ear, watching the crooks carry the loot past his indifferent eyes. One editorial that particularly galled Gilbert was headlined, "Hey Sheriff Rennie, *How About Some Action?*"

"Where'd they find the Chris?" I ask.

"Lake City, Florida. We suspected it would go out of state, but still, I'm surprised it got that far south."

"Who found it?"

"Swear to God, it was parked right by the highway. It had been covered by a canvas tarp that got blown off in that tropical storm down there last week. Local marina owner thought it strange that a pristine antique Chris Craft was sitting in the lot of some guy who sells rusty used farm equipment. Called the state police. Things began moving real fast after that."

"Someone wasn't too bright, or else someone was an amateur in receiving stolen property."

"It gets better, Victor. The guy who owns the farm equipment dealership is singing like a canary. He paid thirty-five grand in cash for the Chris and had a deal to sell it on for a hundred and twenty-eight. It was one day from being picked up and taken to Mexico when the storm hit. Now we've taken down the Mexican buyer, too. And he's not, shall we say, an 'innocent purchaser.'"

"The farm equipment dealer knew the Chris was coming. This was a planned heist, a planned deal. And—get this—*the dealer rolled over on his fence*. Fingered the guy 'up north' he's been buying stolen property from for over ten years. Says the guy runs a big fencing operation out of Green Lake with 'distributors' all over the south."

Gilbert Rennie winks at me and takes a long deep sip of his martini. "Surprise, surprise, Victor. Soon this will all be public knowledge, so I can tell you. Our big-time fence is a guy you have been enjoying drinks with at Happy Hour here at Morton's ever since you came to town."

My mind flashes through a rogues' gallery of my local drinking acquaintances. Mostly Vandals, and a few of the sharper Locals. No one fits my mental stereotype of a squinting Shylock with greasy hair, a stubbly beard, and an evil grin. "Okay, I'll bite. Who's our local dark lord of the underworld?"

"According to the perp in Florida, he's been buying stolen stuff for years from Clarence Causley. Thousands and thousands of dollars worth per year."

I have to laugh. "*Clarence Causley?* Be serious! Gilbert, that guy is my age!"

Gilbert laughs back, loving the moment. "Well, he wasn't always your age, Victor. And apparently, he's been a busy boy, a real fence's fence. He's not a crime kingpin himself, but when it comes to receiving and fencing stolen property, it seems he's been at the top of the local food chain for quite some time now."

I remain stunned and surprised, running a high-speed review of my mental tapes to try to reconcile what I think I know about Clarence—a quiet, personable type, always in gray flannel slacks and a dark blue polo shirt—with this new information.

"But according to what Causley told me when we were getting acquainted, Gilbert, he doesn't need to do this. He told he walked into a big inheritance years ago and has all the money he'll ever need."

"Dunno," says Gilbert. "Maybe he did, maybe he didn't. But he sure is going to need some big bucks for his legal fees."

"Well, Gilbert, I guess you're relieved."

Gilbert pings his index finger off his martini glass, creating a silvery ring. "Yeah, you could say that," he says, grinning.

———

I've come by Gilbert's office because I can't wait for our next Morton's lunch to learn how the great fencing conspiracy is shaking out. This is all just too juicy. I ask how much he is comfortable revealing. Gilbert sits behind the gray metal desk in his office, hands clasped behind his head. He looks like Rod Steiger in *In the Heat of the Night,* only slimmer. I think he quite likes it when I visit him at his place of business. The stiff tension has drained from his posture, warm color has returned to his cheeks. "Ah, yes, Victor, the *Green Lake Register* has transformed me from *incompetent* to *incomparable,* transforming me"—here he makes little quotation marks in the air with his hands—"into a sleuth's sleuth who has used his extensive FBI experience to bring Green Lake's crime wave to a halt.' All this because we caught a fence. You can bet the next time there's a robbery or burglary, I'm gonna be the goat again. But for now, phew! I'm the golden boy! Quite a relief."

"Are you getting some good intel from busting Causley?" I ask in a fascinated whisper.

"Look, Victor. I trust you to keep confidences, but I'm not about to compromise any of my investigations by stepping over the line. So, I'm sure you'll understand if I watch my words. I'm comfortable discussing anything that is of public record, and frankly, I'm also okay telling you anything that I know is soon going to become public record.

"As I'm sure you know, a lot of law enforcement folks enjoy confidential relationships with reporters and folks from the media. I did when I was with the FBI. I had a particularly tight relationship—straight up, of course—with a reporter from the *Philadelphia Inquirer,* and I was okay with giving her various tidbits 'on deep background.' Meaning off the record and without attribution. My higher-ups knew about it, and they were okay with it. In fact, they periodically used my source to plant stories or put the right spin on events that involved the Fibbies.

"I'm comfortable extending the same courtesy to you, Victor, with the same ground rules: we're off the record, and anything I say to you is not for attribution. Put differently, I *may* answer your questions, but I *don't have to* answer your questions. We clear on that?"

"Right as rain," I say. "If I ever push the boundary, just rap my knuckles."

Gilbert laughs and breathes a sigh of evident relief.

"So, you've arrested ol' Clarence, right?"

"I can say yes to that. Right in his living room. Sitting in front of his fireplace. Very cordial."

"What did he say?"

"He said, and I quote, 'Aha.'"

"Was he surprised? Frightened?"

"Taking your questions in order, one: perhaps. Two: no. Very calm, very polite. He asked procedural questions—*What next?* And all that—and I gave him procedural answers."

"What does come next?"

"Well, it's public record that I have filed a local charge, single count of receiving stolen property, just to assert criminal jurisdiction. Asked for cash bail of five hundred dollars. Clarence Causley is hardly a flight risk. But—off the record, Victor—the whole case is going to flip to the feds, because it has a lot of pieces, and it crossed state lines, and the dollar amounts involved are big. I get to go back to writing traffic tickets.

"If you were the Oshkosh FBI office, you'd probably want to pull Clarence's phone records. If you did, maybe you'd find a lot of numbers in Georgia, Tennessee, Kentucky, and Florida. And also up here, in northern Wisconsin and Minnesota. Interestingly, probably no numbers west of the Mississippi River. If I were still with the FBI, I'd start workin' downstream, wedging the small fry, playing 'em off against each other, and using 'em to try to ID major players and traffickers and transportation rings who are working across state lines. That might lead to takin' down a *big* conspiracy, all 'cause of Clarence Causley."

"Is that what the FBI is going to do? All that *workin'* and *wedgin'?*"

"I honestly don't know what their strategy is, Victor. Once a local case gets flipped over to the feds, their people tend to get real tight-lipped. As far as they are concerned, I, the local bumpkin sheriff, have done my job, and now I can just butt out. I'm going to keep sniffing around, of course, and the Fibbies can't stop me from giving Causley a rough time on local charges. But what we got here now is your classic 'two-pronged' investigation. In other words, a recipe for steppin' on each other's toes."

I rise from my chair and reach over the desk to shake Gilbert Rennie's hand. "Well regardless of where the feds take it from here, you've done good work at your end. Nice work, Gilbert. I'm very happy for you, for your cred, and for law and order in Green Lake County. What's Clarence tell you about all this?"

"I can't tell you, but perhaps you can draw some inferences from the frustrated expression on my face."

"Speaking hypothetically," I say—and here Gilbert grins knowingly at me—"why wouldn't he angle to cut a deal? After all, he's just the middleman, right? Not like he's the mastermind."

"Clarence Causley is a proponent of the philosophy *don't do the crime if you can't do the time*. I'm sure he's aware that the standard sentence for a crime such as his usually is a formulaic eleven to twenty-three months. He's got a clean record, so maybe he gets less. Bottom line, he probably doesn't gain much by pleading out."

"Wow," I say. "Ice water in the veins. That's pretty stout for someone his age facing time in the can."

"Yep," says Gilbert.

"Even if the phone records help the Fibbies finger some of the players downstream, seems to me the better question is *who do you figure is upstream?* Who's pulling all these jobs that Clarence has been fencing?"

"If I knew, I'd already be makin' arrests, right? But I got good guesses, and I'm beginning to develop a little intriguing intel. I'm not about to name names, but as far as the type of crimes go, I figure it's different strokes for different folks. I think the Semper biker guys—at least some of 'em—are doing cars and motorcycles and pickup trucks, and maybe they don't even fence a lot of it. Just sell it themselves word of mouth or chop it up for parts. But big-ticket items or items they want to be sure go out of state? I think Clarence would be the one who gets the call.

"Smash-and-grabs are always local drunks and druggies. Clarence gets dialed in only if they find themselves with something really valuable, something with a sizable take even after the fence takes his fifty-percent cut. Heavy equipment? The farm tractors and bulldozers and like that? Man, I have no clue, not around here. Back in Pennsylvania, we identified the gangs that specialized in that kind of stuff, but out here? I'm drawing blanks. I expect I'll learn who they are at some point."

Gilbert pauses, and looks up at the ceiling as if deep in thought.

"Now, hijackings? Like truckloads of tires or cigarettes or computers? I think that's gang stuff, organized crime, just like ol' Bugsy Moran back in the prohibition. You may not think this rural area is ripe for organized crime activity, Victor, but it is. Hell, you're only an hour and a half from Milwaukee, less than two from Chicago. Lots of back roads. So you got organized crime dipping its toe in the water. This kind of stuff isn't new, Victor."

Gilbert leans in toward me, abandoning his breezy tone. His seriousness makes me sit up tall in my chair.

"What is new is these sophisticated, carefully-planned operations with trucks and uniforms and, like, 'Hey, I know when you're out of town and the house is empty.' Like the hit on Rafe's house, with everything carted out like a moving company and his Chris Craft ending up in northern Florida a couple of days later. This is scary territory because these are not opportunistic burglaries or random hits. To me, they're like contract hits by the mob—specific target, carefully planned conspiracy, radios, and sophisticated comms, a lot of moving parts."

Gilbert straightens. "When they see these kinds of elaborate enterprises, these days federal law enforcement guys think RICO. If they'll talk to me, I'm going to try to get the feds to pull Causley into a RICO case. That will frost his apples."

"I don't know what RICO is," I confess.

"RICO is a very scary federal anti-racketeering law. It was designed to allow mob leaders to be charged even with crimes they didn't personally commit, but *conspired with other people to do.* RICO was passed to close loopholes where mob bosses who ordered hits couldn't be charged because they hadn't personally committed the crime."

"Sounds heavy," I say. "As in a sledgehammer."

"Oh, yeah. When a defendant is convicted in a RICO case, he faces twenty years imprisonment *for each count charged in the indictment.* And each 'overt act' that's part of a so-called 'pattern of racketeering activity' is a separate count."

"I'm waiting for you to get to the point," I say.

"Although RICO originally was intended to target just the Mafia, when I was a Fibbie we used it—and frankly, we sometimes abused it—to cover a whole gamut of crime conspiracies. I think the gangs around here that plan and commit a lot of property crimes are engaging in a pattern of racketeering activity that could be charged under RICO.

Now, if Clarence Causley has been fencing for the kind of dudes that are pulling these kinds of heists—and it certainly appears that he has—that means he's caught in the RICO net, too. He's not just some old codger involved in fencing chickenfeed heists.

"As a test case, I'm going to ask the feds to charge Clarence Causley under RICO. That should wake that stubborn old coot up. And he's really not going to love the RICO provision that allows for forfeiture of property used to further the crime. In practical terms, that means the feds could move to confiscate Clarence Causley's farm."

"Wow, that's extreme," I say.

Gilbert shrugs. "Cuts both ways. Sure, Clarence's arrest obviously is a good thing, Victor, but as a practical matter it also spells trouble for me."

"I don't follow."

"His arrest means a crucial part of the supply chain for all sorts of theft has just been taken out. Clarence obviously has been a high-volume fencing resource for the thieves—a lot of stuff has been passin' through him and then, apparently, out of state. If he's out of action, there's suddenly a vacuum—no more safe and respected clearing house for all these different kinds of thieves.

"*Thieves need fences.* They can't traffic stolen property downstream themselves. A lot of these clowns aren't smart enough or connected enough to handle a high volume of high-ticket items, much less the traffic in blue-collar-level stolen goods. But that doesn't mean some of 'em aren't goin' to try. Someone's goin' to try to fill Clarence's shoes. I think there's gonna be turf wars and all kinds of Hatfield-and-McCoy rivalries. I bet there's going to be violence. I think

I'm going to have my hands busy. May be time to hire an additional deputy here in Green Lake."

———~~~———

Two weeks later, there's no martini in front of Gilbert Rennie at our Morton's lunch, but he's most definitely in an upbeat mood.

"My, aren't we jolly," I say.

"Let's just say we're sort of semi-jolly. What we got is sort of a good news-bad news story. The good news is that the Fibbies are having a field day with Clarence Causley's phone records. Kind of a breakthrough. They issued a press release, so I'm free to tell you what's going down. Thirty arrests already, all across the south. All sorts of slimy little weasels falling all over themselves in their hurry to dime each other out. They're fingerin' each other, begging for plea deals. FBI has already recovered tons of stuff, from Lamborghinis to stolen show dogs. And I don't have to do much of anything except be kept in the loop."

Once again I shake his hand. "Loud congratulations from the cheering section," I say. "So, Clarence Causley talk yet?"

"That's the bad news part. Clarence won't sing. Off the record, Victor, I got a polite phone call from Causley's lawyer up in St. Paul. Carl McCausland of McCausland and McCausland. Nine-hundred-bucks-an-hour type, white-collar crime. And McCausland says, 'Like Clarence told you before, sheriff, there will be no singing, no dancing. The feds and southern local cops may be able to take down a lot of low-level jerkwaters, but when it comes to action central in Green Lake, the buck will stop with Clarence Causley. You and the feds can do whatever you want to try to loosen him up, fiddle with the bail, convene a grand jury, and stack the trial dates on top of one another. Clarence will not say one word . If either you or the feds stick phone records in his face, he'll just plead the Fifth. So, Sheriff Rennie?' McCausland says to me, 'don't try to contact him or interview him or wedge him or get to him through his family. If I hear of any... *chicanery* down there in rural Wisconsin, I will ask the court down there to slap you silly. Am I being clear?"

When Gilbert Rennie is angry or intense, a pale vein begins to pulse in the center of his forehead, just as it's doing now. "Okay, if that's the way Clarence wants it, we'll nail him to the barn door straight up, over and over, jury trial demanded in each case. We are going to kill him with legal fees."

"Holy smoke, Gilbert," I say. "You're beautiful when you're mad."

"Yeah, well, now I've really got something to be mad about. And here's more bad news. I'm never going to tell this to McCausland—and please understand that I'm not telling this to *you*, if you get my drift—but the Department of Justice has declined to bring a RICO case against Causley."

"What? Why would they do that?"

"Basically, they say that it's a bridge too far, that this kind of case would stretch RICO beyond the type of enterprises it was designed to attack. They sounded all noble and high-and-mighty, although the DOJ has been guilty of plenty of 'abuse of RICO.' Maybe that's why they're shuttin' us down now. Anyway, they seem to think that all our property crime around here is just small-time heists that should be attacked with state criminal laws, not RICO."

"I'm really sorry to hear that, Gilbert," I say.

Of course, in fact I am not in the least sorry to hear that. Later in our lunch I think of my steaming hot John Deere lawn tractor and tiptoe back into the topic of Semper.

"Gilbert, before, you said that some of the motorcycle, pickup and car thefts were probably Semper things."

"I may have mentioned that, off the record, of course."

"Does that mean that Semper itself acts as a criminal enterprise, or just that some Semper members steal stuff?"

"Could be both. Why do you ask?" Gilbert says.

"Well, one of the Semper guys, Odie Todd, is my yard man, and I want to know if I should count my silverware every time he comes by to mow my lawn."

"I know Odie," Gilbert says. "If he's into bad deeds, it's minor heists. I think your silver tea service is probably safe."

"He works for Gunnar Spaaks at the body shop," I say flatly.

"Yes, he does," says Gilbert Rennie just as flatly.

I pause.

"So, what do you think of Gunnar Spaaks?"

"I feel like you're trying to box me, Victor, trying to get cute with me. I'm not going to go there. I can say this much. As a civilian, I like Gunnar well enough. We've actually talked some. He helped me get oriented in Green Lake. I think he's pretty smart, pretty polite, interesting to talk to. Heavy duty military background. Used to be a jet pilot.

"I find him hard to get to know, but I suppose you could say the same about you and me, right? I can't say the same for his sister. I find Cara Spaaks to be an extremely pleasant, outgoing person, and, in my opinion, quite a gifted artist. You are bound to run into her, sooner or later. You should know, by the way, that Gunnar and Cara do not like each other much. And I mean *really* do not like each other much.

"Now, as the sheriff of Green Lake County, I suppose I have mixed opinions about Gunnar Spaaks. It's no secret that he keeps a tight rein on the motorcycle gang he leads, keeps the members from acting too macho or crazy. And that's a good thing. I 'preciate that—I don't like havin' to play cop and wave my gun around and throw a bunch of Harley hog honchos in my drunk tank every weekend.

"Gunnar can be quite the hard ass if a club member gets rowdy, so I suppose he saves me a lot of trouble. Same's true with the Semper Bar. He's part owner, y'know. Sure, it's noisy and macho and filled with blue-collar types blowing off steam every weekend, but certainly no worse than a lot of the Irish bars I used to see in Philly. I have no doubt that Gunnar is a strong leader, like, iron fist in a velvet glove."

As if lost in thought, Gilbert looks out Morton's big bay window, looks out across Green Lake, today still as glass, shining like one enormous mirror from here all the way over to Sandstone Bluff. "But, as a law enforcement officer, I think it's okay to tell you that, yes, I do have some itchy feelings about Gunnar Spaaks. Clearly, he's a gang leader, but is he a big-time crook? Not that I know of, *not that I can prove.* Right now, I have nothing on him, Victor. I tend to keep a moist finger in the air—that's what sheriffs have to do, you know—but other than an occasional whisper, I haven't heard enough to make me want to sniff too hard or come down hard on him."

Gilbert looks at me intently.

"And why are you so interested in Gunnar Spaaks? *You* got something on him? Something I should know?"

Gilbert continues to look at me intently. I note the vein is still pulsing. *Does he suspect me of something?*

"Not that I can think of," I say. "It's just that a person who runs a body shop, leads a motorcycle gang and runs a biker bar might find his name come up as far as theft and receiving stolen property are concerned. Or when a major-league fence gets taken down and leaves a power vacuum in the local criminal scene."

11

CBX Real Reasonable

MARCH HAS COME IN LIKE A LAMB, and it is an absolutely glorious spring day, warmer than average, bathed under a cloudless blue sky. I am reclining on the veranda with my black puffy jacket on, enjoying a large cup of coffee, a copy of Gibbons' *The Rise and Fall of the Roman Empire* propped on my knee. Why Gibbons? It's long and will take a long time to read, it might teach me something, and the title resonates with my present mood. Up clumps Odie Todd in his usual winter uniform, a red plaid lumberjack's jacket, dirt-stained and torn at the elbows, worn over heavily used overalls.

"Mind if I sit down a sec?"

I mark my place in Gibbons and place it by my feet on the ottoman "By all means, Odie. Surprised to see you. Surely it's not mowing season yet, so what brings you around?"

Odie's clearly uncomfortable. He looks around furtively as if checking to see if he's under surveillance.

"Ah, do you *collect* things, Victor?"

I laugh. "Why yes, Odie. I collect expensive lawn tractors."

"Very funny, Victor. But you have to admit the JD is a great piece."

"From all appearances, it sure is, Odie. But I sense you are asking me something different."

"Well, a lot of people collect things, and, you know, there's a lot of collectors' markets for different kinds of things."

I pause, pondering the best—the safest—way to respond. "I think I'm probably past my collecting years, Odie. When I lived down in Evanston, I used to collect antique pocket watches from around the world, and Magda had an incredible collection of cloisonné Russian jewelry. We'd read all the magazines and flyers and go to auctions. It was a lot of fun, but when we sold the house and went our separate ways, it took a long time for Magda and me to sell off all that stuff. Magda just took her collection to a dealer and dumped it. I found that I could get a lot more if I sold my collection piece by piece. I had over sixty watches, so that took a while. It was a hassle."

I pause for a moment, watching a couple of mallard drakes land off the end of the dock, checking whether it's safe to bring the hens in to nest and lay eggs. "Also, there was another hassle. When I tried to resell some of my pieces, I found out that they had been stolen, that I had bought hot stuff. Cops actually reclaimed some of those watches, so I got nothing for them. Others I had to sell at a steep, steep discount because I couldn't provide provenance—you know, proof of chain of ownership. Ended up almost giving a lot of great pieces away.

"So, to answer your question, Odie, although I have always enjoyed buying nice things, at my age, if I collect a lot of things, someone's just going to have to get rid of it all after I die. So, I'm going to live lean from now on. And as I told you with the John Deere deal, cash is particularly short right now. But why the question? You got something you want me to collect?"

"You wanna buy a CBX?"

I hear a click in my head, like a big key turning in a big lock. The sound of some heavy door swinging open. Wow, I think, it sure didn't take long for the post-Causley era to crank up. I look hard at Odie Todd's sweet dim-bulb face and decide I'm going to play him. "I have no idea what a CBX is, Odie."

"A Honda CBX is a super-collectible six-cylinder motorcycle Honda made in the late seventies. Six cylinders. Big deal among bike collectors. Cost four grand new, good ones are worth a bundle now. Today low-mileage CBXs get over twenty-five grand."

"Why doesn't one of your buddies in Semper buy it, if it's so great?"

Odie guffaws, shakes his head as if amazed at my extraordinary ignorance, and laughs again. He has dewlaps like a basset hound, and he's slinging sweat and slobber my way. "Oh, Victor. You're not from around here, are you? Like I tole you before, Semper is short for *Semper Harley.* That's the name of our motorcycle club, also the name of the bar we own up in Berlin. Nothing but Harleys are allowed to ride with us. *Ever.* Maybe sometimes we let another V-twin, like an Indian or Victory, ride along with us on a tour, but even they can't join the club. And a Jap bike? *No way.* Just sayin' the name Honda is fightin' words for us."

"So how did you wind up with a big old Jap bike for sale?"

Odie's eyes dart around the yard. He lowers his head so that I can't see his face. "It was a...barn find. Ah, up in Rhinelander. Guy dies, they find this 1980 CBX, incredible condition, under a tarp in his garage. *Less than 5,000 miles on it.* The whole bike had been covered with Cosmoline—that's a kind of white lithium grease—to protect against rust and mice. They wipe it down, charge up the battery—original 1980 battery, still takes a full charge—and it fires right up. This bike looks brand new, Victor. Tank looked like it was repainted sometime, but now Gunnar has resprayed it back to the original factory color. Show-quality work. Gunnar heard about it from some bike dudes in Eagle River, said he'd take it on consignment. So, you interested?"

"Well, Odie, I used to be a real car guy and gearhead, and I've had some bikes over the years—a BSA, a Triumph Bonneville—but that was over thirty years ago. I think my riding days are over. This CBX falls over on me at a traffic light, and I'd have to get one of those emergency call buttons that says, 'Help, I've fallen, and I can't get up.'"

Odie's laugh is short and artificial, and he turns back to business. "Buy it as an investment, then."

"I told you when I bought the mower, Odie, that I'm not in an investing mood these days. I'm pretty much running on empty at the moment."

"But you could flip it fast, Victor, get your money out real easy. You could make a real good profit on this piece. You know, play the float."

"'Play the float?' Odell Todd, where did you learn to talk like that? You're quite the salesman, Odie, but twenty-five grand is way out of my league at the moment."

"Oh, it wouldn't be twenty-five."

"Yeah, well what do you have to get for it?"

Odie's eyes narrow. On him, the attempt to look shrewd is ludicrous. He looks away, as if afraid I'll laugh at him. "Eleven-five," he says conspiratorially.

Here we go. I wait for Odie to reestablish eye contact. "Eight," I say softly.

Odie grins. "Ten-five."

"Nine-five or take a hike, Odie. And you got to deliver it here. You or one of your precious Harley-boys is actually going to have to ride it down here and put it in my garage. Maybe you can put a bag over your head as you ride it over so no one recognizes you."

"Okay, I can do that. Only one thing, Victor."

I raise my eyebrows, knowing what's going to come next.

"At that price, you're takin' it on a notarized bill of sale. We don't have a title for it. But in Wisconsin, you can use a bill of sale to apply for a new title. Then you can do whatever you want with the bike."

I look away, trying to figure out how the hell I can quickly lay my hands on ninety-five hundred bucks. I know I'm going to resell the CBX as soon as I can, so I only need a temporary bridge loan. But I know of no one I want to hit up for a loan and thereby reveal just how cash-strapped I am at the moment. So, my only choice is to make a loan to myself; I've got to hit my home equity line of credit. But I give myself a stern internal lecture: *Victor, paying down that HELOC has to be your first priority the moment you sell the Honda. It is imperative that you keep yourself as debt-free as possible.*

I gaze down toward the lake where the two mallard drakes are still bobbing. I let the silence grow heavy. Eventually, Odie says, "So, Victor?"

I turn to him; I want this to sound heavy, so I lower my voice an octave. "Odie, we are straying into dangerous territory here, so I want you to listen very, very carefully, and I want you to communicate everything I'm about to say back to Gunnar Spaaks."

Odie's brow furrows, and he looks confused. Something that he thought would be simple suddenly sounds like it's getting complicated.

"Odie, do I look stupid to you? Like a sucker? Or maybe naïve?"

Odie looks down, not knowing know how to respond.

"*Look at me, Odie.* We both know—and Gunnar Spaaks knows—that I already have purchased stolen property from you. If I get a fit of conscience and decide to dime you and

Gunnar Spaaks out to Gilbert Rennie, you know what happens to me?"

"I dunno," says Odie thickly.

"Probably nothing, except that maybe I have to give up the lawn tractor. Maybe I pay a little fine. Maybe I even get praised for being an upstanding citizen. You know what happens to you and Spaaks?"

"Dunno."

"If you're clean, Odie, probably a stiff fine, couple of years' probation. You got a record, Odie?"

Odie looks away. "Yuh. Ag A-and-B—aggravated assault and battery. Bar fight, Oshkosh, eight years ago. Got ugly and I really hurt a guy. Did a little time in Waupun. Clean record since I got out, though."

"And does Gunnar Spaaks have a record?"

"Dunno. If he does, he never tole me about it."

"Well, let me tell you something. I have lunch with Gilbert Rennie at least once a month, and I can tell you he's pretty steamed about the increase in property theft around Green Lake. He's taken down a big-time fence, ol' Clarence Causley, but he can't get him to sing. *Yet.* Gilbert wants to mount, like, a crusade. Looking to make examples to get people to think twice, to take their burglaries and their robberies somewhere else. He says he's not going to go the probation route for receiving stolen property guilty pleas anymore. He's going to push for jail, and he's got Judge Sugarman very much on his side. As they say on TV, Odie, we got a new sheriff in town."

This is a complete lie, but Odie doesn't know that. His face stiffens. His hands clamp down on the arms of his lawn chair.

"So if I turn you guys in, Gilbert's going to push for some jail time. Even for just misdemeanor theft of a lawn tractor. And he's going to get a warrant and tear your biker bar apart and tear Gunnar Spaaks' auto body shop apart. You just know he's going to find *something.*"

Odie's breathing has become fast and shallow.

"Now suppose I tell Rennie you're trying to get me to fence a hot motorcycle. And not just any motorcycle, Odie. *A motorcycle that is at the center of a murder investigation.*"

Odie begins blinking rapidly.

"Think Gilbert Rennie's going to be interested in that?"

"M-m-murder?" Odie has turned ashen, his voice a coarse whisper.

"Don't play dumb with me, Odie. You know damned well what I'm talking about. I'm not saying you're the guy who strung the piano wire that killed that guy, but in pitching this bike to me, you just made yourself an accessory to murder. So, Odie, my friend, you and Gunnar have just moved from the land of grand theft auto to the land of murder. And now you're trying to involve me.

"Oh, and another thing, a big, big thing. You ever heard of the felony murder rule, Odie?"

Odie shakes his head slowly, carefully.

"Well, I'm no lawyer, but here's the bottom line. The felony murder rule says that someone can be charged with first-degree murder if a killing occurs while a felony is being committed—*even if this person isn't the actual killer.* I understand that it's good for about an additional twenty years in the can."

Odie's palms are sweating so heavily I can see the sheen on them. He wipes his hands furiously on his pants, leaving damp streaks on his overalls.

"So, this has just become a very high-stakes game, my friend. You are not just my innocent yard man anymore, Odie. You're involved in some high-risk action here. I'm sure Spaaks put you up to pitching this deal to me, so now you get to be the messenger back to him."

I pause to add a bit of drama, to create an aura of cold calculation. Odie squirms.

"With Causley out of action, there's a real vacuum. No one to buy all the stolen goods, right? So here's something else you can tell Spaaks. I'm thinking about going into the business of receiving stolen property myself—not just for this particular...*item,* but for other things I might want to... *collect*, especially high-end goods. If I get into this, I'm going to play like a big boy. So, you make it clear to Spaaks that I am not a sucker, and I will not be played for a fool. I'm going to take care of myself at all times. Now, still want to sell me that CBX?"

12

Delivery Day

ODELL TODD SWITCHES OFF THE KEY, and the huge motorcycle sputters for a few beats and sinks into silence. As Odie pulls it up on the center stand in front of my garage, the engine continues a rapid tick-tick-tick as various aluminum parts cool.

"Well, whadya think?" grins Odie.

"Absolutely as advertised, Odie. It's big and it's shiny and it appears to be in beautiful shape. And, jeez, it sure is *red.*"

"You won't be sorry you bought it, Victor. It really is a nice piece."

"Odie, do me a favor. Get it out of sight, please. Wheel it into the garage and park it next to the John Deere mower, okay? I suspect it's not going to live here long, but while it's here, I'm gonna throw a padlock on the garage and hold the key. I know that means you're going to have to get the key from me every time you mow the lawn, and I apologize for the inconvenience. In any event, it won't be long, and after that, we'll just go back to leaving the John Deere in the unlocked garage."

The gravel in the driveway crunches behind me, and I turn to see a vintage mid-60s Chevrolet pickup turn down the drive toward us. This is no rusted-out farm truck; it's a show car. As it pulls up behind us, the sun glints off its deep purple paint and bright chrome wheels and reflects flashes of light against the garage doors. The driver's door opens and a slender man in mirrored sunglasses climbs out, taking care not to rub his sharply pressed jeans on the pickup's running board.

Gunnar Spaaks carefully removes his sunglasses, inserts them in his pencil pocket, and walks slowly over to Odie and me. He probably is under six feet tall, but because of his unusually erect posture and broad shoulders, he looks taller, rangier. Tougher. His bright blonde hair, shiny but not greasy, almost white at the temples, is combed straight back from a pronounced widow's peak. He is quite handsome, with high cheekbones and crow's feet at the corners of his eyes that make him look like he's always squinting. His smile is tight, forced, and artificial. Gunnar Spaaks obviously is not a natural smiler. Even in jeans and a bright blue Amish shirt, there is something military about him. He looks like he is used to being in charge.

On the other hand, standing in my driveway in his creased jeans, low polished boots, and neatly pressed shirt, he hardly looks like the leader of a notorious motorcycle gang, either.

"Victor."

"Gunnar."

"I followed Odie over to give him a ride back and pick up payment for the CBX."

"Well, it's a nice-looking scooter, Gunnar. Your guys detailed it very nicely. Odie, would you be good enough to take it up to the garage for me?"

Spaaks draws an arc in the driveway gravel with the toe of his boot. "You going to drive this beast?"

"Oh, I think not, Gunnar. This is way too much bike for me. But my brother Collie lives down in Georgia and is still young enough to be a bike guy, and I suspect he'll want to ride it some. I'll buy him a nice full-face helmet, the kind you Harley dudes think is sissy stuff, then turn him loose up here for a while. Who knows? Maybe he'll want to buy it from me and take it down to Savannah with him. Or maybe sell it on, if he can find a motivated buyer."

Spaaks nods knowingly, clearly understanding that I am speaking in code. He knows exactly why I'm talking about the benefits of taking the motorcycle out of state. "That's good. Yeah, that would be good. For your brother, I mean. I hear he came a little unwrapped after that plane crash thing. Some road time on a big smooth-runnin' bike might calm him down, clear his head, even if it is just an old Jap bike."

I am annoyed by Spaak's backhanded slap at Collie. "*Be careful, Gunnar,*" I hiss. "Don't let your smart mouth pull you into trouble. You are not talking to some meth-brain in your low-brow biker bar."

Spaaks stiffens and clenches a fist. Then, *good for him!,* he controls his impulse to lash back, and softens his posture. "Sorry, Victor. Didn't know it was such a tender subject."

I let the moment pass. This is no time to make enemies or burn possible future bridges. "And what document are we using to transfer ownership? Odie said you don't have a title to transfer."

"Got a notarized bill of sale here," says Spaaks, withdrawing an envelope from his back pocket. "In Wisconsin, you can use this to apply for a title. In Semper, we do it all the time."

"I'll bet you do," I say with a wry smile. Now Spaaks stiffens again.

I reach into my own pencil pocket, pull out a folded piece of green paper, and hand it to Spaaks. "Here's my end of the deal."

Spaaks' face clouds "*A money order? Deal was cash.*"

"Actually, no, Gunnar. The deal was for nine thousand five hundred dollars. The form of payment was never discussed. There is no way in the world that I'm going to walk around with ten large in cash, and somehow, I figured you would not be keen on my writing you a personal check.

"A money order seemed like a good compromise to me. I left the payee line blank. You can write in your name, or if for some reason you didn't want your name on the document,"—here I cough into my closed fist—"you can either make it payable to the order of cash, or I can put my name on it and endorse it over to you. Your call."

Spaaks looks away for a moment, shakes his head, then fixes me in a hard stare. "I guess you think you're pretty smart, Victor."

"Actually, I am pretty smart, Gunnar, but that's not really the point, is it? We both know exactly what's going on here. I'm not a sucker or a patsy, and neither are you."

I am aware that this is a turning point in my life. I pause, Now or never, I decide. *Time to dive in.* "Gunnar, the moment we close this...*transaction*...we've got the goods on each other. You could take me down for receiving stolen property, and I could take you down as a motorcycle thief.

"That said, let me tell you that I am okay with the idea of doing some business together. But let me be clear, Gunnar. If you ever try to screw me over, I will screw you over times ten. In my time I have played hardball with people whose balls are bigger than yours for stakes millions of times larger than some lowball motorcycle deal or antique lawnmower theft."

I'm rollin' pretty fast here, quite astonished at my momentum, but having an exciting time. So, *this* is what it feels like to be a criminal...

"In addition, Gilbert Rennie is my friend, and I'll bet you do not regard Sheriff Rennie as your friend. As far as Gilbert's concerned, if there's ever a pissing contest about who is a perp and who is a victim, you probably do not want to match your credibility up against mine. I can play innocent a lot better than you can—and certainly a lot better than Odie can. Odie's a sweet guy, but he's a lousy liar."

Odell Todd, returned from garaging the Honda, stares at his feet as Gunnar and I spar. Now his head shoots up and, wide-eyed, he jerks his gaze rapidly between Spaaks and me. Spaaks makes a "down-boy" gesture at Odie with his hands. "Where are you going with this, Victor?"

"I hope I'm going into a demilitarized zone. I have no incentive to bust your chops, Gunnar, and unless you are a lot more stupid than I think you are, you should pause long and hard before ever thinking about busting mine. If we're going to do business together in the future, we would do well to practice mutual respect. I'm not suggesting that we have to like each other, just that we should play the game in a way that no one gets burned."

Gunnar Spaaks cocks his head, and there is a glimmer of humor in his smile. "I take your point, Victor, I get it. I know what's going on here. And like you, I want to be...*constructive*.

"But let me say something back to you, you patronizing, elitist son-of-a-bitch. You gain nothing... *nothing*... by ridiculing my body shop, my bar, my motorcycle club, my courage, or my intelligence. You like to talk about stakes and balls and bucks. Well, I think you should know who *you're* talking to. In this case, that's Lieutenant Colonel Gunnar R. Spaaks, United States Air Force, retired, graduate of the U.S. Air Force Academy, class of 1981. Still hold restricted intelligence security clearance. Flight wing leader, two tours Ramstein, one tour Bagram. I may have moved past my military years, Harding, but in my time, I'd put my balls and brains up against anybody's."

13

Bingo

"BINGO!"

"I guess that means everything went okay," I say.

"Better than that. I really should say bingo, bingo, bingo. Three bingos."

Colin sounds upbeat. *Charged.*

"Talk to me, Collie. But remember you're on a cell phone."

"Assistant groundskeeper at The Landings bought it. Our little baby blew his mind. Fifteen-five, no haggling. Want to know the funny part? Now I hear he rolled it over two days later for sixteen-nine, that weasel." Collie is laughing.

"You're not pissed?"

"Nah. Fifteen-five gives us six clear, and I'm okay with that. If I wasn't, I wouldn't have done the deal. Let him take the risk from here on. If he can get some gravy for himself, more power to him. That's the highest price I've ever seen for that...item."

"Watch your mouth, Collie. 4-G has ears."

"Sorry."

"And how was the drive to Savannah? Six large make it worth your while?"

"Victor, I would have done it for nothing. Long hauls may be strange therapy for PTSD, but it sure works for me. I almost feel human. The edge is off."

"Well, if you like it so much, we can arrange for you to do a lot more. Speaking of which, I want you to get a one-way car rental and hotfoot it up here as fast as you can. Plans are afoot that involve you, little brother."

"Wait. Don't you want to hear the rest?"

"The rest of what?"

"The other two bingos, you turkey."

"Who am I to turn a deaf ear to good news?"

"Okay, first The Landings Club. I talked to Steven Monfried, confessed that the PTSD meant my golf pro days were through, and that we should find a way to wind things down sooner rather than later.

"Actually, I'm sure he was relieved that I brought it up before he had to bring it up. He could not have been more gracious. 'We completely understand, Colin,' and all that. Victor, it turns out they had a package ready. 'Just sign here, we shake hands, the club makes a gracious announcement in the newsletter, and we part as friends.' But that's not the whole bingo. Guess the bottom line."

"Three months' severance and a free set of Ping golf clubs."

"How about a one-year 'consulting agreement' equivalent to my current salary? No duties, no strings, just answer the phone if they need to know where the key to the water main is hidden. Not exactly a retirement nest egg, but it helps take some immediate pressures off. How 'bout them apples?"

"Well, that's a bingo, no doubt about it. Congrats, Collie, although you've certainly earned it. And now I assume you're going to tell me about bingo three, yes?"

"So, I'm sitting in my living room, already feeling pretty chipper, when who should call but George Catterston, that sleazy broker at The Landings' real estate operation. Says he's heard I'm winding things down at The Landings Club, and he wants to '*know what my plans are.*' By this, he means what my plans are for my house. Talk about chasing commissions!

"I say I'm giving some thought to moving north to be nearer to family, but I'm not prepared to sell the house. Escalating property values, and all. He asks if I want to make my house a fully-furnished rental property managed by The Landings Company. I say only if it's a long-term rental. I don't want the wear and tear of a lot of in-and-out short-term tenants. He says they have a Swiss doctor who's looking for a year's lease, maybe two-year, on a fully furnished house. He'll pay thirty-two hundred a month. That pays my mortgage payment and leaves fourteen hundred in my pocket. I say one condition, I retain use of one of the garage bays 'for storing some personal stuff,' the Swiss doc can use the other two bays. George says 'deal,' he'll write it up."

"Colin," I say, laughing.

"Yeah?"

"Bingo, my man. Bingo, bingo, and bingo. At a time when we're both suffering cash flow problems, it's a relief to hear the sound of some cash flowing."

—⁓—

Ten days later, Colin drives back into the Boulders, his southern business done, his new vistas before him. He hasn't rented a car for the trip home, he's bought a car, a ten-year-old ice-blue Jaguar sedan. Twenty-seven thousand miles, for a good price. Colin is pleased as punch.

I sit him down on the veranda. We're sipping the last of my Glenfiddich in celebration of things past and things to come. I figure now's the time to sober him up some, get to the reality bites.

"Collie," I say. "We just made six grand on a garden-variety fencing deal, actually fifty-seven hundred after you deduct the cost of the U-Haul van. How's that strike you?"

"I'm okay with that, Vic. I told you that before I headed down south with the bike."

"And the driving part was okay?"

"I told you, absolutely okay, restorative even. Although I was pretty rump-sprung after thirteen hours on those awful seats."

"Well, I'll tell you how this deal strikes me. *It strikes me as small potatoes.* It would take a lot of six-thousand-dollar turnarounds to clear even a hundred grand a year. And a hundred grand doesn't go all that far these days. For either of us, much less both of us."

Pregnant pause. I wait for the hook to set.

"Collie, I want to know how you would feel about upping our economies of scale—a lot more trips, fencing a lot of bigger-ticket items with a lot bigger margin. And, of course, bigger risks. Just how much are you game for?"

Colin looks at me like he's never thought about this before. "You serious?"

"Serious as can be, Collie. I want to know, like *right now*, if you are willing to engage in a serious criminal enterprise. Nothing that carries the death penalty, but stuff that involves a lot more risk than playing professional golf. If you want to be my co-conspirator, say yes. If this is too rich for your blood, if the prospect of making some serious money—*some seriously illegal money*—is too rich for your blood, just shake your head, and we'll forget I ever mentioned it."

Colin lowers his head, then lifts his chin, and looks me straight in the eye, something he seldom does. "What if I don't do it? What then?"

"Then I do it anyway. I just find myself a different accomplice. Look, Colin, I have to do this. If I am going to keep my house, I need to make some serious money. Frankly, I'd prefer to keep the crime in the family, but I also realize that I am asking you to reset your moral compass."

He lowers his head again. Rubs his chin. Mumbles something I can't catch.

"Say again?"

"I said, how long we gonna do this for?"

"Collie, unless we stumble on Fort Knox and cash out with millions, this is not going to be a short-term deal. This is how you and I are going to make our living. How I'm going to keep my house."

I take a long pause. "And how you're going to pay off your debts and keep you from having to declare bankruptcy."

Collie's head jerks up. "What do you know about my debts?"

"I know as much as I need to know, Collie. I haven't been living under a cabbage leaf. While I haven't been keeping close tabs on you all these years, I have been keeping some tabs, yes. I've got contacts, and a lot of your financial issues are public record. You haven't been particularly discreet."

Colin shoots to his feet. "You bastard!"

I expected this, and I have rehearsed my response. *Which is no response.* Collie stands in front of me, fists clenched, face florid—whether he's blushing or livid I can't tell. "Sit down, Colin," I command, "and get hold of yourself. Let's talk about this like rational grown-ups. Don't play self-righteous with me. You're the one who's gambled yourself into a serious hole. Tell me, Collie, and do not try to bullshit me. Exactly what's the damage?"

I make my patented gimme-gimme gesture with my open palms.

"Buck fifty."

Well, that sucks the breath out of me. This has really gotten away from him. My mole at The Landings Club had hinted that Collie was into high-stakes poker games with a tight cadre of golfing clients, and he thought Collie was now into them for about twenty-five large.

"Oh, Colin…" My voice trails off.

"I know, I know. But after Susan died, I wanted to recoup my losses. Get even, ya know? I bet big and lost big on a real estate packaging deal in Jacksonville. Didn't seem all that speculative, you know? I was just a minority investor. Other guys told me they were puttin' up really big bucks, so it had to be a good gamble, right? It turned out to be a sure thing that wasn't a sure thing. It didn't *feel* like gambling, Victor, it wasn't poker. It was…*business.* Except that it *was* gambling. And it wasn't a level playing field. I got played for a rube. What's more, the guys holding my paper are not being polite these days."

I struggle to still my inner voices, to quell the impulse to become a critical parent driven to bathe the delinquent child in shame and sarcasm. "Okay," I say. "We'll deal with that. *We,* Colin, not you all on your own. But now we've got to factor that debt into our business plan. That and the fact that you've raided your 401(k) and pretty much eaten through your investments. Job One, Colin, will be to keep you out of bankruptcy."

Colin's natural color slowly returns to his cheeks. His labored breathing eases. "So, if I sell my soul to the devil, what's the upside? How much can we realistically expect to make?"

"What would you say if, once we really got up and running, we could each net a couple hundred thousand a year, maybe as much as a half a mil?"

Collie's eyes open wide, showcasing their deep, bright blue, the same as Christine's. "Seriously? Could we do that? Could we really do that?"

"Depends on what goods we fence and who we fence them to. Who our suppliers are, who our downstream clients are."

"Just what kind of stolen property we gonna fence to make that kind of money?"

"I'm speculating here, but given the kind of stuff Gilbert Rennie tells me is getting heisted around here, I hope we're going to see fine art, sculpture, lots of jewelry, maybe some antiques or fancy furniture, oriental rugs, furs, and guns, plus miscellaneous valuable collectibles—stamp collections, first editions, historic documents, like that. I suspect we'll end up doing cars, both current models and collectibles. Maybe a few boats, but I don't really love that too much because you've got to get a trailer and then transport them out in the open. Rennie just snagged a stolen vintage Green Lake Chris Craft back down in Florida 'cause it was just sticking out like a sore thumb on some redneck's used equipment lot.

Colin purses his lips, and blows his breath out loudly. "Okay, and what *won't* we do?"

"Well, at the beginning we may have to take whatever comes our way, but I'd like to push away from low-margin stuff, like lawn tractors, tools, or power equipment as soon as we can. And I definitely want to stay away from heavy equipment, like farm tractors and machinery, bulldozers, and other heavy machinery. Believe it or not, a lot of that kind of stuff gets stolen, Rennie tells me, but that's a specialized niche. It may be big bucks, but I bet the margins stink and the buyers are likely to be hicks and rubes. I don't want to play in that space."

"That's not what I mean," Collie says impatiently.

"What *do* you mean?"

"I mean, *what won't we do?*"

Now I see what he's getting at.

"Colin, we are going to fence stolen property. But we are not going to steal that property. We're not going to commit the burglaries, not going to break-and-enter, not going to commit armed robbery, not going to terrorize people. We're not going to threaten anyone with guns, and we certainly are not going to kill anybody."

"Oh, gentlemen criminals," Collie says, smiling wanly.

"We'll wear ascots to work every day and break for tea promptly at four o'clock. But this is not a cakewalk, Collie. It is going to take a ton of work to get it up and running. We're going to have to develop a network of different kinds of... *end users.* Guys who run art galleries and art collectors and antique dealers. Jewelers. New York. Chicago. Philadelphia. Atlanta. Hilton Head and Savannah. All over Florida.

"Plus, we have to cultivate all those people who are making a pile by shipping stolen goods overseas. All this networking is not going to happen overnight, dear brother, even starting with all your hundreds of golfing contacts and my network of hitters in the construction and architecture world. So I'm thinking we'll probably be straining in the first year unless we luck into some large scores. But if you're willing to think big, and not just deal with penny-ante stuff like stolen motorcycles, the answer to your prior question is yes, in time we probably can get to a half a mil each, year over year."

I see Collie's hands begin to tremble, see him squint. He's imagining things, imagining all the what-ifs.

"But my God, Victor! It's just so risky. I don't want to end up in the can."

"Look," I say. "It is risky, but I'm going to try to play everything as safe as I can. I want to be a very conservative criminal, go for solid scores, but safe scores. Like I said, develop a network upstream and downstream that I trust."

"Are you going to do more deals with Gunnar Spaaks?"

"Depending on what kinds of merchandise he can get to us to fence, I'd say yes, highly likely."

"But can you trust him? Man, he seems like such a weasel to me."

"He and I have already had a conversation about this. Big kid to big kid. Based on the motorcycle deal, Gunnar and I are already in a posture of 'mutually assured destruction,' as they used to say in the cold war days. I'm not saying Gunnar and I are ever going to be friends, but I'm willing to see what develops with various kinds of property he can get."

"And what's that likely to be?"

"Well, with him for sure, it'll include cars. I bet a lot of hot wheels pass through that body shop of his. That means we're going to have to get our hands on a decent trailer—a closed transporter, maybe like the kind race car teams use. They got a lot of extra room in 'em and a lot of storage compartments... for various kinds of things, if you follow my drift. And you, Colin Harding, designated driver, are going to have to get a commercial driver's license. You game to do that?"

"Game," Collie whispers.

"Excellent," I say. "And in that vein, I have some very good news."

He cocks an eyebrow.

"Gilbert Rennie has just arrested the biggest, longest-running fence in this whole mid-Wisconsin area. Cleared out some of our competition, left a big vacuum in the supply chain. At least for a while, we got an open playing field around here, we just got to let the right people know we're playing. I think that's where Gunnar comes in. Not only with selling us the stuff he steals, but in getting the word out. And I think enough people are scared of him that he represents a pretty safe market-maker."

Now Colin smiles. "You call that good news? I call it an IED, like in Iraq. You know, 'improvised explosive device.'"

He shakes his shoulders like a dog sloughing water from its coat, and slugs back the rest of his scotch. "Well, what is it you always say, Victor? *'In for a dime, in for a dollar,'* right? Okay, give me a dollar's worth," he says.

14

Off to The Races

WE JUMP OFF TO A SURPRISINGLY FAST START, Collie and I, working as fast as we can to nail down our fencing M.O., logistics, and client pool. Maybe too fast—I often think that in our ignorance of the finer points of crime, Colin and I often confuse motion with action. It soon becomes clear we need some *discipline,* a consistent set of operating rules and procedures. We need a business plan.

In our eagerness to get the word out that we are "open for business," thus far we've been too indiscriminate in our acquisitions. Despite my aspirations to shoot for the top end of the market, at first we buy almost any stolen item any local thief brings our way, regardless of our final profit margin. I now realize that Collie and I have to stop being a glorified pawn shop. So far, we've handled fine art, modern art, sculpture, jewelry, antiques, new cars, old cars, outboard motors, lawn tractors, flat-screen TVs and top-drawer sound systems, rototillers, fine china and flatware, and mink coats. We've handled some seriously upscale goods. We've also fenced some relatively low-end junk.

I tell Collie we need more fencing finesse. So far, we've worked deal-by-deal and flipped the goods as fast as we can, without warehousing any of them for a while in order to let them "age" and become easier to turn over. And we have dealt only in single items, rather than putting out the word that we'd be interested in goods that come to us in lots, like, for example, a truckload of untaxed cigarettes stolen from a warehouse, or perhaps a hardware store's entire inventory of chain saws.

In our rush to generate volume, we also have not thought enough about margin, about the relationship between productivity and profitability. When Collie realized six grand on the sale of the CBX, I had teased him, suggesting that the deal was "small potatoes." *But was it?* If the sky was going to be the limit for top-end transactions—as long as we could muster enough cash to buy the stolen property in the first place—*where should we set the floor?* At what price point should we say, "Nope, there's not enough money in this deal to make it worth our time and effort?"

Recognizing that we are a start-up, but also that there are only so many working hours in a fence's year, I decide to set an arbitrary benchmark. For now, we will turn down any deal that does not net us at least $10,000. That means if we manage a hundred transactions in our first year, we'll make a million bucks. *Net* a million bucks, because our federal income tax form does not have a gross income line itemizing "income realized through criminal activity." Not great, but not bad, either. Surely enough to save my house.

A good fence steeply discounts the stolen goods received—we never pay more than fifty percent of fair market value when buying—and tries to sell them on for as close to FMV as possible. But I know that I'm often going to take a hit, and that sad truth that gives rise to the fence's mantra: *Some days you eat the bear, some days the bear eats you.*

—⁓—

Without fully understanding what the fencing life would be like, Collie and I find that we have embarked on what turns out to be full-time employment. I'm on the phone constantly, as is Collie when he's not occupied behind the wheel (we use prepaid "burner phones" that we discard every month; my landline phone records will appear simon-pure to any investigator). We find ourselves busy putting out upstream feelers and building downstream contacts for various kinds of high-end goods—several orthodox Jewish diamond experts on Philadelphia's Jewelers' Row, fine art dealers in Raleigh-Durham, Savannah, Hilton Head, and Boston, an antique dealer in Toronto, a chop shop specializing in BMWs and Mercedes just outside Atlanta, and a specialist dealing in oriental carpets in Detroit.

For transporting smaller loads of paintings, furniture, oriental rugs, sculpture, electronic equipment, and such, we initially rent a dull white Chevrolet commercial panel van from Rent-a-Wreck in Oshkosh. Collie and I are quite proud of the false floor we build for the van out of two-by-fours and diamond-plate aluminum panels. We can install or remove this in a couple of minutes, and it provides a sizable hidden storage compartment, which we line with used quilts purchased from the Salvation Army.

At first, we're stymied about how to transport bigger stuff—notably cars and furniture. We could easily rent an open-style car transporter, either a single-car trailer or a multi-car transporter that requires a powerful truck to tow, but obviously, I'm not keen on schlepping hot items across state lines in open view, and the cost of renting the tow vehicle is prohibitive.

We make do with our little white truck until Gunnar Spaaks calls to tell me about Darryl Allmire, whose life has recently suffered a dramatic downturn. Bad luck for Darryl, maybe good luck for Collie and me.

"I'm lookin' to sell the transporter," Darryl says, his words moist and slurred. Darryl's wife Corrinne rises from the corner of the modest living room and reaches in with a tissue to dab a bit of spittle running from the corner of Darryl's mouth. He flicks his hand impatiently, almost imperceptibly, on the arm of his wheelchair to wave her away.

"At some point I want to buy your transporter and your truck, Darryl, but I just can't swing the whole deal right now. But until I can scrape the money together to take it off your hands, let me propose an arrangement, one where you come out way ahead of just dumpin' the rig for whatever you can get for it in a distress sale."

Darryl widens his eyes to express interest, about the most he can do because a broad black band is looped across his chest strapping him tightly to the wheelchair, and a padded strap holds his head tight against a backboard because he can't hold his head up. Darryl Allmire is almost completely paralyzed, capable only of speaking, blinking, and feebly flapping his left hand. He is deathly pale, and he tends to drool.

Until several months ago, Darryl was one of the promising up-and-coming racers on the rough-and-tumble World of Outlaws Sprint Car circuit, where bumping is constant, collisions are common, and so are "endos"—violent crashes where some racer rides over another car's wheels and is launched into a violent end-over-end dance of death, careening, bouncing, and often flying over the outside wall altogether. Darryl was leading a race in Dubuque when a competitor's simple tap on his back tire triggered a mad, gyrating series of violent loops that ended with Darryl's car sitting upside down in the middle of the main straightaway, steam blossoming from his engine. Darryl's neck was broken, his spine was severed, and his life was toast.

Before his accident, rather than springing for one of the big NASCAR-type race transporters, those giant complete-shops-on-wheels semi-trailers towed by glistening Macks or Kenworths or Peterbilt tractors, Darryl had acquired an unpretentious white twenty-four-foot closed cargo/car hauler, which he towed with an equally unpretentious white Chevrolet pickup truck. Now he had no further use for what Collie and I came to call "the Allmire rig." But we sure did.

A reasonable price for the Allmire car hauler would be about eighteen thousand; it's only three years old and in fine shape. And if I really wanted the late-model pickup, another thirty thousand would probably take it. But even if I could take it, I don't want to own another vehicle right now. I don't want to buy it, license it, or transfer it to my name. What I want is to be able to use it when I need it and park it when I don't.

"Look, Darryl," I say reasonably, "how about this? How 'bout a 'rent-to-buy' deal? I would like to *rent* your transporter, and by that, I mean your entire rig, on a trip-by-trip basis until I can get enough scratch together to buy it from you outright. That might be about a year. My brother and I are going into the business of transporting restored classic cars and fancy-ass trailer queens around the country, mostly east of the Mississippi, on a contract basis. We know it's gonna take some time to get our number of trips up to the point where it makes sense to buy our own gear.

"But okay, let's run some numbers. High retail on your rig and truck right now is probably about forty-five grand. But you're a distressed seller, so any buyer's gonna lowball you, right? Someone offers you forty, you're probably gonna take it, right?"

Darryl nods with a short jerky spasm.

"Now consider this. Our average gig is two or three days, maybe twelve to fifteen hundred miles. Sometimes we go to

Georgia or Florida and back. If business is good, we might get maybe four trips a month. So, let's say maybe ten to twelve days a month we're on the road. Between gigs, we'd like to bring the rig back and store it here on your farm. I don't have space for it at my house down in Green Lake. I'd like to offer you a rental fee of eight hundred bucks a day plus fifty cents a mile. All in, you get about between eight and ten grand a month for as long as we rent the rig. We'll pay gas, and tolls. You'll still own the rig and keep it registered in your name, but we'll pay for insurance and any maintenance on the pickup or the transporter. How's that sound?"

Darryl's eyes twitch as he spins the numbers in his head. Finally, he croaks, "Sounds okay."

⟡

As if the transporter deal isn't luck enough, rookie fences Victor and Colin Harding then *really* get lucky. Like a windfall of a hundred and thirty grand kind of lucky. Such a windfall is not enough to magically pull our sorry financial asses totally out of the weeds, but for the moment it will buy each of us some time. Unfortunately, it's a windfall diminished by a painful but highly instructive learning experience about the realities of dealing in high-dollar stolen property.

Out of the blue, in early April I get a call from one "Mike Jones," who asks me if I "sometimes buy things." And if I do, can he come see me? I don't ask how he got my name, and he doesn't offer to tell me. I'm pretty sure Gunnar is in this loop somewhere, but I will probably never know.

"Mike" is about thirty. He's average in every way: average height, average weight, average Caucasian complexion, average brown hair, and average brown Walmart clothes. This guy is clearly not a professional thief. He's terrified. His eyes dart, and his hands tremble. He will not make eye contact. When I direct Mike to the couch in the sunroom, he eases himself cautiously down on the front edge of the cushion as if being asked to perch on a land mine.

Mike is clutching what looks like a cigar humidor. It's a finely crafted box of burnished wood, perhaps rosewood, with attractive inlays, elegant brass hinges, and little legs that look like they came off an antique chair in a doll house. The front hasp, which has a little padlock on it, dangles loosely from its hinge; it has been forced from the face of the box, leaving a little scar on the front finish.

I figure there's no point beating around the bush. "Show me," I say sternly, and he thrusts the box out to me as if it's a grenade about to explode.

It's not a humidor, of course. It's a jewel box. The top lifts smoothly on beautiful little brass struts, revealing a series of little compartments occupied by dazzling bracelets, all no doubt custom-ordered and hand-crafted: a broad curved cuff that must weigh a ton, a tennis bracelet encircled by a row of quite sizable diamonds, and three other bracelets, all bejeweled beauties covered in gems of various sizes and colors.

Nestled alongside the bracelets in long velvet-lined slots are five necklaces of breathtaking beauty. And heft. These are *big* pieces, each with an arrangement of large diamonds set in platinum. One is a choker like you'd see on an A-lister's throat at a Hollywood movie premiere. The others are various iterations on a common theme: lots of ice, designed to drape breathtakingly down the front of some beauty's plunging decolletage. Bathed in the light from my chandelier, the collection flashes and sparkles and takes my breath away.

I wait until I can trust my voice, then say as calmly as I can, "Where did you get these?"

Utterly out of his depth and clearly unsure of his footing, Mike Jones blurts out the truth. "I stole it from the back seat of a limousine that was idling outside of the entrance of the Four Seasons in Chicago. I saw it through the street-side door, opened the door, reached in, snatched the box, and ran like hell. I honestly don't think anybody saw me grab it. I thought it was a cigar box."

"Well, obviously it wasn't," I say drily. "You do this kind of thing often?"

"No, sir. That's what's so funny. I'm not a robber, I'm a third-year student at John Marshall Law School. I just saw this thing, and something went 'pop' inside my head, and... I just grabbed it, you know?"

I couldn't help it: I burst into laughter, which made him recoil in alarm. "And you thought you were stealing a box of cigars?"

"No, man, I thought I was taking a really beautiful box. It was the box I wanted."

"Well, what you got was jewelry. Very expensive-looking costume jewelry."

"What's costume jewelry?"

"It's jewelry that looks pretty, looks flashy, but isn't genuine. It can be real cheap trash, K-Mart trash—obviously fake, just bling, with no real intent to pass it off as the real thing—or it can be really well done. These pieces here are *really* well done. Top quality junk jewelry, you could say. They were meant to fool people, at least from a bit of a distance. But that's not real gold or real platinum and diamonds and gems, of course. All bogus."

I wait for him to call my bluff. He doesn't, and I sense I'm home free. Instead, he asks, "Are they worth *anything*?"

"Sure," I say brightly. "Probably quite a lot, actually, because these are premium-quality knockoffs. They weren't cheap."

"What's 'not cheap?'"

I am totally winging it here, but Mike clearly is deeply mired in ignorance. He's nodding at this tutorial from an old pro. "They probably cost about a tenth of what the real items would have cost."

He blurts out. "Ya wanna buy 'em?"

"Sure," I reply, smiling reassuringly. "But only the whole lot. I'm not going to haggle with you piece by piece. I'll pay one price for everything, pay you in cash. I'm willing to do a deal here and now. Then you get the hell out of here, and we never see each other again. I never do business with the same people twice."

This latter statement is, of course, total hogwash, but inasmuch as I am taking this rube for a major-league ride, I'm not eager to see him again.

Mike Jones nods vigorously. "Okay, okay. How much?"

"If you'll accept hundreds, I'll give you $20,000. If you insist on being paid in twenties, which is inconvenient for me, I knock off two hundred bucks. Take it or leave it."

Mike's eyes grow large. "Hundreds," he says, thrilled at his good fortune.

"And I tell you what," I say. "I'll even let you keep the box."

Yes, in fact, I do have twenty thousand in cash lying around. I have always kept a secret rainy-day fund, a reserve of $50,000 in cash nestled in my safe at home. I have done this ever since 1997 when I was kidnapped from a construction site in Bangalore, India, and held for ransom. Anil Bakshi, who speaks Kannada, the language spoken in southwestern India, negotiated with the gang holding me at a local game preserve and paid five million rupees of his own money for my ransom. That's about $65,000 US dollars. I had international kidnap insurance at the time and was able to reimburse Anil promptly, but after that, I kept a secret cache of cash ready for such emergencies because in most cases, prompt ransom is good ransom.

I regard my cache as a resource of last resort, and now I'm tapping into it to buy stolen jewels. This cuts my rainy-day fund almost in half, and I'm praying there's no serious rain until I can fence the jewels and replenish my secret reserve.

With the purchase of the Mike Jones box comes my first serious test of really big-ticket fencing, of turning the fruits of my taking-candy-from-a-baby con job into hard cash.

How does one turn hot goods into cold cash, dirty money into clean money? The answer, put simply, is to find your place in a continuous food chain of selling...and reselling and reselling, that is, putting as many transactions as possible between the original theft and your own vulnerable derriere. In this case, as a "first-contact fence," I've put myself at the risky end of the chain, a danger for which I exact a sizable price penalty from the perps I must deal with.

Right now, in this Mike Jones rip-off, I'm uncomfortably close to the front end of the laundering cycle. Mike didn't know what he had, but I was pretty sure I knew. I'm no gemologist, but one glance and I saw that I probably had over a half million dollars worth of absolutely gorgeous, absolutely genuine, absolutely traceable gems and hand-crafted jewelry on my hands. But my promising twenty-grand purchase would not represent a coup until the next link in the chain was forged, where some downstream buyer would set the price he is willing to pay for my steaming hot rocks and trinkets. I have miles to go before I sleep.

—◆◇◆—

With the jewel box open before me, contents blinding me with their collective carats, I call my old Chicago construction industry partner-in-crime (back then we used the phrase as a joke), Bjelko Zuerin. Buck Zuerin is a connector, a facilitator. Not a lobbyist, *per se,* but rather the head of a successful government relations consulting firm. I figure he's a good place to start because although I'm pretty sure Bjelko is not a crook, I'm equally sure he knows a lot of crooks. When he picks up, he makes it sound as if he's glad to hear from me, but he can't resist a dig.

"You promised you wouldn't abandon me, Victor, and you have completely abandoned me. *Totally*. Fine friend you turned out to be."

"Guilty as charged, Buck, but you're better off this way. In my retirement, I've turned into a grumpy old man, and you would not enjoy having me as a friend. So, I'm calling to ask a favor, not to say hi."

"I'm all ears."

"I don't know if you know that the harridan and I finally wrapped up our divorce, and I am now trying to rid my life of the last vestiges of all things Magda. Among the things we haggled about in the settlement was a sizable chunk of jewelry. Turns out Magda hates jewelry, *always* hated jewelry, just never bothered to tell me so. Hated every diamond, every necklace, every bracelet I ever gave her to buy peace. In the divorce settlement, she was perfectly happy to drop it all back in my lap—in exchange for cash, of course.

"But here's the rub, Buck. I don't have provenance for all this stuff. Never kept the receipts, never insured it, just let it all sit unused in her safe deposit box for thirty years. Now that I want to sell it, I don't know how to go about it, how to go about getting the best price I can."

"Easy," Buck says. "Start with Charlie Danko in Winnetka. Use my name."

I do. Charlie is cordial but also distant and evasive. He wants no part of this. He tells me to call Jan Ter Horst in New York City—"He knows diamonds." I reach Ter Horst, but he says he's only interested in unset stones, says to call Bruce Roethke in Terre Haute.

On the phone, Roethke is very Swiss, very formal, very guarded. Thick accent. But when I describe what I have to sell, he bites hard. "Take a separate picture of each piece," he says. "Send each picture to me in a separate surface mail envelope. I'll give you the post office box. No email. I'll get back to you with some ideas."

I fire off the envelopes, and after three weeks, just as I'm on the verge of panic, my phone rings.

"We talk straight, okay? I don't like fancy dancing."

"Okay by me."

"Phone secure?"

"As far as I know I'm not on the FBI watch list."

"Don't make bad jokes with me, Mr. Harding. I have no sense of humor whatsoever. So anyway, here's what's what. Want to know about your fancy jewelry? Because I know *all* about your fancy jewelry. I don't know *how* you got those pieces, and I'm not going to ask. Not my business, and neither is what you paid for them. *But I do know where you got them from.* I have the police report, as well as the Chicago Police referral to the FBI, because the authorities know this stuff is for sure going to cross state lines. I know the date and place the jewelry was stolen, I have detailed descriptions of all the pieces, and I have listings of all the hallmarks and registration numbers on the pieces."

This is probably not good news, I think.

"Victor, imagine the best stuff you can imagine. Best stones, best settings, and bracelets, best workmanship, all bespoke, all custom-made. Well, it's clear even from the blurry photos you sent me, *this stuff is even better than that.* My goldsmith friends call it 'Ne plus ultra.' That's Latin for 'there isn't anything better than this.'"

"Gosh," I say. I can think of absolutely nothing else to say.

"So, you want to know what your jewelry is worth? Fair market value—retail value—in today's dollars?"

I catch my breath: I am *intensely* curious. The pause extends forever.

"Conservatively, let's say nine hundred and seventy-five thousand dollars. That's retail. Or let's say quasi-retail, because obviously, if I'm pitching the proceeds of a recent high-profile theft, I'm not going to try to lay it off to Van Cleef and Arpels. Wholesale, if you can call it that, would be a *lot* lower. Under normal conditions, I could expect to get maybe five-fifty when I moved these pieces on, if I was lucky. Still, that's a lot of money, a very profitable deal for me.

"So, the good news is that this is indeed top-drawer merchandise. The bad news is that I can't even think about trying to sell it in the United States. Can't risk it. The feds would be all over me in no time, for sure. You know the Fibbies have a fine arts task force, right?"

"Didn't know that," I mumble. *God damn it, I should have known that by now.*

"In any event, I still want to buy all of it, but you aren't going to like my offer."

"Surprise, surprise."

"No, this isn't just the usual fence's discount, Mr. Harding. I'm not out to screw you, because we may do business again sometime. But you present me with problems I've got to solve, and, sad to say, that's going to cost you a hefty percentage."

"I'm listening."

"So yes, I'm going to have to move it offshore. It'll still fetch a nice price, but getting it there is going to be tricky and expensive for me."

"Where's 'there'?" I ask.

"Probably Dubai, but maybe Japan or Russia. I'll see what kind of interest I can generate in India. Kolkata, Mumbai might work. But I'm thinking probably Dubai. Fast, easy, modern. Thoroughly unscrupulous."

I sigh loudly, rudely. My exasperation is evident. " Bruce, just get to the punch line."

"If this hadn't been such a notorious heist, I would have offered you three hundred thousand dollars for the lot."

"A what? Sixty percent whack? Give me a break, Bruce!"

"I don't give breaks, Victor. *I do business.* And I can't even offer you three hundred thousand. I can only go half that. I'm willing to offer you one-fifty. That's as high as I will go. If we do more business in the future, maybe I can be somewhat more generous."

Bruce Roethke and I complete our transaction in the dining room of the Marriott Courtyard at Milwaukee's General Mitchell International Airport. Bruce has flown in on a puddle-jumper from Terre Haute and will leave to go home in three hours. Ironically, my package of precious jewelry and Bruce's package of precious U.S. currency end up being roughly the same size. Out of the kindness of his heart, Bruce is paying me in twenties, which in everyday life are far easier to negotiate than hundreds. $150,000 in twenties is 7,500 bills and weighs about sixteen and a half pounds—if the bills are new and fresh. Bruce's aren't; clearly, they've been around, so they've picked up a little weight along the way. As for me, I have wrapped the jewels in bubble wrap and placed them in a shoebox, the top held in place by thick rubber bands. I have no idea what my package weighs.

I find that I quite like Bruce, who is very short, utterly bald, extremely well-dressed, impeccably groomed, and very polite. He tells me nothing about himself, and I reciprocate, so we part ways knowing nothing about each other than our contact information. I'm sure he will research me when he gets home, if he hasn't already. I certainly plan to look him up.

In a sweet example of honor among thieves, Bruce buys me dinner, and we split a nice merlot. We part ways with a handshake. As I drive back up to Green Lake, I am awash with mixed emotions. I have fronted $20,000 and realized a net return of $130,000. *Who can quibble with that?* On the other hand, I was forced to sell goods with a fair market value of almost a million dollars for about fifteen percent of that.

Hoo boy, *that* smarts.

—◦◦◦—

I'm sitting at my desk, riffling through the stack of currency I got from Bruce Roethke, reflecting on what a $130,000 looks like in the flesh—not a number on a ledger entry or a line item on a financial statement, but cold, hard *cash in hand.* I looked it up: all U.S. bills are 4.3 one-thousandth of an inch thick. So—I do the math—7,500 of them make a stack a little over thirty-two inches thick.

I feel an intense confusion, an ambivalence, a kind of schizophrenia: *is this a lot or a little?* On one hand, you break a hundred and thirty large into three piles eleven inches thick, and it doesn't look like all that much. On the other hand, 130K is a *lot* of money when judged in terms of the profits Collie and I are realizing from our adolescent fencing operation. But on yet another hand, a buck-thirty seems like chicken feed when set against my present and anticipated financial demands—including the monthly mortgage payment on my beloved house and the monthly alimony payment—*highway robbery!*—to Magda Salveson.

I wish I could just hand Colin the entire buck-thirty and say, "Here, use this to pay off your gambling debts. Let's ease some of the stress on you, my dear brother." But at this point, I can't bring myself to do that. Although Collie and I are enjoying steadily improving cash flow, my investment portfolio balance still looks grim, and I am still trying to follow Stephen Bakshi's demand that I minimize expenses until I can refill the money bin. So right now I'm acting like a cheapskate. I have zeroed out my credit card balances and taken all the cards except my Amex card out of my wallet. I've canceled most of my subscriptions, now decline all pleas for charitable contributions, and buy cheaper cuts of meat and cheaper brands of alcohol. I do not shop online. I rob Peter to pay Paul, carefully picking and choosing what to pay and when to pay it. I feel like one of those cash-strapped fixed-income senior citizens whose plight I have blithely ignored for years, and the experience is profoundly demeaning.

When will I know when things have improved enough that I can afford to buy myself a bottle of Chivas Regal or pop for a porterhouse? How many bucks do I need in the bank in order to feel safe? What standard of living shall I aspire to in the long run?

In addition, I realize I'm in a bind I had failed to consider. Even if my fencing pays off with some solid hits, I may become solvent...*but not liquid.* I can't mail Stephen Bakshi a shoebox filled with a hundred grand in C-notes and say, "here, buy me an annuity that provides a steady flow of income, or invest me in some diversified mutual funds, or build me a nice portfolio of preferred stocks." From now on, I have to operate in two financial worlds—one depicted in the reports on my financial condition that Stephen and the taxing authorities see, and the one defined by the twenties and hundreds I am stashing in my floor safe next to my rainy-day fund.

In the RSP world—*receiving stolen property*—almost all transactions are conducted with cash. The currency of the realm is hard currency, usually twenty and hundred-dollar bills. We generally don't use money orders, cashier's checks, letters of credit, bank drafts, or wire transfers for day-to-day hot property transactions. You can't use your friendly neighborhood bank for laundering because frequent and sizable deposits in your personal checking account will trigger alarms with the regulatory authorities. On the spending side, I can't write large checks for big-ticket purchases, can't maintain huge investment accounts in U.S. banks and move money among those accounts, can't use auto-debit to pay my real estate taxes.

Assuming you know how to set them up, offshore accounts and tax shelters may be nice and secure, but you still have to get your ill-gotten funds *into* them somehow, and I am a beginner at how to do that. In order to wire funds into an offshore account, you have to have an account with a sizable balance to wire them *from*. Easier said than done. That's why time-tested money management techniques— using cash-filled suitcases (despite the risks posed by the modern airport and customs security), or stuffing hundreds of hundreds into your socks or underwear, or wads of bills stuffed in shoeboxes and bankrolls stuffed under mattresses— remain in widespread use among us RSPers. I'm learning that living in a purely cash-criminal economy isn't going to be easy, and I don't want to be caught up in rookie mistakes.

In other words, it's time for Victor Harding to learn a lot more about money laundering.

15

Gotcha

I SLEEP LIGHT, so I get the cell phone on the first ring. My bedside alarm clock says two forty-three. Colin is screaming over the phone, his voice charged and frantic. "Get up to the garage, now!"

"Coming!" I yell back.

"Bring your gun!" he yells.

Old people can move fast if you dump enough adrenaline into their bloodstream. I sprint out the front door and up the driveway as fast as I can run and reach the garage in nanoseconds, my blazing LED flashlight burning a hot circle of white light as I sprint up toward Collie. Now the narrow beam illuminates a large, round dome in front of me. Then I see the dark sweat circles on the dome and a spray of red, greasy fingerprints wiped across the front, and I realize I'm looking at Odell Todd's filthy tee shirt. The dome is his enormous gut, the stains the result of working in the hot sun and pizza sauce that had to be wiped somewhere.

I pan the flashlight upward and see a snake wrapped tightly around Odie's neck. Odie's back is pinned against a large oak next to the driveway, and his hands are clawing frantically at the black coil, even as his legs thrash and scrabble for purchase in the driveway gravel. My light jigs to the side and I see Collie behind the tree, his teeth clenched, his face a mask of strain. In my beam, he looks like a gargoyle. His hands are pulling on the snake from both sides.

Only it's not a snake, it's our soaker hose, and Collie, his knee braced against the back of the oak, has Odie's neck pinioned to the tree with it. "Stop struggling, Odie! Stop it, or I'll choke you 'til you drop!"

Odie continues to strain against the hose, even after I shove my pistol against his left ear. Collie sees the gun, releases his left hand, and the hose leaps free with the snap of a bullwhip. Odie, suddenly unrestrained, flies forward and crashes hard, face-first, into the jamb at the side of the garage door, just below the marks on the wood indicating where a padlock and hasp have been pried off.

Instantly I know what's going on here: *Odie is betraying me.*

Odie bounces back from the impact like an obese bo-bo ball, then plops to the ground on his enormous butt. A gash over Odie's eye swells with the first bubble of blood, and his hand drops to the ground next to him. By pure chance, it lands on a short black crowbar. He picks the iron tool up and stares at it as if wondering how in the world it got there. I hear Collie's arm swoosh through the air as he smashes a thunderous rabbit punch to Odie's right ear, and Odie topples over heavily. He writhes, pulls his knees up to his paunch, and he begins to keen.

Odie's fetal posture leaves his crotch totally unprotected, his genitals protruding from behind his enormous hams. I have only a moment to sense I am spinning out of control, my ears buzzing, and blue stars flashing before my eyes. In a fury that is unprecedented, at least for me, I kick Odell Todd in the balls as hard as I can.

He jerks spastically, gasps deeply, then gasps deeper as I bend down and shove the pistol into his mouth. I push my face close to his, hissing and spitting, stumbling over my words. "You f-f-fat j-j-jerk. You b-brainless b-b-bastard. I warned you never to do this to me. *Never!* Remember that, Odie? Was I not clear? Did I fail to communicate that if you double-crossed me, you were gonna d-d-die?"

Odie has never seen me so utterly out of control. His eyes grow wide, then he squeezes them shut, waiting for the bullet, waiting for blackness. For some reason, his panic calms me, and my rage ebbs. Still panting, I slide the gun into my pocket,and cross my arms over my chest. *I'm going to play this traitor,* I think, *I'm really going to make him suffer for double-crossing me.*

"Where's the Honda, Odie?" I hiss. "What have you done with my motorcycle, you slimebag?"

Now Odie is shaking his head from side to side. He's blubbering. "Th-th-the garage was empty, Victor. The bike was gone when I went in, I swear, I swear."

I turn to Colin, winking at him to tell him to play along. "I bet Spaaks stole it back. I can't believe he thinks I'd put up with that kind of stunt. He must think I'm a real sucker."

Odie waves his arms frantically. "No! Not Spaaks! Not Spaaks!"

"Who might it be, then?" Collie says, cocking his head as if trying to fathom some deep mystery. "Who? You wouldn't do this on your own, would you, Odie? Someone had to drive you down here tonight and drop you off. So, who's your partner in crime, my fat friend?"

Odie goes silent. You can see the wheels turning: he knows he's cooked no matter what he says. He starts to sit up, and Colin and I back off and let him stand. "Crouch," he whimpers.

"Not Gunnar?" I say.

"Crouch. Kerry Crouch. This whole Honda thing has been Crouch's all along."

Ding! A bell rings in my head. I know Kerry Crouch. He's the body filler and pre-paint sander lackey at Spaaks' body shop. He's a skulker, a weasel, a rail-thin skinhead, always muttering under his breath. Greasy hair, lousy teeth. A hillbilly cliché brought to life.

"Crouch *really* hates Japs," says Odie, as if that explains everything, as if that makes everything okay. "Japs executed his grandfather in World War II, and his whole family never got over it. Maybe it wasn't logical, but he hated that guy with the CBX from the git-go."

I'd love to dial Gilbert Rennie right now: *Hey, Gilbert, I've just solved your piano-wire murder for you!* But, of course, I can't. Can't play vigilante hero, can't be the Sherlock Holmes of Green Lake. But that doesn't mean I can't bluff Odell Todd, can't peel this poor sap like a grape.

I pull out my cell phone and wave it in front of Odie's face.

"So, who should I speed-dial, Odie? Sheriff Gilbert Rennie or Kerry Crouch? Kerry Crouch or Gunnar Spaaks?"

"Spaaks," Odie squeaks. "Best you call him." For an idiot, Odie's no idiot. He knows Gunnar and I are in bed together, like it or not. Best plan is to let Gunnar mediate. I dial Spaaks.

Evidently, Gunnar Spaaks also is a light sleeper. He answers immediately, his voice alert.

"Gunnar," I say evenly. "Victor Harding. I've got Odell Todd kneeling in front of my garage here, my pistol aimed at his head. Perhaps you'd like to join us for some conversation."

To his credit, Spaaks does not waffle or play dumb. Doesn't act indignant, doesn't say, "What's this about?" or "Are you shittin' me?" He just says, "Ten minutes."

Spaaks soon arrives in his gorgeous pickup truck and leaves it running with the headlights shining on Odie, on me and Colin, on the torn-up garage door. He steps out, pressed jeans, sneakers, fresh white tee shirt. At three in the morning.

"Whassup?" he says calmly. It sounds both like a greeting and a question. I shine my light on the bent hasp and torn-up garage door jamb and show Spaaks the door that's been slid open a couple of feet.

He nods. His voice is quiet as he looks at Odie—poor dumb, defenseless Odie, covered in dirt, snot, and blood running down his face, hands still covering his crotch. "Into the truck, Odie."

Now Odie is kneeling, head bowed like an American POW awaiting beheading. "Gunnar, I didn't say anything... I...I..."

"Into the *truck*."

Odie scurries.

I turn to Spaaks. "I believe in honor among thieves, Gunnar. If you knew this was going to go down, it changes everything."

Gunnar smiles, a forced, rigid smile, and spreads his hands in a gesture of innocence.

"I didn't, and it doesn't."

"I want to believe you," I say. "Odie says this was Kerry Crouch's idea. Should I believe that?"

"Well, I believe it. Crouch is an idiot, and Odie is an idiot's idiot. Open to blackmail from Crouch for reasons I don't know and don't want to know. I am not these jerks' mother, and whatever reputation you think I have, I am not the head of some evil crime empire. Believe me, Victor, I'm sure gonna let Odie and Kerry know how I feel about getting chased out of bed at three in the morning. And that's it for me. If you want to take further steps, that's up to you."

He turns back toward his truck. I call after him.

"Gunnar." He turns. "Did you know about the piano-wire murder?"

He stops, turns, puts his hands on his hips, and sighs audibly. "Victor, as some wise Buddhist master once put it, '*Un-ask the question.*' Or maybe, 'reframe the question.' The right question is *when* did I know about the murder? And, for that matter, when did *you* know about the murder?

"And if that's not good enough for you, let me speak plainly. Like the other members of my club, I was against including non-Harley riders in our Semper rides. But I had no part in that young man's...*accident.* I will admit that after he was killed, I abetted Kerry Crouch in taking possession of certain stolen property. Why not? The dead guy wasn't going to be using it. You bought that certain stolen property, and any jury in the country would say you knew it was stolen when you bought it from me. That makes me a fence in this transaction. And that makes you a receiver of stolen property. Up 'til now, we have chosen not to turn each other in to our friend Sheriff Rennie. I assume that will continue to be true."

He stretches his neck and runs his hands through his hair. "And I also know some other things, Victor. Despite what you may think, I'm not a stupid or ignorant person. I know about your new 'transportation services' business with your brother. I know about the Allmire rig. I know Colin recently made a trip down south. I know that there is no way a certain Honda CBX motorcycle is still in Green Lake County, Wisconsin, much less in your garage. So that means there's no reason why I would put Odell Todd up to burglarizing your garage. I know your brother is an insomniac and often takes long walks at night and acts as sort of a PTSD night watchman.

"On the other hand, Kerry Crouch probably didn't know any of those things, and God only knows what Odie did or didn't know. I'm happy to give Odell Todd, a loyal employee, if not a trusted employee, a ride home at three in the morning. But as I've told you before, you should stop thinking of me as if I'm some sort of mob boss around here, or that all crime is coordinated by me."

Gunnar Spaaks looks down at his feet, then looks up at me and shakes his head as if disappointed in me.

"Victor, if you want to be a fence, *just be a fence*, okay? Yes, I can steer some things your way, actually a lot of things your way. But you don't need to know all the whats and whens and whos. Not relevant to you. *Don't ask too many questions, okay?* People trust me because I keep confidences, and I'm gonna trust you to keep confidences. Just don't get in over your head, pal."

Spaaks spins on his heel and walks back to his truck.

Collie and I head back down to the house. We talk for a long while after Gunnar Spaaks leaves, killing the better part of a fifth of cheap gin. No more Ketel One for awhile.

Colin and I agree that, all-in-all, it has been a pretty exciting night.

My backyard looks like the African veldt as my fancy John Deere 8500 mower sits silently in the shed. Evidently, Odie has walked off the job. It's been two weeks since Colin threw his garden hose noose around Odie's neck, and I haven't seen hide nor hair of my yard man since.

I dial Odie's cell phone number and am surprised to hear Gunnar Spaaks' voice answer. "Gunnar? I thought this was Odie's phone."

Clearly, Spaaks is not surprised to hear from me. "This is Odie's number, but it's not Odie's phone. It's the body shop's phone. I own it, pay for it. Lent it to Odie to help keep him loyal."

"Where's Odie? My yard looks like a goddamned jungle."

"Odie is...in the wind."

This takes a moment to sink in. "Meaning what?"

"Odie bailed, Victor. Skedaddled out of Dodge in the dark of the night. I guess he got tired of being strangled with garden hoses."

"Well, where'd he go?"

"No forwarding address, Victor. I don't even have a way to send him his last paycheck. You knew, I assume, that Odie had spent some time in Waupun State Prison, yes? Guess he didn't want to run the risk of going back to jail."

"Wow," I say. Then I think, *Well, you shouldn't be surprised, Harding. What would you do if you were in Odie's shoes?*

"Well, where's Kerry Crouch?"

"Right now, he's in the back of the body shop, wet sanding the front fender of a Ford station wagon. Why? You wanna talk to him?"

"No need," I say. "G'bye, Gunnar."

Odie's departure forces me into action. Young Larry Fitzmaurice is happy to pick up the yard job, but he says he won't touch the big John Deere: "A guy could get killed on that monster." I end up buying a new bright orange Husqvarna zero-radius mower for forty-two hundred bucks. I sell the Deere to the Milwaukee Country Club—actually to its chief greenskeeper, Bevar Tilley—for forty-three hundred, cash, no bill of sale, all serial numbers mysteriously defaced. Not much of a profit on spinning the Deere, but I no longer have a hot lawn mower sitting in my garage, and Larry Fitzmaurice is thrilled with the new, absolutely legally-procured Husqvarna.

—————— 16 ——————

Gone in Sixty Seconds

"YA WANNA SEE IT IN ACTION?" It's Colin, calling from somewhere at eleven at night. I can hear the crickets chirping brightly in the background. June in Wisconsin.

"See what in action?"

"Our rig. A pickup. Fencing in action. Gone in sixty seconds."

I'm intrigued, but a little put-off. "I thought I was the contact point, the deal broker, Colin. You booking your own trips now? Aren't we supposed to be comparing notes before taking jobs?"

"You won't argue about this one, Victor. Got a call an hour ago, garage heist, big fat-cat mansion over in Kingston, a work in progress. Not possible to do a lot of advance planning. This was too good to pass up."

"Who? Anyone we can trust?"

"Kenny Longstreth and a couple of other Semper guys. I think Gunnar's behind it, but Ken-Bo is the one who called, says they have to strike while the iron is hot. The owner is away tonight."

"What's the piece?"

"A McLaren 720S. Three years old, nine hundred miles on the clock. Guy bought it from Jay Leno, I'm not kidding."

"We just transporting it, fencing it, or what?"

"That's the good part, Victor. We don't have to front a cent on this deal. Buyer's waiting for it in Memphis with $200K in cash. I haul it down there, then give Longstreth a buck-ten when I get back. He's floating our percentage. Says he trusts us."

"That's a hell of thief's cut, Collie. Since when are we paying over 50%? This could set a bad precedent."

"Victor, think about it. This is not really a fencing deal. It's an...*aiding-and-abetting* deal. We are about to make ninety grand for transporting a car to Memphis where a willing buyer awaits. We don't have to put up eighty or a hundred grand, don't have to hide the thing, don't have to source a buyer or involve a downstream dealer or broker. Whole deal is done and clear in two days. I'm not trying to get too big for my britches, Victor, but I just couldn't say no to this."

He's right. *Who are we to turn down such incredibly easy money?* "Okay, Collie, you win. You made the right choice. And yeah, I'm curious to see the handoff. You gonna pick me up?"

"You're going to have to meet me, Victor. I'll be driving south directly from the handoff, so you'll have to get yourself home. You know where Denbaugh State Park is? Down past Montello? Meet us there. If you get there first, park way in the back with your lights off. We do not want to spook Longstreth."

"You know this guy? Can you trust this guy?"

"He thinks I don't know him, but I know him. Victor, I know the name and have a phone number for every perp who brings us so much as a toothbrush. They don't know I know, but I don't drive anywhere unless all the information is in my little black book. It's my insurance policy. Besides, Gunnar's backing the guy on this one. I don't think we're going to get sucker punched."

I am quite amazed at how quickly and smoothly the pickup goes. First Collie wheels in with Allmire's transporter, makes a big sweeping turn in the parking lot so the rig is facing the street and the loading ramp is out of sight. No more than a couple of minutes later, a nondescript pickup truck drives in, towing a front-wheel-only towing dolly with U-Haul stickers on it. The McLaren is concealed under a dark shapeless shroud.

Longstreth and his boys pull the tarp, and I see why they covered the car: The McLaren is a shocking orange, a real eye-grabber, even in the dark of the night. It reflects the tow car's taillights, it reflects the flashlight Collie is holding, it reflects the stars, it reflects *everything*. Longstreth's lads quickly unfasten it, roll it off the dolly, and push it over to Collie's truck. Then occurs the only moment of friction: "Careful, Ken-Bo," a reedy-voiced kid says. "This is one wide mother, and the side mirrors are about to catch on the transporter's tailgate cables."

Longstreth explodes. "You stupid dickwad, I tole you never to use my name on a job!"

"Oh, lighten up," the kid says. "There's no one here."

I emerge from the shadows. "Actually, I'm here. Hi, guys. Hi, *Ken-Bo*. Victor Harding at your service."

This is probably an unwise move, a bit of unnecessary chutzpah. I suddenly find a pistol pressed against my head from behind. Longstreth calls Collie over from where the McLaren is half-way up the loading ramp. "Who's this clown?"

Colin, bless him, stays supremely cool. "No problem, no problem. This is my brother. I invited him to oversee the transfer. No sweat, guys." Then he laughs. "And he's very bad at remembering names."

Colin is gone within five minutes, easing Allmire's rig smoothly out of the parking lot. The McLaren has been carefully strapped down inside the transporter, shrouded on all sides with thick foam pads and moving blankets. Ken-Bo's boys unhitch the stolen U-Haul dolly and leave it in the parking lot. They vanish into the night, and I start home.

My cell phone rings. "Maybe I shouldn't have asked for company," Collie laughs.

"Well, they certainly got *my* attention," I say, still quivering with the adrenaline shakes. "What next?"

"Overall, GPS says seven hundred and four miles to Memphis. Back roads to Rockford, then pick up eighty, down to interstate fifty-five. Throw on the soft jazz CD, break out the Twinkies, and mellow on down for about twelve hours, counting pee breaks."

"Where's the drop?"

"Get this. The land of the upper crust. Charter Hills Country Club, Memphis, Tennessee. I'm supposed to drive way back into the maintenance area—back behind their mower shed. Some fat cat named Grover Wilmotte should be waiting, pockets bulging with cash."

"This safe? You feel okay doing this alone?"

"It's probably the riskiest part of the whole deal. I get real careful once they've off-loaded the car."

"Got some protection?"

"Oooh, yeah. I'm carrying a Glock Nine, legally registered. Got a nice new carry permit. Also, a military-C Taser. Halogen flashlight that will turn anybody's eyes into raisins. And, of course, bullet-proof vest."

"*Really?*"

"Victor, I survived a plane crash. Think I'm going to let some redneck kill me in a robbery?"

—◦◦◦—

In the middle of the night Collie calls on his cell phone, and the news is not good. I hear road noise, so Collie must be moving, but I also hear a tremor in his voice, as if he's choking back a sob. "They tried to jack me, Victor."

"Where are you, are you okay, what happened?" My words gush out in a torrent.

"I'm okay, really, I'm okay. The load is okay. But I am one *pissed-off son of a bitch!*"

Such vehemence is unlike Collie, who generally is not fond of rough language. "Talk to me," I almost shout.

"I pulled over in a truck stop on highway fifty-five about sixty miles south of St. Louis. Parked way in the back of the truck lot. I'm sittin' in the pickup, eating some fried chicken. Dark Chrysler minivan, Wisconsin plates, pulls up next to me. Skinny guy, long greasy hair gets out, walks to the back of the lot, takes a leak. Then he walks casually over to me, waves, gestures for me to roll the window down. 'Nice lookin' rig ya got there,' he says. Real high squeaky voice. Then he climbs up on the running board, sticks a thirty-eight revolver through the window, points it at the ceiling just to let me see it. Tells me to get the hell out of the truck and stand away from the transporter. Says to just be cool until he calls his guys over from the Wendy's in the truck stop."

"Jesus," I gasp. "What did you do?"

"Well, I was *ready.* When someone walks over to you at a truck stop in the middle of the night, you get yourself ready. Very deliberately, no fast moves, I reached out through the window, pressed my Taser firmly into his cheek, and let this dirtball have it. Taser worked fine, Victor. Guy was launched off the running board like he'd been shot out of a cannon, ended up thrashing around on the ground, twitchin' and gruntin'. All his wigglin' made it hard to stick my Glock in his mouth, but I managed." There's now a distinct twang in Collie's voice; he's sounding real southern right now.

"Did you shoot him, Collie?"

"No, sir, but I certainly got his attention. I also got his thirty-eight and his wallet. I look around, nobody's lookin', nobody's seein' all this. I reset the Taser, plant it solid in the middle of his belly, and give the asshole another round. Result was gratifyin' to behold, I must say."

"Holy shit, Colin. Weren't you scared the other guys would show up?"

"Terrified. I admit it, Victor. completely terrified. But at least I was in command for the moment. And of course I was heavily armed."

"So what'd you end up doing?"

"First, I kicked that jerk as hard as I could in the balls, just like you did to Odie Todd that night up at our garage. Hard as I could, yes, absolutely as hard as I could. I wasn't tryin' to accomplish anything, Victor, I was just making sure he felt some serious pain. Then I got our Gerber combat knife out from under my seat and tore nice long slashes in all four of the Chrysler's tires. It won't be goin' anywhere soon. Then I dragged the robber behind his minivan, climbed into our rig, and headed south. Never saw the rest of his gang. This was about ninety minutes ago, so I'm a long way away from there now, maybe ninety, hundred miles."

"Go through his wallet yet?"

"Not yet. Been too busy drivin'. but don't worry, Victor, I'm keepin' it under the speed limit. I'm not going to get pulled over. But I confess I'm feeling shaky."

"Find a place to pull off," I say. "Let's have a look in that wallet."

The wallet, which Collie describes to me as a bulky bifold affair with a chrome chain and a carabiner to hook it to the owner's belt, belongs to one William Salmon, driver's license address in Wautoma, Wisconsin, which is about thirty miles from Green Lake. Visa card, Master card, courtesy card for Shadrack's Gentlemen's Club in Oshkosh, a couple of business cards: *'Bill' Salmon, Master Electrician, Wautoma, WI. International Brotherhood of Electrical Workers.* "When Only the Best Will Do, Call Mr. Bill."

The wallet holds four hundred dollars in twenties and small bills. And one other thing: a plastic-laminated card that reads *Semper Harley Motorcycle Club, Berlin, Wisconsin, "The Finest Riding the Finest." Please accord the bearer every courtesy.* The card has the address of the Semper Bar in Berlin.

—~~—

It's not as correct to say I prepared for the conversation as it is to say I made sure I *was prepared* for the conversation. That is, I didn't know exactly what I was going to say, but I sure as hell knew how I needed to act. I needed to be in control, stay in control, attempt to exert control. Me, Victor Harding. Retired seventy-two-year-old architect. No prior military service.

This preparation involved sitting for an hour on the sun porch pouring repeated shots from a bottle of Jameson's, and gathering my courage, my wits, resolve, and tactical options. Gilbert Rennie had often repeated a maxim his trial lawyer buddies had recited as a guiding principle: *when commencing cross examination – or any hostile questioning – never ask a question unless you already know the answer.*

And *there* was the problem: I had suspicions, but I did not have answers. Not enough answers. Colin, on the other hand, was beyond suspicious; he was sure he knew the answer: Collie was sure Gunnar Spaaks had teamed with Ken Longstreth to set him up. Had double-crossed him, had put his life in peril. Collie came home from successfully delivering the McLaren with a huge fistful of dollars in his hand and a whole new attitude in his mind: *he was profoundly spooked.* He said he wasn't so sure he wanted to continue what he now was calling his "magical mystery tours." "I still enjoy the driving part, Victor, but I'm not sure I want to go through this hijack routine again. Scarier than being stopped by the cops."

"I hear you," I say.

Under the circumstances, what else can I possibly say?

———

Spaaks picks up on the second ring. "Body shop."

"It's Victor," I say. Not friendly, but not hostile, either.

"Yes," says Spaaks. Not friendly, but not hostile, either. Not a great man for cheery greetings or conversational small talk, our man Gunnar.

I dive in. "Gunnar, do you know someone named William Salmon?"

"Well, I *knew* someone named William Salmon."

"What do you mean, *knew?*"

"Well, Bill Salmon's dead. When he was alive, I knew him. He was a charter member of Semper. Rode a sweet '55 hardtail. But he's been dead almost two years now, Victor. He had a debate with a diesel locomotive at a crossing in Omro. He lost."

So, what do I do now? Play it coy, cat-and-mouse? Try to flush him out? Or full-frontal assault? Well, this is high-stakes game with Gunnar Spaaks, so I take out a hard, direct shot and see how Gunnar responds.

"You knew Colin was making a run this weekend?"

"Oh, sure. 'Course. Sweet-ss McLaren, goin' to Memphis. Ken-Bo Longstreth's heist."

"Did you know Colin got hijacked on the way down?"

There is a long pause. "*That* I didn't know."

Time to test the waters. "Did you know they shot and killed him?"

Gunnar's shock is evident, genuine. "*WHAT?*"

"Actually no, Gunnar, 1 made that part up. Just wanted to see how you'd react. Actually, what happened is that some unknown party drove up to Colin's rig in a Chrysler minivan with Wisconsin plates, stuck a revolver into the cab, told him to stand and deliver."

"What...what happened?" *I'm trying to picture this: Gunnar Spaaks, shocked and surprised. Sweeet.*

"Colin stuck a taser into the perp's cheek and rendered him inoperative. Took his gun, tased him again for sport, gave him a hefty kick in the nuts, then slashed all four of his tires. Took his wallet. That is, William Salmon's wallet. Driver's license, business card, credit cards. And Semper membership card."

1 pause again. "Who do you think might have had Bill Salmon's wallet, Gunnar?"

Error: 1 am giving Gunnar Spaaks too long to think.

"So, you're accusing me of setting Collie up, is that it? That 1 sent some goons to chase him down? That 1 would hijack my own fence on a Kenny Longstreth heist?"

"If you were in my shoes, Gunnar, what would you think?"

"I'd think you ought to be very, very careful who you accuse of robbery, Harding. I'd think you oughta play it very cool right about now, because you are really starting to get my back up."

1 could feel myself heating up. "Yeah? Well, when 1 hear Semper, 1 tend to think of Gunnar Spaaks. You mean to tell me 1 shouldn't consider you a person of interest?"

"Screw you."

"So, you didn't end up with Salmon's wallet after he got killed?"

Gunnar sees a way to de-escalate, a simple way out.

"Nope."

"Who did then?"

Spaaks laughs. He really seems to think that something is funny here. "Damn it, Victor, you really do think I got my finger in every pie around here, don't you? That no one farts without asking my permission? *Get serious, Pal.* I know a lot about the action that goes on around here, both things involving Semper guys and things that don't. But I don't know everything. And you'd do well if you didn't try to pin every tail on my donkey. You just gotta back off, Victor."

On the phone, I can't tell the difference between a sneer and a smile. Maybe Gunnar's trying to lighten things up. But I'm not about to chicken out.

"So Salmon gets crushed. Who ends up with his scooter? Who ends up with his Semper colors? Who ends up with his wallet? His wife? His mother? The funeral home? Or one of his riding buddies?"

"Couldn't tell you. Maybe it's your sweet li'l buddy Odell Todd. He helped arrange Salmon's funeral ride. Or Crouch, Kerry Crouch. He and Salmon went way back. Maybe twenty other guys, including Ken-bo Longstreth."

Now Gunnar Spaaks sighs. He actually sighs. "Victor, this phone call isn't getting you anywhere, all it's doing is getting us sideways. You tell Colin I'm glad he's safe and that I'm pleased he handled himself so well. You tell him that I look forward to sending a lot more stuff his way, to making frequent use of that sweet rig he's using. I'm not trying to screw the poochie here. And Victor?"

I say nothing.

"Go jump in the lake. Green Lake, any lake. Just get off my case. I'm tired of this kind of hassle."

17

Enter Cara

FROM THE MOMENT I STEP OUT OF THE BANK, I can
see that the young lady's outdoor art exhibition is in deep
trouble. This is going to be one mean early summer storm.
The blue sky over the Baptist Assembly vanishes abruptly,
as if a dark gray curtain has been drawn. A roiling avalanche
of clouds chases whitecaps across the surface of Green Lake
and speeds toward the town square. At the exhibition site,
the four white collapsible canopies are now being whipped
by fierce gusts that threaten to rip out their support lines
and send them cartwheeling into the sky. The display walls
thwack back and forth, sending hanging paintings into wild
spinning dances. I see several small watercolors fly off the
exhibit and skitter across the park.

The artist is frantically grabbing paintings off the display
walls and running to heave them into the back of her ancient
Volvo station wagon. I see landscapes, nature scenes, animal
portraits, and a couple of still lifes tossed through the air.
She has completed two trips when an opaque curtain of
rain marches across the marina and heads up Main Street
straight for her. A group of six paintings still hang under the
last canopy, and two are landscapes clearly too large for one

person to carry alone. I dash across the street toward her, gesturing toward the largest of the paintings and pointing toward the entrance of the Salvation Army Thrift Shop across the street. She understands, and in moments we have wrestled the elegantly framed piece through the front door. We head back for the second large painting and are slammed by a sheet of rain just as we wrestle it under the thrift shop's portico. Salvation indeed.

Now the woman grins at me, makes a comical "Sit! Stay!" gesture as if I were a golden retriever, and dashes back out in the rain to grab her remaining paintings. By the time she has heaved the last pieces into the Volvo, slammed the tailgate, and raced back into the thrift shop, she is drenched.

"Wow!" she laughs. "That was some fun! Buy you lunch?"

—•∿∿•—

This is how I meet Cara Spaaks. In the thrift store, she buys a faded purple sun dress and some dry socks for nine bucks and does a swift costume change in the fitting room. Within a couple of minutes, we are seated at a corner table in the Country Bakery. She is an attractive woman, tall, fit, energetic, a bit tomboyish, probably in her early 40's. Her hair hangs down her cheeks in drapes of drenched dishwater blonde ringlets. Her smile is magnificent.

"You, sir, are a life saver! I think I shall call you Dudley Do-right, you know, like the cartoon Canadian Mountie character in the *George of the Jungle* show."

"I am familiar with Dudley Do-right. Better to call me Victor Harding of Illinois Avenue, Green Lake Wisconsin, all chivalry accidental."

She purses her lips, then lights up. "...Illinois Avenue...*Oh!* Then you must be the architect guy!"

"*Was* the architect guy. At your service. Actually, at nobody's service anymore. Let's just call it Victor Harding, retired, Green Lake resident."

"Cara Spaaks, struggling local artist and art teacher."

"Spaaks. There's a name you don't hear every day. I think Gilbert Rennie may have mentioned you to me. Are you Gunnar's sister?"

"Unfortunately."

"Still, this is a coincidence. I've gotten to know him a little bit recently."

Her face takes on a peculiar, pinched look, as if she's biting her tongue. "Well, a little bit of Gunnar goes a long way, and a little bit is all you'll ever get to know. Gunnar is not an open book. He's not an open anything. He gets off on being the mystery man."

"I, ah, gather you two are not close."

"Never been close. These days we work hard just to be civil. But we've grown up to the point where you can put us in the same room without having to get out the dueling pistols. Mostly he leaves me alone, and I leave him alone."

"Guess I'm sorry to hear that. I must say, however, that he did a hell of a job repairing my BMW. Very superior paintwork."

"We Spaakses pride ourselves on our paint work."

"Speaking of paint work, tell me, will the rain ruin your paintings?"

"Think I'm okay. Nothing got too wet. The watercolors were behind glass, and the oils can be wiped down. Rather sad end to my exhibition, though. Today was my last day, and now I'm toast."

"Too bad, because from what I could determine from what I could see of your artwork as it was flying through the air, you are very accomplished."

"Why, thank you, sir! Aren't you *gallant*."

"That big painting we carried in, the long view over the lake, is quite striking. Did you paint that at Xenophon Stakhatos' house?"

She lights up. "You knew Phone?"

"I *loved* Phone," I say. "I know this sounds corny, but he was as deep and genuine a person as I have ever met. Phone had *soul.* I worked in a world of superficial prima donnas and pretentious phonies for decades, and when I met Phone, he restored my faith in, well...*something*. Anyway, for me every moment with Phone was a plunge into a cool, restorative well. Wish I'd met him thirty years sooner."

"Well, my, aren't *you* poetic!"

"Oh, that's me, all right. The soul of a poet shrouded in a dark mantle of cynicism. Look, is that painting for sale?"

"All artists' paintings are for sale, always. Some pieces they may lament losing more than others, but in the end, money trumps all."

"Well, I wasn't kidding about being interested in your oils, that one in particular. I've been doing renovations at my place. Would you be willing to come over to the house at some point and scope out the wall space? Make some recommendations? You really might have a prospect here. I feel strongly about patronizing local talent, especially since I've just recently taken up full-time residence in the locality. I assure you my intentions are honorable."

She grins. "Cool either way. If a distinguished older gentleman wants to tip his hat at me, who am I to take offense? By all means, patronize away."

18

Myth Confirmed

THE LETTER BEARS THE LOGO of the Green Lake Planning, Licenses, and Inspections Department. The logo has pine trees and 50s-era building silhouettes on it. Quaint.

> Dear Mr. Harding:
>
> In response to your recent inquiry regarding any drawings, permits, or plans of work done at 835 Illinois Avenue, Green Lake, when the house was owned in the 1920s by one Adelard Leo Cunin, a/k/a George 'Bugsy' Moran, this is to inform you that no such documents exist. However, I am able to provide some information that may be of interest.
>
> I assume that your inquiry pertains to Mr. Moran's 'escape tunnel' from his house down to his boathouse, which remains a well-known legend in Green Lake. It would be an urban legend, except that nothing about Green Lake is urban, if I may presume to jest. In this case, however, the legend is

true. Such a tunnel does in fact exist. Your house was indeed Bugsy's summer house three owners ago, and we have historical evidence that Mr. Moran and a number of his gang members did take up emergency residence there following the unsuccessful St. Valentine's Massacre assassination attempt on February 14, 1929.

There are no building plans for Mr. Moran's tunnel because technically the tunnel was a landscape improvement, not an architectural project. At that time, no plans or permits or detailed specifications were required by this office for such an improvement. I should add, however, that to memorialize certain conversations with this office, Mr. Moran's Chicago lawyer did write the county a polite letter of the 'this will confirm our conversation' variety. It stated that the Boulders' owner was excavating a 'spill water sluice' (his words), which he described as a kind of storm drain, leading from house level down to the lake. The 'sluice' was to be excavated to a depth of five feet, with a width of three feet. The bottom and sides were to be lined with ten-by-ten-inch creosoted timbers. The letter said that the sluice might or might not be covered over. In fact, of course, it was covered. An open-top ditch certainly would not have served Mr. Moran's purposes.

This office does not possess that letter. We believe the Wisconsin State Historical

Society has it. It's probably either in Milwaukee or at the University of Wisconsin's history department archives in Madison. I saw this letter once, when it was part of an exhibit on prohibition in Milwaukee about ten years ago. It appears as you would expect. It's dated July 1928, onion skin stationery, faded typewriter ribbon, numerous overstrikes. The subject line was 'Project at The Boulders on Illinois Avenue.' It was signed by one James Greneuil, Esquire. Mr. Moran's name is not mentioned anywhere in the letter. I hope this information is of some use to you.

Now I must turn to another most urgent matter, Mr. Harding. When you undertook your recent renovation, your architect and contractor 'borrowed' our file of the originals of your property's historical building plans from the date of initial construction. To date, these have not been returned, and this is simply unacceptable. Please arrange to have our file returned to this office forthwith, or we will be compelled to initiate legal proceedings against you.

If you have any further questions, please do not hesitate to contact me.

Sincerely yours,

Bonnie Lantz

Bonnie M. Lantz, County Planning Coordinator.

19

Lead Into Gold

COLLIE'S BEEN QUITE SNIPPY with me ever since he got back from having a gun stuck to his head at the truck stop south of St. Louis. Like it was my fault or something. Truth to tell, the episode did not help his PTSD symptoms any, so frankly I'm happy he's again on the road and out of my face. At the moment, he's dropping a load of semi-valuable English antiques off at a dealer in Ann Arbor, Michigan, a deal that will make us about eight thousand dollars. Given the promising arc of our fencing enterprise, this trip is barely enough to trouble with, but it's a short trip and I hope it may calm Colin a bit to get back in the saddle.

The dig in my backyard goes easy as pie. It takes me less than an hour to penetrate Bugsy's tunnel. Standing on the edge of the veranda, I can see a clear demarcation line between the luxuriant green turf that has a deep, healthy root system and the paler, yellower grass that runs, like the stripe on a skunk's back, from the front of the veranda down to the rear of the boat house on the edge of the lake.

About two-thirds of the way down to the lake, I drive a steel fencing stake into the green-green grass beside the stripe. One good whack with a five-pound maul drives it in over a foot. Four more whacks and it's down almost to its very end, only a couple of inches of enameled green steel protruding above the top of the grass. Now I place a second stake in the center of the paler grass stripe and swing the sledge hard. The sound is entirely different—hollow and leaden—and the results definitely are different: the stake goes in less than a foot and stops with a dead thud. I swing again. The stake does not move. Ten more shots—hard—and the stake still will not move. *Something is under there.*

A couple of hard shoves on my garden spade pull up the surface sod, and the shovel strikes something hard, unyielding. I push fiercely, scraping grass and dirt away from whatever it is I have struck. Something dull and dark, something wooden, like decking or planking or timbers, appears under my blade.

I have unearthed the tunnel's cover, a solid line of planks leading down toward the lake, each about four feet across and a foot wide. I thrust the shovel under the edge of one beam and try to lever it up. To my surprise, it springs up easily, meaning it had simply been dropped in place without being nailed or fastened in any way. I push the plank up on end and topple it over onto the lawn. A whoosh of dank air strikes me in the face, rich, earthy, and pungent. Grinning broadly, I sit down cross-legged on the sun-dappled lawn to catch my breath. *Whoa. This is fun.*

I visually track the stripe of pale grass leading down to the boathouse. Just uphill from the boathouse, the stripe widens abruptly, framing a large square expanse—perhaps twenty by twenty feet—where the turf is of distinctly different texture and color.

The boathouse's foundation is a poured concrete seawall, and the funny grass square extends directly to the seawall's edge. Except, I notice, where a square concrete pad lies flush with the lawn, its edges overgrown with grass. In the center of the pad is a dark forged manhole cover embossed with several lines of words: *Cleveland Iron Works. Cleveland, Ohio. Pat. Pending. Storm Drain Access.* There is a single small semi-circular opening on the edge of the cover.

It's a long, annoying trudge up to the garage to get the six-foot pry bar and even more frustrating when I insert the end of the bar into the hole in the manhole cover and try to lift it up. No amount of pushing, jerking, shaking, or banging the bar with the five-pound maul budges the cover even an inch, and I decide something must be holding the cover down from underneath.

I walk back up to the house yet again, change into coveralls and muck boots, grab goggles, and retrieve my spotlight. Once back at the hole in the decking on the tunnel top, I drop the stepladder into the darkness and slowly lower myself down. The floor is dirt, but the footing is firm, solid. I switch on the spotlight and aim it down the tunnel. I expect spiders and worms and mouse droppings, but what I see instead looks like a mine shaft, with a series of side support beams propping up the ceiling planking. It's dank, but not damp. Someone must have designed the drainage and ventilation right.

The tunnel is tall enough to walk, but not tall enough to stand upright. I frog-walk down the tunnel until it opens out into a room approximately ten feet square. I must be right behind the boathouse now. Here the floor has been set with bricks in a tight herringbone pattern. Old-fashioned steel library shelves line one wall. These have rusted badly, and the bottom shelf has collapsed, spilling once-stacked bottles of whiskey onto the bricks. I examine a couple: simple pasted-on white paper labels, some of which say Rye, some saying Irish Whiskey. Classic prohibition stuff. I have to laugh, standing here in a rotgut storehouse, rounding out an arc of history that spans ninety years.

On the middle shelf, I see strange shapes cloaked in green rubberized canvas—a stack of flat, circular disks, like Christmas cookie tins, flanked by two lumpy shapes about the length of an umbrella. I pull aside the tarp and gasp in surprise at the sight of two Thompson submachine guns. Their dark stocks are worn to a warm walnut patina, their receivers shine with white lithium grease. I lift one off the shelf and find it surprisingly heavy, even with no magazine in place.

The banjo magazines also have real heft. There are eight on the shelf. I lift one, obviously fully loaded, and find it must weigh at least five pounds. Those gangster-movie depictions of cops and robbers waving their Tommy guns wildly around with one hand are obviously some screenwriter's fantasy. Clearly, it takes both hands to operate a Thompson.

I take a deep cleansing breath. *Bugsy Moran's Tommy guns, imagine that. These things must be worth a fortune. Imagine that.*

I shine my light upward to the manhole cover, and immediately see why I had been unable to pry it up from outside. A single threaded rod has been welded to its center, over which Bugsy's boys had placed a flat steel bar with a hole in its middle spanning the width of the cover. A large wing nut holds the bar in place. *Figures,* I think. *You want to be able to get out of the tunnel, but you sure as hell don't want the bad guys sneaking into your escape route from outside.*

I finger the wing nut and find it turns easily. It too has been greased and then left finger tight. *Don't want to be wrestling with a rusted nut when you're trying to make a rapid escape.* I spin the nut until it drops off, and the crossbar clatters to the floor. The manhole cover pushes up easily, and sunlight floods the hidden room as I push the cover over onto the grass. I squint against the bright sun and turn away from the opening.

Over in the corner, I see a shape that looks like a crate covered with more rubberized canvas. But when I pull the cover aside, I see it isn't a crate, but rather a pallet supporting a neatly stacked pyramid of dull gray lead bars, each about eight inches long, two inches wide, maybe two inches high. I heft one from the top of the pile and find it weighs about the same as the twelve-pound kettlebell up in my home gym.

These ingots are clearly not a professional bit of work. They have been crudely cast, a line of flashing around the circumference suggesting that they had been poured using a two-piece mold. They contain no manufacturer signature, or weight legends, no hallmarks, no index marks. *What had these been used for? Weighting down dead bodies destined for the bottom of Green Lake?*

When I shine my light closely on the ingot in my hand, I am surprised to find brush marks in the dull finish. The lead bars have been *painted*, but why? Lead doesn't need protection; it doesn't rust or corrode. I want to see this in daylight. With a mighty heave, I toss the ingot out the manhole cover, and hear it clunk dully on the cement outside. Then I very carefully push the two Thompsons out onto the lawn and slide four of the magazines out next to them.

Then I start back up the tunnel to my trusty aluminum ladder.

———

With a fresh gin-and-tonic next to me on the veranda, I wipe the grease off the Thompsons and examine them carefully. Both are battle-tested: scrapes and gouges scar the blued finish on the receiver, and there are patches where the finish has been worn through on the stock and the two pistol-grip handles. "M1928" is engraved on the receiver, and on the stock of one of the guns, a fine hand has neatly carved the phrase *"Chicago Piano."* I pull the cocking lever back; it moves easily. The gun has been used often but maintained well. The chamber is empty. I pick up one of the magazines, unsure how to insert it. Several tries later, it nestles into place with a satisfying click. *Look, Ma, I'm a gangster.*

Next, I heft the lead ingot onto the coffee table. Totally unremarkable. Except now I see something I hadn't noticed before. The ingot evidently had landed on its corner when I tossed it out of the manhole. The corner had been slightly flattened when the bar hit, and a small patch of the brushed paint has been scraped away. What now shines through is not the dull gray of cast lead, but rather a bright gleam of yellow.

Each ingot of gold weighs about six kilograms. Six thousand grams. Just over thirteen pounds. About 192 troy ounces. Moran's cache, now my stash, contains one hundred and twenty-eight ingots.

My fingers dance on my calculator. 24,576 troy ounces. The market price of gold is volatile, so I figure conservatively. Today's federal government quote is $1,712 per troy ounce. *Okay, just to manage our expectations, let's be really conservative and figure only $1,500.*

That would be, conservatively, just shy of thirty-seven million dollars. At the top of today's prices, the gold is probably worth almost forty-two million dollars, if I can find some way to cash it all out. I decide that for mental walking-around purposes, I'm going to call it forty mil. Forty. Million. Dollars. *Not bad for an hour's worth of manual labor. About six times what I made in my entire career as an architect.*

Well, thank you, Mr. Moran.

"Glen?" I ask. "I've got a rookie question. Sometimes I see 'karat' with a 'k,' and sometimes I see 'carat' with a 'c.' What's the difference?"

"A carat with a 'c' is a unit of weight. It's usually used to measure the size of diamonds and other gemstones. A karat with a 'k' is a measurement indicating the proportion of gold in an alloy out of 24 parts, so 18K gold is 18/24ths part gold. Me, I deal in karats and not carats." He giggles.

Now Glen Woldow looks up from the sliver of gold I have carved from the ingot with a kitchen knife. He drops his jeweler's loupe into his hand, looks up, and his eyes narrow. "Where did you get this? How did you get this?"

"Rich uncle died," I smile. "My share was a little chunk of this."

"Just how big a chunk?"

"I'm not comfortable saying, Glen. But enough to be a pleasant surprise. Me and my sibs all got some. Please tell me what I've got here."

"What you've got is pure gold, 24 karat fine. Only it's in a very funny form."

"How so?"

"Well, sometime after it was originally smelted from ore and made into ingots, it was melted down again and poured into a mold, but by someone who's a real clod. It has crude grain and a lot of oxygen bubbles and inclusions in it. This is not a product of the Fort Knox smelter, if you know what I mean. I'd say that it looks like someone melted a lot of different stuff together under very dirty conditions, dirty in a jeweler's sense. Still, gold's gold. Once they had their ingots, they painted them with, I think, house paint. Obviously trying to make them look like lead. But they're not lead, Victor. They're fine gold."

"Would you buy it? How much would you pay for this piece?"

"Well, I don't make much jewelry anymore, Victor. Too time-intensive, and I'm not getting any younger. But if you had, say, five ounces of this stuff, I could come up with $7500. But that's probably below market. I'm not a speculator, I'm just a small-town jeweler. If you want to talk to a real gold broker—I mean someone other than the U.S. Government—I can probably get you a name."

"Thank you, Glen. Very helpful. But I think I'll hold off for now. I just wanted to know what I had. I'd appreciate it if you held this inquiry in confidence."

"But, of course," says Glen Loev with a polite nod of his head, his dark blue yarmulke shining in the overhead fluorescent light.

"Pardon the crappy signal," says Tibbets. "I'm driving through a lousy reception area out in the scenic desert, here."

"Mr. Tibbets, my name is Victor Harding, and I'm calling you from Green Lake, Wisconsin."

"Long way from west Texas," says Tibbets.

"My research suggests that you're the man when it comes to Thompson submachine guns."

"Most definitely. I only do Thompsons. And then only the real ones. I don't fool around with any of this new-manufacture replica junk."

"I'd like to make a confidential inquiry."

"In my business, is there any other kind?"

"What would be the approximate value of an M1928, dating to at least 1929, well-used but in perfect working condition?"

"Oh, probably about twenty-five hundred."

"What about a fully loaded banjo magazine?

"No dents, registers slide smoothly, four hundred and fifty bucks."

"What would the value be if the Thompson was previously owned by one Adelard Leo Cunin?"

There is silence on the line, punctuated only by static and the sound of road noise.

Finally, Tibbets speaks, slowly, carefully. "You joshin' me, Mr. Harding?"

"No, sir. This is straight up."

"I would pay—hell, *any dealer* would pay—thirty thousand dollars for Bugsy Moran's Thompson. I'll be straight with you, there's real profit potential here. At auction, such a weapon could top forty-five, fifty. Skip the 'I would' stuff. You got it; I'll buy it."

"What if the provenance is sketchy?"

"What do you mean?"

"I do not have any paperwork on the guns. No chain of title, or documentation. Which is hardly surprising, right? These were gangsters, not gun collectors. But I am the current owner of Bugsy Moran's former lake house here in Green Lake, Wisconsin. He owned it from 1927 to 1939, and I can document that. I'm the third owner after him, bought the house about eight years ago. After the St. Valentine's Day massacre, Bugsy left Chicago in a hurry with a bunch of his North Side gang and turned this place into a bit of a fortress."

"And...?"

"Well, I just found a secret underground storage room built by the gang."

"And...?"

"In that storage room, I found two Thompsons, greased and wrapped, and eight fully loaded banjo magazines. One of the Thompsons has *"Chicago Piano"* carved into the stock."

"Ah, ha. Look, if you'll pardon my asking, are you a respectable citizen?"

"Retired architect. Good reputation. No criminal record."

"You a gun collector?"

"Nope, and I don't want to be."

"Are you willing to prepare a notarized affidavit reciting what you've just told me?"

"Could that get me in trouble with the feds or anything?"

"I don't see any problem. There is a collectors' market for Thompsons or any firearms dating to prohibition days. It's legal. Your weapons are found property, acquired under credible circumstances. Who is going to challenge their provenance?"

A loud horn blast sounds over the phone, and Tibbets cries out in surprise. "Sorry," he says. "I guess I been slowing down as we were talking. Got an impatient semi on my ass. Let me pull over here."

I hear the crunch of gravel, hear Tibbets' engine switch off.

"Okay, lemme think. Look, I'm not trying to jerk you around, but all that we know is that those M1928s belonged to Bugsy's gang. But there's no sayin' Bugsy ever touched 'em, you hear what I'm sayin'? Still, man, that's a hell of a find, and a hell of a story. Look, you get me the affidavit, let me see it before we close the deal, and I will pay you fifty thousand dollars for the whole lot, the two pianos and the magazines. Cash on the barrelhead. Wire it to you, money order, bank check, whatever you want. Deal?"

"Deal," I say. "I think a money order is probably the best way to go."

—⁓—

Fifty grand is not going to save my house, but at this point every little bit helps. The progress of the fencing enterprise is encouraging, and my cash flow schizophrenia is easing up a bit. We've had a couple of hefty deals, but we haven't really hit full stride yet—there's not enough cash flow to sustain both Collie and me, much less attack Collie's gambling debts, which are accruing interest, or even provide a comfortable upper middle class living. We need to ramp up some more, and with increased activity comes increased risk. And, after having a gun stuck in his face, Colin is suddenly showing signs of cold feet.

Who could blame him? Should we pull the plug? Quit while we're alive? I weigh the risks of carrying on our fencing work, particularly if we continue to specialize. If I should get sent off to prison for a spell, who suffers? Other than Magda's alimonial blood-sucking, I am directly responsible for, and accountable to, no one else, although obviously I'm concerned both with Colin's financial situation and his overall well-being these days. I know that a year of Susan's astronomical medical expenses before she died had hit his finances hard. Still, I tell myself, Colin's a grown man, and he should be responsible for his own risk-reward analysis. Frankly, I resent the fact that I have been forced into the role—hopefully temporary—of being my brother's keeper with responsibility for his financial well-being. I'll be happy when he can again fly with this own wings.

I don't think I have to worry about Christine, Colin's twin, because as a well-respected trusts-and-estates lawyer in Manhattan, Christine seems to be doing okay. She's not an equity partner taking a slice of the firm's profits, but I bet she's probably taking home more than five hundred large a year. She lives in a condo on the upper East Side. So, she's sure not dependent on me. I don't have to figure Christine in my risk-reward decisions.

But whoa! Suddenly I now have Bugsy's "lead." Suddenly, I am worth, in round numbers, many many millions more than I was a week ago. So, will this windfall affect my goals, my dreams, my aspirations? Will I use it to alter the face of my retirement, outlast the recession, save my house, buy both myself and my sibs a life of ease?

You bet your life I will. How can I turn down the opportunity to be the family hero? Do I long for a happy ending? *I sure do. Ardently.*

Should I move forward on both fronts? The gold is like... *wealth.* Our fencing activity is like...*income.* Two distinctly different arrows in my quiver. Why the hell not? Now I can move faster, move bigger, think outside of a whole new set of boxes.

I feel the mental click of a decision locked and loaded: *In for a dime, in for a dollar, Victor. Go big or go home. Sure, the risks of continuing to deal with Gunnar and his tribe seem to be escalating, but I must say: this is all pretty exciting. Isn't that what I wanted?*

20

Legal Research

I IMMEDIATELY REALIZE, of course, that my grandiose fantasies face a major liquidity problem. I cannot simply walk into some precious metals market with a bunch of gold ingots and say, "Cash me out, please." First, I have to deal with the threshold question: *Is Bugsy's gold now my gold?*

I sit in the small but impeccably appointed second-floor office of Irwin Schuenke, Counselor and Attorney-at-Law, in Rhinelander, Wisconsin, one hundred and seventy miles north of my house in Green Lake. I'd found his name in the yellow pages.

At first glance, my new lawyer looks like someone straight out of central casting for Oktoberfest. He's huge and Teutonic. In his fifties. Throw some lederhosen on him, have him chug fifteen or twenty steins worth of lager, and this giant is your stereotypic Bavarian Kraut: Blond-haired, barrel-chested, dome-bellied, flush-faced, thick-lipped, lavishly mustachioed. Red spiderwebs of ruptured veins mottle his puffy cheeks. His smile, broad and genial, seems only loosely tethered to his face.

But the details tell another story. His eyes, blue, intelligent, sharply focused on the tip of my nose, send me the message that this guy is *smart*. His diction is crisp, without any trace of what is often called the Midwest nasal twang. His grammar is correct, and his vocabulary is educated. Irwin's wine-colored silk tie is tightly knotted against the collar of his heavily starched white shirt, his nails are trimmed and buffed. He's wearing a Rolex.

This is no two-bit hick-town rube with a degree from some online law school. I'm pleased with my choice.

Irwin Schuenke rests his huge smoldering Macanudo on the blocky crystal ashtray, leans back in his tired leather desk chair, and puts his hands behind his head. "Well, I've done some research," he says.

"Before we start, is this consultation absolutely confidential?" I ask.

"Will be, as long as you don't ask me to break the law or counsel you to disobey some legally enforceable obligation or lie to some court. Sweat not, Mr. Harding. This is privileged communication, lawyer-attorney work product. Besides, this is just a legal research project, correct? You are not asking me to represent you before any tribunal or authority, right? I'm just advising you, but not making any claim on your behalf, isn't that what you told me?"

I sit back in my chair, my hands steepled under my chin. "So, Mr. Schuenke, what's the answer to my 'hypothetical' question?"

I make little quotation marks in the air. I'm sure my impatience is apparent.

"Like most legal things, Mr. Harding, the answer is that *it depends.*"

"Depends on what?"

"On who knows what and when they knew it."

"Oh, give me a break!. You damned lawyers really are all alike."

Schuenke winces. "Want it different? Okay, good news-bad news story."

"What's the good news?"

"Let me take a step back here and tee this up. You familiar with the phrase 'treasure trove?'"

"Only in pirate movies," I say.

"Well, in the law, 'treasure trove' is a legal term for 'treasure that has been found." Schuenke slips on a pair of narrow readers, glances down at his notes, and reads slowly and carefully. "' Treasure trove' is an amount of money or coin, gold, silver, plate...*or bullion*...found hidden underground or in places such as cellars or attics, where the treasure seems old enough for its true owner to be presumed dead and heirs undiscoverable.' Well, Mr. Harding, you seem to be ticking all the boxes. You got the bullion, you got the underground, you know the original owner to be dead. So far, things are looking good for you.

"Now a majority of state courts, including those in Wisconsin, have found that the finder of a treasure trove is entitled to keep it. Some other states say it belongs to the owner of the place where it was found, but you've got that covered too, right? You found it, you own the property where it was found. Your discovery, your money."

I can't keep from grinning. I know I should be keeping a poker face, but well, *damn!* It seems like I've just been told that I'm about forty million dollars richer.

"So, Mr. Harding, the common law looks good for you, and nothing in statutory law or the provisions of the Uniform Unclaimed Property Act says different. I guess you'd call that the good news part."

He takes off his readers and polishes them on his pocket-handkerchief.

"So, what's all this 'it depends' runaround?"

Schuenke sucks in a great bellyful of air. "Well, there's some other aspects of the law we must consider, Mr. Harding. Specifically, the law pertaining to the return of property to its rightful owner, if the owner can be identified. Every state, and that includes Wisconsin, has laws requiring the return of money or property if it is possible to identify the owner.

"Now, even if the owner is not easily identified, most states still require that you contact local law enforcement authorities and place the money with them for a period of time to allow the owner the opportunity to claim it. If the rightful owner fails to surface after a certain period of time, then most states' laws will allow the finder to take the money as his or her own. Doing otherwise is considered theft. And so I have to ask: have you reported your discovery to the police—or do you intend to?"

I throw out my arms in protest. "But that's absurd! Bugsy Moran is dead! There's no way he can ever reclaim the property, so what's the point of reporting it or giving it to the police and starting this 'ample period of time' runaround? Just a waste of time. And at my age, I'm not inclined to waste time."

Schuenke's stare is long, piercing, and patronizing. When he speaks, his voice is soft. "Mr. Harding, you know as well as I do that that gold was unlawfully obtained, that it did not legally belong to Bugsy Moran. That it was, and is, stolen goods."

I feel desperation crawl up my body, feel my face flush, feel my palms begin to sweat. "But...but...but..." A flash of relief washes across me. Triumphant, I exclaim, "There is no possible way to determine the 'lawful' owner of my gold! We're going back ninety years here! A goldsmith has told me that the gold is not in its original form, that it has been put through some kind of amateurish re-smelting process and reshaped into the current ingots. Who can say what its original form was, who its original owner was?"

Irwin Schuenke shakes his head sadly. "Unfortunately, I think maybe I can. Not to an absolute certainty, but to a degree that a court or other finder of fact would find pretty interesting."

I feel myself losing it. I move to the edge of my chair, rise slightly, and place my hands on Schuenke's massive desk. Through clenched teeth, I hiss, "What the hell are you talking about?"

"I am talking about some other interesting research activity I conducted for you. Not legal research, historical research. Research into midwestern heists, specifically gold heists."

I feel my hands grow cold again.

"Have *you* conducted any such research to track down where your gold might have originated?"

I shake my head.

"Well let's see, Mr. Harding. Where in the world might it have come from? Did you think that maybe your melted-down ingots were molded from a bunch of old gold watches and wedding rings and cufflinks that someone melted down in his spare time? Hundreds of pounds worth?"

"No," I say. "I do not know where Moran got the gold. But nobody else does either. Nobody even knew it was hidden in the tunnel. So, tell me why I should care where it came from."

Schuenke sighs. "Let's not spar with each other, Mr. Harding. No point in arguing with me. I'm just your research assistant, providing you with some hard facts. And here is a fact you may find disturbing. Prairie du Chien, Wisconsin is about two hundred and fifty miles from Chicago, about one hundred fifty-odd miles from Green Lake. It's on the Mississippi River, right on the Iowa border. There used to be a prosperous little enterprise in Prairie du Chien called Falk

Brothers Private Mint. It made various things out of silver and gold for wealthy clients, 'bespoke things.' You know the word, 'bespoke?' It means made to order. Falk specialized in silly things like gold medals and gold-plated flatware and custom-ordered solid gold sink fixtures. It also made serious things for various industrial clients in the U.S. and abroad, things like solid-gold contacts for electrical switches and watch cases for Swiss jewelers. Here, have a look."

Schuenke pushes a faded and dog-eared catalog across the desk to me. On the cover, it says, FALK – A RECOGNIZED LEADER IN SOLID GOLD PRODUCT, 1923.

"Anyway, to continue, in the middle of the night on May Fourteenth, 1929, the Falk Brothers Private Mint was robbed. Or, more precisely, it was bombed and then robbed. *Boom!* Someone sets off a hefty explosive, blowing the front gate off its hinges. Several trucks drive in, a bunch of thugs grab the night watchman, and force him to open up the storage vault. From what the local paper said, the heist was fast, furious, and successful. They skipped the silver, and evidently knew exactly what they were looking for, and that was gold. They took three hundred flat 'panels,' as Falk called them. They looked kind of like square waffles. Each one weighed exactly five pounds. Exactly fifteen hundred pounds of twenty-four karat gold.

"Other details were hard to find, Mr. Harding, but I found some. One of the robbers, a young man aged about twenty-five, slipped off the running board of one of the departing trucks and was crushed under the rear wheels. He was never identified, but he had a tattoo on the inside of his right arm. It said, '*Erin Go Bragh*,' that is, '*Ireland until the end of time.*' The tattoo on his other arm was just initials: N.S.G. I think we might surmise that means 'North Side Gang,' no? The police investigation was, by all accounts, woeful. The feds were never called in, because it was not a federal facility, just a private business. The perps were never caught. The story soon faded. The Falk Brothers fixed the place up and continued in business until 1932 when the depression killed the private market for things made out of gold.

"And one last detail, Mr. Harding, but a very important one. The Falks submitted an insurance claim for their losses... and the Fidelity Northern Insurance Company of Dubuque, Iowa paid the claim. The amount was never disclosed, not that I could find. Since 1929, Fidelity Northern has merged and reorganized several times. Today its successor trades under the name Ichiban Hai Reinsurance, Limited. Put simply, Mr. Harding, I think it is highly likely that your gold is rightfully now owned by the Japanese."

Schuenke smiles. "Or maybe not. This is not an absolutely open-and-shut case, maybe your gold and the Falk Brothers' gold is not the same. Maybe Fidelity Mutual paid on some other gold in 1929 and a Japanese claim for recovery would fail for want of solid proof. But I have to tell you, as a small-town trial lawyer, I'd love to put these facts before a finder of fact in exchange for a percentage of any Ichiban recovery. And I wouldn't want to be footing your legal bills as you fought them off. They are a ten-billion-dollar company, with a corporate legal department of a hundred and thirty-four lawyers around the world. My bet, Mr. Harding, is that there's a high probability that you would lose.

"And that, Mr. Harding, is the sum total of my research. I hope you find it useful."

I have continued to lean heavily on Schuenke's desk. Now I use my hands to hoist myself to my feet. I reach into my jacket pocket and pull out a stack of bills.

"I believe you quoted me a fee of a thousand dollars on the phone, Mr. Schuenke, and I believe you have earned it, as much as I dislike the results."

I count out ten one hundred bills and place them gently on his blotter. Then I slowly count out four more and stack them next to the first pile. Schuenke cocks his head and looks up at me, raising his eyebrows.

"Now let me ask you a final question, Mr. Schuenke. Have you ever heard of any place called the Falk Brothers Private Mint?"

He pauses, and coughs into his hand. "Can't say that I recall that name," he says.

"No, can't say that I do either," I say. "Good day, sir, and thank you. I trust our paths will never cross again."

21

Go Ahead, Just Take It

IT'S MID-JUNE, and the face of nature at Green Lake has fully ripened. The summer weather is glorious, and I'm feeling relatively glorious myself. In the several months since we slid into our fencing enterprise, Collie and I have made real progress, and we now have a firm idea of what its upside can be.

Today I have been asked to join a diverse group of folks that Vilma Stakhatos, Phone's daughter, has recruited to help clean out her father's house and dispose of decades of assorted furniture, art, writings, books, outdoor sculpture, and all the junk that Phone had accumulated over the years. Vilma is ready to sell the house, but it's totally unready to be sold.

Vilma sure knows how to arrange a rummage sale. This is a catered event, with waiters in white jackets and blue-jean shorts prowling among us with trays of champagne and assorted Greek finger food. Those of us who want beer have to retrieve it ourselves from a bank of ice-filled coolers in the garage. Vilma also has brought in a dumpster to heave stuff into, and the *Junk Is Us* guys have their box truck there too, taking first grabs on anything being discarded that looks to have any value.

There is a loose, happy vibe to the afternoon, making it feel more like a festive tribute to Phone than a junk-ridden memorial service. People who don't know each other engage like old friends, bonded by their common love for the late Xenophon Stakhatos. It's a sad day and a happy day both, and I find that I am moved by the occasion.

I wander out to the cantilevered deck affording a glorious sweeping view over Green Lake. I sense someone behind me and turn to find Cara Spaaks extending a cold beer to me. "I saw you come out," she said. "I know you old people can't survive without a regular supply of alcohol."

I take a gentle swipe across the top of her head with one hand and make a rude gesture with the other before taking the beer. Cara Spaaks has been very friendly to me ever since I agreed to purchase four thousand dollars of her artwork, the big painting I admired so much on the day of the storm, three other ready-mades, and a commission for a large new piece to go in the dining room. If she is surprised that I insist on paying her in cash, she does not say so, and as a boon to my cash flow issues, she agrees to payment on an installment plan.

For a cash-strapped guy, this purchase might seem profligate. But it's not. It's a classic example of laundering—turning dirty money into clean possessions, which, if need be, can be resold completely legitimately. It helps 'clean the trail' if you 'age' said possessions by letting some time pass before resale, but nothing is stopping you if you want to flip the newly-acquired goods in a hurry. High volume fences do it all the time.

Cara and I had spent a couple of pleasant afternoons scoping my wall space and test-hanging a variety of her landscapes. I very much enjoy Cara's directness. She is smart, sharp (these are not the same thing), and possessed of a wonderfully droll sense of humor. These are traits I find unusual in artists, who tend to evoke meaning visually rather than orally, who tend to be a little...*wifty.* Not Cara Spaaks.

Cara taps me on the shoulder to get me to look at her. "Gunnar's afraid of you, you know," she says.

"Is that so?" I say. "And just how do you know that?"

"Because he made such a point of telling me he *isn't* afraid of you."

"And just how did I come up in conversation?"

"Good question. He knows I sold some art to you, and I think he might be worried that I will divulge family secrets to you, or something. Afraid that you and I will become— *gasp!*—friends."

"Fat chance," I say. "I do not *befriend* bohemian artists. We architects find artists to be...imprecise. Undisciplined. In an exercise of *noblesse oblige*, we simply choose to patronize the arts occasionally."

"Well anyway, Gunnar wasn't too tactful about bringing you up. He said something subtle, like, 'What's up with this Harding guy?'"

"And you said?"

"I said that as far as I knew you were kind, trustworthy, brave, and reverent, and that you obeyed the Scout Oath. I told him to mind his own business. I believe I may have told you before that Gunnar and I are not...well, let's just say that we don't have a lot in common. Also, he's your basic mean-spirited military snob. They seem to feel the need to condescend to everybody who wasn't in some branch of the service. So, anyway, out of the blue, Gunnar says, 'I'm not afraid of that arrogant jerk.' I should tell you, Victor, that this kind of outburst is quite unlike my brother, who likes to be seen as the strong, silent type. In my opinion, Gunnar is fretting about something. I don't know if it's relevant, but I thought it would be fun to divulge a family secret to you."

Before I can reply, Vilma Stakhatos steps out the sliding door to the deck. Actually, she glides. That's what Vilma does: *she glides*. She always is wearing something long, loose and flowing, and she moves like a poem being cast before the wind. I find her enchanting and wish I was twenty years younger so that I could hit on her. "Hi, Cara," she says brightly. "Don't mean to interrupt, but Victor, I wonder if you could look at something for me, help figure out what to do with it. You come too, Cara."

Vilma leads us to a utility carport carved into the hill under the main garage, where a pile of assorted lumber is stacked atop something cloaked under a dirty black tarp. Vilma lifts up the back of the tarp, revealing a strangely shaped car taillight that looks something like a shark's fin. "Know what this is?" Vilma asks.

I move to the car and pull the tarp up far enough to reveal a strange cut-down car door on a two-seat roadster. The door is not made to swing open; rather, it's a pocket door, designed to slide straight forwards into the front fender. I'm no car expert, but I recognize this car from my childhood.

"Vilma, this is a sports car made in the early 1950's called a Kaiser Darrin. It's made of fiberglass, and it was intended to compete with the new Corvette that GM was just bringing out. Also, the much-anticipated Ford Thunderbird. It was a complete failure. It was..."

"*This is the Darrin?*" exclaims Vilma. "I thought Dad had gotten rid of that thing years ago. I had no idea he was hiding it under the garage."

"Why would he hide it?" Cara asks.

"Well, see, Dad always hated the pasty white color of the car, and one night he got good and loaded and repainted the car with a paint brush and some red house paint, including the upholstery. My mother—this was shortly before she died—was absolutely furious, and she told him that she would never be seen in it and that he had to get rid of 'that ugly piece of crap,' as she called it. Dad said he would, but obviously he didn't. I thought it was long gone."

"Well," I say, "Darrins were pretty terrible cars, but they didn't make all that many of them, so I suppose it has some collector's value."

Vilma drops the tarp. "You want it? If you want it, you can have it. Just get it dragged out of here."

I am taken aback; I certainly had not been angling for a gift. "Oh, Vilma," I stammer, "I-I-I couldn't..."

She cuts me off. "Don't play noble with me, Victor Harding. If you can use this misbegotten thing, please take it. I don't want to have to deal with it."

"I'll have it out of here on Monday," I say.

As I head toward my car at the end of the rummage-fete, I find Cara Spaaks leaning against my front fender. "So, what are you going to do with it?" she asks.

"If I can, I'll get it running, have it sanded down and repainted and reupholstered. I can't afford to do a full restoration, but I'd like to turn it into a solid daily driver. This is the sort of thing your brother's body shop probably can do at a reasonable cost. When it's done, I'll get a vanity plate that says 'Phone' and drive the Darrin around on weekends and in parades. I will have glossy broadsheets printed that describe the life of the remarkable Xenophon Stakhatos, and I will hand them out to everyone I see. See if I can make the car into a rolling tribute."

"That sounds nice," says Cara Spaaks.

22

On the Upswing

COLIN AND I DECIDE not to trade in stolen boats, and frankly, I'd be perfectly happy to skip the stolen car trade, too. Ironically, however, our hot car fencing activity has spawned a legitimate sideline for us: transporting exotic and classic cars. Allmire's rig doesn't care what it carries, and Colin says he breathes easier when delivering something that isn't hot.

Moreover, Collie really likes and knows the fancy car guys, and in the realm of valuable automobiles, Collie is in the process of cultivating a trustworthy circle of owners, dealers, restorers, and auctioneers. These guys are located all over the place, often in small towns, and Collie has been busy memorizing his Rand-McNally atlas. Still, even as we work to broaden our downstream network, we know we should not try to be all things to all people.

Through his Florida golf contacts, Collie makes contact with several collectors who move their lavishly restored trailer queens to various car shows and fancy-car auctions. We get a huge boost from Warren Spillman, an absurdly wealthy architect who designed lots of artsy-fartsy buildings that threatened to fall down until I fixed them. I know Warren's secrets—mainly that he's incompetent—and this makes him afraid of me and generally rude to me on the few times we meet.

Now I read in *The New York Times* that Warren has just spent two and a half million dollars on a specially-outfitted Bugatti Chiron supercar that he intends to take to the Bugatti retrospective event at the upcoming Concours d'Elegance in Amelia Island, Florida. I ring him up, and he pretends to be glad to hear from me.

"How's retirement treating you?" he says.

"Sucks, big time," I say.

Neither Warren nor I am good with small talk, so there is a slightly awkward silence, the kind that used to be called a pregnant pause.

"Warren," I finally say, "I see you're going to take your super-Bugatti to Amelia. How you gonna get it down there from Illinois?"

And in strides Lady Luck once again. "Sensitive topic, Victor. I was late booking transportation, and now the only guy I can find needs to drive from Phoenix to Winnetka to pick the Bugatti up and then wants four days to get it to Florida. After he brings the Bugatti back up to Illinois, he wants to charge me a deadhead fee to take his empty rig back to Arizona. This splendid service is accompanied by highway robbery on the price. I've researched transportation rates and insurance, Victor, and this thief wants to charge me double the going rate because of the value of the Bugatti. I'd tell him where to stick it, but the slimebag's got me over a barrel."

"Once again, I ride in to save your bacon, Warren," I laugh. "You are in luck. In fact, you are in unbelievable damned luck."

"Meaning?"

"My brother Colin has retired as the golf pro down at The Landings and is living with me in Wisconsin. We have the use of a very nice, very inconspicuous car hauler, and we have been taking on a few classic car transportation gigs. We could handle your Bugatti, safely and discreetly, at a price that would make your mouth water. Colin drives, he's commercially licensed, bonded, ready to handle every detail. And he's available right now, I believe."

"Is that so?" says Warren.

———ᘔᘔ———

Although our legitimate car transportation prospects are looking up, Collie and I certainly have not stopped using the Allmire rig to transport other...*freight.* For example, it might seem silly to use an entire truck to carry a single eighteen-by-twenty-four-inch welded titanium box, but not if the contents of the box are worth $140,000. I am informed that that's the replacement value, the insured value. I agree to buy the box for $45,000. I arrange to sell it for $75,000, payable on delivery.

I am not going to reveal where I got that box, except to say people would be *very* surprised if they knew who had put out the feelers to me. And I can tell you this: it's quite a rush when the motive for a high-buck burglary is revenge, pure and simple, rather than monetary gain. Pissed-off people do funny things. *Oh, the passions of the filthy rich, the wages of envy, the pure childishness of it all!*

Anyway, following a simple, carefully planned smash-and-grab by some experienced local smash-and-grabbers, Collie will be on his way to Detroit before the victims are even back from their trip to Montreal.

In the Allmire rig, our titanium box is snug as a bug in a rug. On top of the hidden compartment, Collie lashes a tired 1964 Volkswagen Beetle that some banker in Windsor wants to restore and give to his kid. Collie drives the load to Detroit, a long drive in a single day, but worthwhile on a dollars-earned-per-hour basis. The "consignee" drives over the border from Windsor, Ontario, and picks up the box in a blind drop. Collie never sees his face, but the leather satchel he retrieves before dropping off the titanium box contains the proper amount of cash, all fifties, no counterfeit trash. I plan to give the lion's share to Collie, and we agree to drive down to Savannah together to pay off the crooks and loan sharks who set him up.

Before we set off, the phone rings.

23

The Perils of Christine

THE PHONE CALL IS FROM CHRISTINE.

"I'm having a hard time hearing you," I say.

"That's because I'm calling you on my cell phone and I'm sitting outdoors in Central Park with tears running down my face."

"Well, that sounds nasty. Tears do not often run down your face, Christine Harding. What's cooking?"

"Funny you should use that term, because my whole life has just gone up in smoke."

"Christine, what are you talking about?"

"I have just been mugged by my law firm. Beaten bloody and left for dead. Without warning, without...without... *anything.*" She tries to stifle a sob and fails.

"Talk to me."

"Goodman Godfrey just gave me the gate. I am not kidding. New management committee gets voted in, and fifteen contract partners get handed walking papers. *Including me.* They say they can't make enough money from my one-woman trusts and estates practice. So *boom!* They're simply going to stop providing trusts and estates services. Period. Punkt. *Finito.*"

She sniffs, her voice wavering. "I know I'm no rainmaker, but Victor, I've always covered my overhead, and I've been putting in a lot of billable hours with my T & E work. Which they often give away free to fat-cat clients, by the way. Plus, I'm a competent, highly visible woman in New York legal circles, let's not forget that. In addition to the money, I make them, I thought I was worth something to the firm as a diversity symbol. But now suddenly the power structure decides that I'm just some service lawyer who's gotten too long in the tooth. I have three months to wind down my practice and vacate the premises. After eighteen years at Goodman Godfrey, they give me...*three months.*"

Deep sobs now, hucka-hucka-huck.

"They say I can take my portables to a different firm if I want. They'll even help me transfer my files."

Christine voice cracks. "*What kind of insult is that!* They know there's no repeat business for people who write wills. Estates only get probated once. So there *are* no portables, and they know it. So I'm not too marketable under these conditions. Sixty-six years old. Hefty price tag. Man, *now there's* an attractive value proposition to pitch to another law firm."

I am thunderstruck. I know others share my view that Christine Harding is as brilliant as a diamond, as sharp, as radiant, and as multi-faceted. And yes, if the situation requires, the Ice Goddess can also be as cold and hard as a diamond. For years, Christine has been a commanding presence, a class act the firm could wheel out to dazzle prospective clients and trigger conversational pauses in crowded evening affairs. Of course, Christine also can be aloof, cynical, and snide. I've heard her likened to Dorothy Parker more than once. Truth to tell, temperamentally, Christine is a lot like me.

And now she's sitting in Central Park crying into her cell phone.

"God, this really sucks," I say.

"And you know what else?" she says with a snicker.

"No. What else?"

"I was about to call you with some really good news, and instead I have to call you with really bad news."

"What's the good news?"

"Now's not the time to tell you. I'm not trying to be cryptic, but now's just not the time to tell you. No mystery, Victor, just...*later.*"

"Christine, I want you to get out here. Grab a flight, I'll pick you up in Milwaukee. Colin and I will both come down to pick you up. You know he's living here now, right?"

"That's about all I knew. He's been very mysterious with me, but I did know he'd left Savannah."

"So anyway, get yourself out here ASAP, Christine. Harding family reunion. I'm not asking you to relocate, just come visit your older brother. Bring a bathing suit, sit on the dock, get drunk, let the sting abate. Reconnect with your twin. Then tell me your good news."

"We'll think about it," Christine says and ends the call.

I stare at my cell phone. *We?*

24

The Semper Deal

ON A SPLENDID SUNSTRUCK SEPTEMBER DAY, I pull my rented U-Haul pickup into Semper's parking lot, steering well clear of the line of glistening Harley Davidsons stretching in an orderly line in front of the entrance. The Darrin sits behind the pickup, strapped to a car-tow dolly.

Truth to tell, the Darrin is an ugly automobile, with exaggerated 1950s-era swooping fender lines, and tires that look too small for the wheel wells. Ferraris at that time were all guts, growl, and taut sinew. The Darrin is quite the opposite. It's a soft, feminine car, with wide whitewalls on the tires, and a silly little seashell-shaped grille that looks like it's puckering up to kiss you. Still, who was I to complain? The price was right.

I had hoped to be pleasantly surprised when we pulled the Darrin out of its hiding place at Phone's house and I could get a good look at it, but I'm not. The paint-brushed finish is dull and sloppy and crude, and a rime of green-black mold has etched itself into the fiberglass. The carpets are soaked and blackened, and the upholstery stinks of rot. The car may not be salvageable. I want Gunnar Spaaks to have a look.

The Semper Harley bar occupies a two-story farmhouse fronting Route 49 just outside of Berlin. The property is in very good shape: the parking lot has been paved recently, the long veranda in front isn't sagging, and the building is painted an attractive taupe color with contrasting white trim. A large sign, milled out of solid aluminum, hangs from a four-foot bracket extending out from the front of the building: The first line of large letters *reads Semper Harley Motorcycle Club.* Beneath that, a smaller line reads *Members Only, Harleys Only.*

I walk up the stairs and push the screen door open. It's cool and pleasant inside with three ceiling fans turning lazily above my head. I expect the smell of stale beer and cigarettes, but I don't smell anything. The place is spotless. The bar's paneling is real, not some cheapo stapled-on sheets of warped crap-board. The woodwork is nicely crafted, carefully oiled to a dull sheen. This does not look like a biker bar. It looks like an establishment being kept up by someone who gives a damn.

At the moment, despite the long line of gleaming cycles outside, there seem to be no Semper guys or chicks in attendance. I guess a lot of the club leave their scooters at the bar during the week—a real Harley showcase—while they're at work. I stand in the doorway, waiting for my eyes to adjust, waiting for the shit to hit the fan. It doesn't take long.

"You can't come in here." *Caint.* The deep growling drawl comes from deep in the room on my left. I turn and see a short, morbidly obese guy dressed in a soiled tee shirt and farmer's bib overalls sitting at a table in the corner. Long, stringy hair. Reddened, vein-mapped cheeks. Definitely not appealing.

"The hell I can't," I say amiably. "You're registered as a public accommodation, and me, well, I'm the public. I stand here well within my rights."

"Yeah? Well, you can stand there forever, but you'll never get served."

"I'm not trying to get served."

"Just what is it you want?"

"Here to talk to Gunnar."

"Gunnar ain't here. He's down the body shop."

"No, he's not. I was just there. They said he's up here. Gunnar and me, we have, like, a business relationship. You really want to get in the middle of that?"

The fat guy pushes back from the table and is just starting to stand when I hear Gunnar's voice echo down from the balcony over the bar. "Oh, sit down, Mel. This arrogant old man is just jerking your chain."

I turn. "Well, Gunnar. As I live and breathe."

"Okay, Victor. What is it you really want?"

"I wanted to get your thoughts on a car restoration project. I towed my 'project' over to your shop because I thought I'd offer you first dibs. Your guys sent me over here, and now I'm being treated most disrespectfully by your... *caretaker* here. I don't have any use for that kind of treatment, Gunnar. You don't want the work, well, to hell with you and your body shop."

Gunnar Spaaks laughs and lopes down the stairs. He's smiling broadly. He runs his fingers through his bright blond hair. "Oh, Victor, don't get your knickers in a twist. You know you have no business walking in here. So where's this mysterious 'project' of yours? Lemme have a look."

We walk outside to the trailer, and I pull the filthy cover off. Gunnar Spaaks howls with amusement, a reaction that is most unlike him. "A Darrin! Holy smoke, you don't see one of those every day! How'd you find it?"

I cough into my fist. "Acquired it as part of the winding up of an estate."

Spaaks walks closer to the trailer, running his hand over the grainy red finish. "Well, that's a cryin' shame. Why in the world would anyone do that to a car that's sure to become a classic?"

"Alcohol," I say.

"Well, obviously some clown didn't know what he had or didn't give a damn about cars. These Darrins are crap cars, but they're rare."

"If you say, so. You're the expert," I say.

"When did it last run? Engine turn over or is it frozen? Clutch work? Brakes work?"

"Don't know, don't know, don't know, and don't know."

"And you think you want me to do something with it."

"Well, out of...professional courtesy, Gunnar, I thought I'd least see if it was something you'd be interested in taking a crack at."

"'Taking a crack at.' Now there's a phrase you don't hear much anymore."

I turn to leave. "You know, Gunnar, you really *can* be intensely annoying. I'm never quite sure whether you intend that in order to get under peoples' skin, or if you're just gratuitously rude. I'll get someone else to have a look."

Spaaks responds as if he hasn't heard me. "What do you want to do with it, Victor? Do you want to store it, exhibit it untouched as a survivor car, drive it, take it to shows, auction it? What?"

"It all depends on cost. Basically, I just wanted to get it running, refinish the body, redo the upholstery, and use it on sunny days as a driver's car or a parade car. I'm not looking to create something to take to car shows or give to Barrett-Jackson to auction."

Gunnar raises his eyebrows, surprised at my little display of classic car world knowledge. Now he tries to test just how deep that knowledge goes. "And what do you reckon it's worth – or can be made to be worth?"

"You tell me. This is your area of expertise."

"An untouched barn find with a lot of rust might still be worth at least twenty-five grand. A decent runner with solid basic mechanics, maybe forty-nine-nine. Get into a quick frame-off restoration with a freshened engine, it'll fetch maybe in the eighties at auction. A full Roy Hafemeister numbers-matching frame-off rotisserie show-quality restoration, complete engine rebuild, all new nuts and bolts, thirty-two coats of hand-buffed lacquer, well, one just sold at the Mecum auction in Hershey for one hundred and fifty-two thousand."

I take a deep breath. "I know you got to spend money to make money, but I don't have a lot of money to spend right now. What'll it cost to give me a solid runner?"

"Okay," says Gunnar, suddenly much friendlier. "Tell you what. Take your Darrin down to the body shop and leave it there. Give the keys to Kerry Crouch. Tonight I'll go over it in detail, see how much frame rust you got, see if the engine is salvageable, check out the clutch and brakes, stick a new battery in it to see if it turns over, see if the mice have eaten up all your electrics, see if the gas tank is full of sludge, all that basic stuff.

"It may be a lost cause, and if so, I'll beg off. But if I think I can do it, I'll give you a fair price. Understand, Victor, that I run a body shop. A very good body shop, but still, I'm just a body shop. I am not a restoration specialist, and I don't do deep-dive mechanical work on classics or antiques. Just so we're clear."

⚬⚬⚬

The following morning I'm dawdling over breakfast—it's Cal's sourdough hotcake day—when the phone rings. Gunnar is laughing.

"Victor, you really are a dumb shit, you know that?"

"Shall I take offense?"

"Did you look over that car *at all* before hauling it over to me?"

"Okay, Gunnar, you've had your fun. Just talk to me."

"Your car is a 1954, built in May. It is an early car, build number twenty-six. But back to the dumb shit part, did you even think to look at the mileage of your car?"

"No."

"It has *forty-four hundred and forty miles* on it, Victor. Not forty-four thousand. Forty-four hundred. It's barely broken in. Your Darrin's value has just picked up a huge low-mileage premium. Maybe an extra thirty percent. Now, I'm going to hold the phone away from my face, and I want you to tell me what you hear."

I listen. I hear a quiet thrum.

"I don't know, Gunnar. What am I hearing?"

"That is the sound of the Darrin's engine running, Victor. Now that we've blown years of varnish and crud out of the carburetor, it's purring like a kitten. We changed the plugs and oil, put a new oil filter on it, rigged a fuel line to a temporary outside fuel tank, jumped it to a fresh battery, sprayed some ether into the intake, and pushed the starter button. Cranked it for about twenty seconds, and then, *Shazam!* It was running. Not stumbling or stalling or vapor-locking. Just running, smooth and quiet."

I could feel my face stretching into a broad smile. I could almost feel my checkbook breathing a sigh of relief. "What else did you find?"

"Perhaps the best news, almost incredibly good news. This car is completely rust free. Here, in *Wisconsin.* Filthy dirty, but there is no rust on the frame, no rust on the suspension or mounting points, no rust around the heater or radiator, no rust nowhere. It looks like whoever owned it had the bottom coated with rust-protectant right when he got it. That kind of aftermarket tampering makes purists scream, but it sure did wonders for preserving this car."

"Wow!" I can't contain the excitement in my voice, the relief. "Anything else?"

"Nothing that will break the bank. Brake job. New tires. Needs some rewiring."

"So, you feel okay working on it for me?"

"Yeah, I'll do it. As long as you don't want a show car, I can give you a respectable car in pretty much 'like original' shape. New paint, new upholstery, attention to the chrome. I'll add safety belts."

So now it's time to cut to the chase. "Okay, Gunnar, shoot me some numbers. How much is all this likely to cost me?"

"Normally on a gig like this, I like to do time and materials. But given the basically sound condition of this car, I am willing to shoot you a fixed project price. But if we do that, once we agree, we agree. No haggling when the project's halfway across the lake, okay?"

"Do you have a number in mind?"

"For a contract fee of thirty-eight large, I will deliver you a car with a fair market value of at least fifty-five thousand dollars. Maybe more, if the market gets hot and someone wants to pay a premium for that super low mileage."

When I was a kid watching Tom 'n' Jerry cartoons, there was frequently a gag where a little angel argues the case for virtue into one of Tom's ears, and a little devil pleads the case for evil in his other ear. That's where I am now: my little angel reminds me that at the moment I'm only marginally solvent and that it's sheer folly to blow thirty-eight grand I don't have on fixing up an old car. My devil is far more persuasive. He whispers that I'm beginning to make enough fencing money to splurge on the Darrin, and that by the time the car is done, I'll have enough to pay for the restoration. He also whispers that I'm not getting younger, and that in any event, the car will be worth more than I put into it. "You can borrow from your HELOC," my devil whispers. "That's what they're for!"

"Okay, done," I tell Gunnar. "When will it be finished?"

"It will be back in your garage—your *locked garage*—within six months. Perhaps less. I do not like people looking over my shoulder, Victor, but yes, you may drop by occasionally to see how things are going, and I may have to call you at some decision points. But basically, this is a pretty straightforward project. You cool with this?"

"I'm cool with this," I say, ignoring my angel's howls of frustration. "Yeah, I'm cool."

25

Changes

TERRIBLE DREAM: Magda has her archeological team digging up my backyard, and she has discovered Bugsy's gold. She is threatening to turn me in to the government for theft of cultural artifacts, and I am swinging at her head with a leaf rake. I stir in my sleep; think I hear something outside that sounds like tires on gravel. The noise stops, and I roll back to sleep. Before dropping off, I wake-dream that I am shooting Magda point-blank in the head with her own little .25 caliber pistol. *Ping!* Neat little hole, just above the bridge of her aquiline nose.

Collie's off on a road trip, a legitimate run to Boston to deliver a restored 1950s-era Indy 500 race car, nice fee, so I'm alone in the house. For some reason, I awaken earlier than usual, just as dawn brightens the eastern horizon over the lake. I look out my bedroom window and see a car parked in the driveway. It is a metallic gray Maybach, the super luxury big brother of the Mercedes Benz. It's quite elegant, in an intimidating kind of way. Big, expensive. No one I know—no Vandal, and certainly no Local—has a metallic gray Maybach.

There's no one downstairs, where my bedroom is. Barefoot in boxers and a tee-shirt, I tiptoe up the stairs. The door of the big front bedroom is ajar, and I peek in. The hall light is on, throwing a soft band of light across the bed. My sister Christine is propped up against the headboard, wearing a loose-fitting flannel shift. She is sound asleep.

Draped across Christine, with her hands tucked under her head, and her head nestled comfortably in Christine's lap, is another woman. She is utterly nude, utterly relaxed, utterly serene as she presses up against my sister. It looks like she is made of bronze, and the light captures and highlights every feature and curve of her body, her face, her lustrous hair. Her body is graceful, her muscles both smooth and taut, like an Olympic swimmer's. She is totally and completely...*on display,* and I am transfixed.

She senses my presence. Her eyelids flutter, and now she is awake. She cocks her head to look at me. Her gaze is open, direct, and unselfconscious. A smile creeps across her face, a wide, engaging smile, warm and friendly. Deep smile lines appear at the corner of her eyes.

She lifts her hand and gives me a friendly little pinkie wave then presses her index fingers to her lips to make sure I don't speak. I wave back, a shy little boy who has been caught staring and struck stupid. Now, still smiling, this glorious apparition tucks both hands under her cheek to tell me she is going to go back to sleep now. Through all this, Christine remains dead to the world, snoring lightly with her head tilted back. She looks happy, and I am deeply pleased to see that.

So *that's* Christine's good news!

———

This is how I meet Delia Chamberlain. She is married to my sister, turns out she has been for over four months. When the two of them finally come downstairs and we are standing in the living room, I feign being insulted. "So, talk to me. You were afraid to tell me, or you couldn't be bothered to tell me, or...*what?* Christine, you've been out for years. Am I supposed to be shocked that you got married to a woman?"

Christine smiles, a little surprising because she's not generally a big smiler. "My dear self-righteous brother. When you and Magda decided to hang it up, did you call me? Ask my advice, seek my approval? When you closed up your consulting practice and chickened out to sulk up here in Green Lake, did you tell me of your plans before *doing just exactly what you wanted to do*?"

I start to sputter a rebuttal, but Christine thrusts out a hand to stop me. "When you coaxed Collie to move up here to nowheresville and abandon everything he had in Savannah, did we convene a family conference? It's not that I wasn't told about that after the fact, Victor. *It's that I wasn't told at all.* So, you should just get off your high horse."

I try to mount a defense. "Well, you just never seemed interested, Christine. You had your ritzy New York life. When Magda bugged out, what support or sympathy did I get? When Susan died, what did you do for Colin? There he was, alone in Savannah, writhing in agony, and you couldn't be bothered to fly down from Manhattan because 'the summer was too hot?' Give me a break."

Delia's voice breaks in. It's light and musical, with little pauses in her sentences, precisely articulated consonants, and funny emphases. "Here is my *idea*, you two. We should stop this rather negative conversation because there is no *point* to it. I often tell Christine that she is too fond of blame and shame, Victor. And now I say the same thing to *you*. There is nothing to be gained by making people feel *bad*.

"As I see it, we are all facing major *changes* right now. Victor, with your retirement and all, you are in the middle of a *major* life change, yes? Bound to be stressful, yes? And now that Christine has been treated so *badly* at work, she faces major changes, too. Yet here we have some *good* news. Christine and I are *married,* and *we* certainly are facing some major changes. I think it is good to talk about *facing* major changes. And when Colin comes back from his trip, he should talk about that, too. I think this would be a very good *thing* if we could all think about making these changes together, like a family or a *team.* If you will have me, I really, really, *really* want to be part of a real family. And I am sure I can be a major contributor to the team. I think I bring a lot to the party, yes."

26

Oops

IT MAY BE WEEKS before the Altenderfer break-in is discovered. They're snow-birding in Puerto Vallarta. Their nine extraordinary oriental carpets—a ten-by-fourteen super-fine Isfahan, two eight-by-twelve Abadahs, and six smaller silk area rugs—are now settled in the back of the Allmire rig, riding with Collie and me to a new life in Toledo. Looks like we'll net about sixteen grand, an okay deal, but now an amount Collie and I consider only fair-to-middling.

On this Toledo drop, I'm riding shotgun. Literally. I have a sawed-off Winchester 20-gauge shotgun on the floor by my side, a .38 caliber revolver nesting in a belly pack, and a military taser velcroed to the dashboard in front of me. I feel a little silly because I don't know how to use all this armament, but I do feel safe.

After we drop the rugs, we plan to leave the Allmire transporter in Toledo for a couple of days and then drive the pickup truck down to Savannah to pay off Collie's debts. Collie makes it clear he welcomes both the company and the extra protection. We're also going to check on his house and collect several months of rental payments from The Landings Company. We'll pick the Allmire rig up on the way home.

Although the sun is still low in the eastern sky, it's already a glorious morning, and both Collie and I are feeling expansive and friendly. No money discussions for the moment. Collie takes his hands off the wheel for a second, splays his fingers, and stretches his arms toward the roof.

"So, tell me about Gunnar's sister, Victor. You and Cara Spaaks seem to have become big buddies all of a sudden. Is this all just because you're buying so much of her art, or is something going on?"

"Why do you ask?" I reply drily.

"Well, when I've observed you two from a distance, I can't help but notice how you sort of relax when you talk with her. And I must say, she's pretty easy on the eyes, in a tomboyish, outdoorsy kind of way. Do you know if she's seeing anyone?"

I make a dismissive *what a silly idea!* gesture. "Well, she's not 'seeing' me, if that's what you are so subtly driving at," I reply. "I think I've aged out on romantic entanglements, especially where the age gap spans three decades. But yeah, I think she's the real deal. As you've so astutely noticed, I do find her engaging. But not in a romantic sense. I think she's smart. She's upbeat. She's optimistic. Now if you're interested, I could certainly make a formal introduction. I think you could do a lot worse, Collie. And maybe twenty-five years is not too big a span."

I see Collie's hands tighten on the steering wheel. I continue talking.

"One suggestion, though. If you make a move, I'd lose the golf togs, go more Whole Earth catalog, if you catch my drift."

I turn in my seat toward Collie, and put on my most serious look.

"But Colin, *never forget that she is Gunnar Spaaks' sister.* I know they're like oil and water, but still, I'd be real careful in what I say and do around her. If anything you say to Cara somehow finds its way to Gunnar, if only inadvertently, you could find yourself in hot water. In our 'business arrangement,' I have to trust Gunnar, but I don't really trust Gunnar, if you know what I mean. And I sure would not want to have him gunnin' for me, figuratively or literally. He is one tough bird."

I pause, wondering if I should go on. *Yes*, I decide. This is my brother, and I don't want him to get in trouble. Don't want either of us to get in trouble.

"Look, there is another...*factor* you should know about, that you should be *very* careful about. Cara sublets a room in her farmhouse to a woman named Danute Miskinis. Dany, for short. They are roommates, good friends, but Cara has made it clear to me that it's not a romantic relationship, *capice*?

"I've met Dany, Collie. Petite, serious, very reserved. Looks like a Sunday school teacher. A decidedly Greek Sunday school teacher. She used to work for the EPA in Washington, DC. Logistics."

Collie turns to me. "So, what is she doing in Green Lake, Wisconsin?"

"Bad marriage, drunken, volatile husband, lot of domestic violence. Death threats. Cara tells me Dany couldn't get a protection from abuse order, so she simply bailed. Has a sister somewhere around here."

"And I'm supposed to be *very* careful of this woman because why?"

"Because she represents possible danger—to Cara and to you. Just like you, Dany Miskinis suffers from PTSD. She's wound tighter than an eight-day clock. Surely you can relate to that, Collie. Dany does not play well with others, does not do intimacy. Either with men or women. Cara tells me Dany enjoys sex but is not interested in relationships. Says that Dany is not promiscuous, but that she does have a couple of 'friends with benefits' who enjoy her favors on a regular basis.

One of them is Gunnar Spaaks. Cara says there's no romance, just periodic opportunistic interludes. Gunnar does not like it that Dany lives with his sister, but she supposedly has told him that if he wants to get his ashes hauled, he'll butt out."

Collie makes a motion like he's washing his hands. "Jeesh. Thanks for warning me."

"Don't mention it. And I mean that, Collie. *Don't mention it.*"

—◦◦◦—

Toledo is behind us. I'm driving, surprised at how comfortable the seats in the pickup truck are. Still, we have hours and hours in front of us. Conversation turns to business.

"I have to tell you, Collie, when I first got intrigued by the idea of getting into fencing, I didn't stop to think that I'd have to become an expert money launderer, too. I'm no expert on the best way to launder money, so I've got to do some research. I guess one way to launder money is to spend it, but I think we have to be real careful how we throw money around. I guess one good thing is that we look like we're pretty well-off and no one knows how cash-strapped we both are."

Colin taps me on the shoulder, signaling me to look at him. He's got his I'm-worried-about-something face on.

"Does Christine know about what we're doing?"

"Well, I've kept her briefed on your PTSD since the accident, and she knows we've started a specialty transportation business that's bringing in some money, knows that driving all over the place has been good therapy for you. I haven't had time to tell her much more than that. And I'm not sure that I want to tell her much more than that."

"Does she know we are fences who take stolen property across state lines and are likely to end up in federal prison at some point?"

"No, I haven't told her that part yet, you smart ass. Perhaps she'd find that amusing. But probably not. She's deeply infused with Dad's puritan ethics."

"Well, *are* you going to tell her?"

"I don't know, Collie. What do you think? I guess I thought that if she and Delia were going to go back to New York or move somewhere else, I would keep mum about our criminal enterprise. But if they end up living around here, I think we're gonna have to tell them."

"What do you make of Delia? Do you have a read on her?"

"None whatever. Too soon to tell. But obviously, we can't tell Christine without telling Delia. I am not going to suggest to Christine that she keep secrets from her own wife. Probably, I think we should just wait to see what happens with them, get a better handle on whether to keep 'em in the dark or dial them in."

At this moment, as we're cruising comfortably down the interstate, I fall victim to an enormous brain fart and commit a profoundly stupid error.

"And I haven't told them about the gold, either."

"*What gold?*"

In my whole life, I have never had a moment like this, an instant where I've been snared in the jaws of a misstep of this magnitude, so caught out, so mired in deception revealed. I feel myself blushing.

"Oh, shit," I say.

"What gold are you talking about?" Collie knows instantly I have kept something from him. He reaches over, grabs me roughly by the chin, twists my face toward him. *"What gold?"*

I swallow hard. I'm sure guilt is written all over my face.

"*Okay.* While you were making the run to Boston," I sigh, "I began trying to track down that rumor that Bugsy Moran had built an escape tunnel down to the lake. It turned out to be simple. There *was* a tunnel, a lot of people had heard about it, and it wasn't hard to find. I opened it up in an hour. And not just a tunnel. There's a little...*underground warehouse,* just up from the boathouse.

"And there was...*stuff* stored in the warehouse. Prohibition-era whiskey, a couple of Thompson submachine guns...and, uh, maybe about $40 million dollars' worth of gold bullion. Pure gold. Twenty-four-karat."

Colin raises his hands to the sides of his face, pushes on his cheeks so that he looks like a goldfish. I have shocked him into silence.

I try to fill the silence by moving to my practical problem-solving voice. "But Colin, we have an issue," I say, focusing back on the highway. "This is not free money. We did not just win the lottery with no strings attached."

He gapes at me, stunned. He has no idea what I'm talking about.

"It's almost certain that this is *stolen* gold. Looks like Moran's gang stole it in a heist of a private mint over in Prairie Du Chien in 1929. Probably when he and a bunch of his goons were living here in Green Lake for a while after the St. Valentine's Day massacre. Looks like they melted the gold they stole down into 128 crude ingots and painted them gray to look like lead."

I can't tell whether Colin is so red-faced because I have deceived him or because he is trying to get his mind around the idea of forty million smackers cached for decades in our backyard. Finally, he finds his voice.

"But Moran's dead, and his whole gang is dead, and we own the house, and we found the gold. So now it's our gold, right?"

"I had a lawyer research it. Back in 1929, an insurance company paid off the loss. From that moment, *they owned the gold.* The insurance company got acquired, then that insurance company got acquired, and now that insurance company is part of a giant Japanese insurance conglomerate. In short, Collie, it looks like the Japanese own our gold. And although it's an old loss, I'm sure they wouldn't mind getting forty million dollars back."

Now Colin's face darkens again, and his words spill out. "*And you didn't tell me about all this?* What, did you think you couldn't trust me? Or were you just going to keep it all for yourself? What the hell, Victor? What the hell? *Why didn't you tell me?*"

Fortunately, Colin now continues to scream at me, so I don't have to answer him.

"Are you going to tell Christine about the gold?" he shouts. "Or are you going to lie to her about that, too?"

I don't like being attacked, and my customary defensive tactic in such situations is to completely lose control. I'm not pretty when I'm mad.

"You know, mister PTSD victim, maybe you ought to just cool your jets," I shout back at him. "Maybe you'd do well to put yourself in my shoes as I try to figure out how to handle the situation we're all in. *That all of us are in. The whole... Harding...family.*"

I spin and wag a finger in Colin's face. "Look, pal, over the last few months I've been doing everything I can do to both take care of you and try to build some options for both of us, since we're both in a major financial jam. I do not need to have you accusing me of dishonesty, of being a goddamned *liar.*" I spit out the last word.

"You don't know my motives, Colin. You can't mind-read my intentions! I've been nursing a needy off-the-wall cripple, Mr. Colin Harding, and if you don't appreciate that I've been trying to help you, then you are both obtuse and ungrateful. Can't you understand that it might be *safer* not to tell you? That it gave you deniability, that it kept you from being tagged as a co-conspirator?"

Colin tosses his head, then flips me off—a gesture he does not often use. "That's a bullshit argument, Victor, and you know it. Were you protecting me when you shoved me out on the road to transport a bunch of stolen goods across state lines? Was I being protected when someone stuck a gun in my face? Stolen gold or stolen McLarens—tell me, Victor, what's the difference?"

I'm losing this argument, so I affect incredulity. "Wait a minute! Do you honestly think I was *never* going to tell you? That I was just going to hoard all that gold? And just exactly how was I going to do that? Hoard it *and* hide it?"

It works. Colin is stopped in his tracks. And I'm still up at bat.

"And as for Christine, oh cruelly wronged brother, *you tell me*. If you're so damned smart, tell me what to do with our straight-arrow, famous lawyer sister. What would *you* tell her? *When* would you tell her?"

Colin shakes his head. "Whoa, Victor, you've got to consider a few things. First, sister Christine has just been humiliated, and had her lofty reputation torched. So, think about it. How is our proud Ice Goddess likely to react just after she's been crushed?

"Second, although I don't know all the details of Christine's financial situation, how much cash she has put away for retirement, I do know she's a big spender. *Huge spender!* And now she's suddenly deprived of her usual way of making a living. *Bammo! No income!* So, I wouldn't be surprised if Christine undergoes a change of heart...and that pure heart of hers may be a lot harder and a lot less pure than before.

"Third, you say there's a huge pile of gold ingots sitting on our floor? What Christine needs is options, Victor, and now there are millions of them. Think she's gonna walk away from that?"

―∿∿―

Gunsmoke remains in the air for the rest of the trip, and I can't wait for this journey to end. When Colin Harding gets hurt, he stays hurt. When I am attacked, I maintain an indefinite vigilant defense. I hold grudges. So Colin and I do not kiss and make up, do not make peace, do not try to address or resolve the issues of power and authority and respect that go back decades.

Then, out of the blue, as we trundle along the interstate at about four in the morning, Colin momentarily breaks the ice. "Thank you for being there when we paid off my debt. I was frightened of those guys, although I suppose I didn't need to be. They knew they were going to get their money back. Still, I'm glad you had my back."

I want to say, "Is it lost on you that I always have your back, that I have always had your back?" But that's not what I say.

I say, "Don't mention it. That's what families are for."

27

Cal, Meet Delia

BRUNCH IS ON THE VERANDA. Farm fresh eggs, thick-cut peppered bacon, fresh Wisconsin cantaloupe, blueberries with Greek yogurt, mimosas made with fresh-squeezed OJ, and really fine champagne. We're feeling a little jolly but are not yet drunk. Even Christine seems less locked down than usual.

Green Lake's weather is cooperating, presenting us with a comfortable autumn morning, a refreshing breeze, and a lovely light dappling of sunlight through the trees and across the lawn. The Maybach is still parked regally in the drive, and our whole tableau this fine morning is worthy of a *House and Garden* spread. Cal pads out with a replacement platter of bacon and eggs, just in case each of us hasn't ingested enough fat and cholesterol this morning.

"Ah!" I say brightly. "Let me make an important introduction. Delia, this is Calestine Shattucks, my guardian angel and master chef for many years now. Cal runs the house and kitchen like a well-oiled machine, and makes all good things happen. Cal, this is Delia Chamberlain from New York. Christine's wife."

I do not know Cal's views on homosexuality and same-sex marriages, but if she is surprised or disdainful, she certainly doesn't show it. Cal is small and wiry and of indeterminate age in the way that many slender black women are—she looks like she could be anything from forty to seventy. In fact, I know she's sixty-six, exactly Christine's age.

And now she just smiles amiably, and Delia thrusts out her hand for a hearty shake. Cal hesitates a moment before taking it. It's not often that people above her station reach out to her in this way.

"I am *delighted* to meet another woman of color here in lily-white Green Lake," Delia says warmly. "I hope we will become great *friends.*"

I'm not sure Cal knows what to do with the idea of becoming close friends with her boss's sister-in-law. "I am very pleased to meet you too, Miss Delia. Please let me know if there's anything I can do for you and Christine."

We are interrupted by a huge *Plop!* as a passing bird dive-bombs an enormous load of runny white guano square on the roof of the Maybach. "Oh, my heavens, what a mess!" Cal exclaims. "I'll get it, I'll get it." She hurries off to get a towel and a pail of soapy water.

"That's some car, Christine. Gorgeous, just gorgeous." I pause. "You must have been doing well to spring for a Maybach."

"Oh, it's not my car," Christine says. "It's Delia's car."

"Actually," says Delia, "it was my father's car. He gave it to me shortly before he died."

"I'm so sorry," I say. "May I ask what happened?"

"Sure. He was humiliated to death by bankruptcy. That's part of why he gave me the car, to shed assets before the court took them. Then, shortly after the feds indicted him, he wrote my mother a short, rather tone-deaf note, and ingested a massive dose of heroin chased with about half a bottle of

Johnny Walker Blue. They said he was wearing a broad smile and looked quite serene when they found him."

Well, as you can imagine, I am taken aback.

"My God. Was he an addict?"

"Oh, heavens no. He'd never tried hard drugs in his entire life. He just wanted a pleasant exit, and someone told him heroin would be a sweet ride. I guess it was."

"Well, that's a shocker. Had he been depressed?"

"Well, no, Victor. He'd been *indicted.* Was facing a long, hard time in prison, probably the rest of his life. He was seventy-four, so I guess he just figured, 'Why not just check out now?'"

Delia sees my jaw drop, reaches over, and puts her hand gently over mine. "It's okay, Victor. *It's okay.* My father was a crook. Long-time, big-time felon. Very prosperous felon. But the feds finally had him cold, and he really had no defense. Except to die. He thought the prosecutors might feel guilty about driving him to hard drugs."

"What was his particular felony, if I may ask?"

"Oh, you may. I'm not sensitive about any of this. My father's business card said, 'Lloyd Patel, Trader in International Oil Futures'—and yes, he did know a lot about commodities speculation. But what he knew a lot more about were sophisticated multinational Ponzi schemes. He was the consummate con man. His card should have said, 'Lloyd Patel, Golden Fleece Enterprises.' He skimmed millions and millions of dollars off gullible investors, lots of Americans and Swiss guys, but mostly Arabs in Abu Dhabi who thought they were the smartest guys in the room. I thought it was poetic justice when the authorities shut the fund down and all the Arabs took huge losses. I confess I don't much like Arabs."

Christine laughs heartily—an unfamiliar sound to me. I see no trace of the Ice Goddess this morning. "Boy, I'll say. *Delia hates Arabs.* Made me promise I wouldn't do any estate planning for Arabs. Commies, deposed autocrats from former iron curtain countries, banana republic dictators, that's okay. But no Arabs."

I raise my eyebrows at Delia. "Long story, Victor. Relates to Dahlia, my younger sister," she says. "We can talk about it sometime when we're really, really drunk."

"Well, *okay*," I say. "So, your dad's death—how is your mother taking it?"

"Well, mostly she's taking it to offshore accounts in Cape Verde. Through Zurich. She's *expatriating* as much as she can pull out of all dad's other offshore accounts before the U.S. Department of Justice completely cracks the family piggy bank. Cape Verde has no extradition to the U.S., and Alva says it's very pretty there. Found an amazing house on a cliff."

Delia sees how dumbfounded I am. I suspect she's really enjoying the shock value of this conversation.

"Victor, my parents were both crooks, engaged in lifelong...*crookism*. My mother was my father's partner in crime. He ran the scams and was the seducer-in-chief. My mom ran the numbers and the laundering. Alva is a world-class money launderer. I grew up in a life of family crime. They didn't try to hide it from my sister and me. We grew up knowing what they were doing. That can be a bit rough on a kid."

I choke and spit out a mouthful of mimosa. It takes a moment to get my wind back. "Well, your parents sound like...*quite a team*," I manage. "Your mother sounds very... *unusual*."

"Oh, that she is," Delia says. "Based on what Christine has told me about your personality, I think you'll like her when you meet her. Maybe you two lonely senior citizens could even strike up a *thing*."

"I don't quite know quite how to respond to that," I say. "Sounds kind of...incestuous to me."

"Well, I think it sounds delightfully racy!" Christine laughs. "What a stellar idea! Alva could pump some life into Victor before his reclusive retirement makes him dry up and blow away like a fallen leaf."

"Don't be patronizing, Christine," says Delia, with mock severity. "After all, that's what I did with you. Turned some of the lights back on. Let us not judge, lest we be judged."

———

I catch Christine in the downstairs hallway as we're carrying our breakfast dishes back to the kitchen.

"Okay," I say. "Dahlia."

"Oh, you don't know about Delia's early career in modeling. Before she got out of it and switched to making jewelry, Delia was a fashion and jewelry model, very much in demand for exotic photo shoots featuring a woman of color. When she was eighteen, Delia used her New York modeling money to take her kid sister on a trip to see the ol' family stomping grounds in Sri Lanka. When they stopped in Saudi Arabia, Dahlia, who was thirteen, was kidnapped off a tour bus in Riyadh, right in front of Delia. Guys with guns. Delia never saw her again. Delia couldn't get the Saudi police interested in finding her sister until her father paid a half-million-dollar bribe through a cut-out in Zurich. The kidnappers took the money and ran. Cops sat around twiddling their fingers. Dahlia was found in a ditch four days later, gang-raped to death. Any wonder Delia hates Arabs?"

28

On Ajmo's Boat

JUST AS WE ALL SIT DOWN at the card table to tackle a thousand-piece jigsaw puzzle of Mt. Everest, we hear a shout. "Hello, you fellows!"

The call echoes up from the lake, but I'm confused: it's Cara Spaaks' voice, but Cara Spaaks certainly does not own a boat.

"Victor! Colin! Come down, come down! Let's go for a ride!" Cara trots up to the veranda, panting slightly, and points down to my dock. I stand and look down toward the lake. There, bobbing gently at the T-head, is a magnificent forty-foot open launch, its glistening white hull reflecting bright flashes off the lake surface. A maroon canopy extends the full length of the boat, gold tassels rippling in the breeze. The launch's bow is bluff and vertical in the early twentieth-century fashion, and its stern spreads out to a graceful fantail bedecked with an American flag snapping in the breeze. The varnished seats and railings gleam warmly in the August sun. The white leather cushions on the mahogany benches look soft and inviting.

Standing on the dock holding a mooring line is a short, trim man, very dark-skinned, dressed all in white—white deck shoes, creased white uniform trousers, a heavily starched navy-style blouse, and a small white hat with no bill. His teeth are as white as his attire.

I spread my hands in the classic *what-the-hell?* gesture.

"It's Ajmo's!" Cara exclaims with her customary enthusiasm. "It's a replica of the Elco Electric Launch used over at the American Baptist Assembly around the turn of the century. It's an exact copy in every way except that the motor is bigger and it has modern marine batteries. You don't have to charge it up nearly as often. Ajmo had Palmer Johnson build it over in Sturgeon Bay."

For a moment, I'm totally at a loss. Finally, I find words. "*Ajmo?* Cara, what in the world are you doing messing around with someone like that? Everyone knows Felix Ajmo is a former Turkish secret police officer, and he's certainly one of the most obnoxious, most arrogant people in Green Lake."

"I'm not 'messing around' with Ajmo, Victor. I'm simply friends with his wife, Tamara. She commissioned a large landscape from me, and we came to like each other. Ajmo may be a major piece of work, but she's very nice. Anyway, Ajmo's in Turkey for a month, probably planning a coup or something, and Tamara asked if we'd like to borrow the launch for a lake tour. The guy in white is Mahmoud. He's Ajmo's boat chauffeur. So! Y'all ready to go?"

Cara's energy is infectious. I raise a calming hand. "Before we do that, Cara, let me share some news and make some introductions. Then maybe we can all hop into Ajmo's launch and take a trip back to 1900. Come on in and meet the family—*my newly-extended family.*"

Cara skips into the porch. "Hey, Collie!" she chirps. "How ya doin'?"

Sitting at the card table, Colin looks like he's suddenly been bathed in sunlight. He grins stupidly, his Adam's apple bobs like a nervous virgin's at the junior prom. "Why, hi,

Cara!" he says, absurdly cheerfully. "How very nice to see you!"

Christine snickers, and Collie turns beet red.

"Christine!" Delia snaps. "Don't be mean-spirited." She turns to Cara, flashes her killer smile, and extends her hand. "Hi! I'm Delia Chamberlain. I recently married Victor's sister Christine."

"Well, that's marvelous!" Cara exclaims. She turns to my sister. "That means you must be Christine. I heard you were coming out from New York. Welcome, welcome, welcome!"

"Well, thank you, Cara. Did you paint that wonderful piece in the living room?"

"I did, and the other two smaller pieces, the one in the hall and the one in Victor's bedroom. After *much* discussion and debate with Victor. He's quite the demanding client."

"He's quite the demanding everything," says Christine.

"You are very, very gifted," Delia says to Cara, leaning against the card table, careful not to disturb the pieces. "We must talk, 'cause I'm going to commission a portrait of Christine."

"I'm really sorry, Delia, but I don't do portraits. I just can't make 'em work. They never ring true to life. Always look like I've copied 'em from a cell phone snapshot. But I'll tell you what—I would be pleased to gift you a landscape of Green Lake as a wedding present. Nothing already painted, something new to celebrate your new life together."

I start to protest. "Cara, we couldn't possibly ask you to..."

Cara shushes me with a dismissive wave of her hand. "Of course I can. I can do anything I want to. Butt out, Victor. This isn't about you."

Delia squeals with delight. "Oh, Cara! You and I are going to be terrific friends! I love truth-tellers! I accept your gracious offer with pleasure."

"What do you do, Delia?" Cara asks.

"Same thing you do, only with gold instead of oils and pastels. *I create.* In my case, high-end jewelry. I'm a goldsmith and considered a pretty good one. For me, it's all strictly commissions, no store or gallery product."

"Too cool! Might I have seen some of your pieces?"

"Just look at Christine's neck," says Delia.

"Or look in *Vogue*," Christine says proudly. "Particularly the May issue's *Black Beauty Matters* feature. Or maybe the full-arm amulet on Anya Sahnacahnahanh's wrist at the opening of Frank Gehry's new museum last year. Anya's the Minister of Culture for Sri Lanka. She and Delia are buds."

"I get it," Cara laughs. "I'm in the presence of jewelry royalty."

Collie is grinning like an idiot. He's obviously captivated by Cara's directness and lack of self-consciousness, and he lacks the *savoir faire* to hold his cards close to his chest. I'm sure Cara notices. We'll soon see if she's interested. Maybe he's too old for her, maybe not.

"Well, okay!" exclaims Cara. "Here's a plan. We've all got to get acquainted, right? I've got the use of a...*client's* electric launch. Let's all pile in and pretend we're absurdly rich, like Felix Ajmo. I will conduct a leisurely orientation tour of beautiful Green Lake for all you newbies. No need to bring your own booze—the launch has a refrigerated bar, and Mahmoud makes a superb G and T. I had two on the way over here."

Gingerly, we all step aboard Ajmo's showpiece and arrange ourselves around the long central table. It's made of ebony with birch inlays in the shape of five-pointed stars and has ten built-in cupholders, a most welcome anachronism. In 1905 you had to hold your own glass.

Collie is not handling this unexpected encounter with Cara particularly adroitly. Normally poised and passably socially adept—he's a golf pro, for heaven's sake—but right now he's moving awkwardly and self-consciously, as if some outside puppeteer is controlling his moves from a remote-control booth. I feel like patting him on the head like a puppy, telling him everything's gonna be okay.

Mahmoud, smiling warmly, takes our drink orders, and his cocktails live up to his billing. He accepts our praise with sharp birdlike nods and deferential bows. We cast off, and Cara tells Mahmoud to first head west along the shore, toward town, toward the place where Xenophon Stakhatos ended his life. The launch eases along with a quiet hum, leaving barely a wake. Slow and serene. "Rest in peace, Phone," Cara says.

We loop back toward the east side of the lake, starting a big lazy loop that will take us first around the south side of the lake, past Pleasant Point, Evergreen Isle, Sandstone Bluff, Indian Hills, and Green Lake Terrance. Then we'll loop over to the north shore toward Sylvan Shores and back east toward Sherwood Forest. We ride in agreeable silence for a few minutes, sucking our alcohol. Then Cara says, "Delia, would it be rude to ask a question?"

"Certainly not! Ask me *anything*. The purpose of this drive is for all of us to get acquainted, is it not?"

"Are you Indian?" asks Cara.

"Close enough," laughs Delia. "I am of Sri Lankan extraction, although I was born in the United States."

Mahmoud spins from the helm with a broad smile and exclaims, "Oh, excusing me, but *I* am Indian. From Goa. If you will pardon me for saying, I am very pleased to be seeing a Sri Lankan person here in Green Lake."

We all guffaw, and Mahmoud seems relieved that he has not overstepped appropriate social boundaries.

"Where did Chamberlain come from?" Cara asks. "I'll bet that's not a real common Sri Lankan surname."

"Well, my 'maiden name,' you should forgive the horrible term, was Delia Batek. My current name, the one I've been using for years in my business and is now too well-known to change, is a remnant of my first marriage to a fellow named Hugh Chamberlain. Basically a good guy, kind, considerate, smart as a whip. Today, he's a yacht broker in San Diego. Back then he was something of a Bronx slumlord, I guess you could say. We remain friendly."

"What happened?" Cara asks.

I see Christine's face darken ominously.

"Well, the truth is that we deceived each other. We were married for nine years. People kept saying we were 'a fascinating couple.' Hugh walked and talked hetero. No lisp or limp wrist, played it straight in bed. So I was really blindsided when he came out. I suppose he was just as surprised when I told him that I was neither exclusively heterosexual nor exclusively monogamous. We tried to work it out, but what doomed us probably was not just our sexual preferences, but the fact that we had kept such fundamental secrets from each other. I couldn't trust him, and he certainly didn't trust me. When the screaming and name-calling got to be too much, we agreed it was best to step out, you know?"

Cara seems oblivious to the sudden tension in the air. She turns to Christine. "Well, it certainly looks like it's 'all's well that ends well' with you two. How did you guys meet?"

Christine and Delia exchange glances, then Christine moves her hand to her throat, and caresses the choker she's wearing. "*This,*" she says. There is a stunning tube of polished gold around Christine's neck. It's perhaps a half inch in diameter, and it meanders slightly as it encircles Christine's throat, as if floating or flying. As if it's *alive.* The ends of the tube are not connected, but rather overlap by several inches at the front of Christine's throat, each end twisting rearward slightly, as if trying to see the other, as if trying to connect.

"Delia made me this," Christine says in a deep whisper.

"Why?" asks Colin, who sometimes becomes obtuse in moments fraught with meaning or emotion.

"*Because that's what she does.* Because I commissioned it. I saw another of her pieces while I was in London, tracked her down when I got back to New York, and said 'make me something unique, something I will want to wear all the time and never take off.' She invited me into her atelier to watch her make it. That was a very...*very* moving experience for this aging lesbian woman, to see her create something just for me, a unique statement that only a woman would fully understand. That only *I* would understand. I don't know how a piece of jewelry can be a reaffirmation of life, but this is."

"It's a love poem," Delia says simply. "I knew right away. Just swept away. In an instant, I knew I loved Christine, wanted to be with Christine. I heard that people called her the Ice Goddess thing, but that's not what I saw. I loved her intelligence, loved her air of competency, loved her shiny coat of armor, how she could hold her own with anybody. Loved spending time with her. Loved who I was when I was with her. And, of course, loved the sex, too."

"That's probably enough, Delia," Christine says. "I'm sure everyone gets the point."

"God, Delia, you are simply too much!" Cara exclaims. "So, okay, now that you two are together, let me ask Christine a question."

Christine nods pleasantly.

"I'm no expert on gay marriages, and I don't want to put a foot wrong. So, how do you two want people to describe your roles? Is one of you the husband and the other the wife or something like that?"

I'm relieved to have Cara ask. I have been dancing around this delicate question, but Cara Spaaks, with her breezy naivete, seems unconcerned with giving offense.

"Well, I'm the bull dyke," Delia laughs. "Christine is the shy passive one, she throws rose petals at my feet and grovels as I walk into the room." She cracks up.

Christine swats Delia across the back of the head. "We're spouses," she says. "That's all. No gender-related stereotypes, please. No dominant partner, no submissive partner. Just an ordinary lesbian couple who fight a lot and right now are having a hell of a good time."

—*ᴧᴧ*—

The rest of the tour proceeds calmly on the surface—I'm talking about our interactions, not the lake—although it's certainly not without subsurface tension. Christine, Colin, and I have communicated little in recent years, and then at a perfunctory and superficial level. Each of us now finds saying something that "says something" is surprisingly difficult. Each of us presents a brief recap about the circumstances that resulted in our ending up under one roof in Green Lake, Wisconsin. It's all a little forced.

Each of us depicts ourselves as some sort of victim. I of age and ageism. Collie of cruel karma that cost him his wife, dropped an airplane on his head, and cost him both his professional identity and his job. Christine of selfish, greedy misogynistic men.

After this rather muted Harding family show-and-tell—which, after all, is intended mainly for the illumination of both Delia and Cara, not to trigger a deep dive into family waters—Cara, perhaps confused by our subdued effect, proclaims that it's time for a snack, and directs Mahmoud to stop the boat off Greenwyck and let us drift awhile in the center of the lake. Mahmoud produces a fully stocked picnic hamper, and none of us is surprised when the sandwiches and salads are not from the Green Lake Redi-Mart, but rather from the Top Drawer Gourmet Shoppe over in Princeton.

This is, after all, Ajmo's boat, and mediocrity cannot be tolerated.

Between bites, I attempt to turn our 'getting acquainted' conversation back to Delia. Frankly, I want to know more about her mother's money laundering skills "Okay, then, Delia. Earlier you were telling us more about your mother. I'd like to know more about her, particularly if I'm being set up for some kind of blind date."

Delia brightens. "Oh, so now you want 'deep background' on the elusive international crime figure? The fact is, my mother is a pretty fascinating piece of work, for sure, outrageous much of the time, sassy and witty all of the time. To get along with her, you really have to keep your wits about you. Do that, and I guarantee she'll keep your mind alive. People either love her or hate her. She is a woman of deep and intense moods, a bit of Jekyll and Hyde, you could say."

Now Delia heaves a deep, pained sigh. "I'm sad to say that for a long time now my mother and I have moved in separate orbits, even before she moved to Cape Verde. I think she may be a borderline, and I know she thinks I'm a borderline."

Colin looks confused. "What's a borderline?"

Delia sniffs dismissively, as if amused at my brother's naïvete. "You don't know about borderline personality disorder?"

"Hunh-unh," mumbles Colin, now blushing.

"I once went to a lecture where some psychiatrist was asked to define borderline personality disorder. He said, 'although from a clinical point of view, BDP is very complex diagnostically, in everyday life the definition is perfectly simple: *borderlines are assholes.*' Borderlines have deeply dysfunctional personalities, and they often are not aware that they can be almost impossible to live with. They're often overdramatic and volatile. Begin to get the picture?

"Borderlines can be incredibly clingy one minute, then without warning, they'll abruptly abandon a relationship. They tend to be mistrusting and suspicious, not just with romantic partners, but also with friends and family. They're lacking in social judgment and often experience huge mood swings. A lot of 'em end up committing suicide."

Colin sits with his mouth agape. "Jeesh, how do you know all this?"

"Well, my parents, who always seemed to see any problems as *other peoples' problems,* 'didn't like my attitude' when I hit puberty. They forced me to go through a complete psychological workup at the Philadelphia Psychiatric Center."

"What was the result?" gasps Collie, his eyes wide.

"Inconclusive," says Delia somberly—and then bursts into laughter. "You know, maybe sorta-kinda borderline-ish sometimes," Delia laughs again. "But not *all the time.* I can't really see myself as a full-blown borderline—but most borderlines don't, right? That's why therapy generally doesn't work very well for them.

"Actually, I think I'm pretty self-aware—and my self-awareness is probably the best proof that I'm *not* a borderline. Classic borderlines are not very self-aware. But I know I can be pretty intense, and I know a lot of people think I'm an acquired taste."

Delia reaches over to take Christine's hand. "Fortunately, Christine is amused by my eccentricities. That's the tolerance that gay people have for 'people with differences,' right?"

"Delia is definitely *not* a borderline," Christine says evenly.

"How do you know?" asks Colin. *Dunce.* I want to box him around the head and ears.

Christine gives Delia's hand a visible squeeze back. "Because borderlines are generally very unhappy people, and by and large Delia is quite a happy person. Like me, she can be moody, and maybe a little volatile sometimes, but her life certainly is not driven by misery."

There is an awkward stunned silence, so Delia looks brightly around our stunned circle, grabs the reins, and canters on. "A lot of shrinks think BDP is the result of childhood abuse or neglect. Okay, I sure qualify on that score. And certainly, my mother's childhood was pretty shitty—and she's *definitely* an acquired taste. But my mother also is usually pretty upbeat. Maybe she's just a sociopath, not a borderline."

After our afternoon get-acquainted boat, the whole borderline thing would come to be something of a trope, a running family gag. One time, after Collie and Delia had grown used to teasing each other, Collie asked, "Delia, are *you* the girl from the north country?"

"What are you talking about?" replied Delia, perplexed.

"Well, you know, in the sixties Bob Dylan had that song called 'Girl from the North Country.' The first line is, 'if you go to the north country fair, *where the wind hits heavy on the borderline.*' Delia, is that *you?*" This jolly exchange left them both gasping for breath.

But here on Ajmo's boat, given the gravity of our discussion about Delia's mother, I cannot understand why Delia continues to smile.

"I think my mother expects me to reach out to try to make peace. But I think, given how Dahlia and I were treated as we grew up, that my mother should initiate the fence-mending. So...no peace. Right now, I wouldn't say were estranged exactly, just...*disconnected.*

"But I digress. The backstory is that my mother's name is Alva Batek. Like me, she never took my father's name. She was born in Sri Lanka, in Colombo. Her parents, who were peasant sharecroppers, wanted her to be a Buddhist nun, but she did not think much of that idea. She got a student visa to go the U.S, stole airfare from her parents, and ended up getting a degree in economics at Columbia, teaching herself English along the way. She majored in numbers theory and decision analysis. You know, like game theory.

"Alva's education came in handy after she met my dad. He was then at Penn, busy working cons on grad students, so they decided to stay in Philadelphia. My sister and I were born there. My father—funny, I have never thought of him as 'Dad' or 'Daddy'—slid easily into a life of crime, and my mother was perfectly happy to become his accomplice. Over the years, they had a hell of a good run. Nice office in Center City, big house in Villanova on the fabled Philadelphia Main Line, money in the bank. *They liked crime."*

For some reason, Collie again feels he must weigh in. "But with such unusual parents," he says, "you must have had an... *interesting* childhood?" He says it more as a question than a statement.

The question proves a mistake. Delia's tone shifts abruptly. "Well...*no.* My childhood was a complete train wreck. All that fabled Main Line *noblesse oblige* does not apply to dark-skinned Asians, Collie, even if they're born in the United States. Think *any* of those famous private girls' schools on the Main Line—Baldwin, Shipley, Agnes Irwin— *really* embraces diversity? *Hoo, boy.* Those little white bitches found every possible way to make Dahlia and me feel like aliens, like *nouveau riche* party-crashers."

Now Delia's voice rises in volume and pitch, as if she's being wound up by a key in her back. "And my parents? As Dahlia and I grew up, they could not have cared less about us. Just paid the nanny and got back to hustling the bucks and conning the suckers. Our 'family' did not travel on vacation, we did not attend school events, we did not celebrate holidays, we did not hug or discuss ideas or seem to care about each other. Family? *No family.* My childhood, Collie, was *cold.*"

There is a pregnant silence. Collie attempts amends.

"But I must say, you certainly seem to have your act together now."

Delia recoils as if struggling to restrain her impatience. "It's not an *act,* Collie. Not some pasted-on persona. It's a victory, a triumph of survival, as carefully crafted as any of my jewelry creations. As soon as I grew breasts and had my teeth straightened, I bailed. Goodbye, snobby suburbs, hello New York modeling. I was an instant hit, in a Brooke Shields kind of way. Except, of course, that I was black. My first photo shoot was for *Elle,* a four-page spread called *Exotic Bronze.* I was, you might say, loosely draped. My second shoot was for *Esquire.* Wasn't draped at all. We had to have a chaperone there to guard my virtue as they photographed me in my birthday suit."

Delia's voice has taken on a flat narrative tone. "It was a harsh world for a young woman of color, Collie. Horrible, really. Predatory. Superficial. And boring? *My God, it was so boring!* Incredibly stupid women and incredibly narcissistic men. Had an agent at fifteen, and she really shopped me around as a model. I was a novelty, and she turned me into a brand—the gorgeous little dark-skinned exotic. She also betrayed me, ripped me off big time, skimmed a lot of my fees. But I still made enough to live, saved every cent I could. I sure wasn't going to go on modeling forever."

Delia catches Mahmoud's eye and holds her glass up to him, gesturing for a refill. Christine is sitting back on her bench, now tapping her hands lightly together as if silently applauding. I think she is amused to see the rest of us all so caught out, so out of our depth.

"As you might expect," Delia continues, "I had *everybody* hitting on me. Guys, girls, wimps, pimps, queens, Thai kathoeys, producers who 'wanted to take me away from all this' and put me in movies and TV ads. My agent kept trying to sell me, to pimp me. *Pissed me off.* I confess that sexually I was pretty...*active,* but in my whole life I have never taken a dime to let someone have sex with me. I'm a survivor, not a whore."

Now, as if just becoming aware of our stunned expressions, Delia pulls up abruptly, shakes her head. "*Whoa!* I'm sorry, friends. That's *enough,* Delia! I certainly hadn't planned on diving into all this sordid stuff so soon after we met, because I really don't want to put you off or frighten y'all away. But you did seem interested, and there's no reason you shouldn't know all about my background. Twenty-five years ago, I fired my thieving agent. Shocked the hell out of her: *'How could you do this to me?'* Hah! Easy! Goodbye! Go rip someone else off!

"Ever since then, I haven't let *anyone* judge me or box me in or...*victimize* me. I play by my own rules, and I like it that way. I don't hurt anybody, but heaven help anybody who tries to hurt me."

—◦◦◦—

As we near the end of our tour, Delia is particularly fascinated by the historic American Baptist Assembly, now called the Green Lake Conference Center. Cara recites its colorful history in a parody of a tour guide's voice. "In 1888 Jessie Lawson—she was a religious zealot and wife of the publisher of the *Chicago Daily News*—began developing a thousand-acre farm on Lone Tree Point. It evolved into a vast estate, was later developed into a luxury gated resort, and still later was used as an internment camp that housed World War II German POWs. Finally, with the support of Kraft Foods, it was turned into a national conference center for the American Baptist Board of Education. The Baptists' idea of a 'closer walk with God' included a Scottish style golf course favored by Ben Hogan and Sam Snead and the construction of twenty-five fine homes."

As we purr by the homes perched on the lakefront, Delia takes one look at an English Tudor model and exclaims, "Oh, my God, Christine! Wouldn't you just *love* to live here?"

Christine does not answer.

———⁓⁓⁓———

The "Ajmo Tour," as we came to call it, lasts over three hours and results in the consumption of copious amounts of alcohol. Perhaps it is the booze that so enervates us: back at the dock, we drag ourselves out of Ajmo's launch feeling like we've been ridden hard and put away wet. More likely, I later conclude, it is the strain of acquaintance, the challenge of cautious self-disclosure as practiced by intensely vigilant and self-protective personalities. Cara's "informal" lake tour turns out to be a constructive icebreaker, but it sure was hard work. After thanking Cara for her initiative and Mahmoud for his gracious service, we adjourn, too tired even to make plans to sit down to dinner together that night.

Before retiring for the night, in order to settle myself and catch my breath, so to speak, I seat myself at my desk. I leave the lights off. I try to take stock.

I'm surprised that at the moment, I'm feeling exhausted, but optimistic. *Brave new world:* looks like all three Hardings will be living in the same zip code, nearly within shouting distance of one another.

Zounds.

For decades, there has been little to connect us, little to bond us as we drifted into separate orbits. Each of us has grown a little...*churlish* and dismissive when we talk about one another to those not in the room. Because I am the more disagreeable personality, the twins always focused their ire more on me than on each other. But as a family, well, we hardly have qualified as a family. We communicated only when necessary. We celebrated nothing together.

Now, all of a sudden, we are more than proximate. We are inching toward becoming a "found family," as the touchy feelers might say. Thanks to Bugsy's gold and Christine's marriage to Delia, we Hardings are going to be collaborators, co-conspirators, perhaps even codependent—whether Christine Harding is comfortable with that or not. Our fates are intertwined with one another—and with some off-the-wall Sri Lankan woman.

29

Breaking the Camel's Back

GILBERT RENNIE CALLS ME ON THE PHONE, agitated: Must meet *now*. Morton's.

"But our lunch isn't 'til Thursday," I protest.

"*Now*. I got major news."

When I join Gilbert at our favorite table, he is positively vibrating. He's opening and closing his fists as I walk in, tapping his foot on the floor. He's not in uniform; I didn't know Gilbert Rennie even owned a plaid shirt.

"I think we broke the camel's back," he whispers hoarsely. "I think we're gonna shut 'em *all* down."

"Shut who down?"

"Victor, I gotta confess that since the Clarence Causley bust, I have not made terrific progress cutting the amount of property crime in Green Lake County. As you know, I was not able to flip Clarence, either upstream or downstream, and I haven't been able to turn anyone else, either. And the feds are not gonna waste their time and effort bringing local cases one at a time. But still, I thought when we took him down, we'd see a drop in the crime rate. It hasn't been working out that way. It's like some other fence stepped in to take up the slack."

I feel my hands go cold and begin to tremble, but Gilbert doesn't notice. Now he grins triumphantly. "Well, I think the worm has turned."

He slides a little square sticky note over to me. It's bright Day-Glo orange.

Where have I seen that color before?

"I found this stuck to the window of my cruiser last weekend."

The writing is in dark-green sharpie, with the type of stylized print that architects and engineers affect. The note says, *Watch the Epstein house. They're going to hit it.*

"Epstein house?"

"It's over on the south side of the lake. Upscale short-term rental property, log cabin style, seven bedrooms, well-maintained, well-furnished. Owned by Edward and Edith Epstein, who live in Milwaukee, and use a management service up here. Not presently rented."

"And?"

"So we put two deputies on stake out. From the neighbor's garage. Overnight for two nights. Nothing. No action."

"And?"

"And then last night about eight-thirty, in comes a box truck. Guys in blue movers' uniforms start carrying furniture out through the garage. They fill the truck up and drive away. *But they only go about half a mile.* Turn in to a pretty farm, craftsman-style house, white picket fence, big fancy barn. Our guys follow 'em, stay out of sight."

"What happened then?"

"The bad guys unload the truck, and half an hour later, they drive right back to the Epsteins.' Our guys follow 'em. Burglars load the truck up again. Back to the barn again. Back to the Epstein's a third time. Our guys stay at the barn, call for backup, and Ruliscz and I are speedin' out there, sirens off. Only now the shit hits the fan, because just before we get there...*in drive the Epsteins!*"

"Oh, come *on!*" I exclaim.

"Edith starts screaming, and the neighbors dial 9-1-1, but our first team is still over watching the barn. The burglars stick a gun in Edith's face. She faints. Edward rushes over, they pistol-whip him, and put a big gash on his scalp. Believe it or not, Victor, these geniuses, four of 'em, are still loading stuff into their truck when Lee and I roll in, guns out. We suggest to the burglars that we all drive over to the barn."

Gilbert is aglow with excitement. He stands up, putting his hands down on the table in front of me. "What we end up with, Victor, is nine guys out at that farm, all cuffed and quiet. Actually, my guys ran out of cuffs, so half the bad guys get cuffed with baling twine."

I have never seen Gilbert so excited.

"And Victor...*you should see this barn.* It's, like, all newly fitted out. Probably done since Causley got busted. It's spotless. Cement floor, fluorescent lights. The stalls have been turned into carpeted storage bins—there's one for chairs and tables, one for paintings, one for sculpture. Another is filled with banker's boxes, you know, the kind with lids? These are filled with manila shipping envelopes filled with jewelry, watches, wallets. A lot more than just the Epstein's' stuff. Clearly a lot of stuff that's not from around here. This place is a clearing house. Definitely not minor league."

"My God!" I exclaim. "Congratulations, Gilbert! Wait'll the local papers get this news!"

"Oh, I'm not done, Mr. Harding. We head around behind the barn. There's this big metal outbuilding, big overhead door. *It's a chop shop*, Victor. A fully equipped garage. It's got a lift, welding and cutting equipment, four huge toolboxes, and dollies for wheeling parts around. Two Corvettes with the engines and transmissions out. A stack of bucket seats along one wall, maybe twenty. All Corvette. Also, an eight-series BMW, the one that was stolen from the Lawsonia Golf Course last week, big sticker on the windshield. Says, 'Minneapolis.'

"It turns out this sweet little mom-and-pop farm is not locally owned. The owner of record is one Eoin McFarland of Newfane, Vermont. The FBI is on the way to pay him a visit as we speak. The other guys we took down? They're from all over—Wisconsin, Illinois, Minnesota, Indiana, North and South Dakota, Nevada. Two from Chester County, Pennsylvania, where I used to be an FBI agent. All these clowns have records. None can make bail."

Gilbert has run out of breath, and he sits down. The ever-clairvoyant Brianna knows what Gilbert wants right now, and brings him a shot of vodka and a bottle of sparkling water.

"I think we broke the camel's back, Victor."

—⁓⁓—

I call Colin from the restaurant parking lot and get his voicemail. "Call me as soon as you get this. We may have just lucked out big, big time, bro."

When I drive up to my house, I see a Day-Glo orange sticky note pasted to the porch door. In green sharpie ink, it says, *"Collie, got to postpone dinner tonight. Probable customer in Oshkosh. Resched tomorrow?"* It is unsigned.

Collie and I sit on the veranda, drinking single-malt neat. Not really great stuff, but we've put enough money in the bank that I am not buying well scotch anymore. I tell Collie about the Epstein bust. "Collie," I say, "I think maybe it's time to go to plan C."

"Which is?"

"Completely fold our tents for a while, at least once we got those five Yamaha outboards out of our garage and down to Savannah. I think we should go straight, at least for a while, and turn all our attention to the gold action for the time being."

"But if McFarland's out of the picture, doesn't that make us the only show in town? Won't there be more business for us?"

"Maybe so, maybe so. But look at it this way. If we ramp down our operations, and there are no reliable fences for top-dollar stuff, don't you think some of our upstream 'suppliers' may decide to cut back their burglary activity until we re-enter business or they can find another reliable fence?"

I take a healthy slug of the single malt. I can't tell if the burn is from the scotch or the implications of everything that is unfolding around us. "And if this results in the crime rate suddenly dropping in Green Lake County, Gilbert Rennie may conclude that the McFarland gang was the only show in town, and that the store is closed. Result? Rennie declares himself the winner, backs off his investigation of all the burglaries around here, and takes a lot of the heat off us."

"I suppose that's possible," says Collie. "The question is, is it *probable*?"

"This also means that we might not have to disclose the full scope of our criminality to Christine. True, I lie easily, Collie, but after my gold discovery cover-up with you, I do not want to be caught out in another deception with a member of my family, particularly when it relates to Ms. Holier-than-thou."

"You really going to go straight on me, Victor, now that you've turned me into a crook?"

"This isn't honesty speaking, Collie. It's expediency. It's *tactics.*"

"Yeah, well *tactically* I think you're missing a major point. What is your friend Gunnar going to say about us closing up shop? If he's left high and dry without a fencing channel, don't you think he and his chums are going to be seriously pissed off? *Pissed off at us?*"

In what proves to be one of the stupidest misjudgments of my life, I blow off Collie's concern. "What can he say? It's not his call, Collie, it's ours. If Gunnar Spaaks wants to be pissed off, let him be pissed off."

30

The Wedding Party

NOW THAT MY CASH FLOW HAS BEGUN TO FLOW
a bit, I decide damn the expense, I'm going to throw a
celebratory wedding dinner for the newlyweds, although
truth to tell, what I really intend is a family strategic planning
conference. This is the reason I do not invite Cara.

I hire "Feast by Luca" to come up from Chicago to
orchestrate an impeccable luxury dining experience on the
veranda, featuring the haute-est of haute cuisine and some
truly remarkable wines (as in, *Holy cow! What did this stuff
cost?*).

I suggest to everyone that we play dress-up. When I tell
Christine to be sure to wear her gold choker, she snips at me:
"Well, what did you think I'd do?" At the appointed hour of
eight, Collie appears first, looking like a well-dressed golf pro,
with an expensive-looking lime green polo shirt and beltless
lemon-yellow slacks. Collie is a strikingly handsome man, in
a low-key kind of way. Rather like Harrison Ford. Tonight,
he's slicked his hair back with gel and he's wearing his Rolex
on his well-tanned arm. My brother, the cliché.

And he's one very annoyed cliché, his hands crossed tightly across his chest. "I don't understand why I couldn't invite Cara, Victor."

"Collie, I mean neither you nor Cara disrespect. You know I think she's great. But later this evening we're going to talk about some stuff that is not for Cara's ears. Not yet, anyway. By the end of the evening you will understand, I promise."

There's a swish of fabric up the stairs behind Colin, and then Delia glides down the stairway behind him, supercilious and aloof, in a classic model's gait, step-pause, step-pause, step-pause. She arches her neck and lifts her chin high, keeping her eyes half closed, as if she is slightly anesthetized or *incredibly* bored. She's wearing a loose maroon double-breasted tunic that leaves absolutely nothing to the imagination. Double-breasted, indeed. Silk. Swoosh.

When she reaches the bottom step, Delia bursts into laughter and pulls her tunic more tightly closed over her chest so that her nipples disappear from view. "I'm sorry," she laughs, "I just can't do that arrogant model act anymore." Christine follows. She is no model, but she is a tall, graceful woman, and she is striking in a silvery silk blouse draped over linen bell-bottoms. I do not think I've ever seen my younger sister look so elegant.

I stand at the base of the stairs in a newly purchased Cuban guayabera with full, floating sleeves and an elaborate band of embroidery traversing my chest. I feel a little silly, but I must admit that this rather blouselike Cuban shirt is wonderfully comfortable. Cal has pressed a razor-sharp crease into my jeans, and I suspect I look like a high-rollin' Vegas gambler. I tell everyone shoes are optional, and we all opt out. This costume play is fun, I think. All of us acting out, playing party games.

Charged with a festive mood of expectancy, we adjourn to the patio: *What hath Victor wrought?*

I must hand it to Luca. The evening is perfectly realized—the setting, the service, the remarkable quality of the cuisine. This really is among the finest meals I have ever had. It's not just Green Lake good or even Chicago good. It's world-class good.

As this splendid performance unfolds, I keep my eye constantly on Christine, wondering if all this celebratory excess will trigger a WASP-like aversion to conspicuous consumption and make her feel self-conscious. But no, I don't sense trouble. This party is a unique experience, and, after all, it is about *her* and her new relationship.

Our conversation starts loose and gets looser, the jokes get raunchier, the sense of increasing intimacy enfolds us, draws us together. As the wine takes hold (and it's not just any old wine, it's Ruinart champagne and Chateau Lafitte Rothschild), Collie lights up and begins telling golf pro stories, many involving people copulating with people they're not married to. It seems as if a weight is being lifted from him, and I wonder if maybe he's on the way to crawling out from under his PTSD. All in all, this wedding dinner is proving a hell of a trip, and it looks to me like the Harding siblings may be building new bonds, moving in new directions.

Which is exactly the point.

At eleven, Luca appears, accepts our applause, bows modestly. I ask him to clear the table and strike the set, and then I usher our now well-lubricated wedding party out onto the side screen porch. Luca has lit a bunch of candles, laid out snifters and a nice D'Usse VSOP for anyone who's interested. We're all interested.

Now I stand in front of my family and try to look serious, difficult given how smug I feel at the moment. "Okay, this is a different part of our occasion," I start, trying to establish a more serious mood. "I want to conduct some family business that's probably best done when we are all a bit drunk, and I would like you to indulge me.

"I want to ask each of you certain questions, some of which may seem a little peculiar and, frankly, quite nosy. Please don't tell me to jump into Green Lake. By the end of our discussion, the method of my madness will be revealed. Then you can either commit to me or commit me. Will you humor me?"

My family members glance at each other, bemused, amused.

I turn to my sister. "Christine, how much did your gold choker cost you?"

She's obviously surprised at the question. "What?"

"I asked how much your life-changing piece of jewelry cost you when you bought it?"

"I didn't buy it, I *commissioned* it. It's not some off-the-shelf item."

"I'll bet that made it even more expensive, yes? It's exclusivity?"

"Sixty-six thousand dollars."

"Solid gold, Delia? Twenty-four-karat fine?" I ask.

She shakes her head. "Twenty-four karat—which is 99% pure gold—would have been too soft. Very beautiful, but very scratchable and breakable. So I alloyed Christine's piece down to twenty-two karat, which is 92% pure. It's the most common compound used in very high-end jewelry, particularly in India. But yes, Victor, this was the highest-quality creation I was capable of making that would be suitable for everyday use. For Christine, nothing but the best."

"Was that the most expensive piece you made last year, Delia?"

"Oh, heavens no."

"How many pieces of jewelry do you make a year?"

"Somewhere between ten and twenty. Each is a unique design. Each is commissioned. I don't do duplicates or series. I don't do molds. I don't have customers, Victor. I have... *patrons.*"

"What is the average price of one of your creations, if I may ask?"

Delia pauses, and puts her hand over Christine's on the tablecloth. "In the U.S., probably about a hundred thousand dollars. Some less, some more, some a lot more, depending on the purity and amount of gold used and the value of any gemstones. And the amount of time I spend, of course.

"India is an entirely different story. Over there, they use jewelry competitively and extravagantly, as in 'who can wear the most jaw-dropping Haram—that's a huge, sweeping necklace—at this week's social gathering?' Or whose kamarband, Jhumki, or chandbali—these are different kinds of Indian jewelry—set some fat cat back the most rupees? It's a real display culture, yes. Flashiest saris, flashiest jewelry. A *lot* of mine-is-bigger-than-yours blinging going on.

"There's also an additional market over there. Indian women do not have retirement accounts or financial portfolios. Instead, they acquire huge collections of gold jewelry pieces—often *massive* gold pieces—that they store for decades. Seldom wear, just keep it in a vault. This is their form of retirement nest egg. This kind of jewelry is often called 'bullion jewelry,' and often it's made from 24-karat gold. I'm suddenly very much in demand in southern India for bullion jewelry, and I can charge pretty much what I want for a commission. And it's a *lot.*"

"Like, a million?" Victor asked.

"It's happened," Delia smiles, "but usually it's somewhat less than that. But a heavy kamarband or haram requires a lot of gold, yes, whether 22 karat or 24 karat."

"Do you work only in gold?"

"Almost exclusively. Eighteen-karat—that means 75% pure gold—is common in jewelry, but I—and my clientele—regard it is déclassé, even though it's stronger and makes a better gem setting. I much prefer the warmth of purer gold. Like I said, twenty-four is too soft for any but display items. In many of my commissions for clients in India, I alloy pure gold with silver and copper to make it really yellow, which is how they like it over there, so that's how it ends up being twenty-two karat.

"I use gems too, of course. If a client insists, I will use platinum, but I'm not a huge fan. To me it looks cold, and, of course, there are idiots who mistake it for silver, which, of course, ruins the impression of wealth."

"How do your...*patrons* find you?"

"Strictly word-of-mouth. And I must say I got a lot more word of mouth after I won the Medaille Coeur D'Or award four years ago."

"The what?"

"The *Heart of Gold Medal*. Americans sometimes call it the Door-Door, because it's the doorway to *big-time* commissions, magazine ads, free PR. It's a juried annual competition, based in Prague. It's considered the highest award among us goldsmiths."

"Wow," I say. "Let me ask you something. Where do you get your gold for your work, Delia?"

"Gold is gold, Victor. It doesn't matter if you buy ingots on the open market or work through a broker or melt down your grandmother's wedding ring. As long as it starts as twenty-four karat, it's all the same stuff."

"How much gold do you keep on hand?"

"Not much. No point in inviting a burglary. I get what I need when I need it, you know?"

"No, I really need to know, Delia. How much do you usually keep on hand in this atelier of yours?"

"Usually about a hundred thousand dollars' worth," says Delia. "All 24 karat until I alloy it."

Now I pause. Long pause. I wait until my audience glances at one another, and begins to squirm uncomfortably. *What is going on here?*

"Delia," I say very softly, very slowly, "Let me ask you again. Just where do you get your gold?"

Delia pretends to be indignant. "I don't think that's any of your business, Mr. high-and-mighty Victor Harding. Various places, various vendors."

Okay, this is my cue. The big moment has come. Either this is all going somewhere, or else my sister is going to balk. The horse is about to leap off the high-diving platform.

"Delia, do you acquire all your gold legally?"

A sly smile creeps across Delia Chamberlain's lovely brown face, and I think I hear the voices of angels—or maybe devils—singing to me. Meanwhile, Colin Harding has just spit a mouthful of VSOP all over his lap. Those lemon-yellow slacks are history.

"Of course not," Delia says, patronizingly, as if she's saying the most innocent and obvious thing in the world. "I bet five percent of all the jewelry gold that changes hands in the world market has been illegally obtained at one time or another in one form or another. And okay, ya got me, Victor. I must confess that sometimes I know everything's not on the up and up. Certainly, it's a lot cheaper to go down back alleys sometimes. Once the gold gets melted down, who's to know?"

This is the moment to check out where Christine's head is, and I'm pleased with what I see. If Christine is shocked at this revelation, she's masking it. Colin, on the other hand, is clearly surprised—or at least surprised by my timing. I have not forewarned him that I am going to open the great gold kimono tonight. He starts to stand, and I gesture him down.

"Christine, have you ever told Delia about our secret tunnel?"

"What? Why bring that up now?"

"Humor me," I say.

"Well, Delia," Christine says, "back during prohibition, Victor's house was owned by a notorious Irish Chicago gangster named Bugsy Moran. There's long been a myth that there's a secret tunnel from the house down to the boathouse so Bugsy could get away if Capone's gang attacked the house."

"It's not a myth, Christine. I found the tunnel. Opened it up down at the boathouse end."

Christine shoots to her feet. "You're kidding me! That's unbelievable!"

"Wait, my dear. It gets better." I pull a leather sack from behind the living room couch and plunk it on the table. "Guess what I found in that tunnel?"

I reach in, pull out a single lead-gray brick, and hand it to Delia. "What does this weigh?" I ask. She hefts it expertly.

"Six kilos, more or less. Little over thirteen pounds." A knowing smile begins to creep over her face. I put my finger to my lips to shush her; this is *my* party.

I hand it to Colin, who then hands it to Christine. "What do you think this is, Christine?"

"Well, it looks like a hunk of lead, but your theatricality suggests otherwise."

"Smart girl. Look at that corner."

"Yeah, so it's been scraped a little. It's just...*oh...my...God.*"

"I'll spare you the math, Christine. I found one hundred and twenty-eight of those bars. Over sixteen hundred pounds. That means that at today's prices, Bugsy Moran's treasure is probably worth about forty million dollars, give or take. Gold prices fluctuate. Now, if we can only find a way to cash all this gold in, even if we split the proceeds into thirds, we all could probably live pretty comfortably, no?"

Christine looks dizzy.

I smile at her. "Of course, the challenge will be laundering all this gold without getting caught."

"Launder it? But...it's *yours*," Christine sputters. "You found it on your property."

"As I have already briefed Colin, I hired a lawyer—anonymously—to school me on the law of stolen and abandoned property. Bottom line, it's *not* mine. Legally, he thinks it belongs to some Japanese insurance company, the successor to the insurance company that paid off when a bunch of gold was stolen from a private mint in 1929. What that means, my friends, is that we've got to find some creative ways to divest ourselves of forty million dollars worth of 24-karat gold."

All heads swivel to Delia when I ask her, "Do you think you might want to help us with that?"

"Well, *gee*, Victor," Delia says innocently, smile wrinkles creating deep folds at the edges of her eyes. "Wouldn't that be against the law?"

"It would be utterly against the law, yes. And hard work, too. Let's bear in mind that part of your role would be to remelt sixteen hundred pounds of crude ingots into some other form that would provide you with a virtually bottomless supply of material for your jewelry commissions."

"Victor, even if I live to be a hundred, I could never make enough pieces to use that much gold. Not unless I put up a roadside concession stand and sold solid gold bracelets for ten bucks each."

"Good point. But your atelier would be a perfect cover operation for some other gold transactions, no? And no one would ever ask what you were doing with a bunch of gold stashed around the place, right? You might let carefully screened purchasers know that you have a little surplus supply now and again. I don't know if you'd want to try to melt all the gold in one giant operation or remelt a bar or two at a time when you needed raw material for your commissions or customers, but either way, over time we should be able to make *a lot* of money."

Delia is nodding eagerly. Christine's head is clocking back and forth between Delia and me as if we're both mad. For all her brilliance, Christine processes information slowly, carefully. She has always hated surprises. Now she closes her eyes and looks down at the floor, *processing, processing, processing.* I sense that Colin is biting his tongue, waiting to see how his twin sister is going to react.

I say, "Of course, Delia, even if you did a cosmetic makeover on our remelt bars, this would still be stolen property. But the gold would be considerably harder to trace. And you all should consider this. The foundry where this gold was first smelted has long since closed, and the insurance company that originally paid the robbery claim when the gold was stolen in 1929 has long since gone out of business. True, there's a Japanese successor company, but I bet to them, this matter is just a distant loss on closed books gathering dust on some back shelf. I'm sure they have long since stopped looking for it. The gold itself has long since vanished from sight. It has already been repoured once by whoever created these clumsy ingots, and they have been hidden in a tunnel for ninety years. I doubt whether this gold is high on anybody's most-wanted list cold case, even people who work cold cases. I think our chances of laundering this gold successfully are really pretty good."

"Oh, I think so, too," chirps Delia. "And I know something about how to handle behind-the-barn gold transactions."

Christine now appears overwhelmed. I suspect that imagining her transformation from reputable New York lawyer to felon—even a very wealthy felon—stretches her beyond her limits. She buries her face in her hands and shakes her head.

"I can't imagine how we'll do this," she says.

"Oh, I can," Delia says.

I look Christine straight in the eye. "Forty million dollars, Christine. Think about it. Forty million smackers. No matter how we split it, that's a lot of money."

I am surprised to see Christine wince.

31

Open House

THE PHONE IS RINGING as Colin and I walk into my house after a round of golf. Collie plays superbly, his swing smooth and fluid, his putting steady and true. I play poorly, but of course there is no surprise there. It's Cara on the phone, and she speaks in a pressured rush.

"Hey, Victor. I'm so sorry, I completely forgot to tell you guys. Vilma Stakhatos scheduled an open house today at her father's house to show the place. It's going on *right now*. They've cleaned away most of the junk outside and a lot of the yard sculpture, and the realtor has staged the house very attractively. I've lent ten paintings, and they look really good. Why don't all of you hustle on out? Maybe we can get Christine and Delia interested in the house, and I sure want the chance to talk to Delia some more. If she and Christine would ever consider moving out here and maybe Delia creating a studio or something, I've got some ideas."

Cara pauses for effect.

"And one of 'em might be renovating Phone's barn into an atelier. It's big—two full floors—and it's got 240-volt service already installed, so there would be plenty of juice to run her ovens and smelters. Maybe Delia and I could even go in on something together. An artists' collective, like."

"Whoa, you're certainly running at full gallop! Maybe you ought to rein it in a bit."

"But it's such a *great* idea! And think about all the fun we could have!"

Actually, the idea appeals to me. I've been giving some serious thought to what it would be like to have all three Hardings living near each other, if not under the same roof. I'm not getting any younger, and—in a whole variety of ways—the members of the clan could take care of each other as we all get older. This is a novel proposition for me, and my reclusive side has been sparring with a percolating urge for community, for...*intimacy*. Maybe I've had enough of my life of splendid isolation.

"What is Vilma asking for the house?"

"Probably depends on who's buying. You know Vilma. She leads with her heart. Listing price is a million-four, largely because of all the acreage and outbuildings. Can you imagine the developers who'd like to get their mitts on that parcel? Bulldoze the house, throw up three or four shit-for-style McMansions? But if someone promised they'd respect the house and preserve Phone's legacy, I bet Vilma would come down plenty. Eight or nine hundred, maybe? I don't know, maybe even less. Hell, if Christine said she wanted to buy it, I'm sure Vilma would take back financing. And if Delia and I opened an atelier or co-op or school in the barn, named it the Xenophon Stakhatos Fine Arts Center or something, God, I bet Vilma would *endow* it."

"How can Vilma afford to endow anything?"

"I guess there's no way you would know this, not being from around here. Vilma's family owns the Manitowoc Aluminum Foundry over on Lake Michigan. They are this huge manufacturer of metal products that aren't made of iron or steel. Daddy Roman Karaskiewicz took it public in the '70s, and Vilma's two brothers just took it private again. Phone didn't go into the family business; he was the artist in the family, the eccentric in-law. But believe me, he always had plenty of money to play with. And Vilma? She's loaded."

—————

Vilma Stakhatos, tall, elegant, with a wide Slavic face, startling emerald eyes and a flowing mane of dark hair, is prowling the property, making sure everything goes smoothly at the open house. She has spent considerable money to clean the place up, replace some of the degraded siding, and paint the eaves. The lawn has been mowed, the gravel driveway raked, the windows cleaned. The place looks great—both historical and contemporary, both polished and well-worn. The house was not for sale when I moved to Green Lake, or I surely would have bought it. Now it is, and I want Christine to buy it, so I can come and visit, come and prowl around this marvelous property.

My sister Christine has a lot of tells—tics and gestures she thinks mask her behavior but in fact reveal where her head is. When she gets really interested in something, really captivated, she goes silent, purses her lips, shades her eyes with a hand, and feigns indifference. Today she wanders the property for two hours, sometimes arm-in-arm with Delia, sometimes alone. She scopes out all the sight lines, looks down from the deck, looks up from the bottom of the lower yard. Over and again, she shakes her head, starts to walk away, then turns and stares again at whatever has caught her eye. I watch this performance several times and know she is hooked.

Delia is nowhere this reserved. In the course of her perambulations, I hear, "Wow" numerous times. Also "Holy moly," "Oh, man," "Oh, my word," "Oh, come *on*," and "Are you kidding me?" She examines the house inch-by-inch, often pulling out a carpenter's tape measure to scope a room or space. She explores the barn, examines the condition of the beams and dowels that fasten them, checks out the circuit breaker box and electrical service, sticks a screwdriver into the flooring to see if it's rotted, opens and closes the massive sliding doors several times, repeatedly flicks the lights on and off, and finally sits down cross-legged in the middle of the floor as if deep in meditation.

After a while, she and Christine check out the goat pen and then make the rounds of the yard, standing together in front of each of the remaining large yard sculptures Phone welded together from steel plate and junk auto parts. From the deck, I see them kiss several times. It's an open house, so there are a number of other people walking around with cameras and note pads, but to Christine and Delia, all the other people might as well have been in another universe.

As we prepare to leave, Delia steps up to Vilma. "I've got one major problem," she says.

Vilma's brow furrows with concern.

"In all the time I've been in Green Lake, I have seen exactly ten people of color, and except for Ajmo's Indian boat chauffeur, they were all African American. I've been subjected to a lot of racism and a lot of discrimination in my life, Vilma, and I've learned to handle it. But that doesn't mean I want to *bathe* in it for the rest of my life. And I think it's a good bet my political views would be pretty unpopular with a lot of the locals."

Vilma places her arms gently on Delia's shoulders. "That is a fair concern, my dear. After all, you are in mid-state Wisconsin, land of the Germans and the Poles—of which I am one, by the way. And around here a lot of the whites think they are the elite, and they think they rule. And they tend to disdain people who are not like them. Phone was a very swarthy Greek, and he got called a nigger more than a few times.

"Let me just say this. Around here, the 'good people' are like truffles. You've got to dig for them in the forest, root around for them. They don't wear signs, although a lot of us are quite active politically. But I promise you can find fast friends here, wonderful, interesting friends. *Diverse* friends.

"Cara will tell you that Phone and I have long been part of quite an amazing group of stimulating people. Victor is fond of stereotyping everyone in Green Lake as a Local or a Vandal or a Lookamee or whatever, but these people defy being put in neat boxes. We've got academics and professors from Ripon College, artists of all kinds from miles around, reclusive poets, famous novelists, former campus radicals, and the guy who invented the artificial intelligence algorithm for self-driving cars. Even retired geniuses like Victor here."

She laughs brightly as she pictures them, ticking them off on her fingers. "From among us, the Green Lake 'power elite' can choose the threat they most dread. There's the communist red menace, the Japanese yellow peril, the Mexican immigrant tidal wave, all those usurious Jews, all those N-word people, drug-running Colombian gangstas, and, of course, the whole replacement theory threat. We have Indians of both kinds and yes, Delia, even a couple of Sri Lankans that I know of who drive up from Milwaukee. We've got painters, sculptors, welders, wood-butchers, the whole artistic spectrum. We've got thought leaders and thought followers. We've got every brand and flavor of the sexual preference and gender orientation spectrum you can imagine, and some you can't. Get us all together, and we have one hell of a good time."

Delia hugs Vilma. Then, get this, *Christine hugs Vilma.*

When we pile into the Maybach, Christine just stares off into space. "We got a lot to think about," she says to no one in particular.

—◆◆◆—

Vilma's bottom line turns out to be nine hundred and forty thousand dollars. The down payment is to be two hundred and fifty thousand dollars, Christine and Delia each supposed to kick in half.

Then the Titanic hits the iceberg.

Back at my house, Christine asks to speak to me alone, and we stroll down to watch the sunset from the end of the dock.

"Something's on your mind," I say.

"You've got that right," Christine says hoarsely. "Victor, my marriage is in serious danger. And I'm the one who's put it in serious danger."

I am taken aback and shake my head disbelievingly. "What the hell are you talking about? You guys are the very picture of lovestruck newlyweds. What could possibly be wrong?"

"Oh, like everyone, we've got our issues, but one of 'em's really a potential deal killer."

Christine gathers herself, takes a deep cleansing breath, then lets it out in a rush.

"Victor, you don't think Delia's a borderline? Stay tuned for coming events. You're about to see some...*volatility*. I think you're about to see Delia go nuts."

I gape at Christine, mystified.

"Do you remember Delia's speech on the Ajmo boat, Victor? When she said that she will not let anyone victimize her, and heaven help anybody who tries to take advantage of her?"

"Yes, I remember that quite vividly."

"Delia and I really do love each other, but from the outset of our relationship we've also had this thing about each of us carrying our own weight. I don't mean emotionally, I mean financially."

"Yeah? And?"

"Delia thinks I'm well off, and until recently I was...well, at least okay. I'm sure Delia thinks I probably have a few million in the bank. *She* does, and she probably assumes we're on pretty equal financial footing, given the lifestyle we've been living in New York. We've never discussed hard numbers, because supposedly we didn't have to, right? We were both working, it looked like we were both doing well, and it was like, 'You got your pot, and I got my pot, and when we're married, we'll each just ante up equally for our expenses, big and little.'"

"Yeah? And?"

"Victor, do you remember what Delia said about those huge Ponzi schemes her father used to run? All the Arabs he conned? And I assume you also know about the Bernie Madoff scandal, the operation that fleeced all those people who thought they brilliant investors...or at least prudent investors?"

"Yes to both questions," I say.

Christine shrugs, and the import of what she's telling me hits home.

"Oh, no," I whisper.

"Oh, yes," she sighs.

"When? How? How much?" I stammer.

"One of the partners in my law firm—ironically, one of the senior members of the executive committee that just canned me—came to me about eight months ago and said that for several years he had been realizing a fabulous return on a safe and secure offshore fund. He said several of the firm's senior partners had invested heavily in this fund and were seeing a handsome return. I'm sure you know where this is going."

Christine's eyes are dry, but she is shaking her head wearily and her hands are trembling.

"The fund was managed by a couple of Brits who appeared to be on the up-and-up. I met 'em when they came to New York. Very polished Savile Row types, very understated. All 'pip-pip' and 'pup-pup' and stiff upper lip. Had all the answers. Peter Stormouth and Gregory Mansell. Engraved business cards.

"Participation in the fund was by invitation only, *very* exclusive, doncha know. Investors had to be 'qualified investors' under federal safe harbor requirements, and I barely squeaked through.

In order to play, I had to pony up at least three million dollars. Victor, that was pretty much everything I had. I know all good financial advisors say you should diversify your portfolio, but I told myself a happy little story: *Hey, Christine! Think of how this will simplify your retirement planning! And all these other New York lawyers are in deep, and they're no dummies.* The prospectus looked okay; my due diligence did not turn up any red flags...so I bit."

Christine rubs her hands over her face. "And boy, did I ever get bitten. Just before I married Delia, I got the word that regulatory authorities on both sides of the pond had raided the fund, closed it down, indicted the Brits. I was completely wiped out. When the investigators closed in, there was nothing left in the fund to distribute back to the investors. We all got totally screwed. My only consolation is that my scumbag law firm partners got wiped out too, but that's really no consolation. Did those arrogant pricks put me on the street because they were ashamed of what they'd done to me and couldn't bear to look me in the face every day? Part of me sure thinks so."

Given my own recent financial train wreck, empathy comes easily. "Oh, Christine, I am so, so sorry. No one deserves to be shafted like that."

"Oh, but the bad news is not over."

"How so?"

"*I have never told Delia.* Didn't have the guts. Thought she'd never marry me if I was so patently unable to take care of myself. And now what do I do? I want to spend my life with Delia. *But she isn't going want to spend her life with me when she finds out I am pretty much broke.*"

"But. Christine, you paid sixty-six thousand dollars for a necklace!"

"Victor, that took every last cent I had. Totaled my 401(k), used up all my savings."

My mind is spinning. "Okay, I'll admit I'm really surprised, Christine. I've always thought having your financial affairs under absolute control was your...*thing.* But at this point, I honestly don't understand what you're worried about. *We have a plan to acquire all the money any of us will ever need!* And it's not wishful thinking; the pieces are all there. It'll just take some time to get the cash rolling in."

Christine suddenly breaks into sobs, her head bobbing with each word. "*You...do...not...understand.* The issue is not that I might have to rely on Delia's money for awhile. *It's that I misled her.* That's what's going to kill our marriage, just like Hugh Chamberlain's secret about his sexual orientation killed *their* marriage."

I notice Christine does not mention Delia's reciprocal deception about her own sexual proclivities.

"Remember when Delia and I were talking about buying Vilma's house and you heard us 'debating' about whether to keep my New York condo as a *pied a terre,* as a 'performing asset,' as Delia put it? Well, *I don't own a New York condo!* Delia thinks I do, but I don't. I *sublet* a New York condo. I pay rent. And pretty soon I won't be able to afford to pay that. When she finds out, my beloved wife is going to drop me like a bad habit."

"I don't believe that." I say. "I don't think you're giving Delia enough credit, giving the strength of your bond enough credit. Look, Christine, given our prospects, money issues are just not that big a deal."

"*But they are, Victor!* Your gold scam scares me shitless. And you want to know something else? I've *always* been scared shitless. My whole life, my whole career. The great Ice Goddess has feet of clay. Chronic anxiety disorder, my therapist labels it. That's why I am the way I am. Oh, and my therapist says she thinks you and Colin both have it, too."

I feel my hackles rise. "That is *complete bullshit.* Yeah, you're sort of highly-defended, but you've always been an effortless hyper-achiever. All of us have done pretty well for ourselves, so just how crippled can we be? And who is *your* therapist to tell *me* what I have or don't have?"

I'm shocked when Christine grabs the front of my shirt, fiercely pushes her face close to mine. I am not accustomed to such drama.

"Don't you get it, Victor? For once, can't you get past your denial? You, Collie, me—*we're all children of the same screwed-up parents!* The same cold, relentlessly judgmental father, the same anxiety-ridden alcoholic mother. The same 'you've got to live up to your potential' upbringing. It doesn't matter that they're dead now. Their ghosts still rule our lives. None of us has escaped. Each of us has coped differently. You with your relentless cynicism...Colin with his pathetic people-pleasing...me with the whole Ice Goddess act. The world-famous architect, the successful golf pro, the respected New York lawyer—we're all afraid that like in the Wizard of Oz, someone's gonna pull the curtain away and we'll be ridiculed as frauds."

I've got to stop this conversation. I pry Christine's hands off my shirt, step away from her. I need distance right now.

"What *exactly* is it that you want, Christine?"

"I need a bridge loan. I want you to lend me the $125,000 for my share of the down payment on the house. "

Busted. I feel my heart sink.

"Christine," I say softly, "if I had it, I would certainly lend it to you. *Give* it to you. In a heartbeat. Especially because I think it won't be long until you could pay it back. But I can't lend it to you, because right now I don't have it to lend."

Her eyes open wide with astonishment. *"What?"*

"You're not the only one who has suffered a financial train wreck. Believe it or not, my financial advisor became seriously mentally ill and threw most of my portfolio down the toilet. Just like you, I've been pretty much flat busted, Christine. My retirement is toast. I have been struggling to make ends meet, struggling just to keep my house. And don't think about hitting up Colin, because he doesn't have two nickels to rub together, either. He's got his severance from The Landings and some rent on his Savannah house, and after that he's lickin' the bottom of the barrel. And don't even think about asking him to sell his house so you can have your Green Lake dream house—*because he would*, and then I would kill you both. Even before we lucked out with the whole gold thing, Colin and I were struggling to generate some cash flow."

There is a long pause.

"Victor, what aren't you telling me?"

I feel the urge to confess. Let the truth flow forth. Relieve myself of the pressure of continuing the deception.

Nope. Not Now. This is not where or how I want to disclose our fencing enterprise. I look for a way to wiggle out of this moment, so I counterattack. "Well, Christine, what aren't you telling Delia?"

I turn on my heel and head back up to my house.

32

Darrin Do

I STROLL FROM THE BRIGHT SUMMER SUNSHINE
into the cool darkness of Spaaks Auto body, and at first, I see
nothing. When my vision starts to adjust, the first thing I see
is Gunnar Spaaks' startling shock of near-white hair at the far
end of the garage. He waves and starts over.

"You asked me to come over and have a look," I say. "I
know it's not done, but I'm eager to see how we're doin' on
the Darrin."

"Very good shape. Way ahead of schedule, Victor. It just
came out of the paint booth." Gunnar guides me to the back
of the shop to a draped form. He whisks the light blue tarp
off the Darrin with a dramatic matador's sweep, and I can't
help but grin.

"The upholstery's out to be done," grins Gunnar, "and I've
got all the trim pieces at the chrome shop, but I wanted you
to see the paint."

It's gorgeous. The white finish is deep, smooth, flawless.
It has a wonderful iridescent sheen in the bright overhead
lights. Gunnar grins. "The paint is actually a Cadillac color,
Galaxy Pearl Star, except of course this is a lacquer, not
enamel. I'm pretty proud of how it came out."

"You should be, Gunnar. It is an absolutely fabulous finish. I'm very, very pleased."

"Nino, the upholsterer, has found a beautiful set of matched hides for the interior, so the seats, door cards, and dash will all be identical in color and grain. I should also mention that Nino is also making you up a new convertible top. The mice had chewed the old one to pieces. Your new one is going to be a soft beige, with a taupe inner liner. Better than any other Darrin anywhere.

"And what do you think of the wheels?" Gunnar grins.

Now I see what, other than the incredible paint, is making the Darrin look so different to me: the original steel wheels and pitted chrome "dog-dish" hubcaps have been replaced with chrome wire wheels. The effect is very classy, very elegant, very 50's.

I clap my hands on the side of my thighs. "Well, okay!" I exclaim. "You've certainly exceeded my expectations. Have we also exceeded my budget?"

"Of course," says Gunnar, as if this a matter of no consequence.

"Gunnar, we had a fixed-price deal! You're the one who made a big deal about no haggling half-way through."

"That was then, this is now. Once we got into things, there were unforeseen expenses. Like the cost of that special leather."

I feel an intense ambivalence. On one hand, I am bowled over by the Darrin. I can see myself gliding around the streets of Green Lake, eliciting stares and applause. On the other hand, I'm the one that's being taken for a ride by my own partner in crime, a crook who simply does not care if he lives up to his word or not. I'm about to tee off on Gunnar when my mind pulls up the image of all that gold sitting in Bugsy's tunnel. My outrage cools: *Okay, you're being shafted, but now you can afford it—and the work on the Darrin is exquisite.*

"How much am I into you for?"

"Right now, forty-eight five, but we've already paid for the leather. Tell you what, Victor, I'll put an absolute project cap at fifty grand. I'll eat any time over that."

"You bastard," I say.

"It's nice to be loved," says Gunnar Spaaks, deadpan.

"All right, I'll go fifty, you bloodsucker, but that's the absolute ceiling. No more bait-and-switch."

"Okay," says Gunnar simply.

As we're walking out of the shop, I finally bring up what I really came here to talk about. I try to sound off-hand.

"Hey, did you hear about the McFarland bust?"

"Of course," says Gunnar.

"Did you know about these guys?"

"Of course," says Gunnar.

"Well, it was a hell of an operation. All kinds of stuff. *Tons* of stuff. And a chop-shop out back."

"I knew that," says Gunnar.

"Well, what the hell, Gunnar? So, were you using more than one fence, sending these guys stuff, as well as me?"

I'm sure he can see the color rising in my cheeks.

"Look, Victor. I never promised you exclusivity. Do you eat dinner at only one restaurant? McFarland's guys popped up after Causley got busted, and they were serious—made it clear they were capable of moving a *lot* of stuff, not to mention run a top-drawer chop shop that would keep me from having to dick around with disassembling a lot of stolen cars at my place.

"But the stuff he fenced was mostly lower-end stuff than you and Collie have been handling. High volume, but low margin. McFarland was not a class act, wasn't able to cultivate the kind of sophisticated downstream clientele you and Collie have been able to attract. Also, personally I don't like Eoin McFarland much. He's not a stand-up guy, and he did not pay as well you do. So, you and Collie have not really been getting screwed over all that much by having a competitor. With this McFarland bust, there's going to be a real talent shortage, a real bottleneck in the pipeline. That's probably a good thing for you, right?"

I'm very interested to see how Gunnar Spaaks is going to react when I drop the bomb.

"Gunnar, you know, we've got to think about these developments *strategically*. Right now, Gilbert Rennie is *giddy*. He thinks he's busted up the only show in town, thinks that he's stopped the great Green Lake crime wave cold. He expects that all the criminals in the area are going to cut back on pulling jobs because now they don't have any way to fence the goods. But if the level of robberies and burglaries stays high, Gilbert is going to deduce that there's another fence operating around here. He's going to keep digging, keep the pressure on."

"Well, that's your problem, Victor. That's your area of the supply chain."

"Actually, it's yours too, Gunnar. Because Colin and I have decided to stop our fencing operations for a while. Concentrate on laundering some bucks, wait for the dust to clear before starting up again, you know?"

Gunnar stops mid-stride. My news catches him flat-footed, and at first seeing his surprise is a most agreeable sensation. He exhales loudly, combs his hands through his strikingly blond hair. He starts to say something under his breath, catches himself. He stops the f-bomb at the 'f.'

"And here's my suggestion," I say. "I suggest you tell your...colleagues, your.... *minions* to just cool it for a while. All right?"

Gunnar Spaaks turns and glares at me. His left eye twitches, a tic I have never seen before.

"No," he says.

"What do you mean, *no*? Are you telling me that you are ordering Colin and me to continue to receive stolen property?"

"That's exactly what I'm telling you. To hell with your so-called strategy. To hell with what Gilbert Rennie thinks or doesn't think. You cannot leave your...suppliers of high-end goods high and dry just because you and your chickenshit brother suddenly get cold feet. Let me be clear: you two try to shut down the pipeline, and you will be very, very sorry."

I am swept in a tsunami of uncontrollable anger. I push my face close to Gunnar's. "Oh yeah? And just what are you and your redneck gang going to do?" I hiss.

Gunnar does not flinch, does not blink. "I repeat, Victor. You will be very, *very* sorry."

"Are you threatening me, you dime store crime lord?"

"I certainly am. And either I'm bluffing...or I'm not. You want to try me, Victor?"

Before I can reply, Gunnar steps back, cocks his head comically. "Victor, Victor. Why do we keep having conversations like this? Look, the McFarland bust is a great opportunity for you and Colin. Don't waste it. Don't look the gift horse in the mouth, know what I'm sayin'?"

He turns and walks back into the body shop.

33

Things Get Tense

IN A SHOCKING BREACH of accepted burglary operating procedure, Boris Reltne has left his box truck running in my driveway in the middle of the day. He stands at the bottom of my front steps, screaming at my brother, who looks down on him from the veranda. From where I stand in the hallway, Collie appears calm, in complete control of the situation.

"Whaddya mean, you can't take the load? Are you shittin' me?"

Collie stands with his hands stuck comfortably in his pants pockets. "I mean we *won't* take the load. Like we told Gunnar, Victor and I are taking our foot off the gas for awhile, Boris. I'm sure Gunnar mentioned that to you, so don't act so surprised. Furthermore, you didn't call to alert us, you just showed up here unannounced. Not cool, even if we were still buying. But your breaking basic rules is not the issue. Sorry, but we are not presently receiving stolen property. The little sign in the door of the store says, 'closed for renovations.'"

"Well, just what am I supposed to do with a truck full of antique furniture?"

"Not our call. But you could take it down to Milwaukee. Down to Antiques Row. There's lots of action down there.

Or even Madison. I hear there's a couple of guys buyin' stuff in that strip mall just north of campus. Or you could age the goods, Boris. Just stick 'em in a barn or storage unit, let everything cool awhile. Just count us out, at least for the time being."

"You clowns are gonna pay for this," Reltne spits.

"C'mon, Boris. Don't be so melodramatic. You may have to go out of the area to fence the stuff, but that won't kill you."

"Yeah? Well, maybe some people gonna be thinkin' about killing *you*, Harding."

"Boris, there wasn't all this drama when Causley got busted or the McFarland operation got taken down."

"Yeah, Colin, but they were *busted*. This is different. You're jes' *quittin'*.' Hanging a bunch of us out to dry. And I tell you something more, mister big shot. You and your stuck-up brother really think crime is gonna stop around Green Lake because you stop handling stolen property? Man, that's some kind of arrogance. You two guys think entirely too highly of yourselves. Well, just remember this, Colin—*what goes around, comes around*."

———

Days before, Colin and I had sat down at the dining room table, for once without alcoholic enhancement, to discuss our options and tactics. Colin had smiled at me. "The issue on the floor is whether or not we can be forced to continue in criminal activity against our will."

"No, Colin," I had countered. "The issue is how much danger we are in if we continue to receive stolen property from Gunnar and the Semper crowd, and how much danger we are in if we don't."

We agreed that our criminal enterprise had taken a whole new turn, but neither of us was quite sure what road it would take us down. The gold, of course, changed the calculus. Our fencing operation had built real momentum, and we were aware of our solid reputation among burglars and thieves in the area. We certainly would have continued to receive stolen property if fate had not dropped forty million bucks in our laps. But the gold reframed our options, and suddenly our risk-reward analysis looked very different.

"The risk isn't just jail anymore, Victor. Gunnar made it clear that the danger is something worse."

"But is it, though? Maybe Gunnar was just blowin' smoke because we caught him by surprise," I said, hoping that what I was saying was true. "Maybe it was bruised pride thing, Collie. Yeah, we're inconveniencing him if we stop, but he himself said that he saw no need for exclusivity when dealing with fences. Look how quickly the perps shifted gears when Causley got put out of business."

Colin had leaned back, put his hands behind his head. "Victor, do you *really* believe that the lack of reliable fences would lower the crime rate around here and get Rennie to take some of the heat off? Or were you just looking for any argument to make to Gunnar to justify our cutting back?"

"I was just slingin' it," I laugh. "Remember, I have regular lunches with Gilbert, and although he's careful about what he discloses to me, I can tell you that he's not about to ease up. He's made it clear he is just as determined to solve old cases—and by that, I mean heists where you and I bought goods months ago, Collie—as he is to stop the present burglary wave. No, even if we stop now, you and I are not out of the woods. We're still on the hook for the priors."

"Oh, that's reassuring." Collie doesn't laugh. "You mean we don't cut our exposure if we stop? Then why stop?"

"Because at whatever time we have to make the argument to law enforcement authorities that we've gone straight, it will help if we have actually gone straight."

"Good point," Collie says, staring at his clenched fists.

"Look," I say, "the more important question is how much credence to give to Gunnar Spaaks' threats. Do you agree that when he says we'll be "very, very sorry" he's implying serious physical harm, rather than just ratting us out to law enforcement?"

"Of course, it means that. Because Gunnar knows we have the goods on him and that in a pissing match with the law, Gunnar and his gang would come out far worse than we would. And Victor—*here there is a long pause*—Semper has already shown that it is capable of murder."

This comment slides a tumbler into place, springs open a lock that had been jamming my thinking.

"Thank you, Collie! The way you put that sharpens the way we have to look at this threat."

He stares at me blankly.

"We need to decide who, if anyone, we really need to be afraid of. Is it just Gunnar himself? Is it Semper as a whole? Or is the threat going to come from certain individuals within Semper?"

"I don't follow," says Collie.

"Gunnar is always telling me that he is not a kingpin or crime lord, says does not control all the things various Semper members do. Do you think Gunnar personally murdered that kid on his Honda?"

"No."

"Do you think he knew beforehand that someone planned to garrote that kid?"

"No, I think that if he learned about it beforehand, he would have put the kybosh on it. Crime like that threatens the whole motorcycle club. But I'm absolutely positive that he knew afterward who did it."

"Right on both counts. And I think that gives us our answer, Collie."

"You have totally lost me."

"My conclusion is that, despite his threats, Gunnar will not personally commit violence against us. Furthermore, it would be very risky for him to encourage the gang as a whole to commit violence against us. And finally, he will not grant a license for any individual in the club to attack us, I don't care who it is. Why? Because all roads lead back to Gunnar, and he'll be the prime suspect if anything happens to us."

On the basis of this tenuous line of reasoning, Colin and I decide that—Gunnar's threat notwithstanding—we will decline further fencing opportunities for the foreseeable future.

34

The Truth Will Out

ANTICIPATING FUTURE NEEDS, Delia spends eighteen thousand dollars on a humongous new Ajax Tocco tipping furnace for melting and casting gold. Home hobby furnaces cost about five hundred bucks and the biggest ones can process a load of about two kilograms—under five pounds—of gold. Delia's monster, destined for the atelier planned for the barn, can handle up to a hundred kilos. Two hundred and twenty pounds. This furnace has a variety of tip chutes and crucibles that can handle everything from dainty little pours to high-capacity melts—essential if we're going to do big batches when recasting Bugsy bars, as we now call them, into various different forms and sizes. Suitable for either wholesale or retail, so to speak.

"I have some nice ideas," she says over cocktails. "Instead of just melting down ugly bars and making them into prettier bars, I've been thinking about several shapes, several sizes. For my own work, I want to make a supply of thin twelve-by-twelve-inch sheets, so I don't have to roll 'em out when I am shaping jewelry forms. Also, I can cast up a bunch of gem mounts of various sizes. But then I also could get creative, make some bulk merchandise. Not jewelry. *Tchotchkes.* For conspicuous consumers, I can make round solid-gold cocktail coasters. And I can easily make little keychains that look like miniature Fort Knox ingots. Stamp 'em with a Coeur D'Or logo. Price 'em at about a thousand bucks apiece. For other goldsmiths, I can just cast up nice smooth bars in various sizes, and let the word get out that I'm five percent below market. Stampede, for sure."

———

Christine, her face drawn and tense, stands and gestures for me to follow her to the back bedroom. She closes the door, sitting heavily on the end of the bed. She is flushed.

"Well, I told her."

I do not have to be told what the revelation was. "And... so are you two still married?"

"Okay, so it turns out I'm not as inscrutable as I always thought I was. At least not to perceptive people like Delia, people accustomed to having people try to take advantage of them."

"Meaning?"

"Meaning Delia knew that I'd been scammed and cleaned out."

"How'd she know that?"

"Read the paper. Saw how I looked when I read the paper. Saw the changes in my shopping and living habits. Put two and two together. Knew for some time that I was running on empty."

"*Wow.* So, did she go all borderline on you? Does she feel deceived? Betrayed? Pissed at you for not telling her?"

"Nope. No signs of borderline-type insecurity or wild overreaction. Turns out she does not take my deception as being about my taking advantage *of her.* Just saw it as 'bad things happen to good people' kind of thing."

"Why didn't she tell you that she knew?"

"You want to know exactly what she said?"

"Dyin' to know."

"She said, 'Christine, I've lived my whole life in a world of fraud and deception. I know it when I see it. I like to think that no one can pull the wool over my eyes. And that includes you, my love. When you got victimized but didn't say anything, I realized right away that something dreadful had happened, that some part of you was hiding something. I hope this doesn't seem manipulative, but I was curious how it would come out, and how honestly you would handle it when it did come out. As far as I'm concerned, you passed the test. I knew we'd have to get around to the whole money issue eventually, but I did not see your hiding your money problems as a betrayal of me.'"

"Well, that proves it," I say.

"What? *What?*"

"Delia Chamberlain definitely does not suffer from borderline personality disorder."

Christine cannot continue. She starts crying quietly, shakes her head miserably. I go over and sit down next to her. She lays her head on my shoulder. We sit quietly for a few minutes. Finally, in an almost comical hiccupping voice, Christine says, "You want to know how we closed the conversation?"

I nod.

"Delia said, 'you're a very competitive person, Christine, but you and I are not in a competition. We are in a marriage, in the first relationship I've ever had that has really made me feel valued.' Then she said, 'Christine, it is true that I now have a lot of money in the bank. I earned it, and it's mine. You have no *right* to it, but you may have complete *access* to it—and that includes using part of it for a down payment on a house you and I will own jointly. Here's the bottom line, Christine: When we agreed to marry, I did not ask for a prenup to protect my money, and I do not feel the need to have one now.'"

"Holy smokes!" I exclaim. "I need a moment to process all that. But I guess your marriage is safe, eh?"

"Oh, and there's one more thing Delia said, and this affects you and me and Colin. She said that going forward, it was going to be important for all of us—and that may come to include Cara—not to get territorial or jealous of each other when it came to dividing up our profits. Delia said that in the future, allocating the proceeds from our gold-related activity is bound to get tricky, because, in effect, you, Victor, are providing critical raw materials, while she is providing both the labor and the lion's share of the marketing leverage. She said we also have to decide whether to regard the gold operations and the car transportation and storage business as part of one big enterprise or as two distinctly different profit centers."

"What'd you say?"

"Said I'd talk to you about it, but that personally, I liked the idea of everything we do being a single-family business where we dump everything into a common bucket and work off the principle of share and share alike."

Share and share alike? Given my lifelong history of autonomy and persistent self-interest, I find the idea novel, almost unimaginable. *Is this what close-knit families really do?*

—◆—

Collie is on his way back from meeting with Edward Epstein to sign the lease for a two-year rental of the Epstein house on Green Lake, with an option to buy.

After the robbery, Edith Epstein proclaimed that she would never set foot in the house again, and Edward was facing a distress sale when Collie said he was interested in renting a fully-furnished lake property. Done deal: Collie's going to pay $4000 a month, option to buy. Cara Spaaks tells him this is crazy high. "I'm okay with it," Colin tells her. "It's not much more than I'm getting each month from the rental of my Savannah house, and pretty soon I will be in much better financial shape. And I really like the house. With three stories and a four-car garage, there will be plenty of space to store...*stuff*."

What a pleasant development for me! Now Christine's going to have a house, Colin's going to have a house, and I will soon have my own beloved house to myself again, not counting Cal, whom I will always cherish. I breathe deeply. Just because we're suddenly a family doesn't mean we all have to stand in the same room.

35

Laundering 101

ALL THE HOUSEHOLD FURNITURE Christine and Delia ordered has now arrived, and the newlyweds are thrilled. Now Christine, Delia and I find ourselves sitting at a magnificent George Nakashima dining room table purchased from Sotheby's, kicking back, watching the August breeze rustle through the trees, talking about all the stuff we're going to buy. Christine runs her finger anxiously down the condensation on her iced tea glass.

"We're all going a little nuts on the spending here, don't you think?" she exclaims in mock exasperation. "What *are* we doing?"

"We're laundering all the money," I say.

Christine looks up at me strangely. "What do you mean, '*all the money?*' What is there besides the gold proceeds?"

I take a deep, deep breath.

Here we go.

"It's time you knew, Christine," I say. "I have talked this over with Collie, and he agrees we shouldn't hide the truth any longer. He said we have to spill the beans and let the chips fall where they may. His mixed metaphor, not mine."

"What in the world are you talking about?"

"Okay. For some time now, since before you and Delia came out here, Collie and I have been fencing various kinds of stolen property. High-end goods. Colin and I don't steal anything, we just buy stolen goods at a discount and then move them downstream to secondary buyers.

"We started slow but then it ramped up, and the enterprise has continued to ramp up. Cash flow was looking pretty decent. And that's the rub. Fences deal in cash. So suddenly we had cash flow, meaning we had an increasing amount of cash on hand, with the prospect of considerably more. So, I had to learn about laundering."

Christine is shaking her head in disbelief. Finally, she erupts. *"Are you nuts?* Why would you two straight-arrow senior citizens turn to a life of crime at this point in your lives?"

"Two answers—at least for me. I'll have to let Colin speak for himself. For me, reason one was that, like you, I unexpectedly became broke. I faced losing my house. It was that simple: retired or not, I needed to find a way to make a considerable amount of money. Fast.

"Reason two was...*because it was exciting.* I was bored, and this was exciting. You may not believe me, but it's true."

Christine gapes at me, first disbelieving, then scornful. Delia, on the other hand, is smiling ear-to-ear. "Too cool," she says. "This is just *too cool.*" She applauds.

"Butt out, Delia!" Christine hisses. "Victor, you owe me an explanation."

"Christine, I don't owe you *anything.* But since you came clean with me about your financial situation, I'll return the favor. But let's keep one important fact in mind. You and Delia have agreed to enter into a criminal enterprise with Colin and me. So, don't get all self-righteous, okay? The impulse of evil lurks within you, dear sister, my dear, dear financially-strapped sister."

She winces.

"Now the part that's not about money. Christine, because you're seven years younger than me, a relative spring chicken, you don't have any idea what it's like to be me right now. *Oh, but wait! Maybe you do!* Over and above your financial pressures, you're a lifelong achiever who's suddenly been forced out to pasture and is pretty angry about it. To be rendered irrelevant and unproductive. Same thing with Collie after the plane crash. The Landings just writes him off. *So sorry. Goodbye.*

"In my case, I can feel my strength and faculties beginning to diminish with age. Here come the first tinges of arthritis—knees, and left thumb—certainly more to come. Time to change the bifocals prescription yet again. Erosion is all around me. I'm finding retirement so painfully tedious that I can hardly summon the energy to get up in the morning. Here I am, staring death in the face.

"And speaking of staring death in the face, Christine, let me presume to speak for your twin brother, because he and I have chewed this fat at length. Collie should be a dead man, and he knows it. He's been in a wreck, and for many months he's been a wreck. Before he and I 'went into business together,' he was totally emotionally immobilized. Mired in PTSD, he suddenly found something he could stand doing: *driving, just driving.* Then, totally by accident, we find a way to give purpose to his driving: *transporting things, valuable things.*"

Christine shakes her head disdainfully. "What do you mean, 'by accident?' It seems to me that taking up a life of crime is no accident."

"Actually, it was. My yard man, Odell Todd, offered to sell me a hot lawn tractor. Big, big discount. Actually, Odie was shilling for Cara's brother, acting as a straw man for Gunnar.

"Now, just buying a hot lawn tractor was not enough to make me feel like a crook. I felt no guilt about that. Then Odie offers to sell me a very valuable stolen motorcycle. A motorcycle whose owner had been murdered by members of Gunnar Spaaks' motorcycle gang. This was not a low-ticket item. We're talking many thousands here. And if I buy it, I'm certainly not going to keep it. Collie and I talked about taking it across state lines to sell it down south. Which, by the way, makes this receipt of stolen property a federal crime, not a minor state offense.

"So how do we get it across the state line? Collie, thoroughly enjoying the joys of driving...*drives it.* Takes it down to Savannah in a van, sells it, nets about six grand. And you know what? Suddenly, he's feeling pretty good. He knows he's now a federal felon, and still he's feeling pretty good. You know what he says when he gets back? *That was exciting.*"

Christine folds her hands in front of her, as if in prayer. Delia pulls her chair in close to me, eager to hear more. Then the door slams, and in walks Colin. He sheds his jacket, takes one look at us, and knows heavy discourse is in progress.

"Hi, Collie," I say, "I was just telling Delia and Christine how we became crooks."

"Oh, that," he says. "Well, don't let me interrupt you."

"Christine, our car transportation service is a perfectly legitimate business. Collie has made some strong contacts among fat cats in the classic car world who need their big-bucks-mobiles moved around the country, and that little enterprise is proving profitable. Plus, Collie gets to see a lot of neat cars, which really floats his boat. I suspect some of the cars he contracts to move are stolen, but we are not really in the business of transporting stolen cars."

Collie punches me on the arm, none too gently.

"We have also, on a couple of occasions, moved whole loads of furniture and antiques we have 'bought at a discount,' but the margins on this stuff are just average. Particularly antiques—the world of antiques is dying fast. We can make a lot more on the right kinds of smaller stuff. Our transportation rig has a secret compartment in it. Nearly invisible, but big enough to hold, say, furs or various kinds of artwork. Or a whole lot of jewels."

Delia's eyes open wide.

Christine's don't. Her eyes are squeezed tightly shut.

"Hey, I know some people," Delia interjects. "I think I have some interesting contacts in galleries and museums. And we jewelry people are always joking about honor among thieves. There is a lot of grime and crime in the high-end art world, yes sir."

I have to laugh at how readily Delia climbs on board the crime train. "I'll thank you to hold your interruptions, young lady. I am giving my laundering lecture, here. I've studied up on this, so you have to let me show off.

"Laundering is basically a three-part process: *placement, layering, and integration.* Dirty money can't be considered 'clean' until the last step is completed. Placement is trying to slip ill-gotten cash somewhere into the financial food chain. For a lot of fences, the placement of illegal cash means making lots of relatively small bank deposits over time, usually in multiple accounts. This is known as 'smurfing,' and it's a time-consuming pain in the ass.

"If you are somehow able to get your money *placed* someplace—bank, S&L, credit union, investment account, mutual fund—the next phase, '*layering,*' involves shifting your bucks around through a series of transactions designed to create confusion and complicate the paper trail for regulators or investigators. For small fry like Collie and me— and now for all of *us*—the easiest layering technique is high-dollar purchases of tangible goods. Things like yachts, luxury cars, fine art, and George Nakashima dining tables. A large smelting furnace. Or commodities like...*gold*. Oh, but wait! We've already got the gold!"

I can't help myself. I crack up.

"At the final *integration* stage, the laundered funds have become legitimate. Integration is low risk, because it involves perfectly legal transactions—things like selling or transferring high-dollar items purchased with laundered funds, selling real estate purchased with laundered funds, or legitimate purchases of securities and investment instruments. The idea is to hold on to such assets for a while, then resell them and collect a nice squeaky-clean check. And Bingo! You're done."

I pause to see if everyone is following me. Everyone is.

"So, one idea Collie and I have talked about is to start up a perfectly legitimate business and mix our hot dollars in with honest-injun dollars in operating the enterprise. Warehousing and specialty storage are a natural complement to our specialty auto transportation services. Collie is thinking about starting a business where fat-cat car owners could store their precious classics and trailer-queens discreetly and safely. And if the occasional stolen vehicle cooled its hot heels in such a secure venue for a while, why who's to know? Who's to care?"

Christine's head is bowed, and I can't tell if she's on board or not. She looks up, and I see storm clouds.

"I think you're going to end up in jail," Christine says.

"Entirely possible," I say. "I've thought about that, and I'm prepared to pay the piper if need be. But here's the thing: the law does not regard receiving stolen property as being as heinous as *stealing* the property. If we get nailed, even on a big-ticket deal, we probably don't get more than eighteen to twenty-four months. If it's a federal case, you get a low-security federal prison, which is tolerable, if not exactly pleasant.

"Sheriff Gilbert Rennie has recently taken down a couple of high-volume local fencing operations, but he's getting no cooperation from the fences whatsoever. Why? Because they have little to gain by revealing their upstream suppliers and downstream customers."

I nod toward Colin.

"If we are nailed, I think Collie would walk with probation. I fall on the sword, swear he's an unwitting accomplice. He pleads duress, PTSD, the whole tear-jerking works. Christine, I see no risk for you and Delia on our earlier fencing activity. You weren't in on it, didn't know about it, have no legal obligation to inform authorities now that you do know about it.

"And the Bugsy bars? I think that's a probation case if we ever get found out—which I find unlikely. Maybe a fine, maybe some restitution to the insurance company, but I can't see any prosecutor being hot to make a name for himself by taking down a world-renowned celebrity. *Which you are, Delia.* Just ask Martha Stewart. She came out of her... problems with hardly a scar. Even after a hefty fine, we'd still have a lot of money."

I lean back in my chair and put my hands behind my head, trying to make it look like I am nonchalant. "And finally, ladies, I bear glad tidings. Collie and I have decided to climb down from the high wire. We are cutting way back on—if not entirely bailing out of—interstate transportation of stolen property. Collie's PTSD seems a lot better these days, and he doesn't relish driving therapy as much as he used to, although he still loves to rub elbows with all those rich classic car dudes."

Collie flips me the bird, heads for the kitchen. He returns popping the top of a cold Heineken longneck. No PBR—the Pabst Blue Ribbon brew favored by the proletariat—for the golf pro used to having other people buy him rounds. "You make this all sound so clean and neat, big brother. Let me ask you a question that's important to me, in particular."

"Shoot," I say.

"Do we tell Cara? Or, more precisely, *what* do we tell Cara?"

"Yeah, we should discuss that," I say. "Ladies, Cara's brother Gunnar has been our primary conduit for stolen goods. He makes a lot of the referrals. Collie or I get a call from some perp, we arrange the drop and pickup with them, they tender the cash. I'm sure a cut goes back to Gunnar, and I bet he knows about every burglary, robbery, or theft that takes place in the three-county area.

"Therefore, we have an interesting Mexican stand-off. Gunnar and I could rat each other out, but I must say that if the whole shitstorm blew up, Gunnar would come out a lot worse than I would. As I said, I think he's got at least one situation—the dead motorcyclist—where Rennie could pin felony murder on him."

I lean forward, place my hands on my knees, speak very slowly.

"Gunnar is a...very smart guy. And he's also a very nasty guy. He's not above hurting people, including his own sister, who cross him or get in his way. So, Colin, I think you must *absolutely* not involve her in receiving stolen property. You gotta keep her in the dark about the fencing stuff. She needs deniability, deserves to be kept out of our...*thing.*"

Again, I have to snicker, because 'our thing' is the term the Mafia uses to describe their whole network of criminal activities.

"But my opinion is that just by being around us, Delia, and Delia's business, Cara is bound to sniff out the whole story about Bugsy's bars. She knows about the legend of Bugsy's tunnel, and if we show up with a large, unexplained supply of gold, I think she is likely to put two and two together. But we do *not* want to expose her to legal jeopardy. I think that for Cara, the best tactic is to take a page from the US Army's policy about homosexuality: 'Don't ask, don't tell.'

"One last thing, though, Collie. I have a hunch that Cara, who, as you know, does not hold her brother in great esteem, may be into a little vigilante justice. I think she's the one who tipped Gilbert Rennie about the Epstein heist by leaving him the famed orange Day-Glo sticky note. And just how did *she* learn about the Epstein heist? I'll bet Dany Miskinis leaked a bit of pillow talk Gunnar disclosed to her during one of their amorous interludes.

"If Cara did tip off Gilbert Rennie, it was very brave, but also very unwise. She not only put herself at risk, she sure as hell put Dany at risk. So, Collie, I really need to see every one of those cute little orange Day-Glo sticky notes Cara's always writing you. As a matter of fact, I want you to tell her to stop using them altogether. If she asks why, say you hate the stupid color."

I stand, take Collie's Heineken from his hand and take a deep slug. I mimic Forrest Gump's guttural singsong. "And that's all I have to say about *that*."

36

All About Wadcutters

HOW COULD WE HAVE BEEN SO WRONG? So naïve? So cavalier? So unbelievably stupid? I can't speak for Colin, but in hindsight, I am astonished at my dreadful lack of judgment. Collie's and my sophistic denial about threats and risks nearly cost my brother's life. Two near-death events within six months—how I wish I could have spared Colin this tragedy!

They won't let visitors—even family—in to see Colin until two days after the shooting. Green Lake's Grace Cottage Hospital issues a bulletin saying that Colin Harding is awake, alert, and expected to survive. Still, out of an abundance of caution, they are going to keep him in the intensive care unit—a single room tucked back behind the nurse's station in the rear of the hospital—for a few days and keep him isolated.

Maybe they don't want to risk moving him to Ripon Hospital because he's so badly hurt, or maybe they think he doesn't need to be moved to Ripon Hospital because he's not all that badly hurt. Personally, I think they're afraid another attempt will be made on Colin's life, and they think it's best to lock him in a nice, isolated room for his own safety.

The hospital—or Sheriff Gilbert Rennie—isn't taking any chances. When they finally downgrade Collie to a regular room, I am the first to display my driver's license, sign in at the nurse's station, and surrender my mobile phone to the charge nurse. Deputy Sheriff Lee Ruliscz, an affable blond giant of a man, is sitting in a chair outside Colin's room, talking quietly with Cara Spaaks. I give Lee a nod, which he returns politely, and give Cara a hug.

"How is he?"

"How *is* he? *How is he?*" Cara says, her voice hoarse and strained. "He looks like Frankenstein, that's how he is."

I knock on the door jamb and step in. Someone is propped up in the bed, but if the figure hadn't been wearing a lime green golf shirt that Collie can't bring himself to throw away, I could not have guessed his identity. I can't see the right side of his face, but the left side looks like ground hamburger. Three swollen bloody welts traverse his cheek, one starting at the corner of his mouth and disappearing behind his ear, a second starting along the base of his chin and making an angry scabbed track up into his hairline, and the third beginning where Colin's eyebrow used to be and tracing a shallow groove until it intersects the second wound, which looks like a mole has dug a tunnel across Colin Harding's face. Caked blood oozes from each wound's entry point. My brother turns toward me, and I see that the right side of Collie's face still looks like Collie. Taken in profile, he remains a strikingly handsome man. Looked at from the left side, he's a horror.

"Sorry they wouldn't let you in before, Victor. I asked over and over again. They weren't going to let anyone near me, including immediate family. So much for mid-Wisconsin warmth and hospitality."

"Hurt a lot?" I ask.

Collie has a slushy lisp, but I can understand him well enough. "Surprisingly not. Most of the damage is on the outer layers of tissue, and the underlying flesh was not too badly damaged. Whole side of my face is stiff as a board, though. Lots of nerve damage, maybe that's why it doesn't hurt more. May get better, may not."

"How come you're not all bandaged up? From what Gilbert told me on the phone, I expected you to look like the mummy."

"They want to keep the wounds open and 'breathing.' Say there will be less scarring if we let the air do the healing. They're keeping a ton of ointment on the sites, though. And they keep siphoning out the pus. *That's* a real trip."

Usually, I can read Colin like a book. At this moment, I simply can't read him at all, can't tell if he's relieved, or angry, or frightened, or what. He just sits there, his hands resting on the coverlet.

"Better if we skip the small talk?" I ask.

"No, no, it's okay. I don't mind shootin' the breeze for a bit. Nothing else to do at the moment."

"I don't know what question to ask first, *what the hell happened?* or *why aren't you dead?*"

Now Collie tries to smile, but he winces. The effect is not pleasing. "Attempted assassination," he lisps. "About midnight on Sunday night, I had just parked the Allmire rig back at his barn and climbed into your Bimmer. Tap-tap on the window. Somebody's backlit by the halon light on Allmire's house. I can't see who it is or what he looks like. I roll down the window. Before I can even turn my head, I hear three shots, feel three hits, take three shots square in the chops at point-blank range. Man, that's an experience I don't ever want to have again. All I can tell you is that it's.... *shocking.*"

I feel my jaw drop, my eyes widen. Collie keeps talking.

"As I sit there, feeling blood spurting all over my face, I should be surprised that I am alive, but what I really am is amazed that *I'm conscious*. I scooch over to the passenger's side and manage to get the door open, flop out on the driveway. I find that I've got a voice, and I'm yellin' and screamin' for help. Corrinne Allmire rushes out the front door, takes one look and rushes back to get a towel, which she wraps tight around my face, tells me shush-shush, tells me everything's gonna be okay. The rest, as they say, is history. All the right people did their jobs, and here I am at luxurious Grace Cottage."

I can't make sense of all this, particularly the fact that my brother is not dead. "But...but...what...I mean...Was it a pellet gun, or a .22, or what?"

"Victor, I was shot three times in the face at point-blank range with a thirty-eight-caliber revolver." Collie sounds almost proud.

"Holy mackerel!" I exclaim. "I can't believe you're alive!"

"Well, I had the benefit of a little bit of luck," says Collie.

"Yeah, I'd say just a *bit.*"

"No, wait, Victor. Turns out there's a good story here. Gilbert tells me that last week a guy named Danny Mooney from over in Black Earth reports that his brand-new Chevy Silverado pickup has been stolen. Also, two hundred in cash and also his brand-new Smith & Wesson thirty-eight caliber revolver. Said he'd fired it exactly once since he bought it.

"Day after the shooting, Lee Ruliscz calls up Mooney and asks him for any details about the gun. Mooney says he'd been up at his hunting camp on Cable Lake and had squeezed off a few shots at a tree, just to see what the gun felt like. Then he stashed it back in the truck's glove compartment. Lee drives Mooney up to the camp and they look around for the tree. *And they find it!* With three nice round holes in it. Lee digs out the slugs with his buck knife, sends 'em out to the FBI for ballistics."

I sit down on the chair next to the bed. "But that doesn't explain why that thirty-eight didn't kill you."

"Oh, but it does," says Collie. "Gilbert tells me ballistics solved that little mystery, too. Victor, do you know what a wadcutter is?"

"I don't do guns, Collie, you know that." A mental picture of Bugsy's Thompson submachine guns flashes through my mind.

"Gilbert says a wadcutter is a type of bullet that is used only for practice on target ranges. It doesn't have a big, rounded lead tip, like most rounds. It's cut off flush with the end of the casing, just has a light, flat head. That way the bullet makes a nice, clean round hole when it cuts through a paper target. It takes a lot of the impact away from the round, but you don't need impact when you're just poppin' holes in targets at the range."

"I bet I know where this is going," I say.

"Sho'nuff," snorts Collie. "Gilbert calls up Mooney, and asks him what loads he'd put in his new pistol. You know the answer. Whoever stole the revolver saw that it was loaded, but never checked to see what it was loaded *with*. If that gun had been loaded with regular thirty-eights or hollow points, my face would have been totally blown away. But in this case, each round simply hit me in the cheek, burrowed under the skin without smashing into my skull, and then tunneled around to the back of my head, where it exited and fell, energy spent, into the passenger's footwell. Lee found all three rounds, just lying there in plain sight. Gilbert tells me a second set of ballistics came back this morning. 'Course we got a match with Mooney's tree bullets.

"Yup, when I catch the son-of-a-bitch who tried to kill me, I really must thank him for his stupidity. Just before I rip his face off."

37

An Incredibly Stupid Felon

AUTUMN IS UPON US, and Colin is home at the Epstein house. He has requested that I not visit for a while as he heals. It's a painful request, but I understand. Now that it's time to see him, I find him sitting on the back deck winding a fresh spool of fishing line on his spinning rod. He does not stand or turn to greet me, but rather reaches over his shoulder to take my hand.

"Glad you're here," he says. "Good to see you."

"Glad you're here to be seen," I say. "Every day I say, 'I'm glad Colin's alive' to myself, and I mean it."

"We sure blew it, bro. There's too much trust in this family. Too much stupidity."

"Amen to that."

Now he turns to face me, and I'm sure he sees me recoil. The left side of his face looks like a drunken horror movie makeup artist had a psychotic break. The whole left side of Collie's face is flushed a deep red, and two angry swollen welts trace gopher tunnels across his face. Between them is a track of incredibly small stitches, forming a neat seam from the corner of his mouth to the base of his ear. Frankenstein by way of Savile Row.

"Two hundred and seventy-four," says Collie.

"Two hundred and seventy-four what?" I ask.

"Two hundred and seventy-four stitches. Big deal plastic surgeon came down from Minneapolis. Spent the better part of a day on fine embroidery, also spent a lot of time on the muscle and tissue under the skin."

I lean across the table to look closely at the fine, even sutures. "Guy's an artist," I say.

"Kind of you to say so, Victor, and I certainly agree, although I suspect my face modeling days are through. The good part is that it seems he's preserved enough nerve function to allow me some facial expression. The scar will eventually turn white, so will the other welts, so I won't go through life looking like I'm wearing a rigid death mask. Not handsome, but at least I won't scare small children as I walk around town."

"Cara?"

"She's cool. I mean good cool, not chilly. Attentive, but not smothering, you know. I think I'm beginning to love that woman. And she's talked to Gunnar."

"I bet that was an interesting conversation."

"He swears he didn't do it, didn't plan it, or put someone else up to it. Told Cara he'd never be that stupid, knows that killing me wouldn't accomplish anything."

"Does she believe him?"

"She does. Says she knows his truth face. Says he had it on."

"Do you believe her?"

"I do. For the record, so does Gilbert Rennie. He had a serious talk with Gunnar at the station. Gunnar offered to take a polygraph. Said he couldn't guarantee that someone in Semper didn't do the hit, but he didn't know about it beforehand. Said he would have stopped it if he heard about it. If he suspects someone in particular, well, *that* he ain't sharing with our beloved sheriff."

There's a long pause.

"Well, we both know who it is," I say.

"Yes, we sure do," whispers Collie. "Wonder if my taser shots left any scars."

———

I have not seen Sheriff Rennie in the six weeks since the shooting. So I'm pleased when Deputy Sheriff Lee Ruliscz calls to tell me that Gilbert would like to renew our lunches.

At Morton's, Gilbert stands to greet me, extends his hand. Somehow, he looks...*different.* Guarded, a deep furrow between his eyes I'd never noticed before.

We order lunch, I order a martini, and, in a novel twist, Gilbert orders Jameson's, neat.

"Collie?"

"Getting better, but his face still looks like he was put through a meat grinder. Any progress on the investigation?"

"Yeah, there's certainly new information, but I'm not quite sure what it tells me. And I'm not sure it's appropriate to tell you."

"Stop playing games with me, Gilbert. This is my brother we're talking about here."

Gilbert reaches under the table and then carefully places a hefty hunk of something wrapped in a terry towel on the table. When he unwraps the towel and I see the object in a plastic evidence bag, it's clear what he's got.

"Guess," he says.

"I'm betting that's the gun that shot my brother."

"Pick it up, it's okay as long as it stays in the plastic bag. Look at the back of the cylinder. What do you see?"

"Only one bullet."

"Yes. This is a Smith & Wesson Airweight .38 caliber revolver. Holds five rounds. Three were used to try to kill Colin, and they used another for a ballistics test. That leaves one. Now, without shooting yourself in the face, turn the pistol around and look at the tip of the remaining bullet."

"It's flat."

"Yep. That's what makes it a target range wadcutter. That's what saved Colin's life."

"Wow. And just how did you get this thing?"

"FedEx."

"Beg pardon?"

"Delivered to the office Monday afternoon in a nice purple and orange box."

"Surely you jest."

"Nope. Return address said, 'Frontier Justice,' with a street address in Neenah. There is no such entity and no such street."

"I don't get it. Who...how..."?

"Well, it's clear to *me*, Victor. Some insider—although I could not tell you inside of *what*—liberated it, wanted me to have it, wanted to cover his own tracks, make sure he's not in the line of fire, if you'll forgive the pun. And that means that at some point, some other insider is going to be very, very pissed. Some well-intentioned—or at least self-serving— soul is playin' with fire here. *Really, really playin' with fire.* Or perhaps someone is just really screwing around with our heads. Who knows?"

Gilbert raises his hand and waves.

"Brianna, I'd like another Jameson's, please. And give Mr. Harding another of whatever he's drinking."

"Well, this is all pretty hard to believe," I say.

Gilbert tips his chair back against the wall, crosses his arms across his chest. Exhales and shakes his head. "Yeah, well, that ain't all."

I say nothing, just make my patented gimme-gimme gesture with my hands.

"What's the first thing you suppose we did with this pistol, detective Harding?"

"Ran prints."

Gilbert smiles. You can tell that he's delighted with himself. Also with me.

"Very good! You've learned something from our relationship. And just what did we find?"

"Prints."

"Yep. Clear as a bell—right hand. Index, middle, ring finger. Wanna guess?"

"Gunnar Spaaks."

"Nope."

"Kerry Crouch."

"Nope, though that little weasel was certainly a candidate in my mind."

"C'mon, Gilbert, stop jerking me around. Cara Spaaks. Dany Miskinis. Clarence Causley. That fence guy in Vermont."

"Nope, nope, nope, and nope."

"*Gilbert!*"

"Odell Todd."

My heart sinks. "Oh, no. *Can't be.* He's long gone."

"*Definitely* Odell Todd's prints. Right there on the pistol grip. Clear as on a booking fingerprint card."

Now Gilbert drums his fingers on the edge of his tumbler. Raises his eyebrows.

"Only something's a little screwy, something doesn't add up."

I make another gimme gesture.

"Well, when you're right-handed and you grip a pistol, the index finger's on the top, right? On the trigger guard and trigger. Then the middle, then the print of the ring finger on the bottom, usually a little lighter or blurred. Sometimes a thumb partial on the top, sometimes not. In this case, not."

"Okay...."

"Well on our .38, *the print of the ring finger is on top.* Then the middle, o' course, and the index finger's the bottom print. The only way to make that happen, Victor, is to grip the gun upside down. Not very likely, eh?"

"*Oh, come on!*" I snort.

"I kid you not," says Gilbert simply.

In a stunning flash, I realize what this means. "So Odell Todd was not holding the gun! Someone else rolled his hand on to the grip and was too stupid to realize they were doing it backwards."

"You, Mr. Harding, are a deductive genius, and I applaud you. 'Cept I think you got it wrong."

"How so?"

"My theory is that someone cut Odell Todd's fingers off and got 'em mixed up when they were planting his prints on the pistol. The prints are very distinct, very uniform pressure. That's not the way it happens in real life. Also, spacing is not right for someone actually gripping a gun. I grant you this is very bizarre, Victor, but I'm pretty sure this is what happened."

Now Gilbert looks straight at me, and there is a curious muscular tension in his features. "Look, Victor, maybe I'm belaboring the obvious here, I have to say something very serious to you."

For once, I do not play it cute. He's leveling with me, and I owe it to him to listen up.

"I'm way off the reservation here, Victor. There's no way in the world I should be showing you this gun, sharing all this intel with you. I'm doing it because I value your judgment, your input, and also because I respect what you're going through with your brother.

"But Victor, no one else knows about the crossed-up fingerprints except my deputy, Lee Ruliscz. None of the other deputies know, Brianna does not know. Those prints are a huge tell, the kind of clue that can really break a case, get a perp to trip himself up big time. So, I *absolutely* cannot let word get out that there is an incredibly stupid felon out there. Are we clear on this?"

"Gilbert, you have made yourself completely clear. And I want you to know that I respect your trust."

38

Several Short Stories

I STEP OUT OF THE PIGGLY WIGGLY with my arms full of groceries and hear a shout. I look around the parking lot and see nothing but the blazing oranges and yellows of autumn foliage serving as a brightly colored backdrop to the blinding glint of the sun off a silver Ford F150 pickup truck. The driver's window winds down. "Hey, Victor!" the shout comes again. "Like it?"

It's Delia. She's wearing a white caftan, a bewitching contrast with her milk chocolate skin. Sunglasses perched on her forehead, she looks like she's on her way to a photo shoot.

"Like it? It's mine! Does this make me an official Local? Now will people stop treating me like I've arrived from some alien planet?"

"Where's the Maybach?"

"I laundered it!" she shouts loudly, here in the middle of the Piggly Wiggly parking lot, and laughs uproariously. "And I got Christine some laundry, too!"

I walk over and plop my groceries on the front fender, pull on my sunglasses to subdue the glare off the dazzling silver Ford.

"Enlighten me," I say.

"The Maybach was a real sweet ride and all, but it just too much for Green Lake, you know? Too big, too opulent, too pretentious. In New York it was fine, but around here, I'm sure people were thinking that this darkie is putting on airs. So, I decided to get rid of it."

"Trade it?" I ask.

"*Hell, no,*" Delia squeals. "You think I didn't learn anything from your laundering lecture? I sold it for *cash*, used the cash to buy myself and Christine some new wheels that are less conspicuous. More in keeping with our new station in life as solid Wisconsin citizens."

"Well, *this* is pretty conspicuous," I say, sweeping my arm over the Ford. "Crew cab, King Ranch trim package, chrome wheels, looks like all the bells and whistles. Not exactly creeping along under the radar, Delia."

"Well, it's *used*. It's not like I went out and bought a *new* car. Forty-four thousand miles, forty-four thousand dollars. Sales guy told me that was a good price. Was that a good price, Victor?"

"It's okay, but not great."

"Good, I want that Local to think he put one over on the uppity New York nigger. Give 'em an easy win."

"They really don't use the 'N' word around here much in polite conversation, Delia. The Locals are superficially benign racists, polite and cordial to everybody, usually trotting out the 'N' word only among themselves, when they're fretting about 'replacement theory.'"

"Replacement theory?"

"Yeah, the dreadful notion that the white majority in this country is going to be overrun and replaced by various people of various colors. Rural racism is not benign, Delia, it just speaks with a softer accent than the big-city brand. Now the Vandals? *Far more hypocritical.* Talk a good show about diversity and opportunity for the blacks and browns, while keeping their feet firmly wedged against the door. I'm sure you've seen that version in action."

"So far, I really haven't seen either, thank heavens."

"Stay tuned. And watch your back. With your skin tone and your evident wealth, you're bound to incite some strong feelings among both Locals and Vandals. Vilma's right: there *are* a lot of right-minded folks around here. But I also must say that there are a lot of wrong-thinkers, too. Green Lake is as capable of being small and mean as any small town in the deep south. I've been around here long enough to see it in action."

Delia shook her head. "I think you're exaggerating for effect, Victor."

"I sure hope so, Delia, I sure hope so. Anyway, who bought the Maybach?"

"Some old lawyer guy Christine knows named Satuka. You know him?"

"Stan Satuka?" I laugh. "Stan has been driving the same Chevy Impala forever! He must be eighty years old, and his Impala must be a thousand years old. Not exactly your average Maybach guy."

"Well, that dowdy image was his wife speaking. He says she wouldn't ever let him get a new car. But she died from a stroke last spring, and Stan said he wanted to enjoy some real luxury before he croaked, too."

"I can certainly understand that. So, how much did he pay you for it?"

"Well, I said, 'Stan, it's a 2014 Maybach S600, 14,300 miles, asking price one hundred and twelve thousand.' Stan laughs and says, 'Can we bargain? I was hoping to stay under a hundred grand.' And I say, 'Well, I want to make friends here in Green Lake, so ninety-seven-five will take it, but I don't take personal checks.' So now you'll be seeing Stan Satuka at

Tuscumbia Country Club, climbing out of his Maybach with a smug grin on his face."

"Sounds likely," I say. "You said you bought Christine some wheels?"

"Brand new Subaru Outback station wagon, forest green, black leather, sound system upgrade. She absolutely *loves* it. Drives nice. I said she could drive my pickup sometimes, too."

"What do loaded Subarus cost?"

"This one cost thirty-seven-nine, plus tax and tags."

Delia reaches into her pocketbook and pulls out a think roll of bills wrapped in a red rubber band. "So, here's what was left over, Victor. Fifteen grand in hundreds. A gift from my late father, so to speak. To us all. So, I'm gonna let you hold it as sort of a Harding family cash kitty we can all dip into for petty expenses. But before you stick it in a drawer somewhere, maybe you want to break all those C-notes into fifties and twenties, right? You know, laundering best practices?" She breaks into a delighted giggle.

"You are one sharp broad," I say, squeezing her on the cheek.

"Well, I was afraid of getting taken to the cleaners, but instead I took the Maybach to the laundry. I'm feeling pretty proud of myself, Sherlock. *Crime on!*"

———∿∿∿———

Delia Batek Chamberlain, Christine Maston Harding, and Cara Wirtinnen Spaaks are written up in the *Green Lake Citizen,* the *Oshkosh Daily Northwestern,* and the *Milwaukee Journal Sentinel* in a story about their ambitious new not-for-profit artistic enterprise in mid-state Wisconsin, the Xenophon Stakhatos Artists' Alliance and School. "The school will be resolutely inclusive," Delia Chamberlain is quoted as saying, "but we will place particular emphasis on BIPOC artists—meaning Black, Indian, and People of Color."

The articles say that start-up funding was provided by Vilma Stakhatos, Delia Chamberlain, Colin Harding, Victor Harding, and Stanley Satuka, with a generous twenty thousand dollars annual endowment from the Ripon College Department of Art. The XZAAS (which will come to be known informally as just the Alliance) is going to be managed by Cara Spaaks, with studios at Chateau Phone Home overlooking Green Lake and four classrooms at Harding Lodge, the private lakeside residence of Colin Harding on South Lake Road. Appropriate zoning variances have been easily secured. Colin Harding, whose brother is the retired architect Victor Harding, will live on the school's third floor at Harding Lodge and act as chaperone for younger students. Victor Harding is expected to teach design and architecture seminars at the school.

The articles say the Alliance will split its efforts between organizing exhibition opportunities for diverse artists from all around the state of Wisconsin and sponsoring intensive short seminars and workshops at Harding Lodge. Exhibition space will be free, tuition at the workshops will be free, and lodging at Harding Lodge will be twenty-five dollars a night. World-renowned goldsmith Delia Chamberlain predicts a strong reception and proud future for the Alliance. "In some quarters," she is quoted as saying in a prepared statement, "Green Lake has an unjust reputation for being indifferent to artists generally and particularly inhospitable to artists of color. We believe that, on a modest scale, the Alliance will open some doors and open some eyes. Each year, the Alliance will award the Xenophon Stakhatos Legacy Grant to a deserving young artist, regardless of the medium in which he or she works—painting, sculpture, weaving, pottery, smithing, glassblowing, or jewelry."

—⁄∿∕—

Colin and I fly down two-lane country roads at excessive speed in my newly-repaired BMW, Collie driving and me enjoying the scenery, until the sign for Janesville comes up on the right.

"There 'tis," says Collie.

A large beige warehouse sits all by its lonesome in the middle of a huge empty parking lot. Good condition, grass neatly mowed. In the front, it has one small metal door, flanked by a single casement window. No signage anywhere except for a small plaque I can't read from this distance. The faint outline of four-foot letters, now removed but leaving their shadow on the front of the warehouse, says *CoverDale Products, Inc.*

Colin smiles at me like the fox in the henhouse. "Like it? They used to make bedspreads here. Now, wait'll you see this," he says in an excited stage whisper. He drives past the front door, and now I can read the plaque: *Harding Specialty Services.* No phone number, just an anonymized email address. He drives around back, where the only opening is an imposing thirty-foot wide overhead door. I can see that the door has been reinforced with extra steel plates along the sides and bottom. Collie reaches into the BMW's console, pulls out an industrial-sized remote and punches the red button. The door rumbles upward, and I am floored.

The inside of the warehouse is about thirty yards square. It is brightly lit with huge fluorescent fixtures, the floor is highly polished cement, and the whine of industrial dehumidifiers fills the air. My eyes recoil from the jolt of a crazy quilt of color, the kaleidoscopic color of cars, scores of cars, lined up wall-to-wall and floor-to-ceiling. I'm sure I gasp.

"Surprised?" says Colin.

I am, but then again, I'm not. Colin and I have discussed this enterprise, discussed where it should be located, how big it should be, how to finance its operation, how to arrange for ample security, and how to reach out to its particular clientele. All of these are privately-owned automobiles. While at any particular time one or two of them may be hot, our storage facility is not a steal-and-flip enterprise. It's a legit money-laundering machine. It is just what it seems: a very nice climate-controlled garage where astronomically expensive playthings are stored and coddled.

I know these car people. I used to be one. I spent decades as a hardcore car geek, rolling through countless impulsive automotive purchases and memorizing all the monthly car magazines about sports cars, classic cars, and racing cars. I loved cars, I knew cars, and I enjoyed knowing how much my hobby pissed Magda off. "Silly macho stuff," she'd scoff. "Overcompensation for phallic insufficiency. What in the world is the point of racing an automobile?"

Every time she said that, I'd make some withering remark about archeology and then go off and buy a new vehicle with a hundred more horsepower than my current mount.

Before me today, I see exotic cars arranged in neat rows, one row on the main floor and another row above it on shiny black lifts. Some are covered, but most are not, and the reflections off the impeccably polished paint jobs send a myriad of little stars dancing across the floor and walls.

Looking out over this collection of metal, I try some quick math. There are probably sixty cars in the warehouse, each valued between fifty-thousand and perhaps four million dollars. Let's say an average of, perhaps, two hundred thousand bucks. That means sitting in front of me is about twelve million dollars of collectible metal. More to the point, if each owner is paying us six hundred dollars in monthly rent, that means we are taking thirty-six grand to the bank every month. Plus, of course, a few of those bank deposits may derive from other sources of Harding income.

Collie and I have met with Carl Boynton, the president of the Farmers and Merchants Bank in downtown Janesville, explained the operation of our warehouse enterprise, explained why many owners prefer to pay their monthly rent to us in cash, and why many of our deposits therefore will contain a lot of cash. FMB also has lent us the money for warehouse renovation, the build-out of a small, comfortably furnished apartment at the front of the warehouse, and all those shiny black lifts. We're into the bank for two hundred and forty grand, which we are paying off in a convenient—*very convenient for us*—installment loan. Collie and I call it our "WELOC," for "warehouse equity line of credit." We don't own the warehouse, of course; we're renters. We arrange for FMB to remit our rent payment to the warehouse's owner automatically every month. Easy as pie.

Next to a classic Aston Martin race car stands an edgy-looking young man shifting his weight from one foot to the other. He is buff, clean-shaven, dressed in a starched white short-sleeved shirt, wearing pressed marine fatigue trousers and combat boots. He's holding a shotgun. A Malinois—sort of a Belgian version of a German shepherd—sits quietly but vigilantly by his side.

"Victor," Collie says brightly, "this is Seth Bartlett, our on-site representative and security officer. He and Keno here—*the dog lifts his head at his name*—live in the apartment up front twenty-four-seven, guard the cars, take orders for washing, waxing and detailing, and generally make sure that things stay shipshape...and stay below the radar."

Seth does not move to shake hands, and his arms remain crossed over the shotgun held tightly to his chest. His head keeps darting with side-to-side tics, as if making eye contact would be painful. "I'm sure you recognize the symptoms of PTSD, Victor," Collie says. "It's okay to talk about it. Seth knows I have PTSD, knows that's why I went to the VA to source candidates for this job. Seth did an excellent job in Special Forces during two tours in Afghanistan, and he's doing an excellent job for me here in Janesville. Doesn't talk much, but he's loyal to a fault."

Bartlett looks up and offers a fleeting smile. Otherwise, his face is a mask. The blinds are drawn, and there's a ghost in there. The effect is truly eerie.

As we drive back toward Green Lake, I proffer praise. "I'm amazed that you could find a suitable place, make all the arrangements for build-out and find customers in such a short time, Colin. You, brother, really are quite the businessman"—*here I laugh*—"and also quite the money launderer. I hope it's not condescending of me to say so, I am genuinely proud of you, brother. Tell me, how did you fill the place up so fast?"

Colin shakes his head, projecting amazement. "You wouldn't believe the car freak network, Victor, how fast word travels. We must have tapped a very pressing need or very hot market, because our warehouse filled entirely because of word-of-mouth. I made, maybe, twenty calls to my car show clients. After that, it was just a matter of answering the phone. Bingo. Place is filled. Got a waiting list."

—∿∿—

The young dark-skinned woman is heavy, but carries herself with an easy grace, an air of self-confidence. She's going to need it, because here in Egg Harbor, she stands out like a sore Sri Lankan. There is an ample supply of heavy women in Door County, Wisconsin, but precious few people of color. Standing in the doorway of our shop, she's dressed in a dark blue sari with gold trim. Around us, tourists pad by in puffy coats, scruffy vests, and Timberland shoes, pushing strollers and lugging shopping bags. Many turn and stare at this exotic young woman.

"Victor," says Delia, "let me introduce Chaturi Chithkala, an émigré from Sri Lanka and now my protégé. While she schools with me, she's going to run the store for us here in Egg Harbor, although you're going to be seeing a lot of her over at the Alliance, too. Until recently, she was a weaver, but now I'm going to teach her gold. The world will soon have another irreverent Sri Lankan goldsmith."

Chaturi dips her head slightly in deference to my status both as an elder and as her boss. Her smile is every bit as radiant as Delia's. Her voice is sing-song and silky, lightly accented. "May I call you Victor? Delia tells me you are working quite hard to become an informal person, and I would like to contribute in any way I can."

Delia laughs. "Victor, in Sinhala, Chaturi means 'clever.' And Chithkala means something like 'possessor of knowledge.' Roughly translated, her name means, 'I'm a real smart ass.' You're going to discover that she is very aptly named."

Chaturi grasps the sides of her sari and performs a deep British curtsey. The effect is hilariously incongruous. "At your service," she smiles.

Our shop, here in the heart of Door County, is called *D'Or County*. Until recently it traded as Weavers' World and sold Icelandic sweaters and Irish scarves. The recent demise of the woolens store left a slender storefront open on Egg Harbor's main drag into which we slid with our checkbook and our *plan*. Our plan was to insert a clever little money-laundering enterprise catering both to walk-in traffic and an exclusive clientele which on occasion we would spirit in through the back door.

Door County comprises the upper part of a large peninsula sticking out from eastern Wisconsin into Lake Michigan like a thumb. It starts affluent in Sturgeon Bay and gets wealthier—and ever whiter—as you head north to Sister

Bay, Fish Creek, Ephraim, and Bailey's Harbor. Our little shop is in Egg Harbor, which Budget Travel once voted "One of the Ten Coolest Towns in the U.S." Door County pitches itself as a haven for the arts as well as for its scenic beauty, and year-round tourist traffic keeps the local playhouses, boutiques, galleries, bed-and-breakfasts, and pretentious but invariably mediocre restaurants busy.

Chaturi will open the D'Or County boutique each Wednesday through Sunday, ten o'clock 'til nine, and sell horrendously overpriced solid-gold heart-shaped charms, trinkets, key chains, and other tchotchkes, each bearing the elegant *Coeur D'Or* logo of world-renowned goldsmith Delia Chamberlain, to the sucker-bait tourist trade. No jewelry, nothing that can be passed off as a genuine hand-crafted Delia. For those who do not speak French but still carry high-limit MasterCards, a large 24 karat plaque has been placed on the wall that says, "Honor Your Loved One with a *Heart of Gold*."

At the high-profit end of the enterprise, by appointment only, Delia Chamberlain will court prospects for commissioned jewelry pieces in the small, expensively furnished salon in the back of the store that overlooks the harbor. Qualified buyers will be flown up from Chicago or Milwaukee by chartered helicopter, first to Chateau Phone Home to see the atelier, then over to Egg Harbor. After serious discussions about shape, size and cost, Delia will walk the prospect over to a small private dining room in Parador, the local tapas restaurant. There, in a private dining room, a private chef we've retained will provide a meal unlike anything ever seen by any diner who ever walked in Parador's front door. Parador is happy to let our caterer use their kitchen for a thousand bucks a pop. Some splendid wine, some nice post-prandial Armagnac, and bingo, the prospect is whisked back to the helipad south of town and then helicoptered home.

And thus, do we fashion a whole bunch of Door County cash funnels—store rent, tchotchke inventory, cash payments to chefs and various victualers, helicopter fees, and Chaturi's apartment over in Bailey's Harbor (no one in Egg Harbor would lease her a room). In short, we take in some legitimate money, and spend a lot of our 'retained earnings' on various entirely legal things. Classic laundering.

—·ww·—

The next adventure in retail commerce is far less cheery. Delia has driven Christine and me over to the Redi-Mart in her pickup truck, and now she stands third in the checkout line with a cart full of assorted exotic spices, curries, and chutneys. Christine has stayed out in the truck because she finds it hard to disguise her disdain for the Redi-Mart's pathetic selection of cut-rate and out-of-date products. Delia likes to shop there because she likes the owner, one Hrundi V. Pradesh, who specializes in off-brand labels and discounted goods that were probably canned back in the fifties. She also likes it that Hrundi stocks genuine Indian and Asian spices and several varieties of exotic greens not commonly found outside Asian kitchens. They're chums, Delia and Hrundi. They swap curry and biryani recipes, and Delia never forgets to ask how his family is doing back in Bangalore. Today, Hrundi is apologizing to everyone in the checkout line because his antiquated card reader is acting up and going very, very slowly and so he must ask everyone to "please, please, be very patient, if you are willing."

Needing nothing today, I'm standing over at the display case containing various kinds of knives. There's little keychain knives, jack-knives, buck knives, cheap stilettos, and huge frigging Bowie knives with elk horn handles and nasty curvy blades that could gut you a grizzly if you should be attacked unexpectedly. I'm wondering if it would look pretentious for a Vandal in his seventies to carry an eleven-inch blade in an elaborately tooled belt-sheath in an act of open-carry social defiance. Standing directly behind Delia in line, a large, skeevy-looking guy wearing Semper colors and a Rolling Stones tee shirt looks Delia up and down. His body odor is breathtakingly foul; I can smell his stink all the way over at the knife counter.

He leers at Delia. "You pretty good lookin' for a nigruh," he says in a moist whisper. "What kind nigruh are yuh, anyway?"

Delia does not miss a beat, steps back, and looks this huge hunk of stinking meat up and down. She doesn't pretend to ignore him, and she doesn't say, "Excuse me?" or "What did you just say?"

She says, "I'm the kind that has learned not to take offense when some revolting parody of a human being says something that fully reveals just how ignorant and pathetic he really is."

You can see the gears grinding as this troglodyte tries to figure out how seriously he's been insulted. He pushes up against her. And now he rasps, "What did you say?"

"Sorry, Geronimo, there are no repeats. If you want to hear it again you've got to pay extra."

Suddenly seriously out of control, the Semper dude grabs Delia's upper arms, and I can see his knuckles whiten against her dark skin. It is at this point that Hrundi V. Pradesh, or I should say, some dramatically transformed version of Hrundi V. Pradesh, steps from behind the checkout counter. His face is rigid with fury, and his eyes have become dark, intense slits. Now he thrusts a black sawed-off shotgun against the side of the Semper dude's portly torso. His lilting voice is a soft, menacing hiss. He sounds like a cobra singing a deadly lullaby.

"You are letting this fine lady go at this very moment, actually, or you will be dead in a moment. Oh, yes, in a very, very quick moment, you will be completely dead. I will not hesitate to mess you up."

Semper's hands drop.

"That's good, oh yes, that is very good," whispers Hrundi. "Thank you for your cooperating. Now you must sit down on the floor cross-legged and put your hands behind your head. Oh, *please* stop making that ugly face at me. It would be very sad if I shot you in your head because you scared me so much that I am accidentally pulling the trigger."

Protectively, he gestures for Delia to stand behind him. I find her calm unsettling, and a little bizarre. Her expression is utterly blank. Semper is seething. Hrundi's shotgun remains inches from his temple.

Pradesh calls out to me. "Mr. Harding, sir. Am I correct that you are having Sheriff Gilbert Rennie's speed dial number easily found on your cellular telephone?"

I nod vigorously.

"Would you call him for me please and tell him a criminal assault has been taking place inside my place of business?"

By the time Rennie wheels in in his cruiser, Semper has been wrapped with numerous loops of duct tape, several around his ample torso, several more around his ankles. Delia chose the color of the duct tape: hot pink. Over Bakshi's protests, she insists on paying for the tape, saying she will take the rest of the roll home with her.

At the police station, Gilbert Rennie takes statements from Delia and me, separately, in separate rooms. *Oh, Gilbert, ever the cop.*

Delia tells Rennie that she will not be lodging assault charges against Earle Barton "Bart" McKenna, III, but that she would appreciate it if the sheriff would warn him to stay away from her, like, forever. She says she does not want to have to file for a Protection from Abuse Order against Mr. McKenna, but she will if she has to.

On the drive home, I notice that Delia's hands are shaking slightly on the wheel, and, for the moment anyway, she does not seem to want Christine to touch her.

"Protection From Abuse Order?" I exclaim. "How did you come to know about PFAs and peace bonds and shit like that?"

"Oh, Victor, Victor," Delia says quietly. "This wasn't my first rodeo. And *Bart* wasn't my first cowboy. Still, I just hate it when this happens."

39

Love and Other Pleasures

I WALK OUT OF THE FLOWER SHOP and there's Stan Satuka, climbing into his new acquisition.

"Stan," I call. He greets me with a warm smile. He looks more relaxed than I have ever seen him. "How're you liking the Maybach?"

"God, Victor. It's a life-changer. Really. I love driving it, love just sitting in it. I love the look I get from Joel Shlomowitz when he sees me driving by, that pretentious little prick. When I need it serviced, they come and pick it up—*from Madison*—and drop it back off. Please tell Delia how much I appreciate her kind willingness to cut this old man a deal."

"Shall do, Stan. What are you doing downtown? Only mad dogs and Englishmen go out in the noonday sun."

"Ah," he sighs. "Just got my weekly fix."

"Sorry?"

"What, you don't know about Wei Loon?" He points up to a small sign in the second story window above the flower shop. It says, "Asian Massage." If he hadn't pointed, I probably never would have noticed it. I raise my eyebrows and cock my head in inquiry.

"Oh, Victor. You've really been missing something. Utterly *delightful* little woman. Classy, professional. Gives absolutely world-class massages. She does it all: Swedish, deep tissue, Thai, shiatsu, hot rock, aromatherapy. Also, ah, 'special services,' if you want."

He winks. "She really knows what us old farts need. Since I've started weekly massages with her, I've developed better flexibility, lower back pain is gone. Other things work better, too. Best hundred bucks a week I can spend. If you decide to use her, tell her I made the referral. Maybe she'll give me a free session."

—*∾*—

It is Cal's day off, and I've made my own lunch. Made a right mess of it, too. I have blasted bits of red sauce and ravioli all over the inside of the microwave, and my attempts to clean it up have just smeared more muck around inside, where I know it's going to get cooked on and Cal is going to yell at me. I marvel at what a helpless old cripple I'm becoming.

There's a knock on the back door, and there's Cara. For once, she's not smiling.

"Got a minute?"

I sense that this is not the right time for snappy repartee, and simply nod.

"Okay." She sits down and wooshes out a deep breath. "This is a little awkward."

"Earth to Cara," I say. "Hey, it's me."

"Well, you know that Collie and I are really getting into each other. So to speak." She smiles wanly at her pun.

"I really like him, Victor. I'd like this to go somewhere. I don't mind the age difference. But I've always been slow to commit, and there's one issue that has been...concerning me."

"Talk to me," I say.

"Colin gets very evasive with me when it comes to talking about Susan. She's been dead a long time, Victor, and I would have thought he would have come to grips with that—at least to the point where he doesn't get all weird if I even mention her name. Is he still carrying a torch? Is she a Goddess on a pedestal or something? Because if so, I'm not sure I want a piece of that."

I sit down on one kitchen stool across from her. Run my hands through my hair.

"This is a mine field," I say. "And I'm not sure it's my place to characterize everything that happened."

"*Victor.*" Cara is biting her lip.

"Okay, *okay.* I just want to be careful how I frame this. First, Cara, let me say that I did not like Susan. I thought she was unpleasantly passive-aggressive, and I really didn't like the constant guilt-trips she laid on Collie. Courtesy of my overbearing ogre of a father, Collie has always been a real people-pleaser, and Susan pushed that button very hard. I got very tired of hearing him apologize for sins he did not commit. It got particularly bad when Colin hit his hot streak on the professional golf circuit, got some recognition, got some good press. Susan really made him suffer for that."

Cara is sitting stock-still. I have to look carefully to see if she's breathing.

"I can tell you that Christine did not like her either, and in her typically insensitive way, she made that quite clear to Colin. Went so far as to suggest that he should divorce Susan. That did not go over well, and that's one reason Collie and Christine really went their separate ways, even before Susan got sick."

I am finding this conversation strangely hard, like one of those dreams where you're trying to run from a pursuer and your feet feel like they're stuck in tar.

"Susan contracted acute myeloid leukemia. She did not respond well to treatment, went steadily downhill, and was in a lot of pain. At first, I thought Collie was magnificent. Came off the PGA tour, took her to all the specialists, drove her to chemo, tended to her needs. *Nursed her.* Or, actually, *tried* to nurse her. But she wouldn't have it. The harder he tried, the more impossible she became. Blamed him, shamed him, was furious all the time.

"Finally, he just couldn't handle it. Frankly, Cara, emotionally he checked out, although he was still going through the motions. He went back on the senior tour, had the best golf year of his life, went deep into denial. It's fair to say that he abandoned Susan.

"Then they did a marrow transplant. *And it worked!* Knocked her leukemia into remission. But it turned out the treatment eventually also destroyed her liver. Apparently, that happens sometimes with marrow transplants. Technically, Susan died of liver failure, not of leukemia. Some difference, eh?

"So anyway, now Susan's dying, and she knows it. She's vicious to Collie. Collie has a one-night stand with an official at the LPGA. He says something to piss this woman off, she rats him out to Susan. Shortly before Susan goes into a coma, she curses him. *She curses him!*

"And Collie, wouldn't you know, begins acting like someone who's been cursed. His golf game goes to hell, he plummets down the senior circuit pro rankings, he begins to drink too much, begins using rough language around his students, and embarrasses himself a couple of times socially at The Landings. He becomes irritable, hypersensitive, and abrasive. The Landings calls him out, threatening to fire him if he doesn't pull himself together.

"*And Cara, that's exactly what he does!* Collie seems to pull a complete personality transplant, through sheer force of will, as far as I can tell. He's shaky, but he's operational. That's about where things stood when Collie got on that stupid airplane to come up here.

"He survives the crash, we're in the terminal, I'm cradling his head against my chest, he's vomited on his turquoise golf shirt, he's trembling and sobbing, and you know what he says? He says, '*I deserved this, Victor. I had this coming.*'"

I look at Cara. Tears are flooding down her face, staining her blouse. She makes no attempt to wipe them away. Her breathing comes in hiccups. I realize I'm crying, too, realize that I have never had a mental drawer in which to store these horrible events, never resolved the jumble of feelings triggered by Susan's suffering and death.

"*Cara,*" I say. She looks up.

"Cara, Colin Harding is a kind man, a good man. But three times now, first with Susan's death and then with PTSD and then with being shot in the face, he has been completely overwhelmed. Frankly, I'm amazed he's functioning at all at this point. But he *is* functioning, Cara, and I think he's getting steadily better, healthier. I think both his inside scars and his outside scars are healing up. If I may say so, I think you are really helping in that regard.

"Cara, what you choose to do with respect to your relationship with Collie is your business, and I will not presume to tell you what to do. But I will tell you *my* bottom line: Colin Harding is a man who has been through a war, and I think he's something of a war hero. I am quite proud of him these days, and I have told him that. And I'm not known for throwing bouquets around."

40

Grand Theft Auto

SOMETIMES IT SEEMS LIKE my life is defined by phone calls in the middle of the night. This one comes from Gunnar Spaaks. Given the gravity of what he's about to tell me, he seems surprisingly unruffled.

"We got hit tonight."

"What are you talking about?"

"My body shop got broken into sometime after midnight, after Kerry went home. Three cars stolen. One was my 'sixty-five Corvette. One was a 'sixty-four Pontiac GTO I was restoring for a guy. The third was your Darrin. Took a bunch of tools, too. Anyway, wanted you to know."

That's all he says. No, "gee, I'm sorry," or "don't worry, we'll get 'em back." Just dead silence on the phone. He wants to see how I'm going to react.

I mean, really, what do you say at a moment like this? Do you cry *bullshit!* and light the guy up and give him a good excuse to hang up on you? Do you feign credulity, as in, "Golly, that's horrible? Whatever *are* we to do?"

I do neither. I put on my best Sergeant Joe Friday voice: *Nothing but the facts, Ma'am.*

"How'd they get in?"

"Looks like they froze the lock with freon, smashed it with a sledge. Pieces of metal all over the floor."

"Three cars, that means lotsa guys. Looks like a planned heist. Looks like some people were real familiar with your body shop."

"No shit, Sherlock."

"They truck 'em away or drive 'em?"

"Drove 'em. Three sets of tire tracks in the snow. We were able to follow them out to Route 49, then the tracks just blended into the road slush. That doesn't mean they didn't truck 'em away later, just means they didn't load 'em at my place."

"Yeah, well, I suppose they wouldn't load 'em up at your place unless they first put up a big sign saying, 'Don't mind us, we're busy stealing these cars.'"

"Didn't see no such sign," he says in a fake drawl. Laughs.

"What did Rennie say?" I ask.

"I didn't call Rennie. And I'd prefer that you didn't either, Victor. I do not want to report the cars stolen. Not yet. This happened in my own crib, and I don't want the law crawling all over my shop with a bunch of forensics techs."

I feign astonishment. "So, we're just going to sit here twiddling our thumbs?"

"Certainly not. You know better than that, Victor. I'm all over this. I want you to leave recovery to me. I got more guys with more eyes around here than Gilbert Rennie will have in a million years. Someone will whisper in someone's ear. I'll hear about it, and then I'll find the cars. Unless they've been chopped up, which, unfortunately, may be likely for my Corvette but highly unlikely for your Darrin. It needs to be kept in one piece. I'll get your Darrin back, and when I do, someone is going to be very, very sorry. Vigilante justice, hell to pay, like that."

"You don't seem very upset, Gunnar." I let the comment hang. He lets the comment hang. He knows we're busy playing each other. Finally, he gives an exasperated sigh.

"What's the point? My getting all riled up won't change anything. Military taught me anything, it's to stay cool. But don't you think I'm not...*motivated*, Victor. That particular yellow '65 'Vette is incredibly rare. One of only four made with those specifications. If you could auction it with a clean title, you'd get a buck-and-a-quarter, maybe a buck and a half, and that value is only gonna skyrocket some more. The GTO was clean, probably worth seventy. And your Darrin? I don't know, maybe seventy-five or eighty once it's done. I got more skin in this game than you do, pal."

Unless you 'stole' your own car, pal, and have it nestled under a nice warm tarp somewhere.

"Gunnar, the Darrin is not insured. I'm real unhappy right now."

"Probably covered under your homeowner's policy. You should check on that."

"Is this the part where you tell me I can trust you?"

"This is the part where I say, 'we're done here' and hang up."

41

High Crimes and Misdemeanors

I PARK IN COLIN'S HARDING LODGE DRIVEWAY, let myself in through the sliding door on his deck, and, making as much noise as I can, stomp into his bedroom. I switch on the ceiling light, shake him out of a sound sleep. Believe me, he knows I'm in earnest. He gets himself fully awake, pronto.

"God damn it, Collie! Didn't I tell you to warn Cara and Dany to get rid of those Day-Glo post-it notes? Are you trying to get them killed?"

"What are you talking about?" he cries defensively. "I *did* tell Cara. I assume she told Dany."

"Then what the hell is *this?*" I use my thumb to push the bright orange note on to the middle of Collie's forehead. He pulls it off and reads it. The note has a single sentence on it, written with a green sharpie: *Let them sit for a few days, then try Jimmy Griffin's barn.*

"Where'd you find this?" Collie says.

"On the windshield of my Bimmer, when I went out to retrieve my cell phone tonight. You know, the Bimmer in my garage. My unlocked garage. That one"

"She's crazy," Collie says. "I don't know what game Dany may be playing, but to me it looks like Cara's trying to play hero."

"*She's trying to get herself killed, Colin.* Gunnar sees so much as one Day-Glo post-it note, and Cara's dead meat. And so is Dany Miskinis, unless she has enough sense to head for the hills. Cara may write the post-it notes, but Dany's obviously the source of the information."

Colin blinks in confusion. "But why would Cara be dead meat? Why is she at risk? She doesn't live with Gunnar, doesn't write *him* orange post-it notes. You can bet Rennie didn't show Gunnar the Epstein note, and I sure haven't shown him any of the notes Cara wrote me."

"*Notes?* How many have there been?"

"Well, a few. Sort of our jungle telegraph. She leaves them for me where she knows I'll find them."

"You mean, left around where a snooping Gunnar Spaaks or one of his band of merrie men can find them. And they're not hard to spot, are they? They're neon orange, a real eye-grabber. *God damn it, Collie!* Love's given you two a bad case of the blind cutesies and you're both walking through a mine field, going la-la-la. I want you to drive to Cara's apartment right now, grab every one of her damned post-it notes, and flush them all down the toilet. If you want to stay there the rest of the night to protect her, well, that might be wise too. If she can reach Dany, Cara should warn her that she may be in immediate danger."

"You really think it's that serious?"

"C'mon, Collie. Look in the goddamned mirror. You think assassination isn't serious? You don't think something very serious is going on around here?"

"We agreed that Gunnar probably wasn't the trigger man in my shooting, probably didn't set it up."

"*Wake up, Collie! Smell the coffee!* You don't remember Stuart Friend, the guy garroted with the piano wire? You really think Gunnar didn't know what was going on with that? Gunnar has to know that if Cara and Dany are diming him, he's in for a world of hurt. If he thinks his ass is on the line, it's going to be his hand on the trigger."

Colin starts to pull on his pants.

"And Collie, tomorrow I want you to track down that guy in Madison who you said can hot-wire anything. Tell him we need him to work with us on a...*project.* Tell him it's an easy two grand, and tell him he'll have to bring his own flashlight."

—⁓⁓—

My mother didn't bring me up to do this. Here I am, a septuagenarian of marginal strength and fitness, standing out on some country road in rural Wisconsin, with a ski mask over my face. In my hand I'm holding a nine-millimeter Sig Sauer pistol so new it still has the bar code sticker on the receiver. The guy at Targetmaster says I can return it if it turns out I don't like its heft, but not after I've fired it. I'm wearing black pants, a new black Walmart puffy coat, and super cheapo canvas slip-ons that soon will be tossed into some trash can. I've got a taser in my front jacket pocket. To say that I feel out of character would be a huge understatement.

Colin stands next to me, dressed similarly, almost invisible in the darkness, his eyes glinting behind his black ski-mask. He's carrying the cheapest shotgun Targetmaster had for sale. Billed as a "home defense weapon," it is nothing more than a crude Chinese-made twelve-gauge with a short barrel and strange plastic pistol grips instead of a traditional stock. Collie has test-fired it exactly once. Collie also is carrying a silly little kid's toy that looks like a miniature bullhorn. By pushing different buttons on the handle, you can either make it squawk, wail like a police siren, or distort your voice into a robot-like buzz. That's the button Collie's going to push when we pull off our raid. He plans on being the evil voice from the planet Zorg.

Our hot-wire accomplice, one Bryan Frame, isn't bothering with the urban guerilla look. He's wearing brown corduroys, a jean jacket, standard day-laborer shitkickers and, until he covers his face with a red bandana, a bored look. I suppose he feels there's little point in trying to be inconspicuous, because Bryan is six feet seven inches tall and looks like he weighs about thirteen pounds. He's got a small fast-draw police holster strapped around his waist containing a Smith & Wesson thirty-eight. He looks comfortable with a gun on; I'm betting he's fired that thirty-eight more than once. Slung over his shoulder like Pancho Villa's bandolier is a tool belt with various kinds of pliers, picks and vise-grips instead of bullets.

Bryan started off rude when Colin cold-called to recruit him, but suddenly got friendlier when Collie waved the prospect of a couple of thousand dollars in his face and assured Bryan that this was a repossession, not grand theft auto.

"Bryan," Collie had said, "this is a no-brainer: we're reclaiming three cars that were stolen from us. *Our own cars.* If you have to punch out the ignition or hot wire any of the cars, it's two grand. If all you have to do is turn an ignition key and drive a couple of miles, it's still two grand. Basically, we're paying you about a thousand dollars an hour for some extremely light duty. You okay with that?"

Bryan says he is okay with that.

"And if I say that for that two thousand, in addition to being a no-brainer, this is also a 'no-mouther,' do you understand what I'm saying? Loose lips sink ships, Bryan."

"Got it," says Bryan.

Scariest of all is Seth Bartlett. It isn't his clothes, which are, of course, black, that are so frightening. It's the wild west gunslinger's rig strapped low across his hips. Broad wide belt, thongs tying the bottoms of the two holsters around his thighs. As the interior light from my BMW briefly lights up Seth's midsection, I note that his two guns are not the same. His right-hand rests gently on the top of a large revolver with a pearl handle. His left-hand weapon is clearly not a cowboy pistol; it's large and clunky, a sort of dark metallic gray. It looks as if it is made of plastic. I don't ask.

I had told Delia to stay in the car and be ready to hightail it out of here if need be. Yet here she is, dressed in designer jeans and high-heeled boots, hopping from foot to foot and grinning ear to ear. For us stealthy stalker types, it is, of course, a bad thing to be sporting a highly visible smile, but there you are. You gotta take your getaway drivers as you find them. I tell Delia to pull her mask down and keep it down.

We'd had a hell of a time trying to follow Cara's instruction to "try Jimmy Griffin's barn," because we couldn't find Jimmy Griffin's barn. James Griffin was not listed in any print or online directory in the four-county area, and nothing came up when we searched for his name online. He had a criminal record, but it listed an address in Arkansas. We drove around and around, asked around and around, extended our hands, palms down, with twenty-dollar bills pinched between the fingers. Nada. Zilch. Blank stares.

We began to wonder if Cara's post-it note was communicating in code, if perhaps "barn" meant one of the numerous self-storage places over on Highway 41 near Oshkosh. We came up cold until Delia, who would not be denied a supporting role in our caper, walked into Easy Peasey Self Storage in Fond du Lac and asked the young lady behind the counter if she knew of a "car-type guy" named Jimmy Griffin. The woman, amply tattooed and with an oversized ring piercing her nasal septum, seemed unfazed either by Delia's striking beauty or her dark complexion. "Sure, I know Jimmy. He's my cousin. You lookin' for him?"

"Kinda," said Delia.

"This is his day off from Maaco, so he's probably at the barn, getting stoned."

"What barn?"

"His folks' place in Darby Henge, about halfway between Princeton and Mazomanie. Brown double-wide on the street, big ol' white barn out back. Says Norman Clatton on the mailbox, that's Jimmy's stepdad. If Jimmy's there, his old Toyota pickup truck will be parked out front with a 'For Sale' sign on it. Fat bleepin' chance of sellin' that piece of junk.

"Anyway, Norman and Elna-Mary are off down in Naples for a month, and Jimmy's been blowin' his brains out on weed every day. If you see him, tell him he owes me fifty bucks. My dealer is all over me to get paid."

—◦◦◦—

We case the Clatton spread in the afternoon and realize there will be no way to get the transporters in there, particularly at night. It's like a mine field: the place is a junkyard of used-up tractors with flat tires, derelict fifties-vintage Ford sedans, rusted plows, dead washing machines, and various other kinds of junk that will never move or be moved again. We're going to have to drive our cars off the premises, load them someplace else.

This involves uncertainty: We know Gunnar's Corvette runs, and I've heard the Darrin's engine run over the phone. If the thieves drove it out of Gunnar's body shop, we have to assume that the transmission works. But we don't know anything about the GTO's condition. We suspect Gunnar's guys drove it over here, but maybe it's a non-runner and they used a tow dolly. So, we rent a crew cab U-Haul pickup truck and a tow dolly of our own. Delia will drive, and she thinks this is a wonderful lark. We're going to park our rented commercial car transporter about two miles away at Darby Henge State Park, so we should be able to manage things if we have to tow any of the cars away from Clatton's barn.

We don't knock, just barge in, Collie in the lead, me in the middle, Bryan ambling nonchalantly along behind me, Seth Bartlett hanging back, as wired and vigilant as always. The room reeks of weed. Jimmy Griffin, gaunt, disheveled, and wearing a baby-blue jogging suit, is sitting on a couch in front of a monster flat-screen TV, his stocking feet propped on the coffee table next to an empty pizza box and a six-pack of PBR, three remaining. He's watching a rerun of Magnum, P.I., remote in hand. *A perfect cliché,* I think, complete in all particulars.

Griffin looks up at us, all masked and costumed up in our ninja threads. He starts to his feet. Bryan Frame strides over and taps the butt of his .38 lightly on the top of Griffin's head. "Unh-unh," whispers Frame. "Down, boy."

Griffin collapses back on to the sofa. I can see that his pupils are dilated to the size of frisbees. I can't tell whether he's surprised, frightened, or just totally wrecked.

"You gonna hurt me?" His voice is slurred, squeaky. My mind checks the box for totally wrecked.

"Probably not," growls Collie through his comical toy voice distorter. "We just here to liberate some cars. Just be cool, you be fine."

I find Collie's attempt at black gangsta patois hysterical, and I strain to stifle a laugh.

"You got the keys, or are we going to have to pop the ignitions out?"

Jimmy raises his hands slowly over his head. "All three sets are hangin' on the wall rack over there. Please don't kill me."

An idea strikes me. "Did Gunnar say he'd kill you if you messed up on this gig?"

Jimmy shrugs. "Well, you know Gunnar. Look what he did to that other guy with the piano wire."

"Gunnar do that? I thought it was Crouch."

"Well, it was Crouch who strung the wire, but the whole thing was Gunnar's idea."

"Well, Jimmy," I say pleasantly. "We won't kill you unless you make trouble. See, we're the good guys. We're the cavalry, riding to the rescue. I can't promise what Gunnar's going to do, though. Maybe you ought to take some preventive measures, get yourself some protection. Or maybe leave town."

He nods, as if this is an utterly novel idea.

There's a clicking sound behind me, and I turn to see that Seth Bartlett has unholstered his bulky gray weapon and tucked it barrel-first into his armpit. In his left hand he is holding a black plastic case about six inches long, and as the top springs open, I see a neat row of shiny metal cylinders. He removes one, opens the chamber on the side of his strange implement, and closes the slide with a loud click. He turns and aims it at Jimmy.

Jimmy Griffin whimpers and pushes out his hands in futile defense. Then his knees buckle, and he pitches forward over the coffee table, landing face-first on the carpet. Bryan Frame, who seems to know exactly what's going on here, hoists Jimmy to his feet by the scruff of his collar and dangles him so that his toes are just tickling the floor. "Be cool, dude," he says quietly. "This nice man is savin' your life. He's protectin' you from Spaaks, you idiot. He givin' you a 'scuse."

He spins Griffin in the air, rotating him like a piñata so that his back is to Seth Bartlett. As if he does this all the time, Bartlett nonchalantly fires an anesthetic dart into Jimmy Griffin's right buttock. Griffin gasps in pain and horror, and Frame shakes him as if he were a misbehaving dog.

"Cool out, champ. You'll be fine. You gonna be out about two hours, and by then we gonna be long gone. You gonna be the robber what got robbed. Now ain't *that* poetic justice for mister Gunnar Spaaks."

It takes about two minutes for Jimmy Griffin to go limp. When he loses consciousness, his eyes remain open. This is disturbing to me. "God, is he dead?"

"Nope," says Seth Bartlett. "Jes' takin' a little trip to dreamland. Anesthetic just works that way. Won't even have a headache when he comes to." It strikes me that this is the first time I have ever heard Seth Bartlett's voice. It's soft and soothing, pure Appalachia.

We walk to the barn, and Bryan eases up to the touchpad by the side of the large overhead door. "Cheap residential crap," he says. "I could run a diagnostic to pull the combination, but it's easier just to pry the cover off and short the dangling leads to trigger the door motor. And don't worry, this ain't the kind of unit that calls the cops. It's just a combination lock."

Interior lights come on automatically as the door glides to the side, and there are our three cars, lined up neatly in a row, each covered with a soft moving blanket. Five other cars rest under tarps further back in the garage.

We pull the tarps off our cars, and they gleam up at us in the fluorescent light. Bright yellow Corvette, polished black GTO, and my gleaming white Darrin. I'm not surprised to see that the Darrin is complete. The upholstery is finished, and it's wonderful—soft, buttery, smelling like a bespoke British suitcase. The new top is neatly folded under a precisely fitted fawn-colored tonneau cover. The chrome is done, the wire wheels polished and shiny. The car looks terrific, worth every cent I'm never going to pay for it.

Now Seth Bartlett speaks for the second time. "Wow, nice iron," he says.

Turns out we don't need the transporter. The Darrin, Corvette and GTO are operational and will be driven directly down to Janesville, to be happily housed in our warehouse, secure under Seth Bartlett's watchful eye. Bryan pockets his two grand in cash, and we drop him at the transporter. Delia heads back to U-Haul in the pickup. I drive the Darrin, Seth drives the GTO, and I let Collie drive the 'Vette. We're all on a high as we fly down Wisconsin's country roads—the Corvette, hugely powerful with explosive acceleration, the GTO, epitome of the 1960's muscle-car era, and the Darrin, a lousy car but a wonderful slice of automotive history.

We have briefed Seth fully about Gunnar and his nefarious friends, made it clear that Gunnar is to be regarded as *the enemy*. Seth has shoved four shells of double-ought buckshot into his Winchester shotgun and pronounced himself ready for anything. *Semper Paratus.*

———⁓⁓⁓———

The next day, there's a sharp November chill in the air as I slip into my parka. Time to head down to Morton's for lunch with Gilbert. I hear the crunching of driveway gravel and see Gunnar Spaak's purple pickup pull up outside my kitchen door. I know this is bad news. I had thought he might be dropping by, so I have prepared myself for trouble. He climbs out, and there is no doubt in my mind that Gunnar is loaded for bear. He knocks, I open the kitchen door, and Gunnar slides his foot in the door to keep me from closing it.

"Easy, big fella," I say.

"You owe me fifty thousand dollars," says Gunnar Spaaks.

"I owe you nothing until I have a complete car in my hands. That was the price you set."

"Bad mistake, Harding," Gunnar says evenly.

"I don't know what you're talking about," I say.

"You think you're cute? You and your mentally screwed-up brother? You and your goons think you're smart?"

"I still don't know what you're talking about. But now that you're here, I want to know when you're going to get me my finished car back. I want to know how much longer I'm supposed to wait before I file a stolen car report with Gilbert Rennie. I've got it all written up. All I have to do is drop it off to him."

"You are making a very serious mistake, Harding. You are messing with the wrong guy."

"I'm not messing with anyone, Gunnar. I'm just trying to live a nice quiet life as a retired architect and former fence of stolen property. I'm not looking for trouble."

I pause and stare Gunnar Spaaks directly in the eye. Actually, I don't know who this person is who's staring him in the eye, because no Victor Harding I know would have the guts for such a confrontation. *Have I somehow changed, become more courageous?*

"But if I should find myself in trouble, Gunnar, I have something on my side. A leveler, so to speak. Think of it as an insurance policy. It's a little black binder with a lot of interesting names and phone numbers in it. I'm sure your name is in there somewhere. Probably many times. Also other numbers—itemized lists, amounts, dollars, like that. And addresses, too. Right now, the binder's in my safe deposit box, Gunnar. And I've given my bank instruction to give it to Gilbert Rennie if anything ever happens to me."

"You are going to be one very sorry asshole, Harding."

"Like my brother was one sorry asshole when one of your pals shot him in the face?"

"I told Rennie, and I'll tell you. I had nothing to do with that hit. Didn't plan it, didn't okay it, didn't know it was coming."

"But you know who did it, right? So, who's hit was it, Gunnar? Don't pretend you don't know."

"You are doing every damned thing you can to get yourself in trouble, Victor."

Then I say a very stupid thing. "What are you going to do? Go out and buy some more piano wire? You gonna try to take my head off too?"

There is an explosion of motion as Spaaks bull rushes me, pushes me back into the kitchen, bends me backward over the butcher block center island. His hands press down hard on my shoulders, and he moves his face to within a foot of mine. He is hissing like a snake.

"You, my arrogant friend, have just moved on to borrowed time."

I feel an eerie calm wash over me. Maybe this is because I have gone into shock. Or maybe it's because while Gunnar has pinioned my shoulders, my hands have remained free, and I have quietly reached over to the knife rack at the side of the butcher block and slid an eight-inch cleaver from its slot. I slowly position the cold, flat side of the cleaver against Gunnar's cheek and then rotate the blade so that its edge is positioned along the bottom of his jaw.

"Is this how you want to die, Gunnar?" I whisper. "*Is this how you want to die?*"

He releases the pressure on my shoulders, steps back. I move with him, keep the cleaver at his throat.

"Do you think I won't do it? Do you *really* think I won't do it? Come on, try me."

Gunnar raises his hands, palms out. *Submission.* I withdraw the cleaver from contact with Gunnar's cheek, but do not lower it. The pressure of the steel has left a light white line running from Gunnar's ear to his chin.

"Now it's time for you leave my kitchen." I pray my voice won't crack and render my ferocity ludicrous, and to my immense relief, it doesn't. Gunnar backs to the door.

"Oh, and one more thing," I say.

I reach into my shirt pocket and pull out my Sony mini-recorder. It's an old-fashioned model, the kind that holds a tiny microcassette, and it's been running since Gunnar knocked on the door. Gunnar looks at the two little spools spinning merrily in the recorder window.

"I'll send you a copy of the cassette," I say. "Don't thank me. Pleased to do it."

42

Breakthrough

I TURN INTO THE DRIVEWAY at Chateau Phone Home just in front of Cara Spaaks' ancient SAAB. We park side by side, and Colin jumps from the passenger seat of my BMW to help Cara disembark. They do a little cutie-pecky kiss, the kind that signals the world that they're not shy about public displays of affection.

"Do you have any idea what this 'urgent meeting' is all about?" I ask.

Cara shrugs. "Delia wouldn't say, just said to get out here ASAP, said there was something that couldn't wait."

Christine greets us. Her demeanor is striking, so different from her usual dour Eeyore imitation that I'm tempted to yell out, "Hey, what have you done with my sister?" Now Christine wears a broad ear-to-ear grin, and she is wringing her hands nervously, like someone waiting for Santa to come down the chimney.

It turns out Santa is truly on his way.

Christine leads us into the dining room, where Delia is seated at the head of the table. In the middle of the table, a jeroboam of Veuve Clicquot champagne perspires freely, its bright yellow label glistening in a giant silver ice bucket so new the label is still stuck to the side.

"Thank you all for coming on such short notice," Delia says. "We have some very pleasant news to report."

Now Christine can contain herself no longer, and she explodes into delighted laughter. "Actually, great news! Astounding you'll-never-believe-this-in-a-million-years news! Game-changing news!"

"Hoooo-*kay*," says Delia. "Enough preamble. Victor, when we were first talking about my goldsmithing and jewelry business, do you remember asking her how much I said my average commission was?"

"I do," I said, remembering the conversation vividly. "You said they used to average about a hundred grand, but that was before you won the Medaille Coeur D'Or. You suggested that winning the Heart of Gold was going to result in bigger-ticket commissions."

"Very good, Victor! Right on all counts. You get a cookie. At the time, I didn't think you were listening. All right, here's the first bit of news. I have received a firm commitment for a very significant new commission. It's not yet completely signed and sealed, but the particulars have been discussed in such detail that it's quite clear this deal is a go."

Cara, Colin, and I clap politely and reach across the table to shake Delia's hand.

"Now," chirps Christine, "each of you has to guess: what do you think Delia's largest-ever commission was?"

"Unfair," says Cara. "I know that answer, so I have to disqualify myself."

"Oh, just *tell* us," I say. "Please, let's just get to the point!"

"My biggest commission outside of India was two years ago. Seven hundred and forty-two thousand dollars for three pieces, which included a choker, a bracelet, and—I swear I'm not making this up—a matching ankle bracelet. The client was a Russian oligarch named Yevgeny Portochenko, who 'deals in oil.' The commission price was particularly steep because the pieces incorporated a lot of gems that I had to buy. But still, I made out okay on the deal."

Wow, I'll say, I mouth silently.

"Okay," says Christine, "Do any of you just happen to know the name of the wealthiest man in Sri Lanka?"

Silence.

"Okay, okay, that's a tough one, I admit," laughs Christine. "Delia and I have done some research, and it seems that a lot of people think it's an entrepreneur-slash-investor named Avyukt Provastar. Next question. In a recent out-of-the-blue telephone conversation with Ms. Delia Chamberlain, what did Avyukt say?"

We're silent, of course. Now Delia can contain herself now longer. She breaks in, clapping her hands in delight.

"Well, the first thing he asks is how my mother is doing, and I jokingly ask how he *thinks* she's doing after he broke her heart and nearly triggered a divorce from my dad."

"'Lovely woman, Alva' Avyukt says. 'Still very sexy, and so very good with numbers. When I contacted her again recently, she said it would be okay to call you to talk some business that benefited us both. No hard feelings, all that.'

"Then Avyukt congratulates me on winning the Medaille Coeur D'Or, says he's been following my career with interest. Then he says, 'Delia, as one ethnic Sri Lankan to another, I want you to help me make the whole world envy us instead of looking down their bigoted noses at us. If I may be grandiose, I want you to take on the most significant commission you've ever had. I want you to *break through* and ascend to the top step of the throne in the world of gold. And I, Avyukt Provastar, dismissed by many as just an ambitious little social climber up from the poor streets of Colombo, want to be known as the sponsor of your breakthrough. Your Godfather in the jewelry world.'"

Delia pauses to let all this sink in, to give us time to move our mind's eyes from the rustic farmlands of Green Lake, Wisconsin to the lofty aeries of the unimaginably rich.

"So," continues Delia, "I ask Mr. Provastar if he has any particular ideas, and he says oh, yes, he has a clear mental picture both of the piece he has in mind and of the person he wants to display it to an envious world. It seems that Avyukt's current romantic plaything, one Surya Damali, is a gorgeous dark-skinned Indian woman, a 'model of perfection in all respects,' as he put it. He has especially kind things to say about her breasts.

"'Delia,' Provastar says, 'I want you to make an absolutely amazing body necklace, a staggering piece—but oh, oh, so graceful!—made with multiple golden chains that outline and accentuate every part of Surya's glorious torso above her waist. I want a cascade of flat individual golden links, starting with intricate tiny ones that drape lightly across her chest and then get bigger and bigger in concentric circles to become massive signature links that ascend up the center of her body and rise up her chest until they become a choker that stretches her neck and lifts her chin in a wonderful display of exquisite golden power. Do I make myself clear? I want arcs of shimmering gold sweeping wildly across her cleavage. I want grand loops of color to cradle her breasts and fly across her body as if weightless. Overall, I want a piece that makes everyone stop in their tracks. I want a piece that will make women want to worship Surya and make men drool over her.'"

Delia smiles at the memory of the conversation. "I remember saying, 'well, is *that* all?' And Avyukt says, 'no, actually, there's more, Delia. The capper, so to speak.' Avyukt is not a real emotional guy, but now he seems to choke up a little.

"'Delia,' he said, 'I have purchased a quite singular teardrop emerald called the *Lagrima de Atocha*. I want you to incorporate it into the design at the base of the throat.'"

Delia turns, wide-eyed, to Cara, Collie, and me. "Do you guys have *any* idea what that means?"

We all shake our heads. Delia takes a hard slug of champagne to settle herself.

"If this were only your garden-variety one-point-six carat pear-shaped emerald, you'd say, 'okay, that's probably about a mil.' But it's not. *It's the Lagrima de Atocha*—in Spanish that means 'tears of the *Atocha*.' It is a major historical jewel. This emerald was mined about four hundred years ago at the Columbian Muzo mines and sent to Cartagena to be shipped back to King Philip IV in Spain. Only the ship it was on, the *Nuestra Señora de Atocha,* grounded in the Florida Keys and became one of the most famous shipwrecks of all time. The *Lagrima,* then still a four-and-a-half carat uncut rock, was recovered by treasure hunter Mel Fisher in 1986 as part of the historic *Atocha* treasure. Later it was cut into a 1.61 carat pear-shaped gem. *Perfection.* Highest grade. Incredibly deep color. It gets auctioned periodically, and the price always exceeds estimates. Last time around, it was $2.4 million.

"And now Avyukt Provastar owns it. And he wants me to stick it in a giant, three-pound golden *tour de force.*"

"Breathtaking," whispers Cara. My jaw drops.

"Can you do it?" I ask.

Rather than chide me for my insensitivity, Delia just smiles. "*Oh, yes.* Oh, my, yes. I am being given a ticket to make a very famous piece. A piece that will have a place in the world of famous jewels. A piece that will have a name, that will get a new name. No more *Lagrima.*"

Like all of us, Christine is spellbound. "What are you going to call it?" she whispers.

"*The Green Lake*," whispers Delia dramatically. "Catchy name, no?"

———

Unsurprisingly, we manage to kill most of the Jeroboam. "I'm going to London next week," Delia says, slurring her words slightly. "Christine is going to chaperone me," she giggles.

"W*hy* are we going to London, you ask?" Delia asks theatrically. "To finalize the details of the commission, freeze the price and get a deposit from Avyukt. And also, so I can meet the babe this body jewelry is going to be showcased on. I need to meet my mannikin in the flesh, in all her dark-skinned glory. Surya and me, we're birds of a feather, modeling-wise. She's gonna love what I do for her international visibility, and I sure as hell am going to love what she does for mine."

"But I have a lot of design work to do, also some serious number-crunching. In addition to the Lagrima, I'm going to bathe that humongous emerald in a sea of large and costly diamonds, maybe some rubies, too, and I also have to figure out how much of our gold I need to drop into the pot."

Now Colin speaks up. "If this Provastar is as sharp as they say, aren't you in for a hell of a haggle?"

"Oh, we've already settled on the price," Delia says simply. "No prob. We had no problem at all from the moment Avyukt said, 'name your price.'"

"What did you name?" Colin asks.

"Three million dollars," Delia Chamberlain giggles.

In Green Lake, Wisconsin, this is what is known as deep clover.

43

I Knew It

THERE'S A TAPPING AT THE WINDOW, and I see Gilbert Rennie standing there, gesturing for me to come out. I gesture for him to come in. He shakes his head vehemently. Apparently, whatever is happening has to happen outside. I slide on my puffy vest and meet Gilbert out on the veranda. He looks terrible, his face ashen, his shoulders uncharacteristically hunched.

"Sorry to trouble you," he says, although I can tell he's not in the least sorry. Gilbert's face is flushed. His hands are shaking. "I've got two pieces of news, Victor, neither of them good."

Gilbert gestures for me to sit down, and I take a seat on the edge of one my patio chairs. He sucks in a deep breath. "First, I bet you won't be surprised to hear that somebody killed Kerry Crouch. They found his body in a shallow grave in a ditch just outside Ripon. He'd been garroted. With wire. How's that for just desserts?"

"That's not just desserts, Gilbert, that's someone trying to make a point, trying to send a message. Who do you think is good for it?"

Gilbert gives an explosive snort. "Oh, come on, Victor! Don't play coy with me. Whoever bought that Japanese motorcycle knew it was Crouch's caper, and knew Kerry Crouch was a loose cannon. You kill the perp; you kill the investigation. It's that simple."

Maybe not, Gilbert, I'm thinking.

"Crouch worked for Gunnar Spaaks," I say. "Any thought he might be involved?"

"I guess right now I have no reason to think so. I have Spaaks down as a property crimes guy, but I don't have him marked as a murderer."

I do, I think. *If only you knew, Gilbert.* Right now, I don't think Gunnar Spaaks would think twice about killing *me.* If another hit is in the works, I'm betting that I'm going to be the hittee. I'm dying to tell Gilbert Rennie this, but I can't tell Gilbert Rennie this.

"What's the other news?" I say.

"This one is ugly, and in a way, it involves Crouch, too."

I'm absolutely sure I know what I'm about to hear. And I'm right.

"They found Odie Todd's body up in Eagle River yesterday. Stuffed into a culvert under the interstate. Been there awhile. Obvious execution, but the killers weren't even civilized enough to put a bullet in the back of his head. They stuffed a twenty-two into his nostril and pulled the trigger. He got to see the finger move just before they blew his brains out."

I'm glad I'm sitting down, because my knees turn to water. I feel bile rise, wonder if I'm going to vomit all over Gilbert Rennie. I flap my arms as if trying to shoo away bumblebees.

"Another thing, Victor. And you won't be surprised to hear this. *They cut off his hands.* The only good news is that it looks like they did it after he was already dead."

"Oh, Gilbert. Oh, my God. This is all so...wrong, so *unfair.*"

My words make perfect sense to me, because I know a lot of things Gilbert Rennie doesn't. But he gets that look people have when they think something is going over their head. I want to say, "Can't you see they scapegoated Odie? Can't you see they murdered the messenger? Can't you see they just punished his loyalty? *Can't you see, Gilbert, can't you see?*"

But of course, I can't say any of that. All I can say is, "I can't tell you how sorry I am to hear this. Odell Todd did not deserve this."

44

Death of a Friendship

BRIANNA SETS THE STRANGELY-SHAPED BOTTLE in front of Gilbert and me, together with two oversized shot glasses I have brought to Morton's with me. The bottle is filled with a pale smokey liquid that appears thick and viscous. The writing on the label is not English; to me it looks like Arabic.

"I'm not supposed to serve this because this bar did not buy it, and it doesn't have a Wisconsin tax stamp," Brianna says petulantly.

"It's okay, Brianna," I say. "It's part of an ongoing criminal investigation. Just leave it. We are going to take the table over in the far corner, and we're going to be some time. I do *not* want to be disturbed."

Brianna bristles at my tone. "Well, yes, *sir,* Mr. Harding, *sir.*"

She stalks away, shaking her head.

Gilbert gestures at the bottle. "What is this stuff, Victor? And just what the hell is going on here?"

"This was supplied by my sister-in-law, who is of Sri Lankan extraction. This is what she recommended when I told her what I needed it for. It is Sri Lankan arak. The milder Turkish version is called raki. But the Sri Lankan version really piles it on. This particular bottle is *Arak El Messaya*, supposedly the best, in this case meaning the strongest. The Arabs call it Levantine dynamite. It's something like ouzo, but rougher, harsher, and twice as alcoholic. One drinks it in order to get blasted."

"What's this about, Victor? Are you challenging me to some kind of drinking contest?"

"Wish it were that festive, Gilbert. I chose El Messaya because it knocks you on your ass very fast, and when you hear what I have to tell you, you are going to want to be drunk. Me, I will want to be very, very drunk."

"You know I don't like playing games, Victor. Once again, just what is this all about?"

"Let me pour each of us a peg—that's what the Indians call this kind of king-sized shot glass—and I'll explain."

El Messaya takes your breath away. Literally. It sucks the air right out of your lungs and sort of paralyzes your airways so that you are momentarily unable to draw breath. Perfect for the occasion. When I finally can speak again, I turn to Gilbert, who sits with his arms folded, waiting to see what's up. He's curious, of course, but seems composed. But then again, he doesn't know what's coming.

"Thank you for clearing your calendar this afternoon, Gilbert. I've got some weighty matters to discuss with you. It's going to take some time."

I shift in my chair, poised at the edge of the cliff. I had been unsure about whether I could do this, but now I suddenly feel lighter, strangely energized. I take another sip of El Messaya. *Now I'm ready.*

"Gilbert, first of all, I need you to believe how genuinely I value our friendship. I really like you, and I really respect you. I was gratified that sometimes you trusted me with information that was not for public consumption. And that's why this conversation has to happen and why it is the hardest

I have ever had in my life. I am very, very sad to say what it is I'm about to say."

Now I have Gilbert's attention. He says nothing, reaches for his drink, takes a small delicate sip, and winces. He furrows his brow and cocks his head at me expectantly.

"For a long time now I've had information that would be extremely valuable to you, and I withheld it from you. Mostly to protect myself."

"What information?"

"Gilbert, Kerry Crouch is the one who strung the piano wire and killed that kid. It wasn't Gunnar Spaaks or any of the other Semper gang members. Crouch is the one who stole Stuart Friend's CBX."

Gilbert pauses to let this sink in, to ponder the implications of this information. "What does this have to do with you?"

"I'm the one who bought the CBX. Colin and I fenced it down south."

Gilbert Rennie's eyes grow wide. He sucks in a long, loud gasp. "You *what?*"

"Okay, Gilbert. You wanna solve a lot of crimes? Pay attention, because I'm going to put all the pieces together for you."

Now I stop and take a pull from my peg. Too much: I choke and cough.

"Here's the backstory. For the last ten months or so, Colin and I have been fencing various kinds of stolen property. Buying it, transporting it across states lines to sell it, laundering the cash. About the time you cracked Clarence Causley, I stepped up, stepped in, and formed a working alliance with Gunnar Spaaks where he would steer stolen property to me. With his... 'sponsorship,' Colin and I quickly built a reputation among local thieves as the go-to guys for fencing high-end goods. I know you think that McFarland was the biggest fence around here, and he obviously was real busy. But I was buying too, Gilbert, and I must confess there were times when I used the information you gave me—*gave me thinking you could trust me*—either to help set up big-ticket heists or to steer people clear from getting caught."

Gilbert keeps his cool, although it is evident that I have shocked him. His shoulders sag. He sucks in his breath, holds it, then exhales loudly. "Wow," is all he says.

"It actually was Odell Todd who started me off. In addition to working at Gunnar's body shop, Odie was my yard man. Acting as Gunnar's 'agent,' he approached me, sold me a fancy lawn tractor. Confessed that it was hot. But not that big a deal, right?"

Gilbert says nothing.

"Then Odie sold me the Honda CBX. Nine-point-five grand. I didn't know it at the time, but it was a Kerry Crouch deal."

I see the lights go on, and almost hear the pieces drop into place in Gilbert Rennie's head.

"Kerry Crouch killed Stuart Friend. Enlisted Odie to pitch the Honda to me. I bought it, and Collie transported it down south, sold it in Savannah."

Gilbert is both nodding and shaking his head, which makes for a rather unusual gesture, rather like a horse tossing its head when the check rein is too tight.

"But neither Odie nor Crouch knew we'd sold it on. Crouch gets Odie to try to break into my garage, to try to steal it back from me. Probably some kind of blackmail thing, because I know Odie likes me, and wouldn't steal from me on his own initiative. Besides, I'd warned Odie that I would bust him big time if he ever betrayed me.

"But then one night Collie, he's out doing his night watchman thing. He catches Odie in the act of breaking into my garage and beats the shit out of him. Odie caves, fingers

Crouch for the piano wire hit. Given the choice between calling Crouch and calling Gunnar, Odie chooses Gunnar. Gunnar drives over in the middle of the night and retrieves Odie. Obviously, he's not pleased, but he's very cool. Gunnar swears he didn't set up the break-in and also denies he set up the CBX job, although he admits that he learned later that Crouch was good for it. I figure that from that moment, Kerry Crouch was a dead man walking. At the time, I wasn't smart enough to realize that Odie was, too."

Gilbert takes a long, slow sip of El Messaya.

"Gilbert, I could have given up Kerry Crouch to you that night and solved your murder, but I chose not to. Chose to stay in the fencing game, chose to stay in cahoots with Gunnar Spaaks."

"So why tell me this now?" Gilbert whispers.

"Because there's a lot more to this horror story. A while later, Collie is driving a hot McLaren down to Memphis in a transporter we'd been renting from Darryl Allmire. Stops in a truck stop. Tall skinny guy comes up to his cab, sticks a thirty-eight in Collie's face. But Collie's ready for trouble. He plants a taser on the guy's face, then jumps out, picks up the guy's gun, tases the guy again, and gives him a heavy-duty kick in the balls. Grabs his wallet. Slashes the tires on the guy's minivan and gets the hell out of there. If there are other guys helping with the hijack, Collie never sees 'em. You want to guess who the hijacker was?"

"I have a good guess," Gilbert says.

"Hell, at the time, Collie didn't even know who Kerry Crouch was. Collie's never *seen* Kerry Crouch. The wallet, by the way, belonged to a dead Semper guy named William Salmon. Good friend of Kerry Crouch before he got hit by a train."

"Billy Salmon," Gilbert says. "He got killed before I got to town, but everyone says he was a sweet guy."

I clap my hands loudly, and Gilbert's head jerks up. "Well guess who's *not* a sweet guy? You want to guess who ambushed my brother, who set up a revenge killing?"

"Same guess," Gilbert says.

I feel myself fighting to keep myself under control. "Only now both Odie and Kerry Crouch get themselves murdered! You want to guess who's good for *those* hits?"

"So, you think it's Spaaks, think everything adds up. Only at this point, it's all circumstantial. You've just become a valuable 'confidential informant,' Victor, but you're also a self-serving felon. Confessing all this to me is not going to get you off the hook."

"I do not expect to be let off the hook, Gilbert, either morally or legally. I'm a big boy, I can take my medicine. This confession is not one I decided to make without knowing the serious consequences. I do want to negotiate, however, and I also want to collaborate with you on something."

He cocks his head. *Interested, but wary.*

"Look, Gilbert, I don't know if you can get Gunnar for murder or not. But most of my fencing deals came to me through him. Now I'm going to tell you a *lot* about Gunnar Spaaks. And I want to help bust Gunnar Spaaks big time. My brother took three shots to the face because of me. That hit was Crouch's play. But Odell Todd is dead *because of me.* Odie Todd was an oaf, Gilbert, but he did not deserve to die. And they stuck a pistol up his nose and pulled the trigger. Murdered him from the front. *Go on, try to picture that. Picture Odie's last moment on earth, Gilbert.* Spaaks tried to get me to believe that Odie had just left town, run away, because he was afraid I'd turn him in. But I knew better. I knew Spaaks could not let Odie and Crouch stay alive."

"So, if you're right about all this, why hasn't Spaaks tried to kill you?"

"Before, there was no need. We had each other by the short hairs. I knew he was a crook, he knew I was I crook. It was a stalemate. Besides, he was sending me a lot of business. Also, he knew I had *this*."

I tap on a black vinyl notebook sitting in front of me, push it over to Gilbert.

"My insurance policy. You're going solve a lot of crimes with this little book, Gilbert. It's all there: names, dates, phone numbers, merchandise, what Collie and I paid, what we sold it for. You're going to become a local hero because you're going to solve more than twenty crimes, get maybe forty convictions, once you throw all the accomplices in. The good people of Green Lake will probably give you a ticker-tape parade.

"But I want more than that. I want you to nail Gunnar red-handed. I want to set up a sting on Gunnar Spaaks. I want to sucker punch that sucker. I want to see him shocked and helpless. I want to see his face the moment he realizes he's cooked. I want *revenge* for Odie's murder."

Gilbert slides the notebook over to himself, and glances through the pages. "I'll think about it," he says.

—⁓—

Gilbert and I continue to talk for two more hours. The El Messaya has a peculiar effect on our conversation. We both get quite drunk, but we don't try to fight off the intoxication. We both know we need an anesthetic, something to dull the pain. And that's what the arak does.We don't get sloppy drunk or angry drunk or maudlin drunk. We get numb drunk, and it helps us work through things. We remain lucid, don't slur our words or our thoughts. But we are both aware that we are both absolutely *hammered.* Brianna tells us she doesn't intend to let either of us drive home, and confiscates our bottle of El Massaya.

All in all, we conduct ourselves like gentlemen, although Gilbert sighs and says, "God *damn* you, Victor" over and again as I explain the details of our activities. On one occasion he says, "You really make me feel like a sucker." On another, he takes a dirty shot: "Were you this dishonest when you were a big-time architect? Did you deceive people then, too? Didja get some kind of rush out of it?"

I take the shots stoically; after all, he's entirely justified in his anger and disappointment.

"At least I have one bit of good news for you," I tell Gilbert, "a little consolation. Collie and I are out of business. And with Causley out of business and McFarland out of business and me out of business, suddenly there's a real shortage of fences to receive high-dollar stolen property around here. I think you may see a drop off in property crime around Green Lake for a while, because there is simply no one locally to sell all the stolen property to."

Gilbert drops his chin, shakes his head, and smiles wanly. "Well, gee, Victor, that's really great news. Thank you for making my day."

With the aid of the black vinyl notebook, I flesh out a lot of details for Gilbert, filling in a lot of blanks. Several times he says, "So that explains *that,*" and "Okay, now I get it." Truth to tell, watching all the pieces come together and link disparate pieces of his investigation is sort of fun, like completing a jig-saw puzzle. If we weren't sitting, angry and inebriated, on opposite sides of the legal table, we would be behaving like a team.

I tell Gilbert that before we discuss setting up our sting for Gunnar and his chums, I have a proposal for him, one that will assure my cooperation and my testimony. Its's a plan that includes turning custody of the black vinyl notebook over to him. To make the proposal—*our agreement*—work, Gilbert has to get the feds to buy in, to hold up their end in charging and sentencing recommendations, has to assure that there are no double-crosses that would make me scuttle the deal. He promises he can do this.

I tell Gilbert I will agree to plead guilty to one count of Interstate Transportation of Stolen Property, a federal crime punishable by imprisonment for up to ten years, plus a hefty fine. I say I want the United States Attorney's Office for the Eastern District of Wisconsin to waive federal sentencing guidelines and recommend a sentence of eleven to twenty-three months in a federal facility. Citing my lack of a criminal record and recent significant contributions to law enforcement in the Green Lake community, my lawyer will argue for probation, a $5,000 fine, and restitution. I get to put on character witnesses at sentencing. We'll let the judge decide the ultimate disposition. I agree not to appeal. I insist that in the indictment's recitation of our crime, Colin Harding will not be mentioned by name, but will be described as "Unindicted Co-conspirator Number One." No further prosecutorial action will be taken against him.

Gilbert listens to my proposal stone-faced. "You've clearly thought this over, Victor, and now I'll have to think it over."

Now Gilbert shifts in his chair, turns to look out the window again, sighs, then looks back at me. There's a long pause.

"*Victor, why in the world would you do this?* As far as I know you didn't need the money. You've had a successful career. You've pulled your family together up here. You've earned a lot of respect for your part in the whole Alliance thing. You look like you got it all. *So why do this?* It doesn't make any sense. Why would you put everything at risk?"

"You won't believe me," I say.

"Try me," Gilbert says.

"Well the practical reason was I was broke. Courtesy of a catastrophic financial crisis caused by my financial manager unexpectedly losing all his marbles, my whole investment portfolio was wiped out. For a while it looked like I might lose my house. So... desperate times, desperate measures. But there were other reasons to, and although they may sound silly, they played heavily on my mind."

Gilbert looks at me blankly.

"I was forced into retirement just because I was getting old. I still was sharp, but no one would hire an old fart like me. This made me very, very angry. A lot of strong feelings— anger, loss, frustration, fear of dying. I wanted *revenge* against the whole world, Gilbert. Also, I was just plain bored to death. Going stir crazy, as if I was in jail. So...I looked for some excitement. *It was exciting to become a crook.* And, damn my soul, I coerced my weak and damaged brother into joining me. We worked well together, built a bond we hadn't had in years. So, all these factors just sort of came together at once."

Gilbert betrays no emotion. Just stares at me.

"Look, Gilbert, I had a pretty good idea of the consequences if I got caught. Not pleasant, but not horrible, either. So, if my crimes had a cost? Well, to hell with it, I decided I was willing to pay."

Gilbert crosses his arms. "You want me to believe that you'd really risk prison at age seventy-something just to put a jolt in your life?"

"I would and I did. The hardest part was deceiving you."

Gilbert shakes his head as if he's hearing something unbelievably silly. He thumps his wrists on the edge of the table. He takes a sip of arak, looks down at the milky liquor in his glass. "You know, I could grow to like this stuff." He smiles ruefully, an unsettling gesture under the circumstances.

Gilbert pauses and finally speaks, his voice almost a whisper. "I am very angry at you, Victor. And I am very, very disappointed in you. I thought you had more character than this. More...*integrity.* And I'm very sad, too. I don't care so much that you didn't treat me with respect, I can handle that. I'm just sad that I'm losing a pleasant friendship solely because of your selfishness. God damn you, Victor."

"Yes," I respond. "God damn me."

45

After the Fall

GREAT STRESSES often produce paradoxical reactions. I expect Christine to go ballistic when I tell her, Delia, and Cara that I have 'fessed up, that I am I'm about to be outed as a felon. Not so. Christine leans back at the dinner table, sucks down a half-glass of fine Merlot in one gulp, sighs long and deep, and says, "Good work, Victor. Under the circumstances you did the right thing, and I think you handled the situation with Gilbert Rennie very well. I can't be proud of you for becoming a fence, but I can be proud that you've handled yourself like a stand-up guy, as they say on TV."

Delia is more ambivalent. On one hand, because she has had family members operate and suffer punishment as crooks and thieves, my unraveling tale is familiar territory to her. She does not pass moral judgment on me, and she thinks I've negotiated the best deal possible. Like all of us, she is relieved that we've kept Collie from being tarred and feathered.

But she's worried that Gilbert will start sniffing around the legality of Coeur D'Or's activities. That part of our activities is going swimmingly, and she is worried that my confession may somehow derail that promising enterprise. I assure our gang that Bugsy's gold has not been mentioned in my discussions with the authorities and will never be mentioned. No point in going overboard on the whole get-it-off-your-chest thing. As far as the world—and Gilbert Rennie—are concerned, Coeur D'Or is a scrupulously honest enterprise in all regards, and its role in sponsoring and operating the Alliance is much to be praised.

This is important because the Spaaks sting is going to be built around the heist of a mythical delivery of a large cache of gold ingots to Delia's atelier at Phone Home. This fiction makes sense because so much of the Alliance's activity centers around goldsmithing. We also think that it will have powerful seduction potential for Gunnar Spaaks because, first, it will be a direct blow to the detested Victor and Colin Harding, second, it looks like an absurdly easy heist, and third, the supposed value of the goods runs to the millions, even after the fence's discount. Who could resist that?

— 46 —

The Sting

OUR BIGGEST CHALLENGE is to figure out how to get Gunnar Spaaks to "learn" of the gold delivery to the Alliance in a way he finds credible and doesn't make him suspicious. Perhaps we overthink this one a little, but the method we finally devise ends up working like a charm.

A large gray BMW motorcycle with Pennsylvania plates whispers into the Semper Bar parking lot early one December afternoon, its exhaust notes barely audible. It is fitted out for long distance touring, with a tall windscreen, a fiberglass fairing and saddle bags, even a radio. The seat is soft and thickly padded, and the ends of the handlebars are covered with thick protective gloves called pogies. The rider switches off the engine, pulls his hands out of the pogies, swings his leg awkwardly over the high-backed touring seat, and flips the bike's side stand down.

Tall and narrow-shouldered, the rider shakes his arms and legs to drive out the stiffness. He is dressed in what looks like an adult version of a kiddie snow suit. It's olive drab, quilted and heavily padded. The suit has the word "Pagans" embroidered on the back in red eight-inch letters, and the rider's club nickname—his handle—is embroidered in white on his left breast: *Backlash*. The man wears mid-calf military boots, highly polished. The right boot has a knife sheath built into it, out of which projects the handle of a giant Bowie knife, a deadly weapon most definitely not concealed. The rider pulls off his balaclava, revealing salt-and-pepper hair, an oversize Roman nose, and several days' growth of beard.

At the top of the stairs leading into the bar stands Mel Vitriola, the Semper Bar's morbidly-obese resident shield, protector, bouncer, and guard dog. As usual, Mel's face is flushed, and his speech is slurred. His giant gut hangs grotesquely over a leather belt that is dangerously overtaxed.

"You really drive that thang all the way from Penns'vania?"

"Oh, yeah," the rider laughs. "Colder 'n' a well-digger's ass in the Klondike, let me tell you. This ride is something I don't ever want to have to do again."

Mel cracks his knuckles loudly in front of himself, rotates his bull neck as if to free it up for impending conflict, lowers his voice to a growl. "Well, yuh kin just keep on ridin,' because we don't allow nothing but Harley riders in Semper Bar. We all ride 'Murican, don't have no truck with Jap crap or with pussy BMW touring bikes." He gestures dismissively at the big touring cycle. "Get yer German garbage outta here."

"Blow me," the rider replies calmly.

Mel thuds down the stairs, but rather than accosting the rider, he places his grubby work boot on the side of the BMW and gives it mighty shove with his leg. The BMW teeters momentarily, then topples on to its side. There is a crash of breaking glass as its rearview mirror is driven into the pavement. Mel stands back, hands on hips, momentarily triumphant.

There is a flash of movement as the rider slides behind Mel and a peculiar *Zing!*—the sound of the rider's Bowie knife being whipped from its scabbard. A second noise, a sort of *thwup!*, is the sound the Bowie knife makes as it slices through Mel Vitriola's belt and rips cleanly down the back seam of his filthy blue jeans. In a moment, the two pieces of Mel's pants are gathered around his ankles and his red boxer shorts are blowing in the wind. The knife also has put a thin slit in Mel's drawers, revealing a flash of bare buttock, traced with a thin blaze of blood.

The rider crooks his foot in front of Mel's ankle and shoves Mel forward. Hobbled by his dropped drawers, Mel pitches forward and crashes face-first into the side of the BMW. Instantly the rider is on Mel's back, his knife poised behind Mel's ear.

There is a gunshot, and a chip of pavement ricochets off the front fender of the BMW.

"That will do, gentlemen," says Gunnar Spaaks from the top of the steps.

The rider slowly lifts himself off Mel Vitriola, slowly lifts his knife into the air, slowly slides it back into his sheath. He does not raise his hands, does not step back. He makes no move, just stands there motionless.

"Spaaks?" he asks.

"Me." Gunnar says, lowering his pistol. "You are..."

"Hansel Gregg. *Pagans.* Wilmington, Delaware. Drove all the way out here just to talk to you. Got a very rude reception. Disrespectful. Totally uncalled-for."

Mel, meanwhile, has pissed himself and is thrashing around, trying to gather up his ripped pants, cover his bare butt, and see where the blood is coming from. He is a mess, bawling with fear, snot running down his face.

"Mel," Gunnar says softly. "You're a sight, man. Go get yourself cleaned up, have someone put a band-aid on your ass. See if you can recover some dignity."

Mel, still wrestling with his slashed jeans, starts to whine. "But, he..."

Gunnar's voice is sharp, cold. "Mel!" Mel Vitriola backpedals into the garage, trying vainly to cover his buttocks and hide his shame.

Gregg looks up at Spaaks. "Your man takes himself too seriously."

"Well, he's not the sharpest crayon in the box," says Spaaks. "Only got one track on his CD. But he wants so hard to belong, so we let him belong. He usually doesn't push the Semper button quite so hard. I'm sorry you were not treated politely."

"Well, next time, I'd appreciate if you just fire your gun up into the air, okay?"

"Point taken. And we'll fix your Beemer, with apologies for the damage. Now what exactly can I do for you, Mr. Gregg?"

"The question is what I can do for you," Gregg says, starting up the stairs. They seat themselves at a table alone in a back corner of the bar.

"Gunnar, we know about you back in Wilmington. *The Semper man.* Larry Dykstra, who used to ride with you guys out here, now rides with us Pagans in Delaware. Good guy."

"I know Larry," says Gunnar. "Actually, not a good guy. Actually, one mean son of a bitch. You rode all the way out here in freezing cold weather to tell me you know Larry Dykstra?"

"I rode out here to make us all a bucketload of money if you'll just keep your smart mouth shut and listen for a minute."

Gunnar stiffens, then his curiosity gets the better of his pride. He gestures to Gregg to keep talking.

"Look, man," says Gregg. "You, me, we're in the same business. I used to do a lot of jobs with the Johnston brothers out in Chester County, Pennsylvania until they got busted for putting out contracts on their own kids."

"I know the story," says Gunnar.

"You got any contacts out there?"

"Not really, but I can always make a few calls. What's the point?"

"Check me out. Make sure I'm not bullshitting you."

This is the highest risk point of our whole bluff. We're betting that Gunnar won't make the calls, won't check out Hansel Gregg's *bona fides*. If he does try to check us out, he'll learn that both Larry Dykstra and the real Hansel Gregg are presently incarcerated, Dykstra in the state pen at Graterford, Pennsylvania, Gregg in the federal slammer in Allenwood. So here we are at the tipping point: *Will Gunnar make some calls and blow our cover?*

"I may do that. And just why am I supposed to be checking you out?

"Because I'm about to offer you the deal of a lifetime, and I'm gonna want to take a big cut, and my people in Wilmington are going to want to take a big cut."

"What is so big that you should ride your Beemer all the way out to Wisconsin? It's *December,* man!"

"This has to be face-to-face stuff, Gunnar. Emails, phone calls—just not secure enough. So I stole the BMW from an underground parking lot in Philly. The idea was to sell it when I got out here and fly home when we're done with our business. Turned out it was a good approach—lets you and me talk man-to-man and size each other up, lets me in on the heist. Lets me make sure you don't screw it up...or screw me over."

Gregg smiles pleasantly, cracks his knuckles loudly in a clear let's-get-down-to-business gesture.

"Anyway, back in Pennsylvania, the Pagans do some jobs with this guy named Lemuel Dalo. Lemuel Dalo works at the Franklin Mint in Chester County, Pennsylvania. Day job, he's an inventory administrator and invoice processor. And sometimes he gives us some interesting intel."

"Yeah?"

"Yeah. Here's some. You got an artists' collective here in Green Lake. Started by some famous goldsmith broad named Delia Chamberlain. She makes a lot of *very* high-priced gold jewelry, and the artisans in this collective also use a lot of gold in their work. More important, Chamberlain now also sells gold to the trade, not to dentists and like that, but to people who make various products out of gold—solid-gold faucets, solid-gold key chains, solid-gold dog collars, like that. She does some retail transactions out the front door, also slides stuff out the back door at discounted prices to a couple of favored clients. Bottom line, she moves a *lot* of gold.

"This collective is called the Alliance, something like that, and it is Lemuel Dalo's account at the Franklin Mint. He both buys and sells gold for them. Some of it is activity that is not listed in their catalog, if you catch my drift."

"I'm listening."

"Next Tuesday, a load of a hundred and fifty 24 karat gold bars is going to be delivered to Delia Chamberlain's workshop. It's in a barn on a bluff about three miles outside Green Lake. Used to be some famous sculptor's house."

"I know the place," says Gunnar. "I know where that barn is."

"The shipment will arrive in the late afternoon. Only take an hour to unload. There will be no security on the property at all, if you can believe that, except for a dipshit home alarm system. Apparently, these trusting country types don't believe in security guards."

"I know these people," Spaaks says. "One of 'em used to fence high-end stuff for us, then chickened out, left us suckin' some serious wind. And sure as hell, he's going to know this was my play."

"Do you care?" asked Gregg.

"Just the opposite," smiles Spaaks. "It'll be...*rewarding* that he knows I clipped him and his whole family of conceited snobs. And he's boxed: he can't drop a dime on me without me droppin' a dime on him. Anyway, don't sweat security. I'll see to that."

"So, here's what," Gregg continued. "Some of your guys, and me, of course, we drop by and liberate it in the middle of the night. We'll need a box truck, load's too heavy for a van. Your guys are going to be loading about nineteen hundred and fifty pounds."

"No problem."

"Well, maybe one problem. Chamberlain and her faggot partner live in the house. No way of knowin' if they're gonna wake up."

"We got guys with guns. No sweat. Anyway, we'll cut the phone lines before we hit the barn."

"Ever hear of cell phones?"

"Okay, so we'll wake 'em up, baby-sit them while we load the truck. No one will get hurt, no police gonna get called."

"Only now it's a robbery instead of a burglary."

"Doesn't make any difference if you don't get caught."

Gregg makes a jerk-off motion with his hand.

"You got some place you can take the bars?"

"First step would be to get 'em to my body shop, do a tally, but I'll arrange to move 'em on real fast. I know someone who has a barn around here, maybe use that until we can organize fencing. We got a local sheriff who thinks he's Dick Tracy and thinks I'm some big-time crime boss. He'll be sniffing at my ass the moment this gets reported. I will want to be able to give him the squeaky-clean tour of my body shop."

"You got a reliable fence, someone who can come up with five million in cash?"

Gunnar Spaaks pauses, smiles. "That the number?"

"Well, you're welcome to get whatever you can get at your end. This isn't Fort Knox, you know. You're not going to be able to price this by the Troy ounce. Anyway, the Pagans' cut is a four and a half mil. My own cut—as an 'expeditor,' you know, that's why I rode all the way out here—is an additional five hundred K. You get anything you can sell the stuff for over that."

"That negotiable?"

"Why would we negotiate? You stand to make a boatload of money off this deal, so don't be so goddamned greedy. Just do the math. Bottom line, deal is completely non-negotiable, at least at our end. If your fence is a stand-up guy, y'all will do plenty okay. So who is your fence?"

"This guy I was just talkin' about, we used to think he was a class act, but he turned out to be a dickhead. I'm gonna have to find a new banker."

"Well, you better work fast, because my guys, well, we don't always demand cash on the barrelhead, but we're not going to sit around and play the float on five mil, either."

"Understood. Where you staying?"

"Checked in at some fleabag motel called the Dartmoor over by Green Lake."

Gunnar frowns. "You're going to park that twenty-thousand-dollar Beemer in front of the Dartmoor on Route 23 in mid-December? Someone's gonna notice that if you stick around more than a day. For that matter, someone's likely to steal it if you leave it in plain sight for more than a day."

"It's what I got, man."

"Tell you what," Gunnar says. "You leave it here with us, we'll stash it, fix your mirror, buff out the scratches in the bodywork. Then I'll give you ten grand for it. I know that's a steep discount, but as we say at Semper, *'hot brings heat.'* Meanwhile, you drive my Honda Accord while you're here.

And, sorry to ask this, but please take off your Pagan colors and give yourself a clean shave. Buy yourself a cowboy shirt as a souvenir of Wisconsin. Try not to attract attention."

Hansel Gregg, known in other circles as Special Agent David Richter of the Kewaskum, Wisconsin FBI Field Office, nods knowingly.

—⁓—

Back in 1785, in a poetic foreshadowing of Murphy's Law (*"If anything can go wrong, it will"*), famed Scottish poet Robert Burns wrote, *"the best laid plans of mice an' men gang aft a-gley."* And so it goes with us. We thought we had planned a fail-safe, locked down, no drama trap in which the perps would instantly recognize that they had no options and would submit passively to group arrest. We did not count on the rank stupidity on the part of one of the Semper stooges.

Gilbert tries to tell me I cannot attend the festivities, what with my being a civilian and all, but then quickly backs off when I threaten to go mute in front of the Grand Jury. I wouldn't miss this for the world. He finally grants me a spectator pass but warns me to wear a black knit watch cap, keep my mouth shut, and stay out of sight, far away from the action.

The FBI buys a load of one hundred and fifty ceramic-glazed bricks, and the sting team spends an hour spraying them with metallic gold paint. At first glance, the effect is quite convincing. The ad hoc law enforcement task force—local cops in the form of Gilbert and his deputy sheriffs, some state police troopers, and a handful of FBI agents—stack them into a tight little pyramid in a back corner of the barn, behind an ancient hay-baler. This will make the "ingots" hard to access and carry out. They cover them with a blue tarp. Then they position two FBI agents in the loft of the barn, hide four Wisconsin State Police troopers in Chateau Phone

Home's carport, and position two Green Lake Police cruisers on a dirt side road about a quarter-mile down Highway 49. I opt for the loft; Gilbert stands behind the door leading into Delia's private atelier at the back of the barn. Over their protests, we send Delia and Christine over to Collie's house, promising to call as soon as there is news.

Shortly after one-thirty in the morning, a dark red box truck pulls into the end of the driveway, then does a Y-turn and backs in toward the barn. The truck's rear door slides up, and six guys—*dressed in their biker leathers, if you can believe it*—hop out. Two of them head off to check out the house. The rest head for the barn. A beat-up white Honda Accord pulls in next to the truck, and Gunnar, dressed in a starched cowboy shirt and nicely pressed jeans, and 'Hansel Gregg,' dressed in greasy dark blue coveralls, climb out. The two house-checkers jog back, call out, "House is empty!" none too quietly.

From the hay loft, I'm rolling the video on my cell phone as the heisters slide the barn door open and peep in. Gunnar flicks the light switch, and the whole barn is bathed in the bright glow of the barn's overhead fluorescent lights. Not too subtle, these guys, but hey, Gunnar thinks no one is around. The bad guys separate, move around the barn floor looking for their pot of gold.

"Got it!" a tall, incredibly buff guy cries out from the corner, and the others move over toward him. Our man 'Hansel' hangs back. Gunnar Spaaks tugs off the blue tarp, sees the gleaming bars.

"Bring in the hand trucks!" he yells, and three of the thieves wheel in flat orange heavy-load carts they have stolen from Home Depot. Gunnar picks up a bar from the top row of the gold pyramid, examines it in the harsh white light.

He knows immediately something is wrong. He spins around wildly, trying to figure out what he's gotten himself into. His warning shout is drowned out by the deafening blast of a freon horn, the kind boaters use. The four state police troopers spring through the door. Two are aiming big ugly pistols in a two-handed shoot-to-kill grip, the others aim riot guns at the stunned thieves.

"FBI! Freeze! Hands up!" one of the FBI agents in the loft yells. The crooks stumble back into each other in the center of the barn floor, circling the wagons against an attack they cannot possibly defeat. Hands reach for the sky. So far, so good.

Then everything goes south.

Buff Guy reaches back and fumbles for the holster clamped under his vest in the small of his back. "Don't do it!" screams one of the FBI agents in the loft. But Buff Guy does it anyway, ripping his small black semiautomatic free from the holster and starting to squat.

There is a sharp report from the loft, and the left side of Buff Guy's jaw vanishes in a sheet of gore. He flops to the floor, writhing wildly. Much of his face is gone, but his vocal cords apparently are intact, and he emits a horrible, unbroken foamy scream.

I'll say this for Gunnar Spaaks: he thinks fast. In seconds, he has ripped off his cowboy shirt, wadded it up, and stuffed it in the gaping hole beneath Buff Guy's nose. He's shouting, "Don't shoot! We're done, we're done, we're done!"

Deputy Lee Ruliscz, ignoring the fact that he is placing himself in numerous lines of fire, rushes to Buff Guy's side, pinions him to stop his writhing, rips off his own belt, and wraps it swiftly around the gaping wound and Gunnar's blood-soaked shirt. "Ambulance! EMTs! Shock trauma!" he yells, and one of the state police troopers fingers the radio fastened to his upper chest.

Now there is a flurry of barked orders, a chaotic flurry of police action. Even before frisking the thieves for weapons, the Fibbies and state police guys zip-tie their hands behind their backs, one-by-one. A subsequent body search produces four pistols, a huge military knife, and a stiletto in one guy's boot. Also, a small envelope of cocaine and a pill bottle filled with crystal meth.

I am astonished at Gunnar Spaaks' *savoir faire.* He stands quietly, bare-chested, over his fallen accomplice, looking around the barn, taking stock. He sees Gregg/Richter, standing calmly by the barn door. "Hey! What about him?" yells Spaaks.

"Oh, him. He's with us." Gilbert Rennie steps out from behind Delia's door, walks slowly over to Gunnar and his gang. "You are all under arrest," he says calmly. "Deputy Ruliscz, please read them their rights." We then hear that growling *brap!* sound a police siren makes when it's switched quickly on and off. We see the blinding flashes of red and blue lights bouncing off the inside walls through the open door. Two more state police troopers rush in, and Gilbert yells out, "forget the ambulance! Load him in your back seat and get him to Grace Cottage before he bleeds out!" In moments, Buff Guy is gone, leaving a large pool of blood on the floor.

I climb down the ladder from the loft, rung-by-runging it with one hand while continuing to run my cell phone video camera. Gunnar sees me, and I am delighted to catch his expression on video. This will be a highlight of Harding family Christmas parties for years to come.

I walk over, smiling smugly, tasting the venom that washes my mouth, savoring the sting of hatred. Out of Gilbert Rennie's earshot, I whisper in Gunnar Spaaks' ear.

"Hello, you cocksucker. To answer the question you once asked me, yes, I *do* think I'm pretty smart. Oh, and Gunnar? Guess what? We found your Corvette."

47

Due Process

I AM ARRAIGNED SEPARATELY from Gunnar Spaaks and his gang because I am being charged with a different offense. In due course, pursuant to my deal with Gilbert Rennie, I will be charged in a federal indictment and have a bail hearing in Milwaukee. The feds will ask for twenty-five thousand dollars bail, which I will not contest. Meanwhile, Rennie lodges state misdemeanor charges against me alleging petty theft, knowing that I will be released on my own recognizance.

So, at the moment, I'm out of the slammer, and, although I'm fearful of retribution from members of Semper, at least I'm home. As Gilbert requests, I maintain a sort of house arrest, staying away from windows and checking in with him twice a day. I want to know what's going on at his end, he wants to know what's going on at mine. Ours is an uneasy alliance.

I venture out only a couple of times, enough to tell me that in the future I may be in for some rough times in the Green Lake social scene. I'm gassing up my BMW when a car pulls up at the next pump and the driver's window rolls down. Doris Frantz calls out, "I heard about your big 'sting,' Victor. I suppose you're feeling pretty proud of yourself, right? Well, I think you are a slime bag. We don't need people like you in Green Lake." On the other hand, Rudy, the bag boy at the Redi-Mart, punches me in the arm as I check out. "Pretty cool, Man," he smiles.

Delia cannot stop talking about the excitement of the bust and the cleverness of the sting, but the rest of us are feeling pretty subdued. We have just traversed pretty rocky emotional territory, and we all suspect another shoe will drop, although we don't know whether that shoe will belong to the good guys or the bad guys. The story of the bust has hit the local papers, and there's a rush of crime tourists at the atelier. Delia is able to sell each of the "gold" ceramic bricks for two hundred bucks, half of which is donated to the Alliance, half to the Green Lake Police Athletic League. The FBI declines a cut of the proceeds.

We are all having a quiet lunch at my place—Cal's Maine-recipe lobster salad—when the phone rings in the house. Colin rises to get it, and when he returns, he is ashen.

"Gunnar Spaaks made bail," he says, his voice breaking. "Rennie says he posted half a million cash bail, and they have just let him out. The rest of the guys in his crew couldn't make bail, and they're still in the can pending trial."

Christine explodes. "But that's *outrageous!* The man is a murderer! They can't just put a murderer out on the street!"

"According to the judge, Gunnar's bail hearing could only focus on the burglary charge. They couldn't even charge armed robbery because although Gunnar's guys were armed, there was no one home to rob. The Assistant DA tried to bring in the information we have about collateral crimes—namely the piano wire murder and Odie Todd's execution—and the judge said he could not hear or act on unsubstantiated allegations and uncharged crimes. Basically, told the assistant DA to sit down and shut up. So...Gunnar walked."

This was foreseeable. And I know exactly what we all must do. "Christine, Delia, Collie, pack your bags, lock your houses, and get yourselves back over here ASAP. We're going to go to the mattresses, as the Mafia would say. I'm going to call Seth Bartlett up from the Janesville warehouse and have him move into the back apartment to take up guard duty. Also ask him to check your houses a couple of times a day. I'll ask Cal to stay with friends for a while. Colin, I think you should suggest to Cara that she come over here too, but let me leave that up to you. I don't want to presume on your relationship, but I hope she has enough sense to realize that Gunnar's likely to go on a rampage and that she's in real danger."

"How long do you think we'll have to stay holed up?" Collie asks.

"Hard to know," I say. "We've got to see how things play out. Meanwhile, and I do not say this in jest, remember that Bugsy's tunnel leads down to the boathouse, and I've left the manhole cover unlocked. The entrance is through one of those high windows on the south wall of the basement."

—⁓—

Gilbert's on the phone. "You playing games with me, Victor?"

"I don't know what you're talking about, Gilbert."

I'm lying. I know exactly what he's talking about. I agreed to plead guilty and help Gilbert by testifying in every case where I can be a useful witness, but I have not sworn him an oath of truth and fidelity. I'm still feel free to lie any time I want.

"You know anything about a yellow Corvette?"

I go with a half-truth, starting with a parry and a thrust.

"Gilbert, did Gunnar Spaaks ever report an auto theft at his auto body shop?"

"Now I don't know what *you're* talking about."

"I was having Gunnar refurbish a Kaiser Darrin sports car that Vilma Stakhatos gave me. It was almost done when Spaaks called me and said it was one of three cars stolen from his body shop. The other two were a yellow 'sixty-five Corvette, which Gunnar said was his, and a 'sixty-four Pontiac GTO. I told Gunnar to report the thefts to you so that I could get a police report in order to make a claim on my homeowner's insurance. He said, no, he wanted to track the cars down himself, that he could find them before you could."

"Did you get your car back?"

"Not yet, although Collie has put out feelers among his classic car friends, see if it's been fenced out of state."

"And you don't know anything about the Corvette."

"Gilbert, you want to fill me in here?"

"Lee Ruliscz found a bright yellow 1965 Corvette parked next to a meter in front of the bait shop early this morning. It had a big laser-printed sign stuck under the windshield wiper. The sign said, 'Call Gilbert Rennie.' This sounds like something you'd do, part of your whole fascination with laundering."

"Wasn't me," I say. "Sort of wish it was, because this is a cute caper, but nope, I'm not stepping up to this one."

"I wish I was sure I could believe you."

"I don't need gratuitous insults, Gilbert. Just tell me what this was all about. Was the Corvette Gunnar's?"

"Well, Ruliscz calls me out of bed, and I drive downtown, see the note. I run the VIN. According to DMV, Gunnar Spaaks has never owned or registered a Corvette, of any year or color, certainly not this one. This particular Corvette was tracked through NCIS to one Joseph Garr of Naperville,

Illinois. He says it was stolen from a Cubs game at Wrigley Field early last summer."

"You going to give it back to him?"

"Right now, I'm going to hold on to it as evidence of something against somebody at some point. Eventually, Garr will get his Corvette back, and I've let him know that. But for now, it's in impound."

"What did Garr say when you told him?"

"He said, and I quote, 'Somebody up there is going to fucking pay for this, big time.' To put the comment in context, Victor, I have learned that Joseph Garr is a *caporegime* in the East Chicago Damiano family."

"With a name like Garr?"

"Used to be Guarino before he moved to Naperville and became Mr. Suburban. His nickname with his crew is still 'Flash-bulb.'"

"You going to add a charge of auto theft on Gunnar?"

"Can't, not just on the basis of what you've told me. All you said is that you saw a yellow Corvette at Gunnar's. There's no way of proving it was *this* yellow Corvette, even though you and I both know it is. But I have every faith, Victor, that eventually the pigeons will come home to roost."

"Hope you nab the perp, Gilbert."

"Thank you for your kind thoughts, Victor."

I find Collie working in my study. Seth Bartlett is sitting in the TV chair, watching Jai Alai on the flickering screen. A shotgun rests across his knees. Collie looks up.

"That was Gilbert. You can guess exactly what he said. Blamed me, said the Corvette's going to go into impound. Interesting twist: the real owner is a mob guy down in Illinois. He's seriously pissed. All in all, this was one of your cuter ideas, Collie. Sometimes you really are a creative genius."

—◈—

The Semper Bar was, as fire-fighting types would say, 'fully involved in flames' when the first fire engines arrived. They lost control of the raging blaze, called for help, and eventually, units from Ripon, Berlin, Princeton, and Montello all sat around, bright lights flashing in the early dawn, as the two-story building lost the ability to hold up its roof, and the whole place crashed in on itself.

Mel Vitriola, the heavy-set fellow who had greeted me so cordially the one time I had gone into the Semper Bar and who had treated 'Hansel Gregg' so inhospitably upon his arrival in Green Lake, had been asleep—passed out, actually—in the back room until he felt his clothes catch fire. He raced out of the front door like a giant human torch, screaming in agony. He was promptly extinguished, smothered in foam by members of the Green Lake Fire Brigade, as he writhed in the parking lot. With third-degree burns over seventy percent of his body, the Ripon Medical Center reported that he was not expected to make it.

The arsonists had not been fooling around. The fire marshal found six separate ignition points around the building, each using a different accelerant. A *lot* of accelerants. At first, the fire marshal thought that it was solely the heat of the flames that had blistered the paint and melted the rubber on the fifteen Harleys parked in front of the bar. The fire crews had been unable to move them to safety because a heavy chain had been strung through their front wheels and padlocked to the "Members Only" signpost. The fire marshal concluded that five of them had received their own private torching, each with its own personal allocation of accelerant. "This was a very thorough job," he told reporters.

Later that morning, Deputy Ruliscz, acting on Sheriff Rennie's instruction to check out Spaaks Auto Body, found an unexploded pipe bomb under the propane tank next to the little shed where Gunnar stores his paints and solvents. It was an elegant little bomb, carefully constructed, filled with a favorite mob accelerant, jellied naphtha. That is, napalm. The bomb disposal guy said it was a perfectly serviceable device that certainly would have detonated the propane tank, and the only reason it had not yet exploded was because some genius had set the little battery-operated alarm clock attached to the detonator for four o'clock PM instead of four o'clock AM. The bomb expert moved the alarm switch to 'off' and smiled at Gilbert. "Mob," he said, "but not the Milwaukee mob. Theirs don't look like this."

I hear about the fire on the local news and Collie and I drive over to see the sights. There, hands on his hips, stands Sheriff Gilbert Rennie. I walk over.

"You going to try to pin this one on me, too, Gilbert?"

"No, Victor, I know you like to play with fire, but I don't think this kind of fire."

"Well, okay, but if you need me to provide an alibi, just let me know. I've got one ready."

48

Crisis

EVEN FROM FIVE FEET AWAY, I CAN HEAR Cara Spaaks screaming through the cell phone Colin is holding to his ear. "Gunnar broke into my apartment! Totally wrecked the place! My whole place is trashed!"

"Is he there now?" Collie yells.

"Nunh-unh," Cara wails.

"How long ago did this happen?"

"I don't know, I don't know. I was out at the Alliance all morning. Just got back. And I find *this*."

"Lock the door, Cara, and *stay there*. We're on our way. Oh, and Cara, do you know where Dany Miskinis is?"

"Yes, but I'm not supposed to tell anyone."

Collie explodes. *"God damn it, Cara. Tell me where Dany is!"*

"Dany is in Athens. Athens, Greece, not Athens, Georgia. That's where her mother lives. She left last week, after Gunnar got busted."

In perfect unison, Collie and I both exhale. *One less thing to worry about.*

When we arrive ten minutes later, the door to Cara's apartment stands ajar, the screen door hanging by a single hinge and banging against the side of the building in the January wind. Her car is gone. I am carrying a gun, and Collie is carrying the official Boy Scout hatchet he has stashed in the trunk of his Jaguar for some reason. We rush in, Collie yelling Cara's name.

Cara Spaaks is not there.

The place is a mess, but it looks more like everything has just been thrown around than has been broken and smashed. The term Gilbert Rennie uses when he arrives is "tossed."

We go from room to room. For some reason the kitchen is last, and when I go in, I freeze in horror. The door of the refrigerator is covered, top to bottom and side to side, with bright-colored post-it notes. Scores of them, Day-Glo orange, Day-Glo lime, Day-Glo purple, Day-Glo yellow. There's nothing written on any of them, they're just randomly plastered all over the door in overlapping waves of color, some bunches four or five notes thick.

Collie follows me into the kitchen. "Oh, no," he moans.

"Collie, I thought I told you..."

"I did, Victor! I did! I did tell her to get rid of all of them! I did!"

———

We are halfway back to my house when Colin's cell phone rings. I hear the buzz of an official-sounding voice.

"Yes, this is he," Colin says. "Yes, I know my number is her first speed dial."

More buzzing, then Colin screams, "*She's Dead?*"

Colin looks at me, aghast. "Ripon Medical Center ER!" he yells. "Car crash!"

I touch ninety as we barrel down Route 23 into Ripon. We say nothing, but we're both panting, gasping for air. I roar into the ER entrance and slam on the brakes under the portico. Colin is out before the car stops, leaving the car door ajar, sprinting to the ER entrance whose doors glide open silently as he approaches.

"Cara Spaaks!" he yells at the front desk. "Cara Spaaks! Is she dead?"

The curtains part on one of the side bays, and an imposing figure steps out. A three hundred pounder, he's shaped like a professional football lineman: broad shoulders, no neck, buzz cut, huge hands. His rough-hewn face looks like it's been chiseled out of granite by an adze: he's all sharp edges and angular features. He's wearing pale green scrubs that stretch tight across his enormous chest. He steps in front of Colin, places his hands on Colin's shoulders, and stops him dead in his tracks.

"*Okay!*" he yells. "Just settle!" Colin struggles to shake himself free, but the giant holds him fast. "She *not* dead!" the giant rasps loudly . "She been dead but we brang her back! Now you come 'ere and sit down!" His accent speaks of the bayou, of rough times like war and poverty, of rough things like alligator wrasslin' and moonshine in glass canning jars.

He drags Colin over to a couch and forcibly sits him down. I stand a couple of yards away, trembling. I read his name badge. It says, 'Ambrose Pollard, Physician Assistant.'

"I know you her man fren', so I'm going to tell you a couple of t'ings, and you not going to 'rupt me, okay?"

Collie nods.

"Your girl fren' was in a *big-time* accident, man. Someone chasin' her, tryin' to run her off d' road. Cops got a witness. Ol' beat-up pickup, goin' like hell, ram her from behind. She zoom down deep gully, maybe seventy miles an hour. Gully be six feet deep, launches her car inna sky. Wham! Hits a telephone pole headfirst, breaks it in half maybe ten feet offa the ground. Car folds in half, you girl fren' trap inna middle."

Colin's face goes slack. I can't tell if he's taking this in. Pollard shakes him by the shoulder again. "Hey, listen t' me!"

Collie twitches as if he's been zapped with a taser.

"OK, now! Cops, EMTs, fire-rescue guys get there in five minutes, use the jaws of life, cut the top offa car. Got her out *real* fast. Ugly, man. Serious chest damage, foot crushed. Blood pressure droppin' like a stone, meanin' probly internal hemorrhaging.

"She flatline. EMT can't do chest compression, too much trauma, no place to position the defibrillator. *But check this, man!* EMT woman grabs a taser offa cop's belt, zaps your girl fren' on her stomach, *bang!* Gets weak pulse, but at least it's a pulse. They get her to the ER less'n fifteen minutes after accident, take her straight to the OR. They preppin' her for chest surgery, she flatline again. This time easy to bring her back. Defib, *bang!* Back to good pulse, okay blood pressure. She alive, and I t'ink she gwan stay alive. She owe her life to that EMT, dat's for sure. Dat some real fast thinkin' with dat taser."

—◠◠◠—

Colin and I have been sitting in the waiting room for four hours. Christine and Delia say they'll come over, but I tell them to stand fast, that we'll call when there is news. There's no way Cara Spaaks will be receiving visitors, and Collie has all he can handle without having to relate to a lot of well-wishers.

My brother and I say nothing during the ordeal. We're not trying to process events, we are just trying to wait out the clock. I sit with my hands folded tightly across my chest, just trying to hold myself in. Collie perches on the edge of a salmon-colored vinyl couch with his hands on his knees, his head hung low. About two hours in, he suddenly gets the dry heaves and begins to pant intensely. He hyperventilates, his eyes roll back into his head, and he slides to the floor.

The charge nurse barrels over, lifts Collie's head, and clears his tongue. She shoves a vial of smelling salts under his nose—*Do they keep these handy in the waiting room?*—and Collie's head jolts up. "Okay! I'm okay!" he shouts and pushes himself back up on the couch. "I'm okay!" he yells again, waving his arms to shoo us all away.

My legs begin to cramp from sitting immobile for so long, and I'm standing at the nurse's station when I feel a tap on my shoulder. "Victor?"

I turn and see a slender sandy-haired man in pale blue surgeon's scrubs, which are covered with blood. A mask hangs down under his chin. His glasses, which have little cylindrical telescopes attached to them, are pushed up on his forehead.

"Victor, I'm Bob Satuka. Stan's brother. You and I met once at Harry Herder's son's wedding reception. I believe you called me a Vandal, or something like that."

"Bob! I'd forgotten you were on service here. You a surgeon?"

"Yeah, orthopedic surgeon. We got two other guys up there, also working on her. An internal injury expert who's also a chest-cutter, and then we have a head trauma guy. The airbags in the car deployed, but even so, she took a big shot to the head. Look, we're still working on her, and I've got to get back upstairs to finish up, but they said you guys were down here, and I thought you'd welcome a quick briefing."

"Collie, come here!" I call. He wobbles to his feet, staggers, looks like he's going to go down. Ambrose Pollard steadies him and leads him by the elbow over to Bob Satuka and me.

"Guys, I'm dead tired, so I hope you'll forgive me if I just do a quick data dump," Satuka says calmly. "I just can't muster up my tactful bedside manner right now. Here's the scoop: Cara took a huge shot to her whole left side—face, ribs, internal organs. Her left foot was caught in the door sill as the door got crushed in. Foot was pretty badly mangled. Cara went into shock because it was like her body had been hit by a bomb. Not surprising that she flatlined. Let me tell you, that was one quick-thinking EMT. I wouldn't have thought to zap her with a cop's taser. Good thing Cara's super-fit. We'd have lost her otherwise.

"Anyway, here's what's going on. First of all, I think she's going to survive, although she's still pretty shocky. I think Cartelovsky plans to induce a coma to calm things down for a few days. I've been busy trying to clean up some serious foot damage on Cara. Real jigsaw puzzle, but at least all the pieces were there, and I don't think we'll have to amputate. There will be more work to do on that foot later, but I'm pretty pleased with where we stand now."

Satuka takes a moment to catch his breath. I hear a choking sob and see Collie bury his face in his hands. A funny look comes over his face. He rushes over to the trash can in front of the nurse's station and vomits up everything in his stomach with a single gigantic heave. He looks up at us and wipes his mouth with his sleeve. He says nothing, just looks like he's been horsewhipped.

Satuka marches on. "Okay, she has a variety of internal injuries, which is always iffy territory, but John Held knows what they are and where they are. He's sure he has the hemorrhaging under control."

Bob Satuka whooshes out his breath, and stretches his arms above his head. "I got to go finish up upstairs, guys. Bottom line: Cara has suffered major trauma and her body is going to take a long time to forgive that. She's in for considerable discomfort, and a lot of rehab, but she will heal.

"You all should go home. There's no point in staying here overnight. We're going to keep Cara unconscious, and it won't do anybody any good to sit next to her bed and stare at her bandages. We'll keep you posted—and that means both of you, Colin and Victor, too. Mr. Pollard will call you in the morning with an update. By the way, he is far and away the best physician assistant I have ever seen in my life, the coolest head, the surest hands. Iraq war vet, purple heart. You are very lucky he was on call when they brought Cara in."

I move to shake Ambrose's hand, and my fingers are lost in his enormous paw. His grip is—*how to put this?*—long, firm, gentle, and kind. A tidal wave of emotion washes over me, and I cannot speak. All I can do is wave goodbye.

49

Alibi

"HE DENIES EVERYTHING," Gilbert tells me over the phone. His tone is flat, his voice clipped.

"Well, of course," I say.

"Says he has an alibi."

"Who? What?"

"His dentist."

"Pay the guy off?"

"How would I know?"

"You think he paid the guy off?"

"Either that, or he paid someone to run his sister off the road. Me, I'm bettin' the dentist came into some money."

"Yeah, me too. I'm not sure even a loyal Semper guy would sign up to commit what is basically a contract hit. What did the witness tell you? Was he in a car?"

"She, not he. On the sidewalk, opposite side of the street on route forty-nine, just outside Ripon. Said it happened fast, heard an engine roaring, saw the impact, saw Cara's car flyin' through the air."

"What happened to the truck?"

"Just sped off down forty-nine."

"Get any kind of ID from the witness?"

"No ID, no license plate number. Couldn't identify Gunnar on a photo spread. Couldn't identify *anybody* on a photo spread. Driver was wearin' a baseball cap, that's all she could say. The wit was pretty shook."

"I should think so. What now?"

"We churn the wheels of justice as we move toward trial on the sting, with Gunnar Spaaks still wanderin' around on bail, free to commit more mayhem. This has really upset me, Victor, I must say. Spaaks was so insufferable when he talked to me, so smug. Says he ain't goin' anywhere, got himself a good lawyer, is sure he's gonna beat the rap. Says he'll show up, dressed in a nice suit, for all his criminal proceedings. I quote: 'What do you take me for, sheriff? A bail jumper?'"

"Scares me that he's free to prowl around. We're all pretty spooked."

"Everyone still livin' at your house?"

"For the duration, Gilbert. And warning: we are armed and dangerous. Also, we got a security guard, Seth Bartlett, up from his regular job at our Janesville warehouse. Please tell that to your folks, Gilbert. Seth is a *very* serious guy. It's not *'shoots first, asks questions later.'* It's *'shoots first, never asks any questions.'* Am I being clear?"

"Copy. I'll alert my guys, and the state police, too."

So, anyway," I ask, "when's the preliminary hearing?"

"Scheduled in three weeks. I asked the judge to expedite."

"Thanks, Gilbert. Any luck finding the truck?"

"Nope. We're all lookin' for an old blue Ford pickup with right front-end damage. Lee Rulicz is diggin' hard, checkin' the auto salvage places, like that. All he's got to do is find a busted-up front fender. But nothin' so far."

"Wouldn't be surprised if he comes up dry. Gunnar Spaaks runs a chop shop."

"Don't I know it. That truck could be spread all over the Midwest by now."

"Gilbert?"

"Yeah."

"I'm sorry it all came to this. I never thought it would come to this."

"Yeah. I know, Victor. I know."

50

The Green Lake

SURYA DAMALI, NUDE except for the huge gold body necklace encircling her body from the waist up, stands unself-consciously in front of the photographer for the Danish lifestyles magazine "Det Beste." *The Best.* And there's no doubt about it, when it comes to pure animal magnetism, Surya Damali ranks with the best. Delia stands next to her, dressed in a soft white linen suit. Their skin is the same dark chestnut color, only with Surya, you can see a lot more of it at the moment. The effect is quite breathtaking.

Next to her in the Phone Home living room stands Avyukt Provastar. He is a small, polite man, dressed in a dark Savile Row suit, now smiling broadly. "Again, I thank you for the kind invitation to be here for the shoot, Delia," he says softly. "It really is quite special here at your place, and I think it was a splendid idea to schedule the reveal of the soon-to-be-famous Green Lake body necklace at...*Green Lake.* Very creative, but then again, I expect nothing less from you."

Delia beams with pride, eleven on a ten scale. "Glad you could join us, Avyukt. Long way from London, but maybe not all that far from Colombo, *neh?* And my God, man, your PR flacks are tops. They arranged an incredible amount of top-notch exposure absolutely lickety-split. The local hotels are over the moon at the flood of global fashion journalists. They're certainly going to be our friends from now on."

"*Feh*, Delia. It's nothing, really. Just all part of our grand plan...*neh?*"

"Where do you want me?" Surya asks the photographer.

"Well, if we move the couch over a couple of feet, we can catch you reclining and still capture the whole sweeping view of Green Lake. The north light will highlight your curves nicely without making this look like it's a soft-porn feature."

"Fine by me," says Surya. "Just no crotch shots, okay? My beaver is my own business."

Trying to be helpful, the photographer starts to move the coffee table out of the way so that she can reposition the couch and begin posing Surya for the shoot. She picks up a rough gray rectangular bar off the table. "Wow, that's really heavy."

"I'll take that!" Christine's voice barks sharply from the back of the room.

The photographer shrinks back, startled by Christine's tone. "What is it?"

"Just an old bar of lead I inherited. My uncle operated a lead mining operation in Mineral Point, Wisconsin for many years. Source of the family wealth until the lead petered out. We used to have a lot of these bars, but now this is the last one we have. It's an heirloom, I suppose you'd say. Has great emotional significance to the whole family."

51

Two Letters

Dear Alva,

Delia believes that you and I share many traits and interests, and she has strongly urged me to introduce myself to you and perhaps start up a correspondence. I have not had a pen pal since I was ten, but Delia has convinced me that I need to enliven my retirement by cultivating new relationships. I have told her that I'm game, but that she must reciprocate by continuing to foster your attempts at reconciliation. It seems you and Delia have a lot of catching up to do. I have only recently experienced the immense satisfaction of having a family come together, and I see no reason why that should not include you as an extended family member—if you're game. Also, it's time to end the unproductive pissing match about which of you—or neither of you—

suffers from borderline personality disorder. Cheap shots get nobody nowhere.

I don't need to tell you what a remarkable person Delia is, but I can tell you what joy she brings to Christine's life and what energy she brings to everything that happens around Green Lake. Moreover, in addition to the determination she brings to our Coeur D'Or enterprises, she has become the glamorous face of diversity and inclusion in these parts, and her one-woman crusade against the low-key but pervasive racism we have around here is bearing fruit. I believe we may now have a grand total of ten people of color in Green Lake County, and Delia continues to recruit talented immigrants—particularly those artistically inclined. Our lives really are richer for Delia's presence.

As for me, I am a retired architect who used to specialize in the rescue of buildings—usually tall ones—that had been poorly designed and built and that were risking collapse or catastrophic failure. This was admittedly a narrow niche, but it brought a fair amount of excitement and notoriety which evaporated the moment I hit seventy. In retirement, I found that I simply could not "take it easy," and, faced with some serious financial reverses, I strayed into endeavors that I could never have foreseen or entertained. As Delia may have told you, not all of them were legal. I decided to forsake morality for excitement, and that left the gate open for some stimulating new directions. The fact that these activities may well cost me a short spell in prison will not erode my newly-developed fondness for outside-the-box adventure.

Alva, given all that Delia has told me about your life and times (she speaks with particular admiration for your financial acumen), I would welcome the opportunity to get acquainted, compare notes, and even perhaps plan a trip to Cape Verde at some point. And having been assured that you would annihilate me in chess, I hereby challenge you to a couple of games, either virtually or in person. As with many things, I think I am a pretty solid player.

Warm regards,

Victor Harding

—◠◠◠—

Dear Victor,

Delia assures me that you are an arrogant genius with a heart of gold – pun intended – and that I will be missing something if I do not take you up on your chess challenge. You sound like my kind of guy, if I may be so bold. I have some nice friends here in Cape Verde, many of them in the financial sector, but they are not terribly stimulating intellectually, and they lack a sense either of humor or of adventure.

I would welcome the opportunity to compare notes and match wits, but not in the detested emails, please. My background has made me very sensitive to issues of personal privacy and security. If we are going to correspond, buy some high-quality stationery and write me in your own hand, like people cultivating relationships used to do in the old days.

After you get out of the slammer, I think you should hop a plane to gorgeous Cape Verde. Its allure—and of course my charms—may make you want to stay, or at least visit frequently. If and when you do come, do not bring anything with you but your wit and willingness to take yourself in new directions. We can outfit you here with everything you need to feed your sense of adventure.

You have many moves left in life, Victor, on the chess board and off. To start, I'll play black (what else is a woman of color to do?).

Queenside bishop pawn to c5.

Love and Kisses,

Alva Batek

52

Cape Verde

"NICE FLIGHT?" asks Alva.

"Pleasant enough, but I had a bit of a scare when I was going through security at JFK. Guy in front of me, his briefcase gets pushed off the conveyer belt and falls to the floor. Big *clonk*. The TSA guy picks it up and says, 'Wow, what do you have in here, your bowling ball?'

"They ask him to open his case, he gets irate, finally says okay, fine, open it. Looking on, I can see inside. It's a thick catalog for auto parts. TSA lifts the cover, book's hollowed out. And there they are, six neat, banded stacks of hundreds. They haul him away. TSA guy says, 'We're always interested in people who go in for heavy reading,' and all the inspectors burst out laughing."

"I don't know why people try shit like that," says Alva Batek. "They see too many movies. That's why I told you not to bring *anything*, Victor. These guys at TSA or, harsher still at Cape Verde foreign customs, they may be idiots, but they're not fools. Chickenshit like this is not the best way to do things. The best course is to do the dance of the wire transfers. Multiple bounces, multiple countries. Do it right, and you are very unlikely to get taken down. I'll be happy to show you."

Alva Batek looks like a perfectly proportioned miniature human being, nearly a foot shorter than her tall, willowy daughter. She exudes energy in a way that reminds me of the actress Linda Hunt—sharp, vibrant, intelligent, faintly alarming. Her eyes peer deep into you, her smile splits the difference between sly and disarming. Today she is wearing a short khaki skirt, hiking boots, and a flowing, elaborately embroidered Balinese print blouse. She walks very fast.

We head out to the parking lot at Cape Verde's new Cesária Évora International Airport, where Alva's bright red Seat Panda, the Spanish version of a tiny Fiat city car, stands out among rows of quotidian white and silver cars and trucks. I carry nothing but a backpack and my briefcase.

Alva's incredible villa, carved out of a cliff, overlooks a sweeping vista that could be on just about any gorgeous, pristine tropical island. This one happens to be on Santo Antáo, the westernmost island in the Cape Verde archipelago.

"It's off the beaten track, but believe it or not, it has good internet service. My local bank is just across the channel on Sáo Vicente. They have good internet, too."

We're sitting on the veranda, our feet propped up on Ottomans, the air over our heads redolent of marijuana, our Sangria glasses on the third refill. Artur and Gracia hover, ready to tend and pamper. I could get used to this.

Alva wades in. "Okay, sport, tell me how the family is doing."

"We've had some tough innings. All of us have had to weather some pretty extreme challenges. But all in all, Alva, I think the whole extended—and, with my brother's wedding, about to be further extended—Harding family is in pretty good shape right now."

"You must fill me in, Victor. First, Delia—what's to report there?"

"Honestly, Alva, I don't know how Delia does it, how she manages to keep her head on straight. First, she wins the *Medaille Coeur D'Or*, which is not bad for a start, then she blows the jewelry world into the stratosphere with the now world-famous Green Lake body necklace. Phone's dancing off the hook: 'Make one for me! No, make one for *me! Name your price!*'"

"Okay, so she's famous. How's Christine handling that?"

"Well, there's the personal side, and then there's the business side."

"Personal side first."

"Christine is a strange bird, Alva. She can be a real grouch. Don't get me wrong, she and Delia now are getting along well, and Delia has opened Christine up in ways I could never have imagined. But Christine can be so *crabby*. I think that's how she expresses a lot of underlying anxiety. Anyway, she likes to complain, and Delia is constantly calling her on it. I'd say they've had some rough spots, but they seem to have worked out some kind of acceptable accommodation. I'd say the marriage is on solid footing at the moment."

"Okay, now business side. Sounds like Delia is making a lot of money."

"Well, as I said, Delia is at the top of her game. People are flying her all around the world to discuss commissions—and Delia always insists that Christine go too, expenses paid by client. The Door County shop is proving a dandy little money laundry, as is the Alliance. I never realized how easy it is to launder funds through a not-for-profit."

"So, the s Alliance is doing well?"

"Over the *moon*, Alva. Articles, awards, endowments. Applications from all over. Art schools are weighing in with referrals. And we're seeing some truly amazing talent, that's the fun part.

"Christine sort of dabbles in the Alliance's affairs, but she knows it's really Delia's show. So, to keep her mind alive, she has been doing all the back office and scheduling work for Collie's automobile storage and transportation business. That has become a sweet little cash cow, and it both makes us legitimate money and provides a nice back-alley laundering funnel. Not much stress on Collie, which is good for his PTSD, and he and Christine are back to acting like twins. Nice to see.

"Colin's PTSD still creating problems?"

"He suffered a major PTSD relapse after Cara's car accident, but he seems to be managing better these days. Perhaps it's the love of a good woman."

"This fiancé of his, this Cara, *is* she a good woman?"

"She's a *remarkable* woman. I wish you could find some way to come over for the wedding, Alva. Vilma Stakhatos is planning one hell of a bash. I'm told Matthew McConaughey is going to be there. He'd love to hit on Delia, I think, but I don't think Christine would take kindly to that."

"*Prude.* Anyway, I wish I could join you all, too. I'd love to play around with your family, but I'd have to go out and buy a false identity, and I'm just not up for that risk right now. Still, I shouldn't complain. We all make our own bed, right? The wages of sin and all that. I'll just have to keep dragging you back over here."

"You can probably talk me into it."

"And what about you, Victor? You haven't talked about Victor Harding. How are *you* these days?"

"Well, I got a lot better when the feds declined prosecution on my interstate transportation case. *Thank you,*

Gilbert Rennie! He's our local sheriff. I helped him crack a bunch of cases, made him a genuine local hero, and I think he really went to bat for me with the feds. But he couldn't stand to see me get off completely scot-free, so he turned around and charged me locally with receiving stolen property. Under Wisconsin law, it's a misdemeanor, and not a felony, when the property is worth less than twenty-five hundred dollars. He made me confess to buying a lawn mower I knew to be stolen. Five years' probation, five thousand dollar fine. So I'm not a convicted felon, but I now have a criminal record. Rennie's got a twisted sense of humor."

"You ask me, he sounds like a good friend."

"I wish. I seriously betrayed his trust, and he's made it clear he wants nothing to do with me except the occasional polite handshake at social functions. How can I blame him?"

"Sad, but not tragic. So, stop dodging my question. How are *you* these days?"

"Well, I'm a complete outcast, of course. Little kids are told they can't even ride their bikes past my house. I'm used to being disliked, but I can't get used to being spit on. I'm not a convicted felon, but I'm sure generally getting treated like a convicted felon. Both the Vandals and the Locals think I am beneath contempt.

"I've heard rumors that I'm a murderer, that I push drugs, that I take liberties with farm animals. I guess I'll keep living in Green Lake because the rest of the family is there and because there's really no other place to go. Except maybe Cape Verde. The real problem is that I'm on the cusp of being seriously bored again."

"Well, I was hoping you'd say that. Just to keep life interesting, we should play a few games, and I'm not talking about chess. How are you fixed for bucks?"

"I'm not in your league, but I've got a solid beginner's grasp of laundering. Still, I'm just an amateur. Even so, at this point, I guess I have a few shekels to invest in something interesting."

"How many of those shekels are liquid?"

"Well, there's some cash in the mattress, probably about a million and a half to play with. The rest is offshore, and I don't know how to get it back into the U.S."

"Oh, I do," says Alva Batek. "*I do.* Your move, Victor."

53

Just Deserts

GILBERT RENNIE'S POLICE CRUISER follows Christine's Subaru into the driveway as she returns from visiting Cara Spaaks at the rehabilitation hospital. I'm standing at the door when they both step out of their cars. Christine is hostile: "Why don't you stop harassing us?"

There is an intensity to Gilbert's expression that I don't think I've ever seen before. "Why don't you just shut your goddamned mouth for once?" he snaps.

Like many bullies—and let's be clear: when Christine Harding feels threatened, she can act like a bully—my sister can dish it out, but she can't take it. She recoils as if slapped. "What are you doing here?"

"I want to see Victor. No, I *insist* on seeing Victor."

I step out onto the porch. "You keep yelling at my sister, *Sheriff*, what you're going to be seeing is stars."

Ever since I got back from my Cape Verde visit, Christine, Colin, Delia and I have all been living at my house, and everybody is wound pretty tight.

Gilbert glares at me, and lets a few seconds run off the clock for dramatic tension. "Anything you want to tell me, Victor?"

"You keep asking me coy little questions like that. No, I haven't seen a yellow Corvette."

"This is different," he says, and extends his cell phone toward me. "Can you tell me anything about this?"

The photo on Gilbert's cell phone is dark, and at first, I can't figure out what I'm seeing. I take the phone from his hand, and reverse-pinch my fingers to enlarge the picture. Then I see that the photo has been shot in front of the charred bones of the Semper Bar. There is a motorcycle in the center of the picture, but it's not one of the Harleys whose burned remnants Collie and I had seen after the bar fire.

This one is a three-wheeler, a hybrid with a chopper engine and front end, and a shiny black two-wheeled box at the rear. Someone is sitting rigidly on the bike. His feet are lifted up and lashed onto the handlebars, a pose that makes him resemble a rodeo wrangler kicking up his legs like a bucking bronco rider. I look more carefully. No one else around here has hair like that. This is a picture of Gunnar Spaaks.

His chest is bathed in blood.

"Medical examiner did a preliminary even while Gunnar was still tied to the bike," Gilbert says. "His arms were tied behind him, and he had been garroted. *Three times.* Some kind of wire. The killer would pull the wire just tight enough to cut through the skin, then let it go. Move the wire, pull it tight again. *Three times.* Slit his throat three times. Three nice, neat gashes. Spaaks was probably still alive, maybe even conscious, when his killer fired a shotgun into his crotch at point-blank range. He wasn't killed at the bar, by the way. Someplace else, for sure. He was already dead when someone drove this tricycle into place, dragged Spaaks' body onto it, tied his feet to the handlebars, and made an anonymous call to my office."

I don't know quite what to feel. I recoil at the thought of Gunnar Spaaks' last moments. On the other hand, I'm certainly glad he's dead.

"I need to ask you a question, Victor."

I nod.

"Did you kill Gunnar Spaaks?"

"No, sir," I say. "Put me on the box. I'll pass with flying colors."

"Did Colin kill Gunnar Spaaks?"

"I'll not presume to speak for my brother," I say. "But I'm sure he'd be willing to take a polygraph too."

"Well, okay then, that's all I needed to know. For now."

"You think Garr?"

"It's a pretty good theory. Hell hath no fury like a Mafia *Capo* who's been dicked with."

———

At our corner table at the Morton's, Colin hasn't touched his salad, and is pushing his chicken breast all over this plate. He has three empty martini glasses at his elbow.

"Easy, big fella," I say.

"Well, this is all pretty intense," says Collie. "Cara is still pretty freaked."

"Am I supposed to believe Cara feels sympathy for that monster? Someone who tried to kill her? Someone who drove his own sister off the road?!"

"Yes, yes he did, but she thinks his...*manner of death* was pretty sickening. Brutally savage."

"Yeah, well, look at it this way. Someone did you—both of us, actually—a hell of a big favor. Sort of revenge by proxy."

There's a long moment of silence.

"You think Garr?" I ask.

"Why shouldn't people think Garr? Or Garr's guys, anyway. Mafia types tend to get ugly when they're mad. Those guys sure don't fool around, do they?"

Collie shakes his head in disbelief.

Another long pause.

"Collie, between you and me, forever and ever, had you been thinking of doing something similar to our friend Gunnar?"

Colin tilts his chin up to the sky, and sighs. He chooses his words carefully, speaking very precisely. "Do you really think I'm capable of doing something like that, Victor? I'm a retired golf pro, not a Mafia hitman. But Seth Bartlett did once mention we could always count on him for any chores we might need him for."

"Just hypothetically, how much do you imagine Seth's... *chores*...might cost?"

"Who can say? Seventy-five grand, maybe? Maybe paid in small installments over time? Wouldn't that be attractive to someone like Seth? That approach would sort of be like a raise on his present salary, right? Wouldn't the prospect of lifetime employment at Janesville have some appeal to him?"

"So, Seth likes his job?"

"Loves it."

"Colin, can this guy Seth be trusted to keep his mouth shut?"

"Hell, you've seen him, Victor, watched him in action. Not a big talker. But I would trust him with my life."

"Nice feeling, isn't it?" I say.

"What feeling?"

"To be able to trust people," I say.

Acknowledgments

Let's hear it for The Cheering Section, those good souls who provided unflagging support as I wrestled with my debut novel, *Down Wind and Out of Sight*, and then stayed on board as *Old Dogs, New Tricks* slowly took shape, came to life, and benefited hugely from their suggestions, their polishing, and particularly their enthusiasm. I wish every author could experience the energy and warmth of such support.

The Cheering Section bridges various generations and professions, various kinds of relationships and various levels of friendship—all the diverse perspectives a writer needs and craves. Each of your contributions was unique, each was invaluable. You know who you are, but I also want the reading world to know who you are and how much your support has meant to someone who came so late to the whole novel-writing game.

My deep thanks to Pamela Bridwell Cain, Tobey Chier, Felicia Greenberg, Kokila Mallikarjuna, Megan Niño, Vasil and Gina Pappas, Gabby and George Pellinger, Leslie and Andrew Price, my daughters Hollis and Kate Richardson (both biased, of course, but totally candid, oh, yes), David Richter (the model for the David Richter character in *Old Dogs, New*

Tricks, his name and genial likeness used with permission), Jackie and Nick Scharff and Cynthia Shelton. And, of course, the inimitable, indomitable Pamela Woldow—beloved wife, literary critic, publicist, social media maven, and wiper of the author's fevered brow—whose dedication is rivaled only by her patience.

About the Author

AFTER RETIRING FROM EARLIER CAREERS as a trial lawyer and federal prosecutor, mental health lawyer, executive coach, and award-winning Dow Jones columnist, Douglas Richardson has now become an award-winning novelist. The American Fiction Awards named his debut novel, *Down Wind and Out of Sight,* a Finalist in three separate categories—General Thriller, Cross-Genre Fiction, and Multicultural/Diverse Mystery. It won a 2023 Literary Titan Book Award and is featured in the Murder & Mayhem Section of digital marketer Open Road Integrated Media.

A graduate of Harvard Law School, Penn's Annenberg School of Communications, and the University of Michigan, Doug is a Certified Master Coach and author of several successful nonfiction business books. He lives in suburban Philadelphia with his wife, also a recovering lawyer, and their Variety Pack of three delightfully assorted dogs.

For action updates on Doug's life and times, go to:

www.douglasrichardsonnovelist.com